Merry & Bright

A Christmas Anthology

NOCTURNE FALLS UNIVERSE

With stories by

Fiona Roarke
Jax Cassidy
Kira Nyte
Wynter Daniels
Candace Colt
Cate Dean
Larissa Emerald
Sela Carsen
Alethea Kontis

Merry & Bright — A Christmas Anthology
A Nocturne Falls Universe Collection

Published in the United States of America.

Dear Reader,

Is there a more enchanted time of year than the holidays? Wonder seems to be everywhere and the spirit of mankind is renewed by the sharing of the season's joy. Families come together, friends reunite, and for a magical window in time, we remember the excitement we felt as kids.

That doesn't change in Nocturne Falls. In fact, Nocturne Falls at Christmastime is a truly charming place to be. You never know what amazing things will happen, who might cross your path, or what adventure you'll find.

And in the case of these stories, where love and romance will bloom.

I hope these Christmas-themed, guest-authored books will bring you lots of holiday entertainment and warm you up for the season. But best of all, I hope they allow you to discover some great new authors! (And if you like this collection, be sure to check out the rest of the Nocturne Falls Universe offerings at https://kristenpainter.com/nocturne-falls-universe/.)

For more information about the Nocturne Falls Universe, visit http://kristenpainter.com/sugar-skull-books/

In the meantime, happy reading and happier holidays!

Kristen Painter

Contents

Have Yourself a Merry Little Alien 1
by Fiona Roarke

The Wizard's Mistletoe Magic 55
by Jax Cassidy

A Dragon's Christmas Mayhem 103
by Kira Nyte

The Mistletoe Misstep 157
by Wynter Daniels

The Psychics Say I Do 221
by Candace Colt

The Meddlesome Misadventures of Merri and Bright 277
by Alethea Kontis

The Sorcerer's Christmas Miracle 329
by Cate Dean

The Witch's Snow Globe Wish 367
by Larissa Emerald

Magic's Frost 411
by Sela Carsen

Have Yourself a Merry Little Alien

BY FIONA ROARKE

Draeken and Stella Phoenix are celebrating Christmas in Nocturne Falls with a festive holiday party in their new vacation home. Each has a big surprise for the other, but all's fair in love and secret Christmas presents. Right?

1

Nocturne Falls – a few days before Christmas

"I love the white, cold, flaky things that fall from the sky," Draeken said, tilting his head back to catch a snowflake on his tongue as they strolled down Main Street.

"Snowflakes, not white, cold, flaky things." Stella spent a lot of time teaching Draeken about Earth. Back home in Alienn, Arkansas they had a cozy little house and her charming former bad-boy of a husband had fit right into the landscape she loved.

Instead of taking up bauxite mining as he'd planned, Draeken had become an as-needed communications officer for the galactic way station tucked below The Big Bang Truck Stop in Alienn. The facility's communications chief, Axel Grey, had snapped Draeken up as soon as he found out Stella's husband not only had a particularly good mind-nudge ability in general—a crucial skill when it came to keeping humankind in the dark about the extraterrestrials who lived and worked among them—

but could also put the nudge on the supernatural inhabitants of Nocturne Falls, which had a relatively new alliance of sorts with Alienn. Fortunately for the town's vampires, werewolves and gargoyles (oh my!), Draeken mostly used his talents on earthlings in Alienn these days. He'd thwarted a pickpocket and a shoplifter at The Big Bang Truck Stop since starting work there.

At first, Draeken had been disappointed not to get the chance to carry a pickaxe into the mines every day, but he seemed to enjoy his work with Axel sending communications to and from Alpha-Prime. Axel told her he did a very good job and was always upbeat.

When he wasn't working with Axel, Draeken drove a delivery truck part-time and put in a few hours every other weekend at the car wash, just because he liked it so much. He had a keen interest in Earth-style vehicles.

He kept very busy for a man whose family once considered him a loveable scoundrel with a penchant for trouble. Stella was proud to be his wife.

"Right. Snowflakes. Got it." Draeken, gloved fingers tangled with Stella's, dragged her along with him as he moved his whole upper body to nab a particularly large snowflake between his lips.

Stella yanked him straight again. "Come on, Mr. Snowflake Catcher. We still have to pick up a Christmas tree. I hope there will be a decent selection, even though it's so late in the season."

Draeken stopped in the street beneath a lamppost. "So, let me get this straight. Not only do you put huge yellow ribbons around trees when a loved one comes home from a gulag, but you Earthers also chop them down, haul them inside and decorate them during the holidays?"

Stella grinned, remembering her daunting efforts to get that stupid, uncooperative, fat yellow ribbon around an oak tree to celebrate his return from XkR-9, the worst gulag in three galaxies.

"Not to mention the decorated tree-trimming pieces twisted into circles for the front door," he continued.

"Wreathes, you mean. Yes. That's right. We Earthers are obsessed with trees in all forms, limbs and everything."

"I mean, I get it. There are some pretty amazing trees here on Earth. There are so many tall ones. Honestly, I'm obsessed with them, too."

Stella and Draeken resumed walking sedately along Main Street. They had a little time to sightsee and look at all the cool decorations, so different from Nocturne Falls's usual Halloween black, purple and orange. There were dozens of tasks still to be done before hosting their inaugural holiday party two days from now. It was also an open house to welcome friends to see their new home, but mostly about the holiday and themed for Christmas. Stella had done quite a few things toward that goal, but had lots more to cross off her to-do list. Dragging Draeken along was sort of helpful, but mostly he was just entertaining.

Thanks to the magic of the light snowfall, everywhere she looked, it seemed as though an icy wet shine coated the trees, the streets and everyone and everything in it. It was beautiful, but Stella was glad she didn't have to drive in it.

They'd come to Nocturne Falls on their honeymoon several months ago after obtaining special permission to travel outside Alpha-Prime's colony in Arkansas. It had been lovely. They'd loved it so much, they decided to return to Georgia and their other favorite town on Earth—because it was the place that brought them together again as a couple—for their first holidays together, as well.

They hadn't even needed special permission this time.

Recently, the council of elders in Alienn—after consulting with the higher ups on Alpha-Prime—revised the restrictions for folks wanting to visit other communities on Earth.

Nocturne Falls was now officially listed as a secondary "safe" zone on the planet. The leadership in each town had agreed to protect the other's secrets, thus giving a wider range of living space for Alphas who wanted to see more of the planet beyond Alienn and for supernaturals wanting a safe place to visit in Arkansas. Stella suspected that last wasn't such a big deal for Nocturne Falls's residents, since she figured they went where they wanted whenever they wanted. Still, it was a great boon for Alienn residents who wanted to spread their wings, so to speak, and live in a different place on Earth.

She'd contacted Pandora Williams, real estate agent extraordinaire, before the ink was even dry on the new addendum allowing unrestricted travel and access to Nocturne Falls, Georgia, seeking a small two-bedroom place in town that she and Draeken could use as a vacation place whenever they wanted to get away.

The other benefit to their vacation place was it could be loaned out to friends and relatives in Alienn who were eager to enjoy it for the same purpose. Everyone she knew in Alienn, Arkansas wanted to visit the Halloween-themed town of Nocturne Falls and meet supernatural folks.

She glanced at Draeken, who'd gone back to looking at the sky, lining up his next snowflake catch. He seemed to be happy wherever he was.

Her fingers tightened on his. "Are you sorry you moved to Earth with me?" As much as Draeken so clearly took enjoyment in all things Earth, Stella worried he'd eventually come to hate it here or miss Alpha-Prime so much he'd want to go back to their homeworld.

His head dropped mid-catch and the snowflake landed on top of his head. His brows furrowed with concern. "Never. I love Earth. I love *you*. I promise to haul as many trees as you want inside and outside and together we can sparkle them all up until no green shows, if it will make you and your Earther-self happy."

Stella exhaled. "*You* make me happy, with or without trees in our house. And keep in mind that you're an Earther now, too."

He brightened, as if that thought hadn't occurred to him. "That's right. I am." A devious quirk formed on his sensuous lips. "You know what Earthers do a whole lot of, according to Bubba Thorne, that I want to do to you right now?"

Stella grinned as he referred to the burly guardsman who was one of his older brother's best friends. "Let me think. Oh, I know—a public display of affection?"

"That's right. Pucker up, sweetheart. We need to kiss. My PDA capacity is running low."

They shared a lingering kiss as snowflakes fell gently around them, rubbing cold noses together as a finish.

"Break it up you two," a familiar gruff voice said from behind them. "This is a public street."

Back in Alienn, Bubba Thorne typically broke them

up whenever they kissed anywhere other than in their home, calling it a deplorable public display of affection. Bubba was one to talk, since now that he was married to Astrid, she'd caught them in their own PDAs a time or two.

This time, the familiar voice wasn't Bubba's.

"Hello, Sheriff Merrow," she said. "Good to see you."

"You can call me Hank." He nodded pleasantly and asked, "So, are you back for a second honeymoon already?"

Stella shook her head. "We bought a little fixer-upper house so we could spend the holidays and vacations here in our second favorite town. We couldn't resist, now that we're allowed to visit and even live here without special permission from...well, you know where." She gave him a wink and a meaningful nod, not wanting to say "Alpha-Prime" out loud.

"That's right. Alienn lifted the ban on living only in Arkansas, didn't they?"

"Naturally, we wanted to have a place to live in each town," Draeken said. "Nocturne Falls is special to us."

Hank narrowed his eyes. "No Defenders allowed, though, right?" he asked, referring to the Alphas' device of choice in keeping humans from learning about aliens living in plain sight in Arkansas. It didn't hurt the humans, unless one counted a few brief moments of induced amnesia as harm. Stella didn't.

"Right," she said firmly. "I promise we'll follow all the rules. And I hope one day you'll come to Alienn and check it out."

"You never know." Based on his expression, Stella figured it would take an extraordinary reason.

"In the meantime, we are simply tourists from the Midwest."

"Well, that's good to hear. I knew you'd purchased a place. I just didn't realize you were going to be part-time residents so soon."

Stella frowned. "Didn't you get the invitation to our holiday party and open house in two days?"

Hank flicked an unreadable look at Draeken. "It's possible," he said. "The truth is, Ivy usually handles stuff like that. I'm certain she'll let me know at the right time and guide me to exactly where I'm supposed to go."

"All good wives do," Draeken said, and then dodged the elbow Stella shot toward his ribs.

"Well, so that you will know, too, we are throwing a party at our new little vacation house two days before Christmas. I promise there will be people you know," Stella added. "Anyway, I hope you and your whole family can come at least to have some spiced apple cider or hot chocolate. There may even be some Arkansas moonshine floating around if you'd like to try a shot. Kids are invited, but no moonshine for them."

"Good plan."

"However, no babysitters are needed unless you want one."

"I'm certain we can stop by, at least until the baby needs a nap."

Stella clapped her gloved hands, mission accomplished. "Great. We will see you then."

"Merry Christmas."

"Merry Christmas," she and Draeken chimed and continued down the street.

2

Real Christmas trees were still for sale on the open plot of land at the end of Main Street. It looked like business had been good, as only a dozen or so trees remained. Not a huge selection, but it would have to do.

Draeken, who always saw things from a completely different perspective, said, "Wow. There must be twelve or more trees here. You have lots of choices. See? You were worried for nothing."

Stella smiled at him. She hadn't been on Earth for very long in the grand scheme of things, but she felt so much like she belonged it was easy to take the planet's lushness for granted. Draeken had much sharper memories of Alpha-Prime's arid landscape, where even small, sparse trees were a rarity—hence his admiration for what Stella considered a meager selection. Even so, she quickly found one she loved.

The tree was less than seven feet tall. It wasn't a stubby little bush or misshapen. Not too wide, not too skinny, it was just right for their first tree. Stella had a special ornament hidden in her bag to put on this perfect tree for their very first Christmas together. She'd ordered it online and brought it along for this special trip.

She had another, much bigger surprise for Draeken that she couldn't wait to reveal. It wasn't easy to take him off guard—his clever mind had a way of winkling out almost any information he desired—but she was determined. She hoped her revelation would make him happy. He'd given up quite a lot to move to Earth and she appreciated it. She wanted him to know how much.

Stella walked around the lot three more times to ensure the very first tree she saw was the right tree for them. She couldn't find even a realistic contender.

"That one," she pointed to her perfect tree, leaning against the fence with a handful of others.

Draeken pulled it straight, holding on to the trunk a few inches from the top. "Excellent choice, Stella."

She knew he would have said that no matter what tree she selected and a piece of her heart melted just a little more for the man she adored. She loved Draeken's upbeat attitude and enthusiasm. She hoped he'd be as happy and upbeat by the end of this trip after all the surprises she had in store for him.

They paid for their tree and the proprietor wrapped it tightly in a net so Draeken could carry it back to their little house. He slung it over one shoulder like the net held nothing more than air. Stella furtively scanned the area for overly curious humans. Hopefully no one noticed Draeken's better-than-human strength.

Stella already had a place in mind for the tree. In what was considered the parlor of the old house they'd purchased for an amazing deal, thanks to Pandora, was a floor-to-ceiling bay window. It would showcase their holiday tree purchase as though custom-made for the purpose. Maybe that's why it had been designed as part of the original house plans.

Thankfully, she'd brought a stand for a real tree and a few basic decorations from Alienn. Nothing extravagant, just a string of colorful lights to wrap around the tree, some tinsel to add some shine and, of course, the bright green—a special available at The Big Bang Truck Stop only for Christmastime—Maxwell the Martian tree topper she'd purchased right before leaving home.

No tree should be without a little green alien at the top. Maxwell held onto—actually, dangled from was more accurate—the edge of the star with his three digits. The tree topper was pure fun. She spread a white felt tree skirt edged with three tiny rows of green bric-a-brac beneath the tree.

"Perfect," she said.

"I like it," Draeken declared. "My favorite part was slinging all the tinsel on it."

"I knew you'd like that best."

"What are we doing tomorrow?"

"I have a few errands to run. And I want to make Christmas cookies in the afternoon. There's also a parade in town later in the morning."

"I can't imagine what a Christmas parade in a Halloween-themed town might look like. Should be interesting, though, and afterward we should go indulge ourselves at Mummy's Diner."

"Are you going to want to eat blueberry pancakes for every meal while we're here?" They'd eaten there this morning.

"Maybe. What's wrong with that?"

"Nothing. Nothing at all. You can eat as many blueberry pancakes as you can hold." Variety might be the spice of life, but according to Draeken, not when it came to Mummy's blueberry pancakes.

"I'd also like to go into Delaney's Delectables and stock up."

"Maybe we should call ahead so she can be prepared. On our honeymoon, I believe she had to close up for the day after you finished your extensive shopping spree."

"Very funny, Mrs. Phoenix."

"I am simply truthful, Mr. Phoenix. Between you and Bubba Thorne, it's a wonder that poor woman ever gets a day off when the two of you are in town."

"Are Bubba and Astrid in Nocturne Falls?" Draeken asked.

Stella nodded. "I don't know if they are here yet, but they are coming for the holidays, just like us."

"Really?"

Stella tilted her head to one side. "Well, it was supposed to be a surprise, but I don't want you to get into Delaney's shop after Bubba has ransacked the place and be disappointed."

He tugged her into his arms and gave her a deliberately smacking kiss on the cheek. "You're such a good wife. Maybe we should go there before we go to the parade. Beat the rush."

"Probably a good idea, but let's see how our morning goes. We have a bunch to do before our party."

Draeken lifted her hand to kiss her knuckles, this time with a much more serious glint in his eye, and was a whisper from touching his lips to hers when the ancient door buzzer sent an off-toned half-buzz, half-chime echoing through the house.

"Who could that be?" Draeken asked, releasing her. "You don't suppose the kids here trick or treat every night, do you? If so, we aren't prepared. And I don't care what traditions they have in this town, I'm *not* giving up any of my chocolate treats from Delaney's."

"Relax. You don't have to give up any treats." Stella walked to the door and opened it.

Her jaw dropped. It was not anyone she expected. Not at all.

Draeken was about to come out of his skin. He'd planned a huge surprise for Stella. Huge. He worried for day.pngs it wouldn't work out. Hank Merrow had pointed him where he needed to go to make it happen, so he was the only one who was in on it. Draeken was glad the sheriff had managed not to give anything away when they'd met on Main Street. Even so, he was almost convinced something would happen to stop his surprise. Something would keep it away.

But all that worry was for naught. It looked like his surprise had even come a couple of days early, and that was certainly better than not at all.

He followed Stella to the door to watch her candid expression, the word "surprise" poised on his lips.

The look on her face was not as happy as he expected. She appeared, instead, to be shocked speechless. Maybe even a little dismayed. He looked down to see what could have gone wrong. What? No! Now *he* was shocked.

"Mew, mew, mew," said the tiny, adorable black kitten sitting in the basket on the porch. The little feline was cute, no doubt about it, but he hadn't gotten a cat for Stella. That wasn't the surprise he wanted to deliver.

"Sorry!" Both he and Stella looked up at the shouted

apology to see a short, squat deliveryman racing toward them from the street. The man, obviously agile despite his overall shape, leapt over the front yard's knee-high white picket fence like an earthling Olympic runner going over a hurdle. Draeken loved watching recordings of Olympic events from years gone past, so felt qualified to judge.

He was surprised the guy didn't throw his arms victoriously in the air once he got over the fence. The man didn't break stride, though. In record time, he sprinted across their front yard to snatch up the basket with the cute meowing kitten before either of them could touch it.

"So sorry to bother you," he said with only the hint of a gasp. "I have the wrong address." And he whisked the kitten away like it had never been there, climbed back into his truck, shut the door with a bang and hurriedly pulled away from the curb.

Draeken pushed out a sigh of relief as he closed the door. "Whew. That was weird, right?"

"Definitely." Stella narrowed her gaze. "Wait a minute. You didn't buy me a kitten for Christmas, did you?"

He shook his head emphatically. "I swear to you, Stella. I did not buy you a kitten for Christmas." He put his hand over his heart, signifying the Alpha version of a scout's honor promise. "I know you love them, but you're highly allergic."

She couldn't have a kitten, so he'd gotten her something else. Something he knew she'd *always* wanted. Something he knew she *wasn't* allergic to. He couldn't wait to see her face, but his surprise was obviously going to have to wait a couple more days. Draeken's surprise was to be delivered the evening of their party. He couldn't wait to see her expression.

Stella nodded, peering through the window next to their front door, her expression wistful. Draeken didn't want her to be sad. "I did get you something cool, though," he teased.

"Oh?" A sweet smile appeared.

He nodded earnestly. "But you'll just have to wait until Christmas to find out what it is."

"Okay." Her gaze went in the direction of the spare bedroom. She seemed lost in thought, not really seeing anything. She'd been lost in thought quite a bit lately. He'd attributed it to the busy holidays and the trip to Georgia. But maybe not. Maybe it was something else. Did she have regrets? About him? That subject had been on his mind too much of late.

"Are you okay?" Draeken asked, trying to keep his tone light.

"What do you mean? I'm ecstatic." He could see she tried to hide it, but she suddenly looked very tired.

"In the past several weeks you haven't seemed…I don't know what the right word is, but not completely happy is as close as I can come."

Stella shook her head. "I've just been busy at work and with the end of the year and the holidays. Life is a bit more stressful at this time of year, that's all. But now we are on vacation, in our new vacation home, so I promise you that I'm so happy I could burst."

Her communicator buzzed. She took the device from her pocket and checked the message, frowning.

"What's up?"

She sighed. "Nothing really. I had a surprise for you, too."

"A surprise? For me?"

"Unfortunately, the delivery has been delayed until tomorrow or more probably the day after that. I just hope my surprise makes it by then."

"That's okay. I can wait."

"Really? That doesn't seem like you," she said with a growing grin. Maybe he'd been wrong about her melancholy.

Draeken took her into his arms, hugged her tight and asked, "So, are you going to give me a hint about what this surprise is?"

"Nope. You'll just have to wait until it's delivered."

"Okay. The truth is, I can't wait."

"That's what I thought." She left his arms and began to clean up the boxes and packing material left over from the tree decoration supplies. "I promise it will be worth the wait."

Draeken thought he knew what her surprise was. He'd had his eye on a special something for the past few months and hoped she'd noticed his interest. It must have paid off. Whatever her surprise was, he'd love it, especially if it was the electronic dart board he wanted to put up in the garage for when the guys came over.

He'd played with the one on display at the mall for almost an hour. It was amazing. It sang songs. It made fun noises when someone scored. If the dart landed directly in the center, super-duper bull's-eye, celebratory music played. It was the coolest dart board ever.

Stella had to come back for him twice that day at the mall. He rubbed his hands together mentally, certain she would know what his heart desired with regard to boys and fun toys.

Even so, Draeken vowed to be astonished and delighted no matter what her surprise was.

3

They plugged in the colorful string of lights twined through the tree's boughs and turned all the other lights in the house off to watch it twinkle. Not surprisingly, Draeken's stomach rumbled, even though they'd had a big dinner.

Stella left Draeken to enjoy a snack in the kitchen while she crept quietly into the spare bedroom. She looked over her shoulder to ensure Draeken stayed in the kitchen and carefully pushed the door closed without letting the latch make a noise. She'd put a suitcase with something special inside under the bed. It was a clue to her biggest Christmas surprise. She couldn't wait for Draeken to see it.

Stella had more than one surprise for him this holiday season and this one was a doozy. Yesterday, she'd opened the suitcase on the bed and started to get the item out from beneath her folded yoga pants, intent on moving it to a better hiding place in the closet. When Draeken came looking for her, calling her name, she barely had time to throw a blanket over the open suitcase and the unwrapped white box that displayed a picture of exactly what was inside.

She decided the blanket wasn't sufficient. He'd figure out she was trying to hide something in a nanosecond. She grabbed the suitcase, blanket and all, and shoved it back under the bed.

With Draeken distracted by his snack, she had some time to unpack her secret gift, then wrap and hide it so he wouldn't find it. Or if he did, he wouldn't be able to figure out what it was without taking the wrapping paper off.

Stella particularly looked forward to the Christmas holidays. Raised as an orphan, she was so grateful to have a family, at long last, to share this time of year with. Earther colony holidays had been popular on Alpha-Prime before they'd even colonized the planet.

Alpha-Prime was home to a very technologically-minded society. Knowledge, education, bettering the world through technical means and any advancement in that arena was considered the best way to live. Many Alpha traditions had been left behind generations ago.

Because of that loss of culture, several narrow niches of society on Alpha-Prime had adopted Earther colony traditions over the past several decades. Christmas, Valentine's Day and Halloween were the top three, although Alpha-Prime did share some celebrations in common with Earth, at least in spirit. Instead of Veteran's Day, they had Guardsman Day, celebrating all the law enforcement entities on Alpha-Prime. Soldiers in their finest, fully decorated uniforms marched in parades in the center of their protected spheres. Instead of Independence Day, they had Civic Day to honor communities and the spirit of being neighborly—basically, getting along with those in nearby municipalities under the spheres.

Contribution Day, Alpha-Prime's version of Christmas, had more to do with getting together as friends and families at the end of the Earther calendar year to celebrate the blessings of the past year and look forward to the coming one. The definition of family did not have to be by blood, although that was the basis for most celebrations across Alpha-Prime.

Contribution Day was perhaps not as spiritual as Christmas on Earth, but no less important to Alphas. Stella had spent quite a few lonely Contribution Days on Alpha-Prime at the children's home. The staff did their best to make it special for the orphans waiting for a forever family, but it wasn't quite the same.

The two Christmases she'd spent in Alienn, Arkansas with her newfound cousins, the Greys, had been glorious. With seven grown siblings in attendance, Grey holiday gatherings were raucous events. The first year, Stella thought they'd gone completely overboard showing her every single one of the family traditions they had—until last year, when she discovered they *always* went crazy at Christmas. Now she could share all those traditions with Draeken in their new little vacation home. He was her family now, no matter where they spent the holidays.

Stella reached under the bed and pulled out the suitcase with a swift jerk. She lifted it onto the bed. One side of the blanket had folded back to expose her yoga pants. She whipped it off completely to search for what she needed. She took the folded red gift bag from the suitcase pocket along with the white tissue paper she planned to use.

Listening with one ear for any stealthy approach from Draeken, Stella carefully scripted her message to her husband on this, their first Earther Christmas together. She folded the note in half and secured it to the ribbon handle of the bag.

She reached into her suitcase, patted under the yoga pants…and felt nothing. Her heart rate quickened. She lifted other pieces of clothing, feeling around inside the suitcase with an increasing sense of urgency, to no avail. The white box wasn't here. *Oh no!* Had she forgotten it back in Alienn? She squinted, as if doing so would help her think better and shook her head. No. She'd seen it in her suitcase yesterday. That's why she'd had to cover it with the blanket and shove it under the bed. Had it fallen out? She started to kneel, intent on peeking under the bed, and heard a noise from the kitchen. She froze. *What was that?*

Draeken called out, "Stella? Do you want any ice cream?"

She cleared her throat and yelled back, "No, thanks." *Where is the special box with the secret gift inside?* She dropped to her knees, pulled the bed skirt up and searched the darkened space below. Nothing. It was dark, it could be there, just out of sight. Maybe she should get a flashlight. *No time.*

Stella reached under the bed dubiously, feeling around for the lost box while trying not to think about the last scary movie she saw where a character had foolishly done the same thing with disastrous results.

"Are you sure?" Draeken shouted.

Stella startled.

"It's really good ice cream," he continued.

She stood up and put her hands on her hips, staring

at the disheveled suitcase as though intensity alone would make the white box appear. *Where is it?*

"I'm sure," she said in a raised voice. She searched the immediate area with a frustrated gaze.

She noticed a gap between the wrought-iron headboard and the wall and leaned to peer over the headboard. The scrape of chair legs across the kitchen floor stopped her. *Space potatoes.*

Draeken's voice, closer, asked, "Are we going to watch that Christmas movie?"

"Not yet." She grabbed the red gift bag, stuffed the flattened tissue inside and stuck it in the closet on the top shelf.

She slid the mirrored closet door shut and approached the door to the hall, anxiously searching the room for where the box could possibly be. She saw nothing. Absolutely nothing. So frustrating. She was certain it had been right there in her suitcase. She turned in a circle. Nothing. Had she already taken it out? Had she even brought it? *Yes. I think.* Sighing, she looked at the mirrored closet door and wished the box would magically appear. She knew it wouldn't, even in a supernatural town like Nocturne Falls.

Stella pushed out another long sigh of frustration and then the unsteady emotions she'd been battling for weeks settled in for a nice long stay.

The tide started in her chest and moved to her head before she could control it or ward it off. More specifically, tears filled her eyes. She sniffled. She hated for Draeken to see her cry. Explanations would have to be rendered.

Stella rarely cried and she'd already done so three times in the last week alone. Fortunately, Draeken hadn't been around to witness those other times. Now he was about to see a blatant girly response to her frustration at not being able to find the special gift she'd wanted to wrap while he was snacking so he wouldn't find out her really big surprise before she was ready to reveal it.

She brushed at her eyes ineffectually and reached for the doorknob, turned and pulled. She rushed through…and bounced off Draeken's chest. His hands lifted automatically to catch her, so she wouldn't stumble and he looked down at her.

Stella sniffed and the welling tears spilled onto her cheeks.

His fingers tightened on her upper arms. "What's wrong?"

"Nothing."

He grabbed her chin, lifting her face to his. "Why are you crying?"

Without warning, nature gave her an excuse not to tell the truth about why she was so emotional. She turned her head, sneezed hard and sprayed the doorframe before she could get a hand up to shield it.

"I'm not crying," she fibbed, wiping tears from her cheeks with the back of one hand. "I think my allergy to that kitten just hit me."

Draeken wasn't buying it, but he kept that to himself. He hugged Stella close and kissed her cheek, tasting the salt of her tears, wishing he knew how to make her feel better. It would certainly be handy if he could read her mind the way he could the minds of earthlings. Unfortunately, Alphas couldn't read the thoughts of other Alphas. That was likely a good thing, especially at this time of year. Where was the fun in that?

Her arms squeezed around him. "I'm just tired, that's all. We've been busy this trip."

"Yes, we have. Why don't we skip the movie and tuck into bed early tonight? We've got a big day tomorrow."

She nodded against his shoulder. Instead of letting go, her embrace tightened. "I love you, Draeken. I really do," she said, her words muffled. She was so adorable. He was beyond grateful she was his. His wife. His long-lost love.

He kissed her cheek again. "I love you, too," he whispered. *I wish you'd tell me what's troubling you.*

Stella released him to take his hand and lead him out of the spare bedroom toward the larger bedroom they'd claimed as their own.

She took his suggestion and they snuggled together until sleep claimed them. As he drifted off, he hoped Stella got some much-needed rest.

The next morning, Draeken woke up early and slipped out of bed to make breakfast for Stella. Usually, he was barely out from beneath the covers before she was awake, upright and ready to start her day. This morning, she slept on.

He made pancakes because it was basically the only thing he knew how to cook. They were a little lumpy and the one he'd hidden between the other two was a shade overdone, but he wanted to make a gesture. He needed Stella to know he treasured her and would do anything for her. He was so grateful to have the life he lived with her.

He put the plate of pancakes, doused with butter and syrup, on a tray. He added cutlery, a paper napkin, a glass of milk and a cup of coffee, then carried the lot into their bedroom.

Stella woke with a start. Her eyes narrowed, as if she didn't remember where they were. Then the dawning realization swept over her face as she recalled they were in their Nocturne Falls vacation home instead of their place in Alienn. "You made food?" Her smile was so enchanting, he almost dropped the tray.

Stella scooted up to sit against the headboard and he placed his morning offering on her lap. "You didn't have to bring me breakfast in bed, but it's lovely. Thank you, Draeken."

"Happy to do it." Gravely, he said, "I just want to prepare you for the reality of this meal. These are *not* anywhere close to the flavorful experience of Mummy's Diner fare."

"That's okay. I was thinking more about how many pancakes I've eaten this trip."

"Whatever that number is, I'll wager I will think it's not nearly enough."

"Well, I've resigned myself to only eating pancakes while in Nocturne Falls."

"There are worse things."

"Yes, indeed." She cut a section of pancake and took a bite. She didn't spit it out or make a funny face as she chewed. She took a second bite and noticed him watching her. "What?"

"Nothing. I just enjoy watching you eat something I made with my own two hands."

Her lips quirked and she took another bite. "Well, they are pretty good, Mr. Phoenix."

"Really?"

"Yes. Really."

"You aren't just saying that?"

Stella shook her head. "Nope. They're pretty good."

"Even the burnt one in the middle?"

"That's my favorite one. I don't mind a little char on my pancakes."

"You're a good sport, Mrs. Phoenix."

"Aren't you going to have any pancakes?"

"Nah. I sort of sampled and tasted as I cooked."

"So basically you ate the truly charred ones, is that right?" She took another syrup-laden bite.

He grinned. "Yep. Guess I don't mind a little—or in this case, a lot of—char on my pancakes, either."

Stella finished most of her pancakes and said, "This is all I can eat. Want the rest? I need to hurry and get into the shower so we can go out to complete my list of chores."

"Okay." Draeken lifted the tray and she slipped quickly from beneath the sheets, doing a fast walk to the bathroom.

An hour later they were both clean, dressed warmly and walking hand-in-hand down Main Street. First stop, Delaney's Delactables. They walked toward the door just as Delaney flipped the sign in the window from Closed to Open.

"Excellent," Draeken said. "We'll be the first ones in here."

"Let me get what I want for the party and then you can get what you want."

"Fine." Delaney peeked out the window and saw them waiting. Draeken offered a finger wave. To her credit, Delaney didn't frown or make any obvious signs over her chest or head to ward off evil spirits. She opened the door and welcomed them into her shop.

"Hey, you two," she said, sounding exuberant. "Are you shopping for Christmas? Don't forget, we ship everywhere."

"So you'd ship chocolates to us in Alienn? That is awesome," Draeken said to his wife. "How did I not know about chocolate shipping before now?"

Stella shrugged.

Delaney said, "And our special this month is free shipping for purchases of less than two pounds."

Draeken scoffed. "That'll never happen unless I go on a diet or make five separate orders."

Stella elbowed him in the ribs. "I'd like to go ahead and pick up the chocolates I ordered for the party, if you don't mind. And I've decided I want to select a few more, just in case."

Delaney eyed Draeken. Proving she had his number, she said to Stella, "Are you sure about that? I can bring both today's selections and the order with me when I come to the party."

"What are you saying? That I have no self-control?" They both stared at him with what Elise, his new sister-in-law, called a judgy expression. He thought about having that much chocolate so close he'd be able to smell it. The scent winding through the old house would be divine. And how he'd start out intending to only try a single piece and then sleepwalk to the stash and eat it all. "Okay. Fine. Point taken. Bring the order the night of the party. It's clear I can't be trusted."

"Thanks, Delaney."

"No. Thank you, Stella, for having a party where I don't have to find a sitter. I'm looking forward to it."

Draeken stepped up to the glass-covered display of all things good and chocolaty. He made his selections, frowning when Stella limited his order to four pounds. As Delaney wrapped up his order and handed him what he considered a light box of the best chocolate he'd ever consumed in a plastic bag bearing her store's logo, he said, "Fine. At least I can say I got here before Bubba Thorne did."

Delaney made a noise and then cleared her throat as if to cover it up, grinning when he glanced into her face.

"Seriously? He beat me here?"

"Sort of."

"How could he? You just opened the door."

"Well." Delaney drew out the word, clearly enjoying herself. "He called in an order about five minutes before I opened."

"You take phone orders?"

"Yep."

"And you deliver?"

"For a price."

"How much?"

"Two hours of free babysitting for every pound," she said with a practiced delivery.

Stella's small cough turned into a rather loud fit, and she bent over and away from him. Draeken figured she was laughing.

"So Bubba is your new babysitter?"

"Nope. He's picking up his order later today. He told me that when he learned you were in town, he figured he'd better call in the order as soon as he could. Seriously, with customers like the two of you, I could retire early. If I ever decide to retire, that is."

The jingle of the bell over the door kept Draeken from blurting something unfortunate. He'd made that mistake before and planned to never repeat it. As a vampire, she could keep this chocolate shop open until the end of time, or at least until the end of his life. Did she somehow know he'd be a lifelong customer?

Draeken and Stella exited the chocolate shop, leaving behind the delectable scent of chocolatey goodness.

"What's next?" he asked, shoving his hand into the bag and popping a truffle into his mouth.

"Enchanted Garden."

"That sounds cool. What is it?"

"It's a flower shop."

"What are we getting there?"

"I'm going to get a few fresh flowers for the party. I already ordered them, but I need to set up delivery."

"Flowers?"

"Just some centerpiece decorations for the tables, and of course some mistletoe."

"Mistletoe. Is that a flower?"

"Sort of. I'll show you when we get there. I think you'll like it."

"You know what I like."

They passed Mummy's Diner on the way to Enchanted Garden, but Stella gave him a look that said he shouldn't even bother asking to go inside. He simply smiled at her and ate another truffle.

Enchanted Garden featured two big display windows on either side of a main entrance filled with all manner of pretty flowers, predominantly red and white with lots of greenery around them for the season.

They stepped inside and Stella looked up. Draeken closed the door. Stella didn't move. She pointed to a small sprig of greenery and red berries dangling from a white ribbon above the door.

"What's that?"

"Mistletoe."

"Why is it on a string above us?"

"Scandinavian legend and several other ancient human cultures all say that kissing under the mistletoe brings good luck."

"Really? That's awesome. What is the Scandinavian legend?"

"I don't remember all the details, but I'm getting several sprigs so we can hang it up around the house and kiss to our hearts' content."

"Great idea, but I don't really need mistletoe to do that."

"Still, it's a Christmas tradition I'd like to continue."

"Okay. No worries. Buy out the store, if you want."

"You haven't kissed me yet and we've been standing here under the mistletoe for, like, five minutes."

Draeken dutifully took his wife in his arms and kissed her under the skinny sprig of mistletoe like there was no tomorrow. Even more than chocolate, he loved the taste of Stella's kisses.

5

Stella was delighted Draeken took to the idea of kissing under the mistletoe so well. She figured he'd like it.

"What do you think?"

"I'm deliriously happy."

"About the mistletoe?"

"About kissing my wife."

A woman stepped into the showroom from a back room. "Hi! Sorry it took me so long. I had a last-minute shipment arrive."

"No problem." He pointed up. "We were just taking your mistletoe for a ride."

The woman Stella presumed to be the florist nodded. "That piece has given out all sorts of love, affection and fertility vibes today. What can I help you with?"

"Fertility vibes?" Draeken asked Stella under his breath. "Does that mean what I think it does?"

Stella ignored his question and walked toward the woman and the counter behind where she stood. "Hi. I'm Stella Phoenix. I called in an order for several floral arrangements for a Christmas party. I wanted to set up a time for delivery."

"Phoenix. Your name seems familiar," the woman said.

"We are good friends with Astrid and Bubba Thorne."

"Right! Astrid mentioned you. I'm Marigold Williams. This is my shop."

"She told me not to bother getting flowers anywhere else, they wouldn't be as good."

Marigold smiled. "Oh, she's so sweet. She mentioned your party."

"Would you like to come?" Stella asked. "You are more than welcome and if you have kids, feel free to bring them along." She gave their Nocturne Falls address and Marigold noted it on her order pad.

"I appreciate the invite. I'll see if my daughter and I can make it. Let me take you back and show you what I've got so far."

Stella and Draeken followed her to a work area where Marigold pointed out the vases she'd selected along with the beautiful flowers she'd put together for each one.

They were all wonderful. The vases looked like candy canes, with a burst of floral colors leaping from the top.

"I love them," Stella said. "They are just what I wanted. Can they be delivered the day of the party?"

"Sure thing. Let's go look at the delivery book and we'll get you scheduled."

They arranged for delivery a couple of hours before the start of the party and Marigold jotted it down in her book.

"Thanks, Marigold. We hope to see you and your daughter at our party." Stella grabbed Draeken's hand to lead him outside, but he stopped her at the mistletoe and kissed her again before they left.

They spent the rest of the morning checking off a list of things Stella wanted Draeken to experience.

They watched the parade with papier-mâché-covered floats featuring a Christmas theme with a blatant hint of Halloween mixed in. What else could one expect in this town?

Stella was pretty sure the Santa Claus and Mrs. Claus riding by on the sleigh-shaped float sported extra-long canines and pointed ears. Whether they were real or not was hard to say. Either way, the parade was extremely entertaining. Draeken talked about building his own float to drive through Alienn next year. She was certain it would have enthusiastic support, especially if the Grey brothers were able to help out with the construction and also if their aunt Dixie was able to attach some sort of salacious fund-raising event for Alienn's old folks' home.

They stopped by a vendor selling roasted chestnuts like hot dogs out of a cart. Draeken finished his bag quickly and doubled back for a second one. Alpha males had an appetite and a half, while hers was less than robust lately.

She stopped at the Shop-n-Save to pick up ingredients, and they spent the rest of their afternoon baking sweet sugar cookies. Stella let Draeken decorate them, which he seemed to have a penchant for. He was exceptionally creative, with an attention to detail she marveled at. She had a six-piece cookie cutter set with a snowman, a Christmas tree, a snowflake, a candy cane, an angel and a stocking.

As each batch cooled, he went to work covering the cookies with white frosting as a base. Once that was set, he moved to the prepared tubes of colored frosting she'd purchased. The tubes had a few different tip shapes, which was as much as her talent in this endeavor would allow. Draeken, on the other hand, had an artistic ability that made her cookies look like a preschooler with an attention deficit had been let loose in the kitchen.

"What do you think?" he said, adding the final touches to a snowman that looked like a professional bakery had crafted it for the holidays.

"I think you've found another job possibility."

"What's that?" he scoffed. "Frosting manager?"

"No. Cookie decorator. You could probably do cakes, too. I'll bet the Moon Pies Bakery in Alienn would hire you in a minute if they saw these cookies."

His brows scrunched. "I doubt it."

"No. Really. Not only are they colorful and perfect, you're fast. It would have taken me until tomorrow to finish all these. And I would have only been icing them and tossing some colored sprinkles on top. You're really good at this, Draeken. A natural talent."

"Cool. I can be jack-of-all-trades and master of none."

Something in his tone told her he wasn't as casual about the comment as he sounded. "Where did you hear that Earther phrase?"

He shrugged, focusing on putting perfect silver lines on an iced snowflake cookie. "Doesn't matter."

"It matters to me."

He looked up from his task and asked seriously, "Do you think I'm a jack-of-all-trades and master of none?"

"No. I think you're master of all trades and everyone else can suck it."

Draeken laughed out loud. "I love you, Stella. You always make me feel better about myself."

"You should feel good about yourself. You're awesome."

He looked unsure. "I heard another Earther phrase."

"What?"

"Ex-con."

Stella sucked in a breath. "Who said that to you? I will break them!"

Draeken straightened and put his decorating tool down on the counter. "No one, at least not about me. I overheard a conversation in The Big Bang Truck Stop when we were on our way here. An earthling mother cautioning her daughter about her ex-con boyfriend. She told the girl once he got out of jail she should ditch him—whatever that means, but I think it's bad."

"First of all, you are not an earthling and that term would never apply to you. Second of all, you were only in the gulag for a couple of hours and you were sent there undercover to help out the justice system on Alpha-Prime. And third of all, you are not now nor were you ever an ex-con and even if you were, I'd still love you and I'd never ditch you. Never!"

Draeken took her into his arms. "I don't even know what it means, but I'm glad you'd never put me in a ditch." He kissed her face, her cheek, telling her he saved the best—her luscious lips—for last. She probably tasted like frosted cookie. They'd been sampling the broken and overcooked ones throughout the process.

"You taste like cookie," he said, confirming her theory. "I love you and I want to be worthy of you."

"You are. You moved to another planet for me. Nothing says, 'I love you,' like a move to another galaxy for the one you adore."

"You think so?"

"I know so. Trust me. You're stuck with me." *Especially now. Should I tell him? No. Not yet.*

"Good. I want to be stuck with you for forever and a day."

"And on that last day, we'll hug and kiss under the mistletoe and eat frosted Christmas cookies that you've decorated expertly."

He laughed. "Deal."

They cleaned up the kitchen, placed the cookies carefully into containers ready for display tomorrow night and got ready to go back outside.

Tonight she wanted to look at Christmas lights on houses and listen to Christmas carolers sing favorite seasonal songs. When they got home, they were going to hang stockings with their embroidered names on the mantel over the fireplace and wrap some small gifts for any children who showed up to the party.

Draeken insisted on the gifts because, he said, "What kind of Christmas party doesn't have fun gifts for kids? It's a must." They'd selected a stuffed green Maxwell the Martian alien doll dressed in a Santa hat with the current year stitched on the white edging and a red-and-white striped scarf, attached permanently around his neck, whipping behind him. Good for both boys and girls, it was just a little different than what might normally be found in Nocturne Falls. For example, no fangs, pointed ears or fire-breathing capabilities.

As they left the house, Stella snuggled against Draeken's side, hoping he felt better about what he was doing with his life. He'd always had an artistic soul and she wanted him to be happy. She hoped he'd be okay with the multitude of surprises coming his way in the next day or so.

6

Draeken woke the next morning in a much better frame of mind. Stella's swift and protective reaction to his comments about being a jack-of-all-trades and an ex-con had been illuminating. In those tense few moments, he didn't doubt her love for him. She'd been ready to pick a fight with anyone who dared mess with him and he loved that about her.

But something was up. Something was different. He sensed it. He just hadn't figured out what. Perhaps it was the stress of keeping holiday secrets from each other. Hopefully by the time they got back to Alienn, things would return to normal.

Tonight was their party. He looked forward to it. They'd planned a very casual event with snacks and delicious chocolate from Delaney's and something Stella called finger foods—which seemed perfect for a Halloween-themed town—and hand-decorated cookies to go with the presents for the kids. Good food, good conversation, good fun and a surprise for Stella. He couldn't wait.

Holden and Victoria showed up two hours before

the party started to help finish up any last-minute chores and errands.

Bubba and Astrid would be delayed, as Pandora had taken them under her wing to help yet another Alienn couple search for a Nocturne Falls home. Draeken hoped they'd be neighbors or at least find a house within walking distance.

He continued to worry about Stella, but planned his day around catching her under the mistletoe to at least kiss her silly. He convinced himself things would be fine. It alarmed him when Hank, Ivy and their little boy Charlie arrived with Hannah Rose and Stella teared up as she held the baby. Hank clapped a commiserating hand on his shoulder and said—out of earshot of his wife and Stella—that in his experience, women always teared up around babies. He rolled his eyes, explained it was a "woman thing" he hadn't truly figured out, then speculated that maybe it was because his Hannah Rose was the most beautiful baby girl in the state of Georgia. Draeken agreed that must be it.

He sincerely hoped things would go back to normal after the holidays.

The party was smooth sailing. People came and went in a steady stream for the first couple of hours, enjoying chatting, snacking and shots of Arkansas moonshine he and Stella had smuggled in for the occasion, not even bothering to water it down with eggnog. Why would they?

Hank gave them a narrow-eyed stare, but sampled some and conceded the prime hooch would be a welcome addition to Nocturne Falls's adult liquid options.

The Maxwell the Martian stuffed dolls were a big hit with the kids.

Draeken wondered what was keeping Bubba and Astrid, but kept the question to himself. Stella was busy holding Hannah Rose so Ivy could get a bite to eat. She looked so happy he didn't want to interrupt her joy.

If the exuberant comments of their guests on the way out the door were any indication, he and Stella had thrown an awesome party. Draeken was delighted and Stella seemed relieved, though she became teary eyed when the time came to give up the sleeping baby. He'd never seen his fierce warrior so, well, girly, for lack of a better word. Truth be told, he didn't hate her new, softer attitude. It was an intriguing side of her, and proved he still had a lot to learn about his wife.

The party hadn't quite broken up when a loud knock sounded at the front door. "That's probably Bubba and Astrid," Stella said. "Could you let them in?"

"Sure thing." He hoped it wasn't his surprise. If it was, he'd call Stella to come join him.

The room quieted as Draeken answered the door. He popped the front door open, expecting to see Bubba and Astrid. He stared, for an instant only seeing one of the four people on the porch, dumbfounded.

His brother grinned and punched him in the chest. "Hey, old man. How's it going? Earther life looks good on you."

"Riker? What are you doing here?" Draeken felt his grin widen to match Riker's.

"Are you surprised?"

"I am stunned."

"Are you going to let us in?"

Draeken laughed and opened their door wide. He turned and met Stella's sparkling gaze. "Surprise," she said.

Riker stepped over the threshold, followed by his wife Elise, Bubba and Astrid.

Draeken caught his brother in a bear hug. "I can't believe you're here. And Elise, too! All the way from," he only just stopped himself from saying "Alpha-Prime" in front of their terrestrial guests and finished, "back home."

"Thank Bubba and Astrid for picking us up at the airport in Atlanta. And Stella, of course. She orchestrated the whole thing. She wanted us to visit for Contribution Day—I mean, Christmas. We would have been here sooner, but there was an ice storm in Arkansas and we got grounded there."

Elise was the next recipient of Draeken's enthusiastic embrace as he said to Bubba and Astrid, "I thought you two were looking at houses."

"We did," Bubba said. "We drove to Atlanta after touring houses with Pandora."

"Find anything?"

"The perfect place," Astrid said.

"Where?"

"Three doors down from here, on the same side of the street."

"You don't mind if we crash your street, do you?" Bubba asked, in a tone that suggested he didn't care if Draeken did mind.

"As long as you stop beating me to Delaney's shop."

"Not likely."

"Okay, you can still live down the street. At least I know where to go for an emergency chocolate fix."

"Me, too."

Clearly sensitive to the emotions behind the surprise family reunion, the remaining guests thanked Draeken and Stella for a wonderful time and departed, leaving only aliens behind to chat and catch up.

Bubba and Draeken discussed their love of Delaney's Delectables and gobbled up a plate of treats between them, once Stella stopped giving him that judgy, disapproving look. No need to reserve the chocolate treats for their guests.

Riker joined them with a plate of his own special treat. "These are my favorites. I got hooked on them at the Ever After Bridal Boutique while Elise was picking out a wedding dress. I've been dreaming about these little iced diamond cakes for six months."

"Oh, yeah? What flavor?"

"White chocolate lemon coconut."

Draeken eyed the plate and wondered if he'd pull back a stump if he attempted to steal one. Probably. He tried a different tack. "I'll trade you a cherry almond truffle for one of your white chocolate lemon coconut iced cakes."

Riker considered the treat he pointed to and nodded. "Deal."

They each popped a traded treat in their mouths and moaned. "I may have a new favorite," they said at the same time. Then they said, "Jinx!" and punched each other in the shoulder. The Grey brothers had taught them a lot in the short time they'd been together in Alienn, Arkansas.

Bubba and Astrid filled the newcomers in about their new venture in Nocturne Falls.

"I've been assigned to be sort of like the alien liaison between Nocturne Falls and Alienn. Astrid and I will live here on a permanent basis. She can go back to work with her friends at Enchanted Garden and I will manage issues with Alphas living in the area or those who wish to visit or live here.

"Tell them what else you'd like to do," Astrid said. "I think it's awesome."

One corner of Bubba's mouth lifted in amusement. "Since Astrid and I can read human minds, I'm thinking about opening an establishment that offers psychic readings. I'm in negotiations with the leadership in Nocturne Falls to offer the service to visiting humans. We'll have Alphas with the talent for it rotated here to work for a month at a time and see how we do."

"You could offer it to supernaturals, too," Draeken said.

He shrugged. "Can't read everyone."

"Who can't you read?"

"Witches, as it turns out. I've broken out in a sweat trying to read Pandora Williams's mind more than once. Nothing. And then it looks like I'm staring at her. Awkward."

"Huh? Is it all witches or just her?"

"All the witches I've met in town so far. Pandora, Kaley, Marigold, Saffron, Astrid's friend Holli, and last but not least, Corette the wedding dress store owner. I can't read any of them."

"Vampires are easy to read, but I do my level best not to make the effort anymore."

"Probably a good idea. As part of the business, I'll offer an alien matchmaking service for a few special supernatural customers."

Stella asked, "What's an alien matchmaking service?"

"If there are any supernatural folks looking for Alpha mates, my business will help them make the connection." He shrugged. "I think there could be a market for it."

"Right. And you could call it Bubba's Matchmaking Service," Draeken said.

Before anyone could comment, the front door rattled as someone pounded on it. Draeken jerked to attention. His surprise! He'd forgotten all about it when his brother arrived so unexpectedly.

7

Draeken tried to look nonchalant when Stella sent a look his way. He was anything but calm. His heartbeat sped to double when she asked, "Who could that be at this hour?"

"Late party arrival?" he suggested, knowing full well it wasn't. Well, not exactly.

"I don't think so." Stella stood up to go to the door. "The party's over."

Draeken shrugged while holding in his anticipation. *That's what you think.*

Riker gave him a look that said, "I know you're up to something." Stella was halfway to the door. Draeken signaled his brother to be cool as he stood to join her.

"It's only nine o'clock," Draeken said. "Maybe whoever it is couldn't get here until now." He hoped this was going to be a welcome surprise for her.

"Maybe. But this is a small town, just like Alienn. I thought all small towns rolled up the sidewalks after eight o'clock at night."

Draeken kissed her cheek. "Let's see who it is, then we can decide whether to let them in."

Stella opened the door. No one was there. She leaned her head forward slightly and squinted into the darkness. Draeken could barely contain his glee. A rustling sound drew her eyes down. The little fluffy white puppy sat in a basket identical to the one the black kitten had arrived in earlier.

"Woof," said the puppy.

His wife sucked in a breath of surprise. That was the best. "Where did you come from?" she asked. The look on her face was even better than he anticipated.

"Woof," the puppy said again. The joy on Stella's face was something to behold. She was most definitely *not* allergic to canines. Draeken chortled inside, so happy Stella liked his surprise.

She bent down to pick up what he considered the cutest thing he'd ever seen. The wriggling little fluff beast licked her face enthusiastically, letting out little yips of puppyish pleasure. She giggled, trying only half-heartedly to stop the pup's face washing as she stepped out onto the porch and looked around.

"Do you think the delivery guy is about to swoop in and take him to another address?"

"No," Draeken said. "This one is the keeper."

"Keeper?"

"Surprise, Stella! Merry Christmas. I got you a puppy. Isn't he cute?"

She sucked in an even deeper breath of surprise and her face glowed. "He's perfect. How did you know I wanted a fluffy white puppy?"

"You told me once."

"Did I? I don't remember that."

"It was a long time ago, when we first met. You were telling me about where you grew up and about not having any friends at the children's home because they all got families and moved away. You begged the head supervisor for a pet, but she never agreed. You said no pets were allowed, but that you always wanted a cute little white puppy. I thought it was about time you had one."

Stella nuzzled her face into the little beastie's fur as it continued to squirm in her arms and lick her face. She turned toward him. Tears fell from her eyes copiously. *Oh no.*

"Don't cry, Stella." Draeken was at a loss. He'd been so sure she'd like this surprise.

"But he's so perfect. I love you so much. Thank you, Draeken. This is the best gift I've ever gotten."

Whew! "You're welcome." Draeken released a huge breath he hadn't realized he'd been holding. He hugged her and she hugged him back. The kiss was flavored with her tears, but they were tears of joy, so he was okay with that. The puppy started licking his face, too.

"What shall we call him?"

Stella pushed her face into the puppy's neck. "How about Snowflake?"

He laughed. "That sounds about right."

"Also better than White Cold Fluffy Thing. I mean, it could work, but it's such a big mouthful of a name for such a little bit of fluff."

"True." Draeken patted the newly christened Snowflake on the head.

Riker came to stand in the doorway. "What are you two doing out here? I was sent over on reconnaissance."

Stella held out the wiggling little dog. "Draeken got me a puppy for Christmas. Isn't he perfect? I'm calling him Snowflake."

Draeken looked sideways at his brother, expecting some sort of disparaging comment, but Riker grinned. "Snowflake *is* perfect. Who knew my little brother could select such a great gift?"

"What did you get Elise?" Draeken asked.

"Laser scope for her favorite gun."

"Wow. Aren't you the romantic?"

"It was what she wanted." He accompanied the remark with a shrug and a punch to Draeken's shoulder.

"What are we going to feed him?" Stella asked.

"Oh, I got puppy kibble and treats. Also a food and water bowl combination. And best of all, he's been trained to use a litter box like a cat."

"Really?"

He'd believe it when he saw it, but the guy at the animal shelter insisted the puppy was litter-box trained. Win-win as far as he was concerned.

"Well, let's hope so. For my Plan B, I have a good-sized animal carrier in the garage to keep him inside so he won't try to mark his territory. I know you don't want *that* smell in the house for the rest of the holidays."

"True." She shook her head at him in admiring wonder. "You and your Plan B schemes. You've thought of everything, Draeken. Thank you."

"I wanted you to be surprised."

"Check."

"And I wanted you to be happy."

"Double check."

"Mostly I wanted you to love me and be glad you married me."

"I would have loved you and been glad I married you even without the puppy. However, in our brief time together, I've become hopelessly attached to Snowflake, so he stays."

"Good."

Stella put her cheek on Snowflake's back, rubbing her face into his fluffy fur. She carried him inside to show him off to the others, who were all appropriately wowed by Snowflake and his wiggly bodied, face-licking ways.

They all settled down to chat. Stella held Snowflake on her lap. Draeken reached to pat him on the head. Snowflake wiggled off Stella's lap and leapt to the floor, his butt-wiggling dance of joy signaling loud and clear his eagerness to at long last roam free.

Draeken leaned down to retrieve him, but Snowflake had other ideas. In a flash, he was gone, out of the living room and down the hallway toward the bedrooms. The rapid clickity-click of his little puppy nails on the wood floors told them all he was headed for the spare bedroom.

Stella started to get up, but Draeken put a hand on her arm. "No. I'll get him." The sound of puppy nails on wood ceased. It was all quiet down the hall. That might be bad. Draeken hadn't set up the litter box yet.

"Snowflake?" he called.

Riker and Bubba laughed.

"What?"

"He's only been here for ten minutes. You think he knows his name already?" Riker had a point. Draeken looked toward the hallway.

Elise said, "Better go find him quick before he starts marking his territory."

Draeken took a single step to go capture Snowflake, but the rapid-fire sound of puppy nails on hardwood resumed. In an instant, the pup was back in the living room, dragging a small box with a colorful picture on one side.

Draeken tried to grab dog and box, but Snowflake was too fast, dodging his reach like he'd been born to do it. "You sneaky little beast." Draeken realized he'd selected a very wily puppy. That could be good and bad. Good, because he'd fit right in with the two of them. Bad, because that made him, well…wily and unpredictable.

The puppy bounded toward Stella, one corner of the box clamped between his little sharp teeth.

Riker said, "What's he got in his mouth?"

Stella saw the box and her eyes widened to the size of dinner plates. She pointed, her mouth an "O" of surprise. Draeken got the drop on Snowflake, scooping up the naughty little puppy and wrestling the box from him. "I guess it would be a waste of time to tell you not to chew on stuff," he said.

Snowflake said, "Woof," and licked his chin. His wiggly little body never stopped moving.

The corner of box had several puppy teeth marks on it, but hopefully the contents had survived unscathed. He looked at the box more closely and saw a picture of a cute little bunny family—a mama bunny, a daddy bunny and a cute little baby bunny wrapped in a little blanket. "Who's this for?" Draeken asked.

The room went silent.

Stella, eyes still wide, said in a small voice, "Um…you."

"Me?" Draeken's brows furrowed as he tilted the box to read the description on one side.

Riker grinned at him. Elise also grinned. Bubba and

Astrid grinned. What was everyone grinning about? He looked at the box again and read out loud, "Some bunnies, a soon-to-be new parent's keepsake ornament."

He tilted his head as he tried to puzzle it out. "Who's about to be—" And then he understood everything. "Wait. Is it us?" He felt *his* eyes widen to the size of dinner plates.

Stella nodded slowly. "Yes."

Draeken couldn't immediately grasp the concept of pending fatherhood. "Was it because of the fertility vibes from the mistletoe at Enchanted Garden?"

"Um...No. I was this way when we got to town. What do you think?"

Draeken shook his head in wonder. He walked over and gently dropped Snowflake in Riker's lap. Instantly, Snowflake sped his little puppy forelegs up Riker's chest until he could coat his face with puppy slobber.

Draeken turned to Stella. She rose from the sofa, looking verdant and perfect and beautiful. Now her uncertain mood and attitude and the crying made sense. She carried his child. His. Child.

Draeken looked into her eyes and spoke from his heart. "Stella, I think we will make awesome parents." He couldn't hold back any longer. He grabbed Stella and hugged her tight, then released her just as fast. "Sorry! Are you doing okay?" He put a hand on her belly, as if that would help protect his coming child.

"I'm fine. Just tired and, you know, *really* tired all the time, like I need to take a nap every hour on the hour. And stupidly emotional." Tears rose in her eyes as though just saying the word held the power to make them appear on command.

"Well, I can't wait for us to be parents."

Riker said in mock complaint, "Way to be favorite son, Draeken. Mom and Dad will probably move to Alienn the minute they find out their first grandchild is on the way."

Stella laughed. "They are always welcome."

Draeken looked deep into her eyes. "Best present ever."

"Really?"

He nodded.

"Even more than that electronic dart board you wanted?"

He laughed. "Yes. A baby is so much better than a dart board." Then he added, "But if you got that, too, I'm not taking it back."

"Bad news. They were out of stock for the holidays."

He shrugged, chiding himself for feeling disappointed that he wouldn't get the toy he'd coveted. He was going to be father. Wow.

"Good news, though," his woman said. "The back order will arrive sometime after the first of the new year."

"Awesome. You are the best wife, Stella."

"And you are the best soon-to-be-bunny dad ever."

They kissed and kissed and kissed until Bubba groaned exaggeratedly from the sofa, muttering about public displays of affection running rampant even in Nocturne Falls.

Draeken didn't care if all the people in three galaxies saw him kissing his wife. It awed him that this wonderful, strong, independent woman had chosen a scoundrel like him. And now she was giving him a child. It was more than he could have dreamed possible when fate reunited him on Earth with the woman he'd loved and lost on Alpha-Prime. All it had taken was a spaceship crash, a certain beautiful woman on a mission and a magical place called Nocturne Falls.

Stella gasped out a laugh when he broke their kiss to sweep her off her feet.

"Riker, happy to see you. Snowflake's stuff is in the animal crate in the garage," he said over his shoulder. "Everyone else, glad you could make it to the party. See you in the morning. Say good night, Stella."

Her lips spread in sexy anticipation as he carried her to their bedroom. Tunneling her fingers through his hair, she whispered against his lips, "Good night, Stella."

The End

The Wizard's Mistletoe Magic

BY JAX CASSIDY

Sent on a holiday gift giving mission, Kearney Maclachlan, wizard and royal bodyguard, reluctantly returns to Nocturne Falls where a fateful encounter with intuitive street artist Kaia Wyntir takes them on a journey to reclaim past memories and truths that may finally melt a warrior's frozen heart. Unexpected miracles lead to everlasting love, all thanks to a kiss under the mistletoe.

1

Kearney exited the Hallowed Bean and took a sip of the black coffee. It tasted just as addictive as he'd remembered. His sour mood instantly vanished as the liquid warmed his insides. It had been two years since he discovered this magical brew in Nocturne Falls, and it became a staple for every visit.

"Been a while old friend," he said to the paper cup in his hand, before finishing off the drink and discarding the empty cup into the nearby trash receptacle.

He had to admit, this quirky little town with its supernatural residents had grown on him. Although it celebrated Halloween 365 days a year, the prominent orange and black decorations weren't overshadowed by the addition of snow flurries. Somehow, the wintry weather seemed to give the festive mood a livelier boost for the tourists and its citizens. He blew out a cold stream of air and noticed there were more folks out than usual. He quickly side-stepped a googly-eyed couple and allowed them to pass without running into him.

Humbug.

Kearney scowled, his inner Scrooge returning. He

could do without the excessive jolliness this year. This season always held too many memories he'd rather bury. The dull ache crept back into his heart, reminding him of a past he'd never forgotten. His lips stretched into a thin line as he made his way down Black Cat Boulevard. He shoved his hands into the pockets of his pea coat and walked in the direction of where his car was parked several blocks away.

It was hard to believe that the last time he'd taken off from his official duties was exactly a century ago. Not by choice back then and not this time around either. Was it so bad that he enjoyed the demanding position as the personal bodyguard and guardian to Ace Conall, the wizard prince of the Kingdom of Draíocht? The fast-paced lifestyle left him little time for distractions or dwelling on things that didn't serve him. He had no complaints about working non-stop because he viewed the lad more as family than a mere obligation.

Marriage to Luna had transformed Ace to a dedicated family man. Having a mermaid/heiress wife of a luxury resort in Mer Haven kept him quite busy these days. Especially now, more than ever, since their daughter Aquarius was born. Kearney hated to admit that being in Nocturne Falls may just be what he needed right now. He might as well make the most of it, and perhaps a month of freedom would allow him some uninterrupted R&R time.

However, before he could start his forced mini-vacation, he'd have to drop off holiday presents to their good friends Keke and Rock Winthorpe, the unicorn shifters. The couple had already promised him the use of their rental cottage, but he'd forgotten to inform them of his much earlier arrival date than previously arranged. It wasn't unusual for them to keep the place vacant during the holiday season in case family or friends decided on unexpected visits. The newlyweds were an easy going pair so he knew his unexpected appearance wouldn't be an issue.

Kearney relaxed as he passed the familiar shops and the unique street lamps with their angled metal cobweb shaped brackets. This was a welcome change from Mer Haven where he couldn't turn a corner without running into a mermaid—literally! He'd also grown accustomed to all the nautical paraphernalia and beachside vacationers. He couldn't complain because there were stellar perks that came with the move. He owned a secluded beach house and a nice piece of property on the island that boasted beautiful sunny weather year round.

Since he didn't have any solid plans for the day, he wasn't in a rush to get to the cottage. Kearney decided to stop off at Bell, Book & Candle to pick up some reading material. The local bookstore was one of his favorite spots to hang out. He could spend endless hours absorbed in a good novel there. This place was special, mainly due to the proprietor, Agnes Miller. She was a real interesting woman from her personality to her looks. Recalling the kind bookseller put a smile on his face.

Agnes had a short, chic, silver-gray bob with teal and purple streaks and baby bangs. She wore big, round, black-rimmed glasses that made her bright blue eyes more prominent, reminding him of an animated character. Chatting with the woman was always pleasant, but he was most impressed by her wealth of knowledge when it came to book recommendations.

Kearney lifted his gaze and in the distance he noticed the green striped awning that matched the exterior paint colors of the bookstore. He approached the store and slowed his pace, stopping not far from the street artist who'd set up shop on the sidewalk near the door. He couldn't help noticing the lovely green mistletoe with its glittery red ribbon hanging from a rod above the easel. The paint stained wooden stand held a breathtaking painting that depicted a happy scenario of a little girl on a carousel. The little fist tightly held onto strings that belonged to a cluster of balloons floating above her. Beside the decorative horse stood her father with a bright smile and cotton candy in his hand.

The dreamy style was reminiscent of Degas' ballerinas, with a contemporary spin that meshed perfectly with the classic techniques. What made the piece stand out was the pop of bright colors and use of varying thicknesses of the abstract lines, which made for compelling elements in the artistic storytelling.

The petite, dark-haired woman took one last look at her work and appeared to be pleased with the final product. She signed her name at the corner of the canvas before submerging the paintbrush in a jar of liquid on the small table beside her. She wiped her hands on her apron and pushed back the seat to stand up.

"It's a stunning piece," Kearney praised. "Quite inspiring, actually."

As she turned to respond to his comment, the smile on his lips was quickly erased.

Kearney felt like he had been thoroughly gut punched. He held his breath as he gaped in recognizable disbelief at the beautiful vision innocently returning his gaze. This was the same face that had haunted him for the past century.

2

"Saoirse—"

"Excuse me?" Kaia tried hard not to drool at the super-hot man talking to her.

His face had paled as if he was staring at a ghost. He seemed to struggle to catch his breath as he brought his hand to his chest. For some reason, his action made her heart ache in response.

Her eyebrows knitted together in concern. "Are you okay?"

The man seemed to be frozen in place, except for the strange expression she couldn't decipher. Heaven help her, but she was worried the handsome stranger was having a heart attack right in front of her eyes.

"Can I get you anything?" she asked loudly and her voice jolted him out of his daze.

He seemed to recover and mustered a weak smile. "I—I'm fine, lass," he answered in a thick Irish brogue.

Somehow she wasn't convinced. Heck, she was known to leave clients speechless with her art, but none had dropped from cardiac arrest. Not if she could help it. She prayed he wouldn't be the first.

"You want to sit down for a second? Or would you like some herbal tea to warm up? It's organic." Kaia gushed, reaching for her thermos on the ground. Why was she so nervous?

He held up his hand to stop her. "I'll be fine, Miss—"

"If you're sure," she replied.

"I'm sure." He nodded, his coloring started to come back.

"WHEW." She grinned. "I suck at CPR, anyway. Probably would've had to ask Agnes to do the honors of reviving you…if it had come to that." Her comment elicited a laugh from him.

Sweet candy corn! He appeared even more handsome than from first impression.

"Sorry for the scare," he added. "Must be the jet lag."

Kaia saw something in his eyes. They were sad. Distant.

"No worries. Crisis thankfully averted." She held out her hand, not thinking. "I'm Kaia Wyntir." She'd forgotten to put her gloves back on after the painting session when he'd distracted her.

"Kearney." He reached for her hand, holding on for a few seconds longer than customary. Not that she was complaining, since his gentle grip felt nice. Firm. Calloused, yet masculine.

"Kearney Maclachlan. Pleasure to meet you." The way he'd said the last sentence in that yummy accent sent a delicious shiver across her skin.

Suddenly, she realized her error.

A flash of fragmented images and intense emotions assaulted her. Nothing made sense except for the yearning. The kind that made her long for a love so deep that her soul ached, leaving her feeling hollow.

She quickly pulled her hand away, breaking their connection. Kaia felt frazzled until reality came back into focus.

"Um, yeah," she responded awkwardly. "Nice to meet you, too." Her fingers still tingled as she tried to appear normal. She quickly yanked the gloves out of her coat pocket and pulled them on. She continued to feel his warmth seeping through her skin, heating up her internal temperature a few degrees. It was her turn to remind herself to breathe. She'd never been affected by anyone's touch until now. Oddly, it stirred up familiar sensations yet she'd never met him until now. She brushed it off as the unexpected energetic connection they'd shared.

Kaia changed the subject to avoid his eyes. "Oh, and thanks for the compliment." She motioned to the artwork. "It's for clients who should be back soon to pick it up."

"Mind if I take a closer look?"

She shook her head. "Nope. Help yourself." Kaia was grateful for the chance to calm her overactive nerves.

Kearney thoughtfully peered at the canvas, leaning in for a better inspection. He observed the details in silence, and after some time, he straightened up. "This literally transports me..." his voice faltered. Appearing to search for the right words, Ace thoughtfully continued, "I can't recall the last time I've felt...I've felt such a personal connection from art. Your work showcases the most vulnerable aspect of a person through their own eyes. It's *their* memories and *their* emotions shining through and everyone can relate to the message somehow."

Kaia blushed. She'd received many compliments for her work before, but this time, when he conveyed those things, *like that,* it sounded so intimate.

WHOA. Her thoughts were taking off in a direction they shouldn't. She crossed her arms, stepping back to distance herself from the man. He may be charming, but she wasn't looking for a holiday fling. Kaia was only in Nocturne Falls for a few weeks and the chances of entertaining any romantic notions were out of the question.

She glanced away and was relieved to see her client Nick approaching them.

"We're back," the older man announced. His teenage daughter trailing behind, her eyes and attention glued to the cellphone screen.

"Just in time." Kaia smiled. "Have a look and tell me what you think, Nick."

The man seemed to mimic Kearney's physical actions from earlier, taking his time on the details, yet his eyes grew misty as he stood silently staring at the canvas. The daughter had grown impatient of waiting and finally lifted her gaze away from the phone to address her dad.

"Just pay the lady so we can go…" her voice trailed off as the artwork caught her eye. She clutched the phone, and as if in a dream, she walked over to stand beside her dad. Her eyes locked on the images.

"How did you know?" Nick choked up as he spoke, "That was a memory I've always cherished."

The girl slid her cell into her back pocket and she hesitantly took her dad's hand. "That was our last father-daughter date when I was nine-years-old. Remember?"

Kaia couldn't help grinning. The healing process was

beginning. It wasn't too late to mend their broken souls.

"I'd never forget that. I've been wrong." Nick squeezed his daughter's hand. "I miss those days, Joss."

"Dad, can we do that again? Have a father-daughter day?" She leaned her head against his arm. "I think mom would've wanted us to."

Nick nodded. "I think you're right, honey. Maybe this is her way of reminding us."

Precious moments like these never got old. Kaia turned her face away to wipe her eyes. She knew the piece revealed the last happy outing the father had spent with his daughter. That was also the year his wife had died. Seeing Joss was a painful reminder of the loss of his childhood sweetheart. He'd poured himself into his work and their father/daughter relationship had deteriorated. It never occurred to him that their love had carried on through Joss.

Kaia tried not to get over emotional at witnessing the newfound connection between a parent and his child. Days like these made her cherish her gift even more. It was rewarding to see the reaction of clients when they acknowledged their true heart or dearest wishes. Sometimes they just needed a little nudge. A wake-up call. In fact, her magical paintings were meant to heal wounds.

Too bad, it couldn't heal hers.

Nick turned to Kaia. "I can't thank you enough. Your art is worth way more than you charge!" He grinned and pulled out his checkbook, filling it out before handing her the paper. "Do you mind if we take it with us now? You won't need to deliver it to the hotel later."

Kaia shoved the check in her pocket without looking at the amount. "Yes, of course."

"Can I carry it, Dad? Please?" Joss begged.

Nick approved, "You certainly can, honey."

"Just hold it by the hook when you carry it. You won't drop it or get paint on yourself," Kaia instructed, carefully demonstrating her technique. She then helped the girl to get a firm handle on the art. Afterwards, they exchanged hugs and goodbyes as she watched the happy customers go on their merry way.

Kearney's deep baritone broke through her thoughts, "What would it take to have one of my own?"

Her eyes widened. "You?"

"Yes, me," he laughed. "How could I pass up on the chance of having an original custom piece after seeing that?"

She chewed on her lower lip. A part of her wanted to refuse the request, but the other part reminded her that nothing was a coincidence. This man needed healing and it was her job to take on the mission. Her mentor had emphasized that she couldn't turn away anyone who was led to her. That was the number one rule she couldn't break, or else her gift would be taken from her. If that happened, she would never be able to recover her memory. She'd never know where she came from or what she truly was.

Kaia gave him a big smile. "It's your lucky day, I just had a cancellation and you earned the spot."

"'Tis lucky, indeed." He winked. "How does this work? I mean, I've never worked with an intuitive artist 'who heals the soul'." He had recited some of the verbiage from her sign.

"First…" She took a step toward him. "You have to be open to the truth that's in your heart." She swallowed and continued in a soft voice, "You also have to be completely vulnerable so that I can paint the answers that you're searching for."

"Wow. That sounds profound, and somewhat terrifying." His eyes locked on hers.

"Oh, believe me, we're just getting started," she announced.

He chuckled. "I'm intrigued."

"Second..." She pulled off her glove and took another step closer. "You have to trust me."

Kearney's face grew serious. She may not know what he was thinking, but even through his smile, she could see the raw pain buried deep within those ocean-blue depths. She'd had a taste of his anguish and she wanted to delve into those dark waters.

"If I must trust someone, I suppose it should be you," his voice practically dripped honey.

OH, BOY.

Kaia shivered, feeling the magnetic pull between them, and she suddenly questioned the no fling thing. What was the harm in a brief winter romance? They'd both get something out of it, and when their time together came to an end, they'd go their separate ways. Easy peasy.

"Ready to begin?" She wanted to give him a fair chance to change his mind. Or maybe hers.

His eyes flashed in interest and he bared a perfect smile. "Oh, I'm more than ready. Are you?" he challenged.

Game on.

Kaia chose to ignore the tiny voice in her head that screamed she was in way over her head. Wasn't she on vacation, after all? She mentally convinced herself to follow the advice she'd given others. *Live a little.* She couldn't remember the last time she'd actually done anything for herself.

She supposed she'd been searching for answers for years now, without a break, and there was nothing in the rule book that said she couldn't have some fun. As long as she continued to pursue the truth, she knew every person she encountered, every story she unraveled through a painting would lead her one step closer to the right person, someone who'd eventually know something—*anything*—about her.

Besides, she wasn't one to retreat from a challenge. Not as long as the memories of her past were on the line.

She held Kearney's even gaze. "There's no going back," she warned, more for her own benefit.

"Aye, lass," he agreed. His blue eyes turned a shade darker as if he, too, wasn't about to back down.

3

Kearney expertly threw a flat stone and watched it skip across the surface of the water, creating tiny ripples where the object had briefly touched. He needed something to do to calm his racing heart. No matter how many times he replayed the meeting with Kaia, he couldn't shake off the uncanny resemblance.

Saoirse was dead.

He needed to accept the truth. When was he ever going be free from the guilt of losing her?

"Yet—" he paused.

He shook his head at the ludicrous thoughts. He was definitely going mad. How many times had he met someone who resembled his late wife during the past century?

Too many to count.

The interaction with Kaia earlier had been entertaining. One thing was for sure, her carefree nature and candidness was nothing like Saoirse. They were total opposites. Where Kaia offered warmth, his wife had been cold.

Kearney expelled an agonizing breath as he stared

off into the calming waters. He'd always been fond of the lake that separated the homes, yet still connected the neighbors through a single path. The residents of this private community were essentially like family. That's why he enjoyed the visits to Nocturne Falls. It was also a short distance into town when he needed to escape the solitude for a few hours.

He wiped his hands on his jeans and decided to head back to the Winthorpes' house to retrieve the presents from the trunk of his rental car. He shivered despite wearing a heavy jacket. The temperature had dropped a few degrees as evening approached. He wondered where Rock and Keke were. They hadn't made an appearance yet, so he opted to find the spare key to settle in. If he had to wait any longer he'd surely freeze to death. He'd bring the gifts over in the morning and sort things out.

As he walked to his cottage carrying an arm full of boxes and gift bags, he looked forward to starting the fireplace to cozy things up. Maybe catch up on some reading. There were plenty of options from the stack of novels Agnes had given him. The idea of a low-key evening sounded exactly his pace after the long day he'd had. He spotted the spare in its regular spot and quickly made his way in, kicking the door shut behind him with his booted foot.

"A hot shower would be good," he announced to the empty room as he pivoted around to put the presents on the hardwood floors. That's when he glanced up and caught a flash of very sexy legs running down the stairs.

Apparently, someone had already beaten him to the punch.

"Who the h—" the woman gasped in mid-sentence. "KEARNEY!"

He knew that voice.

His eyes moved slowly upward, finally resting on her face. His breath caught in his throat. How could he not stare at her beauty? Kaia was barely clad, wrapped tightly in a fluffy white towel. Her damp hair clung to her tanned skin as droplets of water dripped onto her shoulders.

He didn't question why she was there because, at that moment, she was the most gorgeous creature he'd ever seen. Kearney's face split into a boyish grin. "Well, this is one heck of a welcome."

Rearranging the logs with the iron poker, Kearney wanted to keep the fire burning steadily. He watched the dancing flames while he waited for Kaia to get dressed and return to the living room. He hadn't gotten much information out of her except that she was visiting from Hawaii, and that she was a childhood friend of Keke's.

"Tell me again why you're in my cottage?" Kaia asked from behind him.

He stood up and turned to face her. "Seeing as I'm friends with Keke and Rock, I had pre-arrangements for the use of this place for a couple weeks."

"Is that so?" She quirked a brow, looking unconvinced. "Then why didn't I know you were coming? They'd promised it to me." Her arms were crossed in an effort to appear intimidating.

Clamping his lips together, he tried not to laugh at her attire. She was adorably dressed in a matching thermal pajama set printed with cats in Santa hats.

Kaia threw up her hands in irritation. "Fine. Let's try to figure this out." She kicked off her cat slippers and took a seat on the sofa, tucking her legs under her.

"How about some herbal tea? It's organic."

She rolled her eyes. "Very funny."

He enjoyed teasing her to keep things light. Kearney had brewed some from her stash while she'd been upstairs. He reached for the two steaming mugs on the fireplace mantel and handed her one before taking the recliner across from her.

Kearney cleared his throat. "Seeing as I've arrived a few weeks earlier than scheduled, I'm prepared to find alternate accommodations."

She took a sip of the drink and gave him a guilty look. "It seems that I'm also at fault. I haven't told Keke I wanted to extend my stay. I'd planned on leaving a few days after Christmas which would've coincided with your visit."

"So we're both in a bit of a pickle," he noted.

"I guess in all fairness, since this cottage has five bedrooms, I'm willing to share."

"That's mighty generous of you."

"It's plenty of room for the both of us." Kaia's lips curled into a seductive smile. "After all, we're both adults."

Kearney swallowed hard at the invisible lump in his throat. "Yes, we are." Was it suddenly hot in here or maybe he was wearing one too many layers?

"Hope you don't mind that I'll be doing most of my work from home."

"Not at all. I'll do my best to stay out of your hair," he promised. "Don't think you'll be getting out of my commissioned order, though."

"I never turn away a paying gig." She sat up and placed the mug on the coffee table. "So we're good, right?"

"Aye, roomie." He raised his mug in salute when a loud noise grasped their attention.

The front door swung open as Keke and Rock tried to squeeze their way through the narrow space at the same time. It would've been comedic if he hadn't detected the apparent baby bump she was sporting.

Kearney jumped to his feet. "Feck, there must be somethin' in the water." He threw his hands up, "I'll have none of that."

Keke laughed, then squealed and rushed toward him for a hug. He gave her a gentle squeeze.

She pulled away and pursed her lips. "You're early!"

"You're glowing!" he beamed. "Motherhood has done you good."

"And you're forgiven." She smacked him on the chest. "For now."

He stepped away briefly to shake Rock's hand, then changed his mind and yanked the guy in for a manly bear hug. "It's been a while, my friend. I see you didn't waste any time."

Rock chuckled, "You're next, old guy. You did catch the bouquet at our wedding."

"Bouquet? Breaking tradition, huh?" Kaia walked over to join in on the hug fest.

"C'mon, now." Kearney rubbed the back of his neck. "I was only minding my own business."

Keke turned to her husband and gave him a goofy smile. "I told you they'd be able to figure something out."

He wrapped his arm lovingly around her and nodded. "Yes, dear."

Everyone laughed and they spent the next few minutes catching up and discussing the misunderstanding. Kearney arranged to bring the presents from Luna and Ace over in the morning.

The married couple was about to leave when Keke exclaimed, "Oh, I'm having a holiday dinner at my house tomorrow night. Now that both our dear friends are in town at the same time, there's just so much to celebrate."

"She's right. It's not often that we have guests, now that the baby is coming and my winter schedule has slowed down," Rock agreed.

"Don't you mean you need some 'bromance' in your life before you're elbow deep in baby spit and dirty diapers?" Kaia joked.

"Guilty." Rock chuckled. "On that note, I better get Keke home before she scratches the whole thing and turns it into a lady's night."

"We can't have that." Kearney held the door open for them. "Goodnight, kids."

The room was filled with awkward silence once the couple left. He turned around but hadn't expected Kaia to be standing so close. She stumbled back and his arm shot out to catch her, pulling her against his body.

She expelled a half-gasp, half-sigh. Tipping her chin up, her eyes locked on his.

All his senses were on red alert and he couldn't deny how good it felt to hold her in his arms. They may have just met this morning, but when he looked at her, he saw the similarities and doubts they carried. He could see a woman who was guarded yet wasn't afraid to take chances. The fire in her eyes was every reason for him to want to get to know her better.

He wasn't a fool. The chemistry was blistering between them from their first meeting. Yet this time, his wants and needs were different. He wasn't searching for a passing fling. He wanted Kaia, that's true, but in a way that was beyond the physical. His eyes raked over her face as he cradled her soft body in the folds of his arm. He knew her tremendous worth and wasn't about to let her go. That's why he planned on getting to know everything about this woman.

Kearney was willing to let go of the past…a destructive love that had only been filled with heartache, in order to finally heal his broken soul.

Her lips parted, then Kaia licked her lips before speaking. "A—are you hungry?" Her question came out as a breathless whisper.

His mouth stretched into a broad smile and he quirked a brow in interest. "That depends on what's on the menu."

Kaia wiped at her forehead and realized she'd smudged paint across it with her pinky. She'd been up all night working on the artwork since she'd had trouble falling asleep. Darn the man! Every time she closed her eyes, she'd see Kearney's devilish grin and the suggestive response he'd given.

"Ugh." She rubbed her hand on the worn fabric, caking on another layer of color to the already paint-stained apron. "Focus, Kaia! FOCUS."

In addition to the brushes, she reveled in using her hands and fingers as an organic tool for blending and building textures. There was something magical about smearing the wet paint, grazing her fingers across the surface to form curves and shapes. Filling the image with her personal energy to help bring the healing to life.

Kaia raised her arms over her head, stretching as she mentally critiqued the first phase of the design. This was not her usual style but it matched the person she was creating it for. There were more details and emotion in the aggressive motions and color palette. Truthfully, she'd had a difficult time interpreting his memories and wishes. Kearney was like an unsolved puzzle. Pieces of shattered glass she needed to put together to form an entire picture. It was frustrating because she couldn't finish the painting without more information.

Who was this woman that had captured his heart?

Her chest constricted and she blamed it on the late-night snack binge.

Kaia's eyes fell on the sketch of the woman, her silhouette was distorted, her face unclear. She sighed as she recalled all the men she'd dated over the years. None had ever come close to this sacred love that cut Kearney so deep. That's the kind of love she craved. Yet, she'd lost her memory a century ago, so there was no telling what kind of life she'd led before then.

That memory of her resurrection was still fresh in her mind. Kaia had awakened on a bed of leaves and flowers to the aroma of fragrant medicines. She was brought back to life by the elder Morrnah, the Hawaiian *Kahuna*, a shamanic healer and ancient sorceress. The woman she regarded dearly as a grandmother, yet she couldn't return Kaia's memories back even with all the magic they'd cast.

Time was the only cure.

During those difficult years, she'd learned to harness her own abilities. She'd transformed the knowledge she'd been taught to apply in her healing artworks. Kaia had perfected her skills for survival and to adapt to the changes that came with the modern world. She'd met Keke ten years ago during a visit to Hawaii. She'd gotten lost in the forest and stumbled across the unicorn shifter by accident. Thankfully, their shared supernatural secrets helped forge a lifelong bond of sisterly friendship.

Kaia's eyelids started to droop from sleep deprivation and she forced them open. She took one last glance and noticed the image in the forefront of the canvas. The man's eyes were the one thing in focus and the rest of him was an abstract blur. There was no mistaking that it was Kearney. His intense icy-blue eyes were unforgettable.

She concentrated on the man's energies, opening her spiritual connection to receive any new visions that would bring more clarity. Focusing all her strength and having nothing came through; Kaia reluctantly gave up in frustration. Her rigorous attempts to connect only left her with residual heightened emotions that were unnervingly difficult to shake off. Kaia sensed unfinished business and heartbreak. This passion deserved closure, yet something troubled her about this mission. She couldn't seem to put a finger on it and it bugged the crap out of her.

Maybe the attraction between them was no more than a mutual desire for connection, to be set free, but Kaia never disregarded her empathic nature. These powerful feelings compelled her to uncover the truth. Partly out of curiosity, but mostly for Kearney's sake.

She promised, "I will find your answers."

The house was all decked out for the holidays, complete with an enormous Christmas tree, lots of candles and fairy lights, stockings hanging from the fireplace, and plenty of poinsettias and mistletoe strategically placed throughout. In the background, soft music played while Kearney stood staring out the window at the lake view, a glass of whiskey in is hand. He'd wanted to dress a little more appropriately rather than daily attire, so he'd chosen to wear a dark buttoned-up dress shirt, black slacks, and a pair of leather shoes that matched the ensemble.

Everyone had been buzzing around and the women politely refused his offer of help. He could hear the kitchen bustling with productivity as he brought the glass to his lips.

Stasia, the peculiar catering chef and reaper next door, was making final preparations for the dinner. Keke was at the table rearranging the place settings and food dishes. Her husband was upstairs in his home office taking an emergency vet call. Professor Hyde, the cursed pueo owl, was on the counter reading the local newspaper, *The Tombstone*.

And, Kearney was left waiting.

He peered through the window up at the stars. They were glowing brightly across the night sky in an even path that was both dreamy and graceful. He hoped the sky would remain clear so he could show Kaia later from a better viewpoint near the lake.

His forehead crinkled as he frowned. Checking his watch again, he wondered what was taking Kaia so long to get here. Did she have car trouble? Maybe worse? He forced himself to stop dwelling on the negatives and took a hefty sip of his drink.

When he'd gotten up this morning, he'd found a note that she'd be working in town all day. He took that as a sign, giving her space. Kearney had spent the day splitting firewood and even did some reading, but he'd been restless. In fact, he was dead tired. He hadn't slept a wink knowing she was sleeping a few doors away.

Maybe staying together was a bad idea. At this rate, he'd turn into an insomniac.

The creak of the door opening made him twist around, almost spilling the alcohol. Kearney's mouth fell open and he quickly clamped it shut to hide his shock. Kaia was a vision of ethereal beauty, rivaling the striking Fae women who visited his world. She slid off her double-breasted wool trench coat and revealed a simple, yet elegant red satin shift dress. It had a low neckline with straps that crisscrossed at the back. Her hair was a messy up-do pinned low at the nape of her neck. Her makeup was a flawless, natural look, except for her luscious mouth. The lipstick color was a deep seductive crimson that enhanced her plump lips.

Professor Hyde whistled and Kearney gave him an irritated glare.

"Wow! You look gorgeous!" Keke exclaimed.

Kaia's cheeks flushed from the compliment. "Thanks. I hadn't planned on getting all gussied up."

"You look like a work of art." Stasia said as she walked in from the kitchen. "Is this dress rehearsal for the holiday gala? Why didn't I get the memo?"

Kaia laughed and shook her head. "Basil at Hair Scare wanted to give me a makeover as an exchange for the painting I made for her last week."

"Seems like you've rendered Kearney speechless," Stasia half-teased. She gave him a knowing look and crossed her arms.

"I'm afraid it's true," he agreed good-naturedly, moving closer to them.

Rock bounded down the steps and whistled. "Who'd you invite to dinner? I thought Kaia was coming?" He winked at her before giving Kaia a hug. "You look great."

"Now that we're all here, let's get this party going," Keke announced.

Professor Hyde flew over to a vacant chair and the group started to head to the table.

Kearney stopped Kaia. "Would you like me to take your coat?"

She gave him a shy nod and handed it to him. "Yes, thank you."

His eyes never left her face as he spoke. "It's true, you're absolutely stunning tonight." He straightened up and walked away before she could respond.

Kearney rounded the hallway and hung the jacket up in the closet. He gripped the handle of the door, needing time to calm his racing heart. How could he be so smitten by someone he'd only met not more than forty-eight hours ago?

She'd enchanted him.

This incredible woman had made him feel things again, and *that* frightened him. Did he have the right to pursue Kaia when he wasn't sure if he was completely over Saoirse? Would he ever be? He didn't know the answers to those questions, but what he was a hundred percent certain of—*he wanted her*.

Kaia's high heels got caught between the cobblestones and thankfully she clung to Kearney to steady herself. He'd held her hand while she disengaged her shoe from the pesky hole. Now that her feet were firmly planted on an even spot, she kicked off the source of her problems. Her hand hadn't moved from his sturdy bicep so she reluctantly released him.

"I don't know how women can wear these things all day," she commented sourly.

"Two reasons," he offered. "*One.* It makes you taller. *Two.* It tones your calves." He gave her a smug smile.

"Know-it-all." She stuck her tongue out at him. "Where are you taking me?"

He shook his head. "Not going to tell you unless you accept a piggy-back ride."

"No way!"

"Yes—*way!*" he mimicked. "I don't want your feet to get dirty. Not when you're dressed like that." Kearney turned his back toward her and squatted. "Get on, lass."

Kaia hooked her fingers through the loops of the heels and shrugged. "Fine. I'm only doing this because I want a piggy-back ride."

He laughed at her tone and she hopped on. He almost buckled backward. "Jeez. I'm not a horse. And I thought women were supposed to be more graceful," he kidded.

"I'm not any woman," she snickered.

"I can see that."

He stood up and Kaia's crossed legs were wrapped firmly against his tight abdomen as he held on to her. She leaned forward, her body pressed closer to his back, her arms secured loosely around his neck.

"Now that you've obediently complied, I'll tell you where we're going," Kearney stated.

"Real nice of you."

A gust of wind made him shiver and she opened her coat, wrapping it around them both.

Kaia grumbled, "Why didn't you bundle up?"

"We're only a short walk away and I hadn't planned on a detour home," he supplied.

She tilted her head; her face snuggled against his neck, her mouth close to his ear. "You're too much, Maclachlan." She could feel his smile and it made her stomach flutter.

He carried her in silence for a few minutes and they soon reached the area he'd mentioned. She wanted to hold onto him much longer but she swiftly disengaged herself from his warm back.

They were standing in a patch of grass at the edge of an overhang that overlooked the lake. He pointed up at the sky and she gasped in excitement.

"The stars look so close! Look at all of them." She twisted her neck to see his face. "They're AMAZING!"

"Aye, they're a beaute." He inhaled deeply. "It's perfect," he said on an exhale and turned to look at her.

Her teeth were chattering through her wide grin and her cheeks were burning from the cold, but she didn't care. This was something she hadn't seen before. Of course, she'd seen stars but this view was as enchanting as the paintings she created.

Kaia's hands were numb from the chill and she shoved them into her coat pockets. Her fingers felt something rub against them and she pulled the item out of her left pocket.

"What's that?" Kearney asked.

She laughed. "Someone slipped a mistletoe twig in there."

"You don't say? Those crazy kids," Kearney said as he blew into his hands.

Kaia bit the side of her mouth and she raised the fresh sprig over her head before tapping him on the shoulder. She was feeling happy and she could easily blame it on the drinks she'd had, but she knew being in

Kearney's company was naturally intoxicating.

He narrowed his eyes at her action. "What are you doing?"

"We might as well make good use of it." She got on her tiptoes and dangled it over their heads. "You a scaredy-cat?" she goaded playfully while she continued taunting him.

Kearney shrugged and grabbed her by the waist and planted a tantalizing kiss that squelched all thoughts from her head. She wrapped her arms around his neck and kissed him back.

His kisses were tender as if he was holding back. Just as quickly, he let her go.

"Time's up," he said.

She rubbed her temple to reduce the ache, but it didn't help. Her head was spinning and she thought it was from the exhilaration of their lip-lock action, until she swayed on her feet, and he reached for her.

"You okay?" His face revealed his concern.

"I'll be fine. Just need a minute." Kaia couldn't seem to make the strange images disappear from her mind's eye. It was as if her memories were merged with reality and the two were short-circuiting. She found it difficult to distinguish or process the information.

Just as swiftly, she was back to normal.

"That was some kiss," she teased. "Swoon worthy." She snickered at her own joke.

He rolled his eyes at her. "Anyone ever tell you that you're corny?"

"Yes, but it's only because they don't have a sense of humor. Except for Keke."

He noticed some loose strands falling out of her up-do, so he tucked them behind her ear.

She gave him a goofy grin and tipped her head back for another look at the stars. The wind was kicking up and she shivered. "I could stare at them forever," she said happily.

"Maybe next time," he said through chattering teeth. "Right now, we need to get back before we freeze our arses off."

They both burst into laughter.

"Good idea," she agreed. "My legs are already turning into popsicles."

"Then we'll just have to melt them."

Catching her by surprise, she squealed when he scooped her up in his arms and tossed her over his shoulder. Her laughter echoed and didn't subside as he easily carried her away from the lake. Within seconds they were back in the comfort of their warm cottage.

5

They were sprawled in front of the fireplace on a plush rug, legs outstretched, and their feet growing toasty from the fire. Mugs of hot cocoa sat on the floor beside them as Kaia listened to Kearney's rich tone read poetry from a Robert Frost collection.

She interrupted him before he moved onto the next page. "Can you read something else? Frost is wonderful, but some of the poems are a bit of a bummer."

"All right, then. Hmm…let's see what else we have." He sorted through a stack of books and pulled a small vintage one.

He cleared his throat and recited Lord Byron's "She Walks in Beauty".

Kaia was hooked on the lyrical way in which he pronounced each word. He made the romantic words jump to life. She leaned back against the floor and closed her eyes. He finished the last sentence and she absorbed the sound of crackling fire as she let the poetry sink into her head.

"Was that enough romance for you?" Kearney shut the book and put it aside.

They were both casually dressed in pajamas for the impromptu indoor camping. Her eyes flew open when she realized he was tucking something under her head for support. Kearney had rolled up a throw blanket and made it a makeshift pillow.

She stared up at the ceiling. There were so many things she wanted to know about him and somehow she managed to ask the questions out loud.

"Why are you so kind? Is this really who you are, or is this all an act?" Kaia clamped her mouth with her hands, rolling over to stare at him.

He shook his head, answering without hesitation, "Sadly, this is truly who I am."

"So why are you still single then?" She sat up and crossed her legs yoga style.

"I could ask you the same question," he returned.

She furrowed her brows and jutted out her chin. "I'm being serious."

"Me, too," he responded but her expression seemed to make him laugh. "All right. I'll tell you."

Kaia rubbed her hands together. "Gimme all the juicy details."

He laughed a rumbling laugh.

"C'mon now. As roomies, this is as real as we're gonna get if we want to know each other better."

Kearney motioned his head in slow nods. "As you wish." He took a deep breath and started, "Many…many years ago I was married."

She waited with bated breath for him to continue.

"I loved that woman deeply." His voice lowered. "Sadly, I fear she had found comfort in my mate's arms while I was away at war."

"You don't have to tell me," she said.

"No, I need to tell you." He took her hand and threaded her fingers through his.

The simple act made her heart constrict at his vulnerability. He was giving her his complete trust and that was exactly what she'd needed to finish his painting.

"I'd rushed home even though I'd barely recovered from injuries. I'd been so elated to see her again." His voice broke. "I was told of her betrayal and didn't believe it. I went to investigate, but discovered she'd killed herself when her lover left her." His eyes were filled with hurt and unshed tears.

Kaia's heart broke at witnessing the burden of his anguish all of these years. He had trusted his wife and she had destroyed him. Leaving him with not so much as an explanation for the reasons that motivated her to stray. He'd been left carrying that torture and doubt regarding their failed marriage for a century.

"Oh, Kearney." Kaia didn't think, she clasped his face between her hands and stroked his cheek with her thumb.

He turned his face and pressed a tender kiss against her palm, and that one action was all she needed. She leaned in and their mouths connected. The kiss was electrifying, spreading through her body and squelching the emptiness she'd felt.

Kaia responded without thought of consequences. She understood his pain. She needed to heal as badly as he did and what they were sharing wasn't more than just friendship. They were comforting each other. Taking chances together.

Kearney was surrendering to the unknown, yet she wasn't sure she was ready to.

His mouth was a drug and she was falling into his

spell. Slipping into a delirious state of bliss. Every kiss turned more intimate, every stroke of his tongue grew deeper. Bolder.

Out of nowhere, the throbbing took root in her head. Then the pain increased in its intensity until it was unbearable. She pulled away, trying to fight off the agony within, when the vision blasted through her. All the images and emotions returned in slow motion, as if the film had rolled backward until each piece of the puzzle came together. Making sense.

She cried out, clutching at her heart. She fought for air and took huge gulps of oxygen to fill her lungs, but it didn't seem to be enough. It didn't register that Kearney had gotten on his knees, holding her tight against his body while she resisted. She could hear him speak but couldn't make out what he was saying through the excruciating headache.

His voice broke through the muffled barrier.

"Breathe," he commanded. "Just breathe!"

After several minutes of his soothing instructions, Kaia calmed down enough to seize control of the rhythm of her breathing. She slumped forward and buried her face against his chest. Her cheeks were wet with tears but she gathered the strength to push away.

She couldn't look at him directly. When she regained her voice, her words came out raspy and barely audible as she confirmed, "I am Saoirse."

"Let me get this straight." Keke stopped her pacing and took a seat across from Kaia at the table. She made hand gestures as she spoke. "Kearney was married, but his wife betrayed him with the best friend. Then the jerk abandoned her and she threw herself off a cliff. After that, Kearney met you and you're really her?"

Kaia was impressed her friend had said that all in one breath.

Stasia placed three mugs of tea on the table during Keke's long-winded recap. She snatched the two mugs up and returned to the kitchen.

"Where are you going?" Keke called after her.

A few minutes later Stasia came back with an opened bottle of whiskey and two shot glasses. "I figured we needed something stiffer if we want to try to decode that mess of a story."

She slid Keke the tea and gave Kaia the alcohol before holding hers up in the air. "Sorry Keke, you're on an extended alcohol hiatus."

"No offense taken." She lifted her mug.

They all clinked glasses and drank up.

Kaia shoved her empty cup at Stasia. "Hit me again." She was in the mood to forget the truth. It was funny how she'd searched for answers all these years and now that she knew, she was more lost than ever.

"This isn't a bar, y'know." Keke smirked.

"It is tonight." Kaia jiggled the glass. "Drinks all around, bartender."

Stasia shook her head and refilled the order. "Why don't you go over the story again? At least I'll understand your version."

Keke frowned but leaned in to listen to Kaia's rehashing of the complicated tale. During their discussion, she'd consumed more alcohol than she thought she could handle. Somehow Stasia appeared to hold her liquor too well.

Kaia heaved a sad sigh and the heartache resurfaced. "There are still things I'm not really clear on. There's something missing in the story Kearney told me about Saoirse."

"You are Saoirse," Keke corrected.

"Right." Kaia nodded. "I forget. I'm her—his adulterous wife."

Stasia shook her head. "Before you put a label on yourself, you need to gather the facts. I agree that the story seems like there's something missing."

"It's strange that I remember a lot of things, yet I feel like two completely different people. Who is the real me? Which life do I live? Even though I've recovered most of my memories…it still feels surreal." Kaia shook her head in disbelief. "I'm still shocked at the fact that I'm a freakin' Fae! It might take some time to absorb that particular revelation. Not to mention the fact that Kearney is a wizard and we had an arranged marriage to keep the peace between worlds—but that's a whole other can of worms!" She suddenly felt the anxiety and pressure building as the facts gradually sunk in. "There's so much I need to do now that I know who and what I am."

Stasia pulled out a chair and sat. "Fae or not, this is really about you and Kearney. There's plenty of time to take care those things later."

"You lost your memories, and not once have you used your Fae magic, so there's no way any of us would have known." Keke crinkled her nose. "Besides, everything came at you all at once, which can be overwhelming. You simply need to give yourself time to absorb and heal," she said lovingly.

Kaia let out a frustrated groan. "In my heart. In the very core of my soul…I *love* him," she professed.

"I know, sweetie," Keke reached over and patted Kaia's hand.

Stasia suggested, "Maybe it's time you finished Kearney's painting. That could be the unfinished business you have."

Keke wiped a tear from her face. She sniffed and said, "I agree. The answers will be revealed now that you have your memory back."

"It's true about the saying, 'ignorance is bliss'. At least when we both didn't know who I was, our relationship was really, *really* good."

"It will be again." Stasia gave her a confident smile. "Just as the gift you provide others, you must also allow your true heart and dearest wishes to surface."

Keke stood up gingerly, her hand rested on the round belly. "I'm totally in agreement with Yoda over here. I don't think you're a cheater, and I bet my sweet stash of uni-dust that it's the—," she used air quotes, "*'supposed'* lover that did Saoirse in."

"What if you're wrong and it's all true?" Kaia drained the last of her small glass. She was really feeling the potent liquid make its way through her system. Instead of numbing the pain, she was hit with nostalgia and longing. How could she have loved Kearney so much and betray him? Her intuition told her it didn't ring true.

"It's always the lover," Keke insisted.

Kaia pushed out of her seat and stood facing the women. Her hand balled tightly in a fist at her side. "You're right. I'm not going to wallow in defeat. That's not my thing. I'm going to get to the bottom of this!" Her finger shot up in the air and she swayed from the effects of the hard liquor.

"If you're not careful, you'll be landing on *your* bottom," Keke whinnied then snorted.

"That was actually a funny one this time," Stasia commented but she didn't even crack a smile.

Keke lightly rubbed her stomach and gave the reaper an incredulous look. "Are you ever going to be normal?"

"Nope." Stasia glanced at her watch and let out a quick breath. "I'd love to stick around, but I've got to blackmail a prospective employee in eleven minutes and eleven seconds."

"Wish I could do your job. Seems less complicated." Kaia blew out a puff of air. She was troubled over being branded with the scarlet letter. The pounding in her chest validated what she was feeling. She bellowed out her thoughts, "I am NOT a cheater!"

"Now that you've established what you're not, why don't you go paint?" Stasia pointed in the direction of the empty room that led out to the garden at the back of Keke's house.

She gave the woman a crooked smile. "I—I'm just a wee bit tipsy." She squinted, demonstrating with the use of her thumb and index.

Stasia eyed her meaningfully. "That's the best time to create. When you're at your most vulnerable."

She knew the reaper was correct. Losing her inhibitions would make her open up to the visions. Perhaps she hadn't grasped the information because she'd been guarded. In the recesses of her mind she knew who she was and that was the key to the actual truth.

Thankfully Rock had moved all her stuff over to the spare guest bedroom and the unfinished room housed her temporary art studio. Kaia had chosen to leave when the tension mounted after her confession. Kearney had been confused and furious at the news. How could she blame him? In his mind, she'd been dead and now that she wasn't, he needed time to readjust. Just as she did.

Now that they were apart, she had a chance to sort out the memories that were partially restored. There were crucial fragments missing and she needed to locate them in order to salvage the relationship between her and Kearney.

Snatching the whiskey off the table, she drank straight from the bottle, swallowing the rest of the contents. Grinning from ear-to-ear, she was elated to discover her mission.

Kaia was determined to capture Kearney's heart and win back her husband!

6

The sun crept up over the horizon and soft light filtered through the oversized French doors. Kaia had been working non-stop to finish the painting Kearney had commissioned from her. From the start, she knew his loneliness. She lived it. The yearning inside of her had transformed just as the darkness of the night flowed into a new dawn, the images took on new shapes and deeper meaning. She leaned in close, her nose almost touching the piece and she made one final loving stroke with her pinky across the surface. Her heart no longer lost within the shadows of the past.

Sitting straighter in her chair, she gazed at the completed canvas with new eyes. Not caring that the tears continued. The guilt had vanished and was replaced by sympathy. The beautiful and haunting faces staring back at her provided a powerful conclusion she was now ready to face.

"There are two sides to every story," she murmured below her breath.

Kaia felt her courage waver, but she succeeded to knocked loudly on the door. She waited nervously on the porch and was prepared to stand there as long as it took for Kearney to give her a chance to speak. She didn't have to wait long because it swung open and the expression on his face was masked. Unreadable.

They stood for a few seconds without speaking.

"I was on my way to see you," he volunteered, slicing through the tension.

Even though his clothes were disheveled, hair tousled, face unshaven, Kearney was the handsomest man she'd ever laid eyes upon.

"Can I come in?"

"Yes. Yes, of course." He pulled the door wider and she walked in carrying the large wrapped gift.

She took a few steps in and stopped. Her eyes landed on the canvas propped back against the unlit fireplace. Her hand flew to her chest, stunned and happy all at once.

"I've been an idiot," he admitted. "All those years I thought you'd betrayed me. Maybe that was my way of keeping your memory in my heart forever. Believing you weren't going to be in my life was painful. It also gave me a reason to live—so I could find you now."

Kaia was too choked up to say anything. She handed him the present and he took it with trembling hands.

She clasped her hands in front of her. "I finished it for you."

He gripped the item as he talked. "I'm sorry, Kaia. I should have believed in you. *In us.*"

She shook her head and took a step toward him. "No. I'm sorry I couldn't remember."

Kearney set the package aside and hugged her tight.

"Oh, darling. I don't care in what century or what name you go by, you'll always be *my* wife."

Tipping back her head for a good look at him, she was overjoyed by his words.

He bent his head and pressed his lips against hers, whispering, "I love you. I always have. I always will. Wizard's promise."

"I love you so much, Kearney." She kissed him back with all the emotions in her heart. "Fae's promise."

"I'm a lucky man to find the love of my life twice in one lifetime," he proudly announced.

Kaia nipped at his chin, planting kisses along his jaw and his hands slid to her hips. He picked her up, her lips never leaving his while she wrapped her legs around his waist. He carried her to the bedroom and laid her down. Their kisses more fervent, more urgent. Her body lit up as she clung to him. He tasted even sweeter now that she knew she belonged to this amazing man. They were stronger now and there was nothing that could ever come between them again.

He pulled off her sweater and she returned the favor. Her hands grazed over his toned abdomen, gliding up his muscled arm. She wanted to touch all of him to memorize everything about him. He was real and she was never going to let him slip through her fingers again.

In the next moment, they were both flinging clothes across the room, hastily stripping off every piece of fabric in their hand's way, until their bodies met. Skin-to-skin.

Kearney cradled her head as he kissed her against the mattress. "I wanted you so badly the first moment you offered me herbal tea." He laughed. "The tipping point was when you were in that red number. Trust me;

I took a heck of a lot of cold showers after that."

"You'll never have to take another cold shower again." She traced a finger along his lower lip and he shivered.

"You're killing me, lass."

Her lips curved into a seductive smile. "You have me now."

"Aye, that I do, Kaia." He gave her a quick peck on the lips. "And…you have all of me. Forever."

They took their time rediscovering each other. Exploring and pushing the limits of how much love they could share with one another, making up for lost time. This was their beautiful beginning and they were able to heal all their wounds together.

Many hours later, they sat on the sofa comparing the two paintings side-by-side.

The original was unfinished but it was an exact duplicate of the one Kaia had made for him. Before she had arrived at his doorstep, Keke had given him the aged artwork. She'd found it in the attic and remembered how she'd come to possess it. When the two women had become friends, she'd found the art in the dumpster at Kaia's studio. She'd kept it and it wasn't until her room was used as a studio that she thought to return it. That's when she noticed the uncanny resemblance to the man on the canvas. It was Kearney's face all along. Even before Kaia had met him, she'd always carried her love for him in her heart.

The memory loss never could erase her feelings for him.

He'd matured mentally and spiritually so he was never truly angry with Kaia. He knew it was directed at himself and his inability to protect her. The separation allowed them to fall in love all over again. It wasn't an arranged marriage that ended in tragedy. This time around, it was an organic love that blossomed between two good people. Growth and wisdom taught him about forgiveness and taking chances. Happiness was on the other side of fear. There would be no more searching.

Kearney could honestly say he'd never planned on leaving Kaia. A love so strong couldn't easily be discarded. He needed space to do some soul searching so he could have a fulfilled life with her in it. In this century! His dearest wishes had come true. The proof was the woman he held in his arms.

"You know I would never cheat on you. It was Deaglan who murdered me."

He stroked her hair as she recounted the tale again. "Aye."

"In his jealousy over you, he couldn't understand why I didn't want him. He poisoned me and covered it up with a story he wanted to believe. Saoirse died that day, it's true." She sat up and took his hand. "What we had was not the love I longed for. Right now, this is what I'd dreamed it would be. Just you and me." She raised his fist to her lips and kissed his knuckles. "We're free to choose who we want, yet we chose each other all over again."

Kearney gave her a tender look. "I guess we always knew the answers."

"What happened to that asshat, anyway?" Kaia frowned angrily.

He reached over to smooth the creases on her forehead. "The 'asshat' that was Deaglan got his just desserts. His wife stuck a dagger through his heart when she discovered his infidelities."

"I can't deny that sounded almost satisfying. He deserved a slow, agonizing ending for the century of pain he inflicted upon us." She raised her finger to her throat and pretended to slice across it.

"You're scaring me, lass."

She laughed. "I'll show 'em not to mess with a Fae who's married to a wizard."

"On that note." He got up and dropped to one knee. "Let's do it right this time around. Be mine. Make me the happiest man on earth and marry me, lass."

"Is that a question or are you telling me?" A fat tear rolled down her face.

He reached into his pants pocket and pulled out mistletoe. He shook his head and shoved it back into his pocket, fumbling for the ring. "Will you marry me, Kaia Wyntir?"

Kaia sprung up and held out her hand to him. "The anticipation was killing me," she teased.

He slid the object on and she peered down at him with an enormous smile. "Yes! I'm all in!"

Kearney grabbed her and kissed her with all the pent-up passion stored inside. She matched his kisses with equal emotion. When they finally separated, her expression made him pause. "What's the matter?"

She gnawed on her lower lip. "Um, wait until you meet my grams, Morrnah." Kaia shivered. "You'll have to get through her to get the girl."

He signed, "Is there never a dull moment with you, love?"

"How boring would it be without a little adventure here and there?" She grabbed his hand and gave him an innocent look before leading him toward the stairs. "Let's start practicing now."

Kearney wasn't a fool.

He waggled his brows. "I could use lots and lots…and *lots* of practice."

THE END

A Dragon's Christmas Mayhem

BY KIRA NYTE

Firestorm dragon Zareh is a Christmas virgin, but that doesn't stop him from doing his best to conjure up the perfect holiday celebration for his beloved lifemate, Kaylae. The fact she's keeping something from him is tearing him apart. Their ancient enemies could strike at any time, bringing with them menace and mayhem. But that's a tangible enemy. Can their love overcome some unexpected Christmas mayhem of the personal kind?

1

Zareh Lutherone turned his hand over, admiring the stunning sparkle of the diamonds along the gold band. The sales associate waited patiently behind the counter, her eyes glittering almost as brightly as the diamonds in anticipation of a solid sale.

Alazar Brandvold sidled up to Zareh and leaned an elbow on the glass display case. "Two things, my friend. One, Kaylae isn't a jewelry girl and, two, you really shouldn't have waited until Christmas Eve to buy her a gift." His signature smile spread across his mouth as his eyes glowed with a contented love Zareh understood completely.

He and his closest friend were two of the eight remaining Firestorm dragons in existence, and the only ones lucky enough to have found lifemates. Now, Zareh had to figure out how this whole Christmas thing worked for the sake of his beloved Doe. The endearment suited her, even though it had started out as a diminutive of Jane Doe when she wouldn't share her real name on their first meeting.

Zareh pressed his lips together, gave the diamond

band one last consideration, and handed it back to the sales associate with a small shake of his head. "Thanks for your time."

"Of which you're running short on," Alazar said, tapping his watch. "Stores close early today. Not everyone procrastinates, because they have other plans tonight. Dinner plans. Christmas Eve party plans. Drink spiked eggnog until you're passed out plans."

Zareh scowled as they left the shop. Despite the chill in the Georgia air and the swollen gray clouds that promised a magical snowfall to start the Christmas holiday, his dragon's blood kept him comfortably warm. He glanced up and down the street, noticing for the first time that Nocturne Falls was not bustling with the usual tourists dressed in Halloween costumes. Those who, like him, were busy pulling together the frayed ends of pre-holiday preparations wore festive Christmas attire, from Santa hats to elf shoes and everything in between. He also wasn't blind to the true elves who came and went from Santa's Workshop—the grand toy store housed in an austere warehouse a few blocks away.

"Where to now?" Alazar asked.

"I'm not sure."

"Ah, blind together." Alazar fell in step beside Zareh, twisting to avoid barreling into a couple strolling down the sidewalk. "Insight please?"

"You're right. Doe doesn't care for all the baubles and glamour. She likes simple. I'm going to stick with simple." He shot Alazar a glance. "What did you get Ariah?"

"A kitchen." Alazar shrugged. "You know how she is. Pretty grounded and all. Not into the fluff."

Zareh snickered. "Certain the kitchen wasn't for you?"

"Nah. I've been teaching her how to cook. Her request, of course."

"I can't believe you got her a kitchen for your first Christmas. Isn't it a little over the top?"

Alazar laughed. "Buddy, don't go dissing my gift when you haven't managed to get your lifemate anything."

Zareh detoured down Black Cat Boulevard and slipped into Delaney's Delectables. The rich, sweet aromas of chocolate, candy, and other confectionary goodies filled the shop. Christmas music flowed from hidden speakers. A subtle scent of pine wound its way through the intricate sweetness.

The shop exuded Christmas.

As did the owner, in her floppy Santa hat bordered with thick white fluff decorated with holly and bells. He was vaguely surprised to find Delaney Ellingham working, her happy predisposition and holiday spirit on full display for the thinning flock of customers. She had hired a few assistants over the last few months, but still kept her hands and feet fully engaged in her business.

Even on Christmas Eve, it seemed.

Delaney handed the customer at the cash register a prettily stuffed bag, and her eyes lit on the newcomers. "Zareh. Alazar. What're you two doing here? I thought you'd be enjoying the holiday with Kaylae and Ari." Her smile stretched to her eyes.

"Mr. Romance is desperate for a gift." Alazar nudged Zareh with his elbow. "He's a Christmas virgin."

Delaney laughed. Zareh managed a thin grin directed at his friend.

"I'm flattered that you find my confections gift-worthy, Zar, but I don't think this is what you'd like to give Kaylae for Christmas." She lifted a small silver tasting tray from the cashier counter and held out the sample-sized sugar-dusted truffles. "Although she might enjoy these. They're cocoa mint truffles with sugared peppermint dusting."

Zareh helped himself to a sample and popped it in his mouth. The chocolate melted over his tongue, releasing the fresh essence of mint. Definitely a combination his sweet Doe would moan over.

"A dozen of those," Zareh said without hesitation. Delaney gave him the smile of a satisfied proprietor clinching a sure-thing sale. "And the usual."

"Perfect." Delaney disappeared in the back room.

Alazar leaned back against the counter and crossed his arms over his chest. "How's the decorating going at the new place?"

"Decorating?" Zareh snorted. "We've barely made a dent unpacking the boxes. There's been no time to decorate. Besides, I'm not sure how to decorate for this holiday. I've never ventured about during this crazy season, let alone taken interest in these human traditions. It's not something we ever celebrated in The Hollow. You know that."

Alazar's eyes narrowed. "Kaylae hasn't mentioned a tree? Ornaments? Lights? I mean, I dunno, Christmas stockings to hang over that ridiculously big fireplace in your new living room?" A sharp, exasperated groan left his lips. A rare wash of seriousness overcame his expression. "Pardon me for offering my advice, but I think you need to consider the *holiday* more than the gift at this point. This is her first Christmas without her father, without her old life. Her first Christmas with you, in your new home. Make it special. *Memories* are priceless gifts."

Zareh cocked a brow at Alazar, and clicked his tongue against the roof of his mouth. "Almost six hundred years in the bag as friends, and this philosophical side of you continues to surprise me. What man has Ari dug up from the cave in the months you've been living in our homeland?"

Alazar shrugged, winked, and pushed off the counter as Delaney returned with two boxes of treats. "The same one you've always known, brother."

The off-the-cuff response struck a chord with Zareh. His good-natured, funny—albeit with a sometimes misplaced sense of humor—friend had always managed to keep the majority of the Firestorm dragons in check before the war came to The Hollow, their precious homeland far from the human world. He had a talent for easing tense situations with his charm. When the Baroqueth slayers murdered his Keeper, Alazar buried his pain and guilt. It was only recently, when Ariah came into his friend's life, that Zareh realized the lengths Alazar had gone to hide his pain and keep the rest of the dragon clan from unleashing fire when their tempers got out of hand.

Being Firestorm, tempers were definitely quick to snap, especially when it came to the welfare of family and loved ones.

"Dare I ask if you have any plans for Christmas Eve, Zareh?" Delaney asked as her fingers skated over the computer to ring him up.

"Of course. He's planning to spit a Christmas hog in his fireplace, apple in mouth and all," Alazar said. Delaney's eyes went wide before she burst out laughing.

Alazar shook a finger at Zareh. "You made sure that hog wasn't a werehog before you stuck it, right?"

Delaney covered her mouth, eyes dancing as she tried to contain her laughter. Zareh rolled his eyes and shook his head.

"Don't pay a moment's heed to this giddy fool, Delaney. There is no hog, no apple, and certainly no spit in my fireplace. However, one thing I don't have that I hope you might be able to point me to would be a Christmas tree. And perhaps some decorations?"

Delaney composed herself, dabbing at the corner of her eye, and cleared her throat. "There are a few shops along Main Street that may still be open and have some decorations left this late. As far as trees, you might get lucky at the live tree stand adjacent to Mummy's Diner. They had quite a stock at the beginning of the week. Many locals seem to wait until the last few days to pick up the real ones." Delaney shrugged. "Why, I don't know. I love the smell of fresh pine in the house. Really brings the Christmas spirit home."

Zareh didn't know why either. He was running partially blind when it came to the holidays, with a comedian as his wingman. Where he ended up all depended on the joke. He made a mental note to research all holidays throughout the calendar year to be better prepared for the next one.

"Thanks, Delaney." Zareh flipped open his wallet. "How much do I owe you?"

"Ten dollars even."

Zareh scoffed. "The real total."

Delaney smiled. "Merry Christmas, Zareh. Consider it my Christmas gift to you and Kaylae. She'll definitely appreciate the chocolate."

Grumbling under his breath, Zareh fished out a ten-dollar bill and handed it to her. "Don't make a habit of discounting me or I'll have a word with Hugh."

"Oh, I can see the result of that now," Alazar said, squaring his shoulders in perfect mimicry of Delaney's vampire husband's very proper posture and crisp British accent. "'Darling Delaney, you mustn't cheat Zareh out of paying full price for his purchases.' To which Delaney replies, 'Handsome Hugh, try my latest creation and let me handle my business.'"

"Dear gods, grant me patience and strength so I won't be tempted to spit and roast dragon this evening," Zareh muttered, grabbing the two boxes of treats. Delaney laughed, accepting a hug from Alazar over the counter.

Alazar clapped Zareh's shoulder and headed toward the door. "Merry Christmas, Delaney. To you and your family," he called back.

"Behave, Al." Delaney rounded the counter and gave Zareh a hug. "You, too. I know that no matter what, Kaylae is simply happy to have you."

"I hope she always feels that way."

The way things were going of late, he wasn't as certain of that as he used to be.

"A little more to the right?" Kaylae suggested. Her brows furrowed and she bit her thumb knuckle as she tried to gauge the exactly right position for the china cabinet in the living room. Ariah and Pandora flanked her, their heads tilted in opposite directions.

"Um, Kay, I don't think it'll get any more centered

than that," Pandora said. "I used a measurement spell to get it exact. Perhaps it's the slope in the ceiling that is throwing it off?"

Ariah twirled a dark strand of her A-line cut hair between her fingers. "I think you should've stuck with the buffet instead of the cabinet and installed shelves against the far wall to display your china."

Kaylae dropped her hand and sighed. "I don't even *have* china. We got the china cabinet because we had to have it for a formal dining room."

"Says who?"

Kaylae cast a glower at Pandora. "Really? Who?"

The two women stared at each other for a long moment before laughing. Ariah moved closer to the cabinet, her focus intent.

"Why don't we put it against the far wall? The ceiling angle is straight across and not sloped over that wall and the windows are far enough apart that the bulk won't block them."

"Remind me again why the women are doing this work and not the men?" Pandora asked. She looked at Kaylae. "Want to give it a try?"

"Sure. And if it doesn't look right, I'll make Zareh return it."

Pandora murmured a spell in a soft, wispy voice. The cabinet lifted from the floor and slowly floated over to its new location before settling down. Ariah clapped her hands as though they'd actually done the hefty lifting and folded her fingers against her chin as she contemplated it. Pandora released a low breath.

Kaylae's shoulders slouched.

She didn't like it against that wall either.

Heck, she didn't like it. Period.

Gotta get yourself under control. It'll be different in a few weeks.

She loved the piece when they purchased it a month ago. Just like the dining table and the chairs. And the living room set.

All of which bothered her now.

Her stomach churned with frustration. "So, yeah. I think I'm done reconfiguring for the day. It's Christmas Eve, I have no idea where my husband is, what we're going to make for dinner, or how we're going to celebrate this holiday, but whatever."

Kaylae flung an arm to encompass the expansive living room in her new home.

"I mean, look at that. There's nothing. Not a single Christmasy thing in this house. Closing on this place four days before Christmas, trying to move everything in and make it livable, much less festive, might have been taking on more than I could handle. I feel like I'm living in an impersonal cave."

Ariah's brows rose, gold-laced brown eyes shimmering in the dim light pouring through the windows. "Honey, I live in a cave. This is *not* a cave."

Kaylae waved away her friend's attempt to lighten her mood and slipped through the ginormous butler's pantry into the even more ginormous kitchen. Acutely aware that Pandora and Ariah had followed her, she opened one of the wood-covered fridge doors and rifled through the odds and ends that made up her sparse food stock. No turkey. No ham. No trimmings or desserts. Nothing.

She opted for a bottle of water and pulled two additional bottles out, tossing one each to Ariah and Pandora.

Catching Ariah's eye, she said, "Alazar's home at The Hollow is certainly not what one would consider a cave. *In* a cave, sure, but *not* a cave. He's made your home opulent and beautiful and warm and cozy. Everything this place is not."

Pandora's brows wrinkled over her stunning green eyes and she chewed her lower lip, not saying anything. Kaylae sighed as she realized she'd inadvertently taken a jab at her friend. Pandora had worked closely with Zareh and Kaylae from the blueprint of the home straight through to the closing. This house was as much an investment for her as it was for Kaylae. She'd spent a lot of time ensuring that Kaylae and Zareh had the perfect home. It wasn't her fault that Kaylae was having a difficult time settling in.

Kaylae took a swig of her water, the cold liquid cooling her riled belly and her rising temperature. She was so over the hot flashes, too. They could stop anytime.

"Pandora, that was no slight against you. I'm sorry. I'm just stressed out. We should've waited until the new year to close, that's all." Her throat constricted as she battled a swell of emotions. "It's just that Christmas was always warm and special in my family. My dad decorated the house to the rafters. Christmas festivities started late afternoon Christmas Eve and didn't let up until we passed out from exhaustion Christmas Day. It was a special time when the rest of the year posed challenges. Now that he's...well..."

Kaylae coughed, trying to clear the ball of emotion from her throat. Her eyes stung at the memories of Christmases past, when the trials of life were locked out in the cold while she, her father, and her uncle celebrated without reserve.

A weight plowed into her chest. Her heart thumped hard. Over seven months ago, her father and uncle were killed protecting her. She never got to say goodbye. This was her first Christmas without them.

But now she had Zareh. Her beloved lifemate. Her darling, tender dragon.

Her hour-late dragon.

Where he could be as four o'clock rolled around was beyond her, but his absence left her to simmer in her pot of growing frustration. She was beyond ready to commit some mayhem when he deigned to walk through the door.

Swiping her forearm over her wet eyes and the chunks of dark waves that had fallen free of the messy bun, she gulped down half the bottle of water, let out a harsh breath, and shrugged.

"I don't want to keep you two any longer. Thanks for your help today," Kaylae said, plastering on a fake smile.

Pandora folded her arms over her chest. Ariah rested most of her weight on one leg, hip jutting out, fists on her hips, water bottle in one hand.

"What?"

"Do you think we're leaving you alone on Christmas Eve? Not until Zareh returns," Pandora said.

"Damn right. Lonely holidays and I were intimate way too long. No one deserves to feel like that," Ariah added.

Despite the sadness, frustration, irritation, and confusion roiling inside her, Kaylae's mouth quirked up. Ariah's hardships were gut-wrenching and inspiring at the same time. The woman possessed a fierceness that balanced her vulnerability to a T. Alazar could not have been granted a more perfect lifemate had he begged the gods for one.

Pandora tapped a finger in the air. Kaylae braced herself. She recognized that pinched brow, pursed lip look anywhere.

"I have an idea. It's too late to try and get Christmas lights from any of the stores, but I can probably work a spell to simulate the fairy lights that decorate Nocturne Falls. Oh, let me call Cole and see if he has some spare time before he picks me up to stop at the tree stand and see what's left." Pandora all but bounced on her toes—squeezed as they were into fashionable four-inch heeled pumps—and dug her cell phone from her pants pocket. "I'll call my mother to see if she has any extra food items and—"

"Hey, Pandora, wait. I appreciate the thought, but it's Christmas Eve. You shouldn't be here. You have Cole and Kaley, and your family to spend it with. Next year will be different for me, I know that." Touched by her friend's eagerness to help, she managed a genuine smile as Pandora's excitement fizzled. "Seriously. I'll have an entire year to plan a grand holiday celebration. I'll make up for what's been lost this year."

"I can't possibly leave you here with nothing."

"I have a house and some food. Far from nothing." She gave a small laugh. "Besides, I think all of the stress has taken a toll on me. I need to lie down for a little while and recharge."

After another ten minutes of convincing Pandora she would be fine, Kaylae walked her to the door, gave her a big hug goodbye and waved her off. She returned to the kitchen to see Ariah perched on one of the counter stools. The other woman's beautifully strange dark eyes pinned her with a curious look.

"What's going on with you?" Ariah asked before Kaylae had a chance to speak.

"Nothing. Been a hectic few days, is all."

"Uh-huh."

Kaylae rubbed a hand against the side of her face. "Really. Nothing but stress."

"Okay." The other woman's skeptical stare said otherwise.

Kaylae leaned her elbows against the countertop, dropped her water bottle, and folded her hands together. "All right. There is something."

"I know that."

"Of course you do." She loved Ariah like a sister, just as she loved Alazar as a brother. With sisterly love came sisterly aggravation. Ariah's keen sensitivity to the feelings of others, particularly Kaylae's, triggered a small bout of that aggravation, which she tried to ignore. She knew Ariah only wanted to help. "I haven't said anything, and I think keeping it bottled up inside is driving me mad."

Ariah lifted her water to her mouth. "Bottling things up can drive a person crazy."

Kaylae knew her friend spoke from experience. She weakened. It would be so good to confide in someone. "Promise not to say a word?"

After she swallowed her sip of water, Ariah capped the bottle and leveled her gaze on Kaylae. "You know me better than to have to ask that."

"It's a secret."

"For how long?"

Kaylae swallowed back the rise of bile in her throat. "For as long as I feel it necessary to keep it a secret."

2

Zareh stepped back and admired their handiwork. Alazar brushed his hands together as he finished hanging the last ornament on the tree, and came to stand beside him. For a long moment, the two of them took in the results of the work they had put into decorating the living room he and Alazar once shared as roommates.

Twists of pine-and-metallic garland trimmed with a mixture of clear and multi-colored lights graced the mantel and doorways. Mismatched ornaments dangled from the boughs of the live tree, sparkling amidst the sparse foliage.

The tree stand had run out of most of its inventory, but not all. He found a shop on Main Street that still had some decorations, and bought up their inventory. Santa's Workshop bustled with last-minute shoppers and pre-Christmas preparations from the elves. Zareh liked the festive touch of falling snow inside the warehouse, but was disappointed to learn it was magic he couldn't replicate at home. Well, so be it. The sky had begun to release its own snow on Nocturne Falls, and that would have to do. He settled for some nutcrackers, plush snowmen, and other toys he could use as decorations instead.

Executing the decorating part?

"Hey, at least we tried," Alazar said.

Zareh cringed at Al's blunt statement. This was why he let Kaylae handle decorating the new house. He lacked any sense of design.

He had to admit, the garland draped over the walls looked like a five-year-old's artistic mess. They'd used nails to hang the stockings over the fireplace because he hadn't thought he needed the holders one of the associates suggested.

And that tree?

"She's going to hate it." Zareh groaned, rubbing his eyes. "I hate it. It's hideous."

"Zar, you're on borrowed time now, so it will have to do. It's almost five. It's snowing and sticking. You told Kaylae you'd be back at the new place by three." Alazar pressed his lips together. "I've already received a month's worth of text messages from Ariah demanding to know where we are. I can only hold her off with the elusive responses so long. I think we're on the fast track to creating a Christmas Eve disaster. I don't want to be forced to sleep alone as a result."

Zareh winced at the thought of Kaylae trying to text and call his phone, which now rested at the bottom of a lake back at The Hollow. He had retrieved it after dropping it into the shallow water only to toss the worthless thing back into the lake when he realized it was fried.

He had a gut-twisting feeling Kaylae wasn't going to buy that excuse.

"You're so helpful in bad times."

"You know you have a friend in me."

Zareh growled. "Are you offering to be the main course?"

Alazar smirked. "Now, now. Don't get your tail in a knot. I had the foresight to know you'd be down to the wire tonight. That said…"

He beckoned, and Zareh followed him into the dimly lit kitchen. He leaned against the doorframe, arms crossed and booted toe planted against the floor. He hated the foul mood his poor planning and even poorer execution put him in. Kaylae didn't deserve this, certainly not when he had more than enough time to plan, had he been more attuned to her quiet hopes.

Unfortunately, his beloved lifemate's mood as of late had kept him on his toes. He couldn't understand what was bothering her, and she refused to talk about it, insisting, "It's nothing, love." Each time those words were spoken, he sensed the lie behind them.

He tried to coax her to share, and failed. He tried to beg and earned nothing but a smile, a kiss, and the sight of his beautiful Doe's backside as she disappeared into their bedroom. Alone. He tried to tread the edges of her mind, his dragon disconcerted by her behavior, and found himself shut out.

He'd thought it was anxiety over waiting for their move, but then they closed on the house and she went hot to cold and back again without warning. He found her crying quietly in their new bedroom, but she adamantly insisted there was nothing wrong.

He was lost. As close as she was, he felt her slipping away. The feeling of helplessness was more than maddening.

So, he remained in the kitchen doorway, unwilling to hold his breath that anything could turn this night into something Kaylae would be excited about.

Alazar opened the fridge doors, stepped to the side, and spread his hand to indicate the full contents. Zareh's brows rose, as did he off the doorframe.

"In a jam? Well, my friend. I brought ham." Alazar snickered at his lame Dr. Seuss-ish joke. "And turkey, sweet potato pie, an array of vegetables, mashed potatoes, roasted potatoes, rolls, you name it."

"What the heck?" Zareh asked.

"I told you I got a kitchen for Ariah. We had a blast in it before heading here to unload the results. All I have to do is warm everything up, which shouldn't take long, and we've got ourselves an amazing Christmas Eve dinner. Oh!" Alazar pulled a few of the platters out of the fridge and placed them on the island. "And I brought ingredients for breakfast in the morning. Got you covered, food-wise, brother."

Zareh had moved to the fridge by the time Alazar was through with his menu rundown, the knot in his stomach disentangling with relief. Maybe this wouldn't be as terrible as he imagined. He only hoped Doe would forgive him for his lack of punctuality.

"You never cease to amaze me, Al. I think I'm going to be in your debt for a while after this stunt." Zareh stole a glance at his watch. "Think we can get the women and surprise them now?"

Alazar closed the fridge as his cell phone vibrated audibly in the pocket of his jeans. He pulled it out and looked at the screen. Zareh didn't need to hover to know Ariah had texted again.

"Damn, bro. I think we're both going to be in the

cave tonight." Alazar's cheeks darkened as he rubbed a hand over his tied-back russet hair and let out a long breath. "Ariah's pissed."

Zareh sighed. "Yeah. I'm not holding out hope Doe is letting this fly. These last couple of weeks have been tough on her."

"Well, let's go get them before we both become the main course, and not in any pleasurable way."

"I can't believe they're ignoring us. What is wrong with them? Do they not know that we worry about them? And Zareh. He's never late. He doesn't know the meaning of late."

Kaylae slowed for the stop sign, the tires of her new BMW 1 series taking a moment to gain traction on the slick road surfaces. She wouldn't be out in this weather looking for him if Zareh had come home when he said he would. Seriously, he couldn't answer a damn text? Or twenty of them? Didn't he know she worried about him?

She navigated the snow-dusted roads through the swollen flakes that obscured her view. Her wipers did nothing but smear the heavily falling snow across her windshield.

Despite her focus on the road in front of her—thankfully, it was deserted of traffic, since most people had enough sense to stay indoors, unlike herself—she didn't miss Ariah's increasingly obvious concern with each glance her friend threw in her direction. She might have taken her frustration to an unnecessary level, considering the enemies of the Firestorm dragons and their Keepers remained elusive and at large. The Baroqueth slayers had been quiet for too long, especially as they knew Zareh and Kaylae remained in Nocturne Falls. The last time silence stretched like this, Alazar and Ariah became targets. Alazar nearly lost his life.

Silence in the world of Firestorm was often a warning.

Like silence among kids. You know all crap is going to the hands of destruction.

Or so she heard from mothers she'd come to know in town. Silence was never a good thing.

Including Ariah's prolonged silence since leaving the house.

Her friend had one leg curled beneath her on the seat, her scarf wound around her neck and chin, and a knit cap pulled over her stylish hair. Her eyes were as piercing as lightning bolts, belying her calm exterior. Kaylae learned real fast when they met that Ariah's eyes spoke more than the words that came from her mouth. She could lance with a glance.

Kaylae looked one way, then the other, trying to decide which leg of Main Street to scour first. After another moment of hesitation, she turned right and headed toward Howler's—one of Alazar's favorite haunts when he was in town—and in the general direction of Mummy's Diner.

"Tell me again why we're driving around in the makings of a blizzard on Christmas Eve when this town has shut up good?" Ariah finally asked, turning her back to the door and her attention on Kaylae. "Honey, this is a little extreme. I'm sure they have a very good explanation for why they're late."

"Sure. They're building snowmen. They're having snowball fights. They're fighting off Baroqueth." Kaylae sucked in a deep breath and let it out slowly, hoping to calm her nerves. She really needed to get hold of herself.

"Whoa, girl. You need to relax. Why don't you pull over and let me drive, huh?"

"I'm fine." Kaylae tightened her grip on the steering wheel, holding desperately to her sanity. Ugh. What a Christmas Eve.

They rolled up to Howler's Bar and Grill and she scowled. Big surprise. The parking lot was empty, and a Closed sign wishing patrons a Merry Christmas hung in the window. She headed to Delaney's sweet shop. No luck. Hallowed Bean was dark, except for twinkling fairy lights shining through the snow. Every shop she passed was closed for the holiday.

Even the gargoyle fountain hot spot was quiet, the square empty of the usual tourist horde. Not a single person. The fake stone statue gargoyle was in place, the one Nocturne Falls used during the holidays or on any occasion when one of the real gargoyles couldn't stand duty to entertain the tourists.

Kaylae felt a touch on her shoulder and jerked away in surprise. Ariah lifted her hand in a sign of surrender.

"Sorry," Kaylae muttered, turning the car around and pulling to the side of the road. She threw the vehicle in Park once it faced the way they'd come and slumped in her seat. She tried to gather her emotions, the ones that seemed to be driving these irrational actions and filling her eyes with tears far too often lately.

"Kay, listen to me. The boys are fine. You know if they weren't, we'd have seen Cade or Syn or one of the other Firestorms. Someone would have come straight here. Maybe they went out of town to get some last-minute things and are taking it slow coming home. The roads aren't pretty. And before you say anything about them not answering texts or calls, I'm sure they don't want to be distracted on the road. And if they're too far away, telepathy won't work. So, why don't we head back to the house and wait?"

Ariah wrapped a hand tentatively around Kaylae's wrist and eased her molded fingers off the steering wheel.

"And that means I'm driving." Ariah shooed Kaylae away from the steering wheel. "Come on. Out with you. I'm not sitting on your lap the entire ride home."

Kaylae snorted out a short laugh and shook her head. "Can always count on you to lighten the mood."

"I learned a thing or two from Alazar. I was more than ready to give up the dark and dreary after a decade of miserable living." Ariah gave Kaylae's shoulder a playful shove. "Out. Now. The snow is coming down harder and we still have to make it up that darn hill into your endless driveway."

Kaylae and Ariah switched seats, belted in, and Kaylae settled back to try and relax. She fought hard to keep her crazy emotions in check. Sure, it was the first Christmas without her father and uncle, and that was difficult enough. She knew deep down in her heart that Zareh was perfectly safe, but his persistent avoidance on this particular night hurt more than it made her angry.

Despite Nocturne Falls' commercial area being eerily quiet, Kaylae kept her eyes peeled for any signs of Zareh and Alazar. The wind had kicked up in a matter of minutes, sending whorls of white to blind their view. Ariah cussed under her breath as she leaned forward to peer out the windshield. Kaylae had to blink away the dizziness the swirling snow stoked. She glanced at the speedometer and sighed. At this rate, they'd make it home in time for breakfast.

"Just an FYI, your expensive little piece here sucks in the snow."

"Zareh wanted to change out the tires yesterday, but we ran out of time."

Ariah's nostrils flared. "Still, for the price tag on this machine, you'd think the thing would handle snow a little better."

"You seem to be handling it well." Kaylae cranked up the heat and suppressed a shiver. "The car, that is. On that note, why aren't you worried about Alazar?"

"If I have to worry about Alazar, I'm in trouble. As far as the car, you *do* remember that hunk of metal I drove down here from North Carolina a few months ago? Yeah, I drove *that* in the snow." Ariah snickered. "Not that this is much better, but there's a bit more control." She cast a glance at Kaylae. "They were on their own for centuries before we turned their worlds upside-down. They are fine."

Kaylae studied her friend's delicate profile. The wisdom that often came from her mouth—or on the whip that was her tongue, if circumstances demanded it—was not lost on Kaylae. She was a year younger, but where Kaylae had been sheltered her entire life, Ariah swam with the worst sharks in the ocean. She knew ugly. Kaylae did not. At least to the degree Ariah knew it.

"I think this holiday is a wash. We'll do it right next year," Kaylae said, resigned.

"Aw, girl. Where's your Christmas spirit? Don't throw in the towel so early. It's only"—Ariah glanced at the clock on the dashboard—"six."

"My spirit is curling up for a nap. It'll keep me warm

when I call it a night once we're back home." Her hopes of a sorta Christmas Eve went the way of the wind-blown snow. "Besides, I still have Christmas Day to spread that merriness."

The car fish-tailed more times than Kaylae could count. After a while, she stopped counting, trusting her friend's skill behind the wheel—until they came to one of the first inclines leading up the hillside toward the residential areas of Nocturne Falls, and her new home with Zareh.

She felt the back tires slip and the car roll back even as Ariah cautiously gave the engine more gas. Gripping the seat and the door handle, she glanced behind her. The snow was too thick to see anything out the rear window but the reflection of taillights against the pristine white.

"I'm going to roll back and see if I can't get traction enough to get up this incline. Hang tight," Ariah said, laying off the gas and reversing the car down to level road. "How deep is the ditch on your side?"

"I don't know and I don't want to find out tonight."

"Neither do I." Ariah tapped the brakes as the car slowed in its roll. She threw the car in Park and climbed out.

"What are you doing?" Kaylae asked.

"Gauging the road, since I'll be going it blind." Ariah soon dropped back into the driver's seat and pulled the door closed with an audible shiver. She turned off the headlights to cut the glare on the falling snow, left the parking lights on, and popped the car into drive. "Here goes."

Every muscle in Kaylae's body tensed as Ariah pressed down on the accelerator at an even pace. The car moved forward, tires connecting with the pavement, and they began a promising climb up the incline. Kaylae counted each beat of her heart while she held her breath.

Should've stayed home. What was I thinking? And putting Ariah in danger? Inexcusable.

"Come on, girl. Come on," Ariah whispered to the car. She flexed her fingers against the wheel.

Kaylae closed her eyes as her stomach rolled.

"Almost there."

"Good," Kaylae breathed.

Without warning, the back end of the car swung out. Kaylae's eyes shot open. Ariah maneuvered the wheel, her expression as calm as her expert movement. The car jerked as the tires fought for traction. Ariah eased the wheel in the direction of the fishtail, but it didn't help.

"Damn it. I can't get traction."

The front end began to slide to the left. Ariah tried to correct, fighting against slick road and gravity.

"Oh, boy."

"Don't say that," Kaylae squeaked.

"I can't get control." Ariah turned the wheel in the direction the car was sliding. The car turned, and kept turning until they faced downhill. The tires bumped over the low-running curb—the curb that separated the road from the small patch of grass beside the ditch.

"Ariah!"

"I'm trying!"

Kaylae planted her feet on the floor, instinctively trying to apply the brakes. "The ditch!"

"I know!"

"Zareh!" As she let out the mental cry, Kaylae squeezed her eyes shut again, fingers digging into the seat and the handle, and braced for impact.

3

"Doe? I'm home," Zareh called out, slipping into the unnaturally quiet house. Alazar hung back on the porch, most likely trying to get in touch with Ariah. "Kaylae?"

As he moved through the open, tall-ceilinged foyer into the living room, his skin tingled. Instantly, he knew Kaylae and Ariah were not anywhere in the big house, but even so, the residual energy of their essences was anything but welcoming.

"Doe, where are you?"

He paid close attention to the telepathic line he and Kaylae shared, but silence answered him. No need to panic. Telepathy became a moot point when there was significant physical distance between them.

That raised another question. Where was his lifemate that he could not reach her telepathically? And in this terrible weather?

"Anything?" Alazar called into the house.

"Hold on." Zareh rushed through the living room, the laundry room, and to the door leading into the attached garage. He switched to his dragon's sight to see through the darkness. His heart plummeted into his gut when he saw the empty spot beside his SUV. Slamming the door shut, swallowing down the thin curls of smoke that rose into his mouth from his throat, he returned to Alazar. "They're gone. Took the car."

Alazar rubbed a hand down his face and groaned. "Perfect. Any idea where they would go in this lovely weather? And in that not-so-snow-proof can you bought her?" He waved his cell phone in front of Zareh. "Ariah's not answering."

Zareh scowled. "I wouldn't answer you either if you kept ignoring my texts."

"I haven't ignored them. I've...been vague in my answers, thanks to you. More than I can say about your responses."

"The Hollow. Lake. Phone. The last two don't mix." It wasn't his first phone causality, and it certainly wouldn't be the last. It could have happened on a better day, though. "We've got to locate them before something happens. Can you reach Ari telepathically?"

"No."

"Can't reach Doe either."

"Well, let's get sky-bound, shall we? It's perfect flying weather," Alazar said, his voice dripping sarcasm as heavy as the sky dropped snow.

Zareh hopped off the porch and moved away from the house. He released himself to his dragon form, his body swelling, his bones twisting and remolding. His burnished red scales slipped over his skin, which thickened to a leathery texture and provided an added layer of warmth. His shoulder blades thickened and stretched upward until he flapped his wings once, twice, stirring the snow immediately around him. As his head and body finished transforming, he snaked his long neck around to find Alazar already rearing back on his hind legs.

Together, they launched into the fast-falling snow. Zareh used his thermal sight as he scoured the grounds below, seeking any sign of Kaylae's car or the women. He stamped down any possibility that their ancient enemies—the Baroqueth slayers—had chosen this particular evening to launch another attack. The deadly sorcerers had been quiet for months, but Zareh and Kaylae's location was no secret. He knew it was only a matter of time before they made another attempt to capture and coerce them both.

If they found my Doe, if they dare harm her...

A burst of smoke sieved through his fangs, weaving between the sheets of white that fell from unseen clouds. The faint silhouette of Alazar's formidable figure disappeared through the dense snow to his right, though he could still hear the strong flap of his friend's wings.

"Kaylae, sweetheart. Can you hear me?"

He wove through the sky, heading along the streets he knew Kaylae would drive to get to town. The residential section of Nocturne Falls was nothing more than a blanket of white from this height. He could barely make out the houses, let alone any of the smaller details. Lights were nothing more than a glint that quickly drowned beneath the white cape. The snow fell too hard, too fast.

Zareh dropped closer to the ground, keeping a few feet above the tall Victorians along Shadows Drive, too worried about his lifemate to care if anyone saw him. As he veered to the left, away from the wealthy landmarks, a faint zing in his mind caused him to slow.

The familiar warmth that accompanied their mind-speak bond poured through his body. His Doe was close, within a mile or so. He followed the low resonating hum of their connection, determining his direction according to the strengthening or weakening of that connection.

A moment later, Alazar descended on his left, flying a few feet above him. A plume of gray escaped his friend's wide nostrils to be quickly absorbed in the snow. He looked at Zareh and his massive jaw tipped once in a nod. Yes, he had a connection as well.

"Zareh!"

The shrill cry filled his head, unleashing the dangerous beast inside him. He tucked his wings tight against his body and dove toward his lifemate's fear-filled mental scream. A pulse flowed along the bond, echoing the up-tick of Kaylae's heartbeat.

"I'm coming!"

As Zareh's own desperation threatened to strip him of logical control, he spotted the first sign of heat in the dense white snow. He heard the squeal of an engine.

He pushed his body faster, cutting through the wind currents until he could see the car.

And the ditch the back end crept precariously close to.

Zareh twisted sideways as he bulleted toward the car. Throwing his wings out enough to slow his flight and not overshoot his target, he extended his claws, digging them into the fiberglass siding as the BMW began to tip into the ditch. The high-pitched shrieks from inside the car drowned out the painful screech of his talons scraping through frame.

The car jerked in his grasp. Wings flapping

powerfully, claws sunk into the hood, Alazar yanked the car back toward the road as Zareh maneuvered it from the rear. Together, he and his friend landed, securing the car's front bumper against a thick tree, away from the street.

Through the windshield, Zareh caught Kaylae's wide eyes, her mouth slack and her face a few shades paler than normal. She threw open the door and scrambled out of the seat, struggling briefly with the seatbelt as she tore it off. Zareh reached out to steady her, but she shoved his claws aside, made it a few more feet before slipping and falling to her hands and knees, and...

Zareh instantly reined in his dragon and returned to his human form. He rushed to Kaylae's side, dropping to his knees beside her in the snow to hold her dark waves away from her face as she lost a vicious battle with her stomach.

"Love, you're okay now." He stroked her back with his free hand until she had calmed enough to sit back on her knees, breathing heavily. Zareh wiped tears from her damp eyes. "What were you two thinking, coming out in this?"

Kaylae rubbed the corners of her mouth with two fingers and cleaned those fingers in the snow.

When she turned her beautiful blue eyes on him, they were brimming with anything but happiness to see him.

He swallowed.

"Where have you been?" Her voice was low, lethal. Zareh fidgeted on his heels. Kaylae shrugged his hand off her back and his heart nearly cracked. "You said three. It's six. You ignored my calls and texts. It's

Christmas Eve and I've been waiting in that monstrous house for you with no one but Ariah, who's listened to every complaint I've spit out. Where. Have. You. Been?"

"Are you hurt, love?"

Kaylae's brows shot up. "Really? You're going to completely ignore my question?"

Zareh was almost certain he'd prefer her screaming at him over this deadly calm tone. It left his blood chilled and his skin warming over his cheeks in what he could only imagine was discomfort. He, Zareh Lutherone, second oldest living Firestorm dragon, embarrassed. Put in his place by his little Doe.

"I didn't ignore your calls, love. My phone fell in a lake and isn't working."

Her eyes narrowed to slits. "That's as bad as, 'The dog ate my homework.'"

Zareh's brows wrinkled. Dogs ate food, not paper. "Uh…"

Kaylae scowled, waving his curiosity aside as she climbed to her feet. He hopped up and tried to reach for her hand. She tucked it into her coat pocket and glowered at him with moist eyes.

"Ahh, thank the gods. Looks like all is well in the land of Lutherone."

Alazar's light-hearted interruption couldn't have been more ill-timed. His clueless friend stepped right up to them, Ariah tucked beneath his arm, and flicked a finger between Kaylae and Zareh.

"Ariah doesn't like the cold, so I think it's time we head back to the house and settle in for a proper Christmas Eve. What do you say?" Ariah, who appeared content pressed against Alazar's side, smiled.

"It's Christmas Eve. There's much to celebrate," she

said. Zareh almost missed the way Ariah's gaze lingered on Kaylae before lifting to meet his eyes. Something in her stare caused an unnerving tingle to ripple down his spine, leaving him both curious and unsettled. "But you two *are* unacceptably late."

Kaylae's jaw set. "I think I've had enough celebrating for one day." She shot a short glance at Zareh. "Just bring me home."

Zareh looked helplessly at Alazar. Alazar buried his face in Ariah's knit cap for a few moments, shunning his silent plea for some advice.

"Kay, let's forget the tardiness and enjoy the rest of the night." Ariah reached out for Kaylae, who took her hand. The corner of Zareh's mouth twitched. His sweet Kaylae refused his touch but was willing to find comfort in her friend's. He'd royally screwed up. "But let's not do it out here. This storm is a doozy."

Zareh waited for Alazar to change into his dragon and draw Ariah into his chest with one huge taloned claw to protect her from the storm during flight. Zareh gave Kaylae a few moments alone, hoping she would finally give him a chance to apologize.

When she kept her back to him after Alazar took to the air with Ariah, Zareh stepped up behind Kaylae and tentatively rested his hands on her shoulders. "I'm sorry, love. I would never hurt you intentionally."

"Where were you?" she asked again, her voice barely above a whisper.

"Let me show you." He dipped his head and placed a kiss on the top of her head. Snow clung to her dark strands, a cool whisper against his lips. "It was supposed to be a happy surprise."

Kaylae bunched her hands into fists, keeping them tucked deep in her coat pockets. After a short flight tucked close to Zareh's hot dragon body—why did the man have to possess the power to melt her anger without much effort?—she stood on the walkway, staring at their old house on Crossbones Drive. Confusion set in as quickly as the cold, now that Zareh no longer had her wrapped in his natural body heat.

Okay, so part of that was her own doing. She remained stubbornly separate from him, her grudge anchoring heels deep in her unstable emotional state. She was really beginning to hate this lack of control over her own feelings.

Trying not to make it obvious that she couldn't keep her eyes off his handsomeness—seven months did little to dull the fiery attraction she felt for him—she opted to move closer to Ariah. And hesitated. Her dear friend was ensconced in Alazar's arms.

You should be in the same place, with Zareh.

A sigh escaped her lips. Her shoulders slumped. Slowly, she twisted and squinted through the merciless snow, her heart doing the strange double-thump thing it always did when she laid eyes on Zareh.

Zareh's moss green eyes glowed, lit by some magical inner light, and held steady on her. Snow clung to the wide berth of his shoulders, covered by his soft leather jacket. His hair, midnight black and brushing his nape, acted as a refuge for snowflakes, enhanced the sharp contours of his gorgeous face. What most people saw as edgy and rough, she knew to be tender and loving.

Right now, he wore a heavy burden on his expression, one that she had caused.

"You two can dance in the snow, but we're heading inside," Alazar announced, leading Ariah to the front door.

"We'll be right behind you," Zareh said.

Kaylae watched his fingers moving at his sides and sensed his desperation to touch her, but he refrained. Her shoulders slumped more.

"I'm sorry, Kaylae." Zareh pressed his lips together for a moment. "I know I upset you. I wanted to do something special for you. For us. Christmas traditions are, well, not my specialty. I haven't any idea how Talius celebrated the holiday." A sharp breath escaped her dragon as he said the name. "I know you miss your father, love. I miss my Keeper. I was hoping to keep him alive in the holiday for you." Zareh rubbed a hand over his chin. "I have this horrendous feeling I've failed. Miserably."

Tension began to drain out of her arms and fingers. She couldn't stay mad at Zareh.

"You could've called. Alazar's phone didn't go for a swim."

"Yes. And I should have, but I didn't. I didn't want you to detect a secret from me."

Kaylae licked her lips and cringed inward. She really needed to rinse her mouth out. "I need to use the bathroom."

Zareh took her forearm in a gentle grip as she turned toward the house, bringing her to a stop. His touch singed her skin through several layers of clothing, leaving her to simmer in the fire he stoked. He stepped in front of her, facing her, and molded one of his warm hands against the side of her face, his thumb stroking her lower lip. Instinctively, Kaylae pressed her cheek against his palm, loving the feel of heat and strength in his touch, the tenderness beneath the iron-forged will and fierce protector.

She closed her eyes, giving herself over to the man who cradled more than her cheek. He cradled her heart, her soul, the very reason she breathed. Without Zareh, she ceased to exist.

She squeezed her eyes tight against the swell of tears that threatened to pour over the rims when Zareh's lips touched her forehead. He lingered, his kiss gentle and endearing. She sucked her bottom lip between her teeth, leaning into him, wanting him, needing him to encompass her and assure her all would be okay.

"I love you, Doe. Everything I do is for you." He leaned back, his hands gliding down to rest on her lower back. She willed her tears away and met his piercing gaze through the sheets of snow. "Everything, love."

"I know," she whispered. There was nothing Zareh wouldn't do for her, including giving his own life for hers.

"Ready to go inside?"

Kaylae nodded, sidling up against Zareh's side. There was no mistaking the way the tension flowed out of him as he settled his arm around her shoulders and held her close.

"Would you like to tell me why we're here and not at the new house?"

Zareh glanced down at her, the smallest hint of a grin touching the shadowed crease at the corner of his mouth. "You are horrible at hiding your feelings about our new place. It's not a home, I know. It'll take time to become a home. But here?" Zareh led Kaylae up the steps to the door. "We have months of memories within these walls. Let us make our first Christmas memories here as well."

Kaylae failed to keep her lips from quirking in agreement. Her love for Zareh swelled to bursting as guilt churned in her gut.

Zareh opened the front door and guided her into the warm interior.

Kaylae gasped. She lifted her hands to her mouth as she soaked in the glittering living room decorated with haphazard strands of Christmas lights along the wall. In the corner leaned a pitiful live tree donned with an array of ornaments, tinsel, and more strands of colorful lights. The fire flickered full and hot in the fireplace, setting the room aglow in succulent orange-yellow. Mismatched statues and Christmas decorations crowded the mantel. Four stockings hung from nails hammered into the polished wood.

As she did a slow turn to survey the cozy living room, she couldn't suppress the small laugh that escaped her lips. More random Christmas statues and decorations cluttered the coffee table and the corners of the room. A pine garland hung over the window. Christmas tree-shaped pillows shimmered on the sofa.

Zareh shrugged when she made the full circle back to him. "I don't possess your keen eye for style and design, but I hope we can turn the mess I've created of these decorations into a beautiful Christmas to treasure forever."

Kaylae dropped her hands from her mouth. "Is this what you've been doing all day?"

"Surprise?" His brow furrowed, his sharp-featured face taking on an expression that might have been a cross between uncertainty and child-like hope.

Kaylae threw herself into his body, nuzzling her face against his shoulder. Zareh's strong arms came around her, encasing her in his unique scent of spice with a hint of fire.

"Thank you," she breathed into the leather jacket. "Thank you, Zar."

"Anything for you, love. But there's a little something more."

Kaylae leaned back and looked up at Zareh. His lips curled into a devilish half-grin.

He took her around the waist and led her toward the kitchen across the foyer. "I recall you sharing a story about your father making a feast to celebrate Christmas Eve. You said it was a tradition to have ham?"

Kaylae's stomach twisted. A memory of her last Christmas with her father flashed through her mind. He had never skimped on tradition, and the meal had always fed them for days. They would go to sleep with full stomachs and continue the celebration Christmas morning with an exquisite breakfast.

She sucked in a shaky breath and released it with a controlled exhale.

"Yes. And every possible side you could imagine."

With a gentle hand on her lower back, Zareh ushered her into the kitchen. Kaylae's attention was drawn immediately to Alazar and Ariah. The lovebirds were tangled up in each other's arms, sharing a kiss that ramped up the temperature a few dozen degrees.

She began to smile—oh, she knew all too well the powerful pull and desires that came with the lifemate bond—but her stomach lurched. Her nostrils flared as the potent aroma from the masterful spread of food split between the dining room table and the kitchen island filled her nose, leaving a foul taste on her tongue. Sourness lingered in her mouth from her upset stomach after Zareh and Alazar rescued them from the ditch.

"Oh no." Kaylae shot Zareh a panicked glance before she shoved by him and tore down the hallway to the bathroom.

5

The muffled clearing of a throat held him in his place. His dragon coiled, sensing Doe's distress, but Zareh planted his feet where he stood. He'd count to a hundred before he followed after his lifemate, giving her enough time to compose herself.

He'd never seen a look of such raw panic cross Kaylae's face, even when they'd faced their enemies, and it didn't sit well with him.

"You told me she liked ham, Zareh."

Zareh scowled. "I think you need to go back to what you were doing, Alazar, and let me handle Doe."

To the fire with counting.

Zareh took off after his lifemate. If she was ill, he needed to know. She'd been through enough these last couple of weeks. He didn't want what remained of tonight to go the way of the toilet.

The sound of the toilet flushing greeted him as he reached the bathroom door. He didn't hesitate to knock on the closed door.

"Kaylae, what's the matter?"

"Nothing. I'm fine."

He gritted his teeth. Lies and more lies. It seemed Doe had something big to hide from him. Something that was starting to put a rather infuriating wedge between them.

Was she regretting their bonding? Regretting their unbreakable promise to each other? The mood swings, the tears, the lies, the secrets.

He wouldn't be able to live with Doe resenting him, but living without her was unthinkable.

"I think this is a little more than nothing, love."

"Stress. Still shaken up about the car."

Zareh dropped his head. Another lie.

He listened to her wash her hands, spit a bunch of times, and turn off the faucet before pulling the door open. Zareh scrutinized the pallor that had taken over her face, leaving her skin tinged with gray. Her eyes sparkled with moisture. Her lips were red and irritated.

She smiled wanly, and he bristled, unable to continue with the farce.

"What's going on?"

A faint crease formed over her brows. "What do you mean?"

"I think we both know what I mean. Let's quit the charade. What are you hiding from me?"

Zareh tried to put a slight edge of command into his voice, but he couldn't muster the strength. All he wanted was his Doe back. Her trust in him. When had she stopped trusting him?

He crossed his arms over his chest, silently noted the slow drop in Kaylae's gaze, followed by a defeated dip of her head. Her fingers knotted together at her waist. He listened to the quickening of her heartbeat and the shortening of her breaths.

Against his mind, he received splattered flashes of colors and muddled thoughts that made absolutely no sense, but the tension in each flash was undeniable.

"Did the Baroqueth threaten you?" If those damn sorcerers were using his woman as a tool against him, it would take more than an edict from Cade, the Firestorm leader, to hold him back from his revenge.

Kaylae sighed and shook her head. "It's nothing like that."

So she *was* hiding something.

Zareh unfolded his arms and rested his hands on Kaylae's slouched shoulders. He stroked the sides of her neck with his thumbs, hoping his touch would relax her enough to confide in him.

"You know that I will never leave your side. I will never abandon you for any reason. Whatever it is you hide, know we will face it together. You're the breath in my lungs and the blood that flows through my heart. I need you, love. Tell me what I can do, what I *must* do, to have you back, happy and content."

Kaylae tilted forward to press her forehead smack center in his chest. She said quietly, almost too low to hear, "I'm scared."

Those two words shredded him to pieces. He pulled his lifemate into his arms, his body, and held her in his protective embrace.

"Sweetheart, what are you scared about? The Baroqueth? The house? What can possibly scare you to this extent when I protect you?"

"Zareh, I really don't want to have this conversation in the bathroom doorway."

"I'm willing to forget the bathroom for a better understanding of what's been going on that you can't trust me enough to talk to about."

Kaylae jerked upright, her beautiful multi-hued blue eyes wide. Her lips worked silently until she cleared her throat. "Why would you think I couldn't trust you?"

Zareh lifted a brow. A deep red flushed her cheeks.

"You two lovebirds doing okay?"

Zareh rolled his eyes to the ceiling, then turned to flash Alazar a tight smile. His dear friend forewent his usual casual expression for one of true concern. His gaze slipped to Kaylae, lingered for a moment, then returned to Zareh. The small exchange put Zareh on the defensive.

He glanced at Kaylae. "We were just returning to the dining room. I hope the table has been spared any inappropriate servicing?"

Alazar snorted. "I have more class than a dining room table, brother." He shook his head. "At least when it's about to be used for dining purposes."

Kaylae stifled a small giggle behind her hand. Zareh wiped the images Alazar placed in his head away and motioned with an outstretched hand toward their evening meal.

"After you."

Zareh kept a half step behind Kaylae, observing every inch of her from head to toe. His lovely Doe. His body ached and his mind twisted. He would let this go tonight for the sake of enjoying the holiday. They faced enough mayhem day-to-day. Tonight and tomorrow didn't need to be part of the complicated, and dangerous, life of a Firestorm dragon and his beautiful Keeper.

As they arrived in the kitchen, Zareh noted the slight stiffening of Kaylae's shoulders and heard the audible swallow as her gaze slid over the food. He stepped up beside her and caught her lowering her hand from her stomach.

Her face had paled again.

"Wine, love?"

"Um, no. Water. Water will be…fine."

She swallowed a few more times on their way to the dining room table, where he pulled a chair out for her. Ariah's sharp gaze landed on Kaylae from her seat across the table, concern flashing in her gold-laced eyes.

Zareh ignored the exchange and went to help Alazar in the kitchen.

Despite the calm, easy movements that came naturally to his friend while in the kitchen, a strange unease seemed to keep his back a tad straighter.

"Did Ari tell you anything about Doe?" Zareh asked under his breath.

Alazar shot him an unreadable glance. "Mouth is sealed, even if I did know."

"Thanks a lot, brother. Where do your loyalties lie?"

Alazar dished out a side of rosemary potatoes, clinking the serving spoon loudly against the plate. He lifted the full plate and shoved it toward Zareh with a bright smile.

"Merry Christmas Eve, brother. Feed your woman."

Zareh scowled, waiting for Alazar to finish preparing a second plate before he returned to the dining room to serve Kaylae and Ariah. He made a trip to the kitchen for drinks, his plate, and settled at the table with Alazar.

Unfortunately, with each bite of food, his appetite went the same way as his beloved lifemate just a short time ago.

6

"I don't think you should wait until tomorrow, Kay. He looks like he's about to lose his skin to scales and go all fire-shooting."

Kaylae nodded, turning away from the sickly image reflected in the mirror to face Ariah. Her friend's eyes glowed with sympathy, her delicate face etched with worry.

So far, she'd done nothing but ruin Zareh and Alazar's endearing attempt to make Christmas special for her and Ariah.

Her heart swelled to near bursting with emotion, but her body allowed little time for her to show any love and appreciation before throwing her into an unwarranted mood swing or worse.

She just finished worse. Again.

"Perhaps Zareh and I should go home so we won't ruin your evening."

Ariah shoved her playfully. "You two go home and our evening *will* be ruined. So, you're staying. Just...don't wait."

Kaylae nodded again.

"Hey, listen. Nothing about this Christmas is anything you or I might have expected, but it has been the best so far. Look at us. We have men we love and adore at our sides. We have their love in return. We're together, the four of us. The guys cooked and decorated—"

Kaylae arched a brow. Ariah laughed.

"Okay, so it's pretty bad—"

"But the effort is admirable."

"Completely admirable. And so sweet." Ariah sighed, a smile lighting her face. "Zareh wanted to do everything to make you happy. He knows you're hurting with the absence of your father and the uprooting to the new house right before the holidays. He tried hard, Kay. He deserves to relax tonight."

Wise words from her friend in a time when she struggled to straighten out her thoughts. Ariah and Alazar were perfect together. The balance, the wisdom, the fun-loving go-with-it attitude. Where they were equals, Zareh was Kaylae's foundation. Her strength and protection.

"Okay. Let's get this night on the right track."

After a few minutes to freshen up and make herself look presentable—again—Kaylae and Ariah returned downstairs. Zareh stood in front of the fireplace, a hand braced on the mantel, and stared into the flames. Every few seconds, a flame would lick toward him as if drawn, but immediately sink back into the orange-yellow blaze. The glow cast his face in a breathtaking creation of sharp and rough edges in shadows. His dark hair fell over his cheek, his eyes obscured by the thick strands.

Faint gray curls of smoke curled out of his nostrils with each exhale, giving away his strong emotions.

Kaylae moistened her lips, absorbing the waves of tension and careful control pouring off her dragon.

"At last, you've decided to stop primping and preening and return to us." Alazar edged by Kaylae and Ariah, holding a tray with four cups of eggnog. He jutted his chin toward the cup set a few inches away from the others. "That's yours, Kay."

Kaylae mustered a grin and accepted the beverage, but didn't dare take a sip of the rich drink. She took a second cup and saucer, and brought them to Zareh. His half grin failed to impress her as he took the offering from her hand.

"We can retire early. You're not feeling well," he said softly, his sharp gaze watching her closely. Kaylae shook her head.

"I'm feeling fine."

His eyes narrowed.

"So, my understanding from Zareh is that it was Talius's tradition to open a single gift on Christmas Eve?" Alazar asked. Kaylae looked at him, settled on the sofa with his ankle resting on his knee, eggnog on his thigh, and his arm loose around Ariah's shoulders. Her friend was tucked comfortably against his side.

Kaylae smiled. "Yeah. We'd all open one gift before we went to sleep, and the rest in the morning."

There were no presents beneath the precious Charlie Brown tree, but presents didn't matter to her. The man beside her was all that mattered. Zareh Lutherone. She wanted for nothing as long as he was in her life.

"I think Kay should be the first to give Zareh a present," Ariah said, her brows rising. "Right, Al?"

Alazar smirked. "Oh, yes. I couldn't agree more."

Zareh cast the floor by the tree a glance. "There are

no presents to give, so I'm not quite sure how this exchange is going to occur."

"The gift isn't beneath the tree, silly," Ariah said.

Kaylae rolled her eyes and placed her eggnog on the coffee table. "No, it's not."

Zareh didn't speak, confusion darkening his green eyes.

Kaylae faced him, tucking a wave of hair behind her ear. Heat spread up into her cheeks from her neck, the fire only a few feet to her right amplifying the sudden warmth that struck her. Nerves rattled for no reason. Why would she be nervous?

Because you're scared.

There would be nothing easy about this. Nothing at all.

"I, well, I was going to wait until morning, but Ari talked sense into me."

Zareh's gaze cut to Ariah. Alazar's hand tightened on Ariah's shoulder and his lifemate winked.

Kaylae let out a short breath and squared her shoulders. "I know I haven't been myself lately, but you need to know it has nothing to do with you."

"Oh, boy. Here it comes," Alazar taunted. Zareh's lip curled in a scowl.

Kaylae caught his face in her hands as he turned to glare at Alazar, diverting him back to focus on her. She held him steady, gazes locked.

"I love you, Zar. More than anything in this world, or any world. I exist because of you, and I feel terrible for the way I've treated you lately. I had no idea why I was acting the way I was. None." She rethought that. "Well, I speculated, but I refused to believe it until yesterday."

"What happened yesterday?" Zareh asked, his voice soft, gravelly, breathless.

"I went to the clinic for some blood work to make sure I wasn't sick with all the junk going around."

Zareh frowned. "You're not sick, are you, love?"

"No. At least, not the way you mean." Kaylae leaned forward, pressing onto her toes, and brought her mouth close to his ear.

"Our line is going to continue, Zareh." She squeezed her eyes shut. These darn tears were really getting old. "Your baby grows inside me."

Ceramic shattered. Kaylae gasped and jumped back, staring at Zareh. He looked dumbfounded, his hands empty, his cup and eggnog casualties on the wooden floor.

For the first time since meeting Zareh that fateful afternoon at Howler's over seven months ago, she witnessed her dragon tremble. When he reached for her face, his fingers shook in the tender grip along her cheeks.

"You...you're..."

Kaylae nodded, pressing her lips together to hold back the sob that pushed up her throat and resigned to the tears that spilled down her cheeks.

"Pregnant," Zareh whispered. A crease formed on his forehead and he tilted his head toward the sofa. "Did they know before me?"

"I threatened her if she didn't tell me what was wrong with her. But, if it's any consolation, she only told me a few hours ago," Ariah said. "Alazar dug around in my head and happened on the information when we got to the house."

"I wasn't supposed to know until now, but I don't

like it when Ari is all tied up in deep thought and concern." He kissed his lifemate's temple. "Not when I'm trying to kiss her into oblivion and she's preoccupied."

Zareh shot Alazar a short glance. "Is that how the dining room table was spared?"

"Pretty much."

"What are you talking about?" Ariah interjected.

"You don't want to know," Kaylae said, lowering Zareh's hands from her face and leading him away from the mess on the floor. A surreal glaze coated his eyes and faint tremors continued to tease his fingers. She almost felt bad for him.

"Oh, I think I do."

"Zareh thought you and I did a little pre-dinner dance on the table," Alazar said. Ariah choked on her eggnog, a thin dribble of the drink streaming from the corner of her mouth. Alazar dabbed it away with a napkin from the tray. "Yeah, that's what I said, too."

Zareh took Kaylae by the waist, circling her until she faced him, flush against his body. He brushed the hair away from her eyes, tipped her chin up, and captured her lips in a sweet, gentle kiss.

"We're going to have a baby?"

Kaylae smiled against his mouth, loving his innocent wonder as he spoke into her mind. *"Yes. We're going to have a baby."*

Zareh's arms tightened around her as his tongue swept through her parted lips in a kiss that weakened her knees. Heat filled every cell of her body, the familiar craving for her dragon conquering her queasy stomach. She pressed up on her toes, arms wrapping around his neck. She played with the silky ends of his hair until

Alazar's exaggerated throat-clearing cut through the moment.

Zareh gave her bottom lip a gentle tug as he ended the kiss. Kaylae sighed, savoring the flavor of Zareh's mouth against her lips, and tucked her head beneath his chin.

"You said you were scared. Are you frightened about the child?" Zareh asked, his voice a caress along her mind.

"I'm scared because the Baroqueth are still out there, hunting us. It isn't about you and me anymore. It's about you, me, and our child. I fear for our child's safety in this world."

Zareh kissed the top of her head and whispered, "There is nothing to fear. No harm will ever befall our child."

"You're a Keeper, Kaylae. You are lifemate to a Firestorm. That child will be the most protected child in this world and our own," Alazar said, all humor gone from his voice. "Fear for nothing."

"He's right, love." Zareh nuzzled the top of her head. "You have nothing to fear and every reason to be joyous."

"You know, you could sell that humungous home and come back to The Hollow."

"Alazar."

"It's just a suggestion."

Kaylae smiled. "For the moment, I like Nocturne Falls. It's a place of firsts for me. The place I learned who I was, what I was, and where I fell in love." She looked up at Zareh as she said the last part. He grinned. "Yes, I would love to move to The Hollow, but for now, I want to enjoy this town and what we have built. What we are building."

"Anything you wish, Doe."

"I wish one more thing." Kaylae leaned back to smile toward Ariah and Alazar. "I wish for us to have a very special Christmas from this moment on."

"I don't think that's going to be a problem," Alazar said, pushing to his feet. "I'll get more eggnog." He scrunched his nose. "And a rag so your klutz of a man can clean up his mess."

"I think we need some Christmas music, don't you?" Ariah reached for her iPhone. She pulled a portable speaker from her purse and plugged it into the phone. "Time to get jolly."

"I don't think anything can make me any more happy than I am right at this moment." Zareh pressed a kiss to Kaylae's forehead. "I have my beautiful lifemate by my side and the future glowing in her eyes as it grows in her belly."

"Oh my, such a romantic."

Kaylae laughed at Ariah's teasing comment. "You have no idea the romantic this guy hides under that mean shell of his."

"I've gotten a pretty good handle on him over the last few months." Ariah placed her phone and speaker on the coffee table. Christmas music began to flow through the house. Alazar returned with another round of eggnog and two rags, one of which he dropped over the mess on the floor.

"I think tradition calls for a toast, does it not?" Alazar asked, his attention split between Ariah and Kaylae for confirmation.

Ariah handed out the eggnog from the tray and nodded. "Yes. I believe it does."

Kaylae snuggled back against Zareh's chest, his arm loose around her waist. Together, they lifted their cups.

"A toast to love and friendships to last an eternity," Ariah said. "And to the gifts we are graced with through our trials and our bonds."

"And...to Christmas mayhem, because who are we without a little ripple in an otherwise calm sea?" Alazar added.

Kaylae laughed. "I think we come with more than a ripple."

"Tsunami. Firestorm dragons and Keepers bring with them tsunamis."

Zareh chuckled. "I'll toast to that." They all clinked their cups. "And to a very Merry Christmas."

Kaylae sipped her eggnog, enjoying the company she kept—her closest friends, the promise of a new life, and the one man who was her heart and her soul.

She couldn't ask for a more perfect Christmas.

THE END

The Mistletoe Misshap

BY WYNTER DANIELS

Psychic hairdresser Amethyst Powers wants to keep the peace in her quarrelsome family, even if that means dating the wealthy vampire who could help her father's fledgling business. She'll get over the great guy she really likes. Superhuman mechanic, Dustin can't believe his luck. When the purple-haired siren who broke up with him gets stuck, he helps her out. They share an intimate dinner, and one amazing kiss. But is she willing to buck her family's wishes in the name of love? Sometimes all it takes is one part mistletoe and one part luck.

1

"I suppose you can't give me tighter curls like Grace did when she used to do my hair."

A headache flared to life behind Amethyst's eyes as she removed the last perm rod from her mom's hair, and tossed it into the wheeled cart next to her station at Hair Scare. "I could have if you'd mentioned that before we'd processed the perm."

Her mother shrugged. "It's fine, honey. Maybe next time you do my color you can make the brown a little darker, too. Grace had forty years to become the fantastic hairdresser she was. You've only been at this for three. Give it time."

Ami bit back a retort. Why bother? Her mom knew everything, and if Ami contradicted her, it would only lead to an argument. Her parents quarreled enough for a hundred people—mostly over money—although both had been known to pick a fight about almost anything.

All Amethyst wanted was peace, for those around her to get along.

The front door opened and a chilly breeze blew through the salon. "Delivery." A young man wearing a purple jacket with the logo of Enchanted Garden, the local florist, came inside and set a gorgeous floral arrangement on the reception counter.

"Maybe those are for you." Her mom sat up taller in the service chair.

Not likely. She was finished with romance. Of the few guys she'd dated, none had measured up to her mom's expectations, and the last thing she wanted was to start any more family arguments. Better to just remain single for now.

Petra, the new receptionist, who happened to be Ami's bff, pulled a few one-dollar bills from the register, and handed the tip to the delivery guy before he left. Then she adjusted her glasses and read the name on the envelope. "Darcy." She fluffed her auburn curls. "Nobody's surprised, are they?"

Probably not, since half the staff were psychics.

Two of the other hairdressers groaned in unison as Darcy crossed the room to get the bouquet. Wearing a huge smile, she sniffed the calla lilies and pink roses as she carried the vase to her nail station.

Amethyst squelched a tiny pang of envy. Darcy deserved her happiness, it merely made Ami sad knowing that no man would make *her* that happy. Dustin's face flashed in her mind, but she immediately banished it. No sense in dwelling on something that could never be.

"That's sweet," her mom said. "From Darcy's husband?"

"Fiancé." Ami used the blow-drier on her mother's hair.

"What about you?" Her mother narrowed her eyes at Amethyst's reflection in the mirror. "You're not still dating that grease monkey, are you?"

Her mom had loudly registered her displeasure, so despite the fact that Ami had liked Dustin—a lot—she'd stopped seeing him. If only her mom hadn't lost her own psychic abilities, she could have seen beyond Dustin's blue-collar job. Then she'd know what a great guy he was. In fact, he was way more than a mechanic—he happened to own the auto repair shop down the road from the Shop-n-Save. But that hadn't been good enough for Colleen Powers. She'd had dollar signs in her eyes for as long as Ami could remember. Not that it mattered anymore. "I already told you I wasn't."

"Good, because your father's hoping to get financial backing for his mop-cycle from a certain handsome vampire." She waggled her eyebrows.

Amethyst wondered what her dad's latest invention had to do with her. "And?"

Before her mom could explain, Petra came over and handed them each a red envelope. "Excuse me, ladies. I want to make sure you both got an invitation to the salon's holiday gala. With me in charge of it, I can assure you that this year's event is going to be the best ever, and our first masquerade party. You have two weeks to find the perfect mask, although with Amethyst's purple hair, she'll be easy to pick out, mask or not."

Her mom grabbed Amethyst's arm. "Wouldn't it be wonderful if you took Lawton to the gala?"

Ami racked her brain to figure out who her mother was talking about. Despite the fact that Amethyst was empathic, her mother had always been one of the most difficult people for her to read.

Petra beat Amethyst to the punch. "Who's Lawton?"

Spinning the chair around to face them, Amethyst's mother sucked her lips into her mouth as if she was holding back some secret magic spell. Unfortunately, she didn't keep her lips sealed for but a moment. "You met him at our house a few weeks ago, Ami. He's that handsome vampire, remember? And he's wealthy as can be. Most of them are, you know. I wonder if that scrying mirror of yours would show you if you two were destined to be together."

Amethyst vaguely recalled the vampire with the bleached-blond hair. She'd stopped by her folks' house to say hello, and realized they had company, so she'd left after a few minutes. She'd barely spoken to him, except for a cordial hello.

Her mother spoke to Petra. "Lawton and Amethyst would make a wonderful match. His family and the Ellinghams go way back, although you never see Lawton during the day. I wonder how the Ellinghams manage that."

"Keep your voice down, Mom." Amethyst craned her neck to check the nail stations. Everyone who worked at Hair Scare had some sort of supernatural gift, although they kept that fact on the down-low when there were any regular humans within earshot. Plus, both Elenora and Delaney Ellingham came regularly for manicures and pedicures, but thankfully she didn't see either of them.

Her mother waved away her concern, and continued speaking to Petra as if Amethyst wasn't there. "Anyhoo, Lawton Langford, III is perfect for my Amethyst. He's quite tall, has thick blonde curls, and what a dresser. All his suits are bespoke. Granted, he's probably a lot older than Ami, but you know how vampires are. Immortality keeps them young looking."

Amethyst narrowed her eyes at her mom. "Don't most vampires who marry mortals turn their spouse into vampires, too?"

Her mom's complexion paled. "Not always."

Ami thought back to the night Dustin had come over to meet her folks last month. To Dustin's face, her mom had been sweet as candy. But the moment she'd gotten Amethyst alone, she'd let loose.

"That's the man who works at the auto repair shop." Her mom jabbed a finger at Amethyst. "A grease monkey. Oh, Lordy." She dropped into a chair and panted as if she was about to pass out.

"Actually, he owns it," Ami retorted. "What's the difference? He's a nice guy."

Her mother fanned herself. "Here we go. You're following in Emerald's footsteps, aren't you? As if your sister didn't destroy us enough. Are you trying to be the final nail in my coffin?" Setting a hand over her heart, she gasped. "I don't think I can take anymore. What have I done to be so despised by my own children? You should end your relationship with him. If you don't, I might not make it."

Amethyst shook herself out of the painful memory. She'd done what her mother wanted, as she always did, but that time the cost had been so dear. Merely thinking about it made her want to cry.

As her mom rambled on about Lawton, Amethyst opened the envelope and glanced at the invitation.

Bubble, bobble, toil and tribble. Came one, come all,

Trip the light fankastic at the Nocterun Fills Holiday Gaal.

Amethyst couldn't read another word. Petra knew

better than to print something without having it proofread. How many copies of the unreadable invitations had her friend already passed out?

Leaving her mom and her best friend for a moment, Amethyst hurried to the reception area and grabbed the stack of red envelopes from behind the desk. Returning to her station, she found Petra whispering to her mother.

When they saw Amethyst, they broke apart, as if they'd been conspiring about something. Oh, lord. She hoped they weren't planning another surprise party for her birthday, as they had last year. After her sister had stormed out of the house, and her mom had taken to her bed, the rest of the guests had quickly left, and Amethyst had ended the evening in front of the television, drowning her embarrassment in a huge slice of red velvet cake from Delaney's Delectables.

She touched Petra's shoulder. "There are a couple typos on the invitations, sweetie. I can redo these for you on my break."

A pink flush rose on Petra's cheeks, and Amethyst immediately regretted saying anything. When they'd attended Harmswood Academy together, Amethyst had been her friend's tutor, although Petra still had trouble with her writing and her spell casting, thanks to her dyslexia. Just last month she'd attempted to cast a locating spell to help a customer find her lost keys, but instead of them turning up, keys belonging to everyone in the salon at the time, had disappeared. What a fiasco!

"Sorry," Petra said. She grabbed the envelope from Amethyst's mom. "I'll get one to you later, Colleen. It's our first masquerade party. All the clients and staff are invited."

"How fun. Thank you, dear." Her mother patted Petra's hand, and Amethyst was even more convinced that the two were definitely up to something.

"A masquerade party will be just the thing to lift Amethyst's mood." Petra headed away.

What was her friend talking about? Her mood was fine. Maybe she was a little down about not being able to go out with Dustin anymore, but she didn't think she'd brought any of that regret to work with her. Hmm. She spun the service chair back toward the mirror and went back to work on her mom's hair.

"Perhaps if you invite Lawton to the gala, that'd put a smile on your face." Her mother lifted a penciled-on eyebrow at Amethyst.

She bristled as she teased her mom's hair. "I hardly even know who he is."

"I understand that, but as I said, he's in a position to really help your father. Dad's worked so hard on the mop-cycle. All he needs is the financing. Trust me, honey, this will be the one that makes your father a household name."

Amethyst's dad had invented at least two dozen machines, and her mom had always been positive that each was going to be 'the one' that would take off, and allow her to retire early from her job as an administrative assistant at Harmswood. Yet none had made it past the prototype stage. Each new invention had caused financial setbacks, and eventually more arguments.

In her mind's eye she pictured herself as a little girl, pillow over her head to keep from hearing her parents yelling at each other. Heck, she'd attended the beauty academy at sixteen in order to be able to afford to move out the moment she graduated high school. Even though her mom had talked her into renting their garage apartment, at least it was far enough away to give her some measure of privacy and independence, and most importantly, she didn't have to hear most of their altercations anymore.

"I don't know what help you think I could be," she said. "Me going on a date with a man won't convince him to fork over money to Dad."

Her mother patted Ami's arm. "Oh, but it might. He insinuated as much after he met you."

Ami froze and met her mother's gaze in the mirror. "So this is *his* idea? That's kind of icky, Mom."

"And going out with a man who gets automotive grease under his fingernails isn't?"

Channeling her inner yogi, Ami drew a calming breath. She wished she didn't feel compelled to always give in to her mother's demands. Someday… "Dustin's nails were always clean for our dates. But like I just told you, that's over."

Her mom ignored the comment. "If only I hadn't lost my own psychic abilities, I'd be able to tell you what man you're destined to be with."

After a bookshelf had fallen over and whacked her mom on her head a couple years ago, she'd not only lost her psychic gift, but her personality had changed as well. She'd always been difficult, but after the accident, it was as though every negative aspect of her mom's personality was on steroids. Although for Amethyst and her sister Emerald, the loss of their mother's psychic powers had been more of a relief, since she'd always used her fortunetelling abilities to tell her daughters what they were doing wrong.

"You've been the good one since you were a little girl, the one we could count on, unlike your sister. Which is why I suggested Lawton make an appointment with you for a haircut. You two could get better acquainted. And then who knows? Maybe he'll ask you out so you can be more comfortable together before the holiday party."

Amethyst tamped down a groan. "Sounds as if this is a done deal." Her mother never let anything go. Ami should probably just give in and accept her fate, but a vampire who dyed his hair? Ugh.

Petra returned carrying a cup of coffee. "Here you go, Colleen." After setting the drink by the mirror, Petra just stood there, apparently unaware that she was in Amethyst's way. Fluffing her red locks, she grabbed one of Amethyst's scissors. "My bangs are a little long." She snipped the ends then took a backward step, which gave Ami just enough room to continue working.

Her mother's aura shifted from its usual brown and gray, to pale yellow. The suddenness of the change gave her pause. What had just happened to switch her mother's guardedness and insecurity to optimism?

Her mom and Petra exchanged a knowing glance, the second time in the last half hour. As Amethyst contemplated what the looks could mean, Petra bumped into her back.

"Oops, sorry." Her friend set the scissors down on the counter.

Ami picked them up and was about to dunk them in the sanitizer jar when she thought she saw a few strands of her own purple hair between the blades. Before she could question Petra, her friend slipped away, toward the reception area.

Weird.

"Amethyst will be with you in a few minutes," Petra said from the front desk. "Have a seat."

What the...? Her mom was her last client of the day, or so she'd thought. She stole a quick glance toward the sofa and glimpsed the back of a man's head. His bleach-blond hair left no doubt as to the man's identity. Ami's stomach lurched.

Boy, her mom sure worked fast. Ami hated that vampire's auras were so difficult to make out, since she used that information to make a quick judgement about people, at least about what kind of energy they had.

Her mother tugged on Amethyst's arm, forcing her to lean in closer. Keeping her voice to a whisper, she reiterated how important it was to Ami's father that Lawton invest in his invention. "I don't want to frighten you, honey, but our money is tight—like borderline bankruptcy tight."

Amethyst gulped. "I had no idea, Mom. I-I can pay you guys more for the apartment." She'd been renting the space over their garage from them for several years, mostly to help them out. Sharing a place with Petra would be a lot more fun, but when she'd mentioned wanting to do that a few months ago, her mom had broken down in tears, so she'd stayed put.

Shaking her head, her mother sighed. "That won't do it. We need a big break. We need one of Dad's inventions to take off. And in order for that to happen, he must get major financing, the sort that someone like Lawton can provide."

Ami slid a glance toward Lawton, and her shoulders sank from the weight of what her mother had just shared with her.

After she finished with her mom, she swept up her station, pretending not to listen when her mother spoke to Lawton in the waiting area.

"Amethyst is looking forward to getting to know you better, Lawton," her mom said.

"She won't be disappointed," he replied.

Oh, boy. He sounded way too full of himself. Definitely not her type. Dustin's face flashed in her mind. He'd been totally her type.

"Night, y'all." Petra waved to no one in particular. "See you tomorrow."

"I'll walk with you, Petra," her mother said.

Ami glanced around the room. She was the last one there, and in a moment she'd be alone with a vampire. Thankfully none of the vampires in Nocturne Falls were permitted to feed upon humans against their will, and she had no desire to be a blood donor tonight.

Hoping for the best, she pasted on a smile and waved Lawton over to her chair. "Nice to see you again."

As he strode toward her, he skimmed his gaze over her body. She had a sudden desire to take a long, hot shower.

Before sitting down, he took off his jacket, and carefully laid it over the chair in the neighboring station. "You think it'll be safe here?"

Ami raised her arms in surrender. "I can promise you that I won't attack it."

His blank stare let her know that he didn't have much of a sense of humor. Or if he did, he didn't care for hers.

She draped a cape around him and swiveled him toward the mirror. Nearly an inch of dark roots contrasted with his dyed blond hair. "Just a trim?"

He brushed an invisible spot off the cape. "Have other people worn this…thing?"

No, she wouldn't give in to temptation and say something snarky. "Yes, sir. They're reusable."

"None of the VODs share any part of our costume."

The nylon cape was hardly the same thing as the pricey cloaks the town's Vampires on Duty wore.

"Do you have a new one?" he asked.

Drawing a breath for patience, she nodded. "Of course."

"Which reminds me. My shift starts soon, so I hope you can do this quickly."

"The sooner I get started…" Fixing a smile on her face, she searched through her cabinet until she located a new cape. She made a show of removing it from the plastic sleeve then draped it around Lawton.

For Dad, she told herself. She loved her father dearly, and she desperately wanted to see him succeed. Lawton apparently held the key to her dad's future, so she'd swallow her pride and do her daughterly duty.

2

Dustin Ruiz locked the last bay door then shut off the lights and headed inside the retail area of his auto repair shop. He frowned at the Christmas tree, which his employees had set up right in front of a display of his best-selling light truck and SUV tires. Not that he had anything against the holiday, but he had a business to run.

Jeez, his inner voice was starting to remind him of Scrooge. In truth, he just wasn't feeling in much of a merry mood lately. Since his family was up north—not that he had any desire to see them—and he didn't have a woman in his life anymore, he'd most likely spend Christmas alone. Well, not completely alone. At least he had Spot.

When he'd started dating Amethyst last month, their chemistry had been off-the-charts hot right from the get-go. He'd been sure that by now they would've been making plans for the holidays. Instead, she'd broken things off with him after less than a month, insisting that she didn't feel the same about him as he did about her. But he knew mutual attraction when he saw it.

What he didn't get was *why* she'd suddenly pulled back when it was clear that she hadn't wanted to. Women had always baffled him, starting with his own mother.

He rubbed the bridge of his nose, and forced his thoughts back to the present. The tree did look good there, so maybe it was the display rack that needed to move. With a glance out the windows to make sure no one was around, he slid the tree aside then picked up the tire display and relocated it to the opposite corner of the room. Sometimes his superhuman abilities came in handy, although he had no desire to demonstrate them in front of tourists. Not that he showed off his strength or speed to locals, either. Some of them knew, which was no big deal in Nocturne Falls where so much of the population was…unusual. It was what had brought him to the town several years ago—a place where he didn't have to be afraid that if anyone found out about his powers, they'd make him their personal science project.

Another glance at the tree reminded him of the fact that when he was a kid, his folks had rarely put up any decorations at the holidays.

His father's voice played in his head.

"We don't have time to waste on silly nostalgic traditions like Christmas trees," his dad said. "We're doing important research here. Our results could open all sorts of scientific possibilities."

Dustin had pleaded. "Just this once? We didn't put one up last year, either. All the other kids get to celebrate holidays with their families. Why can't we?"

His mother had grabbed his arm and yanked him to her. "People who are…unusual often have to make sacrifices. You're different—better—than all of your friends."

Only he hadn't wanted to be better. He'd only hoped

to not be so lonely. He shuddered at the memories.

With a final glance around the retail area to make sure everything was tidy, he closed himself in the small office to tally the week's receipts. The numbers were good—better than good. Business had been fairly steady all year. He'd be able to give every one of his employees a sizable holiday bonus. They deserved it.

The familiar tinkling of the bell on Spot's collar pulled his attention to the pet bed in the corner. The Tuxedo cat yawned and stretched on her way over to him then leaped onto the desk and parked her furry black butt on a stack of mail.

"I haven't even opened any of that," he told the feline as if she'd understand. "There might be something important in the pile."

Spot curled up right where she was, her white front paw landing on the Christmas card he'd bought to send his parents. His gut automatically clenched. All he'd ever wanted was a normal life. But with his mom and dad both being research scientists who'd studied him as if he were a lab rat, rather than loved him like a son, his childhood had been far from normal.

They'd told him that he'd accidentally been exposed to the fumes from several chemicals they'd been testing, and that was what they suspected had changed his DNA, and given him the extraordinary abilities he now possessed. Yet how could he be sure they'd told him the truth? Especially after they'd published some of their research, and had parlayed the fame from the paper into lucrative fellowships at a major university in the northeast.

He extricated the card from under Spot's paw, and relocated it to the other side of the desk. "Let's go home, girl." The moment he got up, the cat hopped down and followed him out of the office. He was about to leave when his cell beeped with an alert from the auto club. He could pass the call on to another garage, but if there was a stranded motorist close by, he'd just as soon take out the wrecker and help. Wasn't as if he had any evening plans.

Checking the message, he noted that the call was just down the road, in the parking lot of the Shop-n-Save, a purple Mini Cooper that wouldn't start. He'd only seen one car matching that description in town—or ever.

Amethyst.

His pulse kicked up a notch. He quickly donned his coveralls then returned to the service area and lifted Spot into the cab of the wrecker. She waited for him to slip on his jacket and climb in before meowing at him and pawing at the glovebox.

"Okay, okay." He opened it and took out the foil pouch he kept inside. "Dr. Shlick is gonna lecture me about your weight at your next vet appointment."

Unfazed, the kitty licked her lips as he pulled out several cat treats and set them on the seat. Spot gobbled them up as if Dustin hadn't fed her less than two hours earlier.

Shaking his head, he checked the mirrors—not only to be sure they were positioned correctly, but also to make sure he looked okay. He combed his hair, popped a mint into his mouth, and for good measure, used the cologne he kept in the cab. Couldn't hurt.

A few flurries stuck to his windshield as he drove. He pressed harder on the accelerator knowing that Amethyst was extra vulnerable to the snow and cold in her convertible.

When he found the car, Amethyst was leaning against it wearing a dark dress with no coat. There was no mistaking her unique style, from her high-heeled ankle boots to the half dozen bangle bracelets on each wrist. Nearly every one of her fingers glittered with a ring or two. Under the streetlamp he could see that her lips were trembling from the cold. His chest squeezed. Grabbing the small woolen blanket he kept behind his seat for just such occasions, he headed over to her.

Her eyebrows shot higher when she realized it was him. "Sorry, Dustin. I'm sure you hate coming out in weather like this, and so late in the evening."

God, she was even prettier than the last time he'd seen her. She appeared so vulnerable standing there in the parking lot of the closed supermarket, with a dusting of snow in her hair and on her eyelashes. Half an hour earlier there might have still been some Friday-night trick-or-treaters on the street, but by now they were gone.

Waving off Amethyst's apology, he closed the distance between them and wrapped the blanket around her shoulders. Had her shiver been a product of the cold, or did she still want him as much as he did her? "Don't be silly. If I didn't do this for someone I care about, who then?"

Her cheeks—already pink from the low temperature—deepened to crimson. She swallowed, but too quickly, backed away. "Well I...I appreciate it. I stopped at the store to pick up something for dinner. I was only inside less than ten minutes. When I came out my car wouldn't start up."

"Why don't you wait inside the truck with Spot? I've got the heat cranking."

A big smile lit up her face. "The cat's with you?" Her blue eyes sparkled when she turned her gaze toward the wrecker.

"Always." Just being near her heated his blood. He took her hand and started toward his truck with her, inwardly smiling at the familiar jingle of her bracelets. "Don't slip on the pavement. It's probably icing up already." As he opened the door for her, he breathed in the scent of her hair—like fresh-cut strawberries.

She got inside and let out an excited squeal when Spot jumped into her arms.

The sight of his two favorite females together warmed him from head to toe. A pleasant ache settled low in his belly. He cleared his throat. "I'll be back." He headed to her car and tried to start it.

Click.

The wrecker was close enough so he could try jumping her battery. The charge held for a few minutes, but when he stepped on the car's gas pedal, the headlights grew brighter, and got dim when he eased off. He couldn't let her drive away knowing the car might strand her again.

He got back inside the truck, rubbing his hands together to warm them up. "Could be the alternator. I'll tow it wherever you want."

Her lips bunched to one side. "Can you do it at your shop?"

His pulse sped up. Since when did the prospect of fixing an alternator get him excited?

Since it meant seeing Amethyst again.

He tried for a nonchalant shrug. "Sure, but since tomorrow's Saturday, I might not be able to get the part. If it is the alternator, I can have it back to you by Monday afternoon. I'll hook it up to the computer and run diagnostics to be sure."

She snuggled Spot closer and nodded. "Would you mind taking me home after we drop off my car?"

"Course not." The more time he spent with her, the better. Not that he held any illusions that she'd changed her mind about the two of them, but maybe he'd at least get some answers about why she'd called it quits with him.

That little voice inside him nudged him. In truth, he sought more than answers. If he knew what the problem had been, there might be a way to fix it, or possibly refute her reasons.

After they towed the Mini to the garage, he parked the wrecker then gestured toward his personal pick-up. "My Toyota's over there."

Still wearing the blanket around her, Amethyst carried Spot to the truck. "I really appreciate the lift."

The pleasure was all his. Didn't matter how much he'd tried to make peace with the idea of their relationship ending. Having Amethyst so close reignited his desire, and reminded him just how great they'd been together. He unlocked the pickup and opened the passenger door for her. As she brushed past, their gazes met and held.

Every nerve and muscle in his body strung tight. Despite the chill in the air, an inferno flared to life inside him. He had to give it his best shot. "Hey, you want to stop and get a bite?"

Her lips flattened but he could see interest in her eyes. After a long pause, she set Spot on the seat. "Last time I checked, cats weren't allowed in restaurants."

"She'll be perfectly fine staying here at the shop." He

offered up a silent plea that Amethyst would acquiesce.

She caught her bottom lip between her teeth and tucked a purple lock behind her ear, revealing long, dangly silver earrings. As if he needed a reminder how sexy she was. Finally, she squared her shoulders and smiled up at him. "Oh, why not? I'm starved."

He resisted the urge to do the touchdown dance in the middle of his parking lot. Instead, he lifted Spot off the seat and headed inside with her. In his office, he got the cat situated with a bowl of food. Then he stripped off his coveralls and returned to the truck.

Amethyst was seated inside the cab. Edged in moonlight, her features were even prettier—from that adorably turned-up nose to her cat-shaped eyes. "You're sure Spot'll be okay here?" she asked.

"Positive. I'll get her after we eat. Trust me, my office has all the comforts of home, at least for her." Without waiting for more objections, he circled the vehicle then got behind the wheel. A few minutes later he parked outside the Poisoned Apple.

Amethyst wolf whistled. "Wow, fancy."

He'd chosen the place since it was where he'd taken her on their first date, but she didn't need to know his reason. "I'm in the mood for their chicken fingers and fries. Do you mind?"

"It's fine. One of my favorites, actually."

A hostess with pointy ears sat them in a booth.

Dustin waited for Amethyst to slide across the burgundy leather seat before joining her. This was just what he'd had in mind. The high sides of the booth gave them ample privacy, and the small oil lamp in the middle of the table set a perfect mood for rekindling romance. He just hoped she was open to it.

A server came over to take their drink order.

"Moscato?" Dustin asked Amethyst.

Her eyes lit up with reflected candle light. "You remembered."

"How could I forget anything about you?"

A rosy flush settled on her cheeks.

"I'll have a draft beer," he told the server. After she'd melted into the background, he returned his attention to the beautiful woman across from him. "I like what you've done with your hair. It's a little longer, I think. Gorgeous."

She gave him that beautiful smile, complete with dimples. "And yours is shorter. I heard you came into the Hair Scare on my day off and had the new girl cut it for you."

He shrugged one shoulder. "I didn't want to make you uncomfortable. Although I've got to admit, I like how you cut my hair better."

She tilted her head to the side. "I don't mind doing it. You don't have to avoid me."

The notion of seeing her so soon after she'd broken up with him had been too hard. Of course, he could have traveled a few miles to a nearby town for a different salon or barber shop, but he hadn't. He'd been hoping that their break up was temporary, so why bother trying a new place?

The server dropped off their drinks and took their dinner orders, which diffused the slight tension that had set in.

"You have no idea how glad I was that you got there so fast tonight," Amethyst said. "The temperature dropped like twenty degrees as soon as the sun set." She sipped her wine, eying him over the top of the glass. The air between them sizzled with electricity.

He yearned to take her hand, to taste her lips again. "This sounds terrible, but I'm glad your car broke down. At least that gave me the opportunity to see you again."

A deep line crisscrossed her brow. "Nothing's changed, Dustin. I appreciate you coming to my rescue tonight, but there can't be anything between us."

His mood hit the floor. Why had he entertained the possibility that he could spark her interest again? She'd been clear enough when she'd told him she couldn't date him anymore. He just had to accept that and move on. Problem was, he hadn't been able to get her off his mind a month after she'd dumped him, and he had no reason to believe that would change.

3

An unbearably heavy weight pressed Amethyst's chest. Dustin was such a sweet guy. Breaking up with him had been so difficult because she'd been crazy about him. Still was. But her mom had gone into one of her states when Ami had resisted her directive to stop seeing him. So she'd given in, as usual.

Being with him tonight, though, staring into those soulful amber eyes, she wasn't sure she could stick to her guns.

She flashed back to the conversation she'd had with her mother at the salon earlier in the day. Her parents were counting on her to go out with Lawton. If she bucked, not only would her mother make her life a living hell, but her folks would undoubtedly start arguing again. No, she had to do her duty to her family and help secure Lawton's financial backing.

The waitress arrived with two platters piled high with French fries and strips of chicken. When the server left, Ami couldn't escape Dustin's heated gaze. Heck, she didn't want to. In the dim light, his aura was easy to read. The green color confirmed that he loved animals and nature, but the gray tinges around the edges showed a guardedness, which was understandable, considering that she'd already hurt him once before. Knowing she'd been the cause of his pain absolutely killed her.

As she ate, Dustin barely touch his food. His appetite had always been even bigger than hers, which was saying a lot. Yeah, she'd hurt him all over again. She cleared the lump lodged in her throat. "It's really good. Aren't you going to eat?" Despite her regrets, she was still hungry. She dipped a chicken finger in honey mustard and took a bite. "The sauce is amazing, even with the potatoes. I've been craving it for weeks."

His half-hearted smile didn't reach his eyes. "Yeah, I had this last time we were here, on our first date, remember?" The deep timbre of his voice brought her back to that magical night filled with so many firsts.

They'd held hands, and later shared a spectacular kiss. She'd walked on air for days after, counted the minutes until she'd be with him again. Just being with him now was stirring something up inside her, a longing for him.

She tamped down her desire. "Sure. How could I forget?" He'd brought her a pink rose when he'd picked her up, and he'd been the perfect gentleman all evening, catering to her every wish. Being with him was so easy—unlike her parents' relationship, which often reminded her of a boat trip through the Bermuda Triangle. The waters might be choppy or smooth, but at any given moment, you couldn't be sure if a giant squid would take out the whole vessel without warning.

Dustin took a drink of his beer. "It's all Spot's fault."

She laughed. "Definitely." The first time she'd

brought her car to Spot On Auto Service for an oil change, she'd fallen in love with the cat for whom the place had been named. When Spot had wandered into Dustin's office, Ami had followed, and found an incredibly hot guy seated behind the desk. Something sensual had ricocheted between them in that first moment—a zing of powerful desire. They'd started talking, and discovered that they had so much in common—they were both foodies with a passion for baking. They shared a love of cats, and both enjoyed bike riding. He'd asked her out before she'd left.

Now that she was here with him, remembering how great they were together, staring at that handsome face, she considered telling her mom that she couldn't date Lawton. How could she go out with anyone else when her heart belonged to Dustin?

When she'd done Lawton's hair, all he'd talked about was himself—his big, beautiful home, his affinity for expensive clothes, and fine wine. At least he'd taken her up on her advice to return his hair to dark brown, his natural color.

The server came back to clear their plates. "Can I interest you in our famous apple pie for dessert?"

Amethyst never refused sweets, but since Dustin hadn't made much of a dent in his dinner, she figured he'd skip it.

"Want to split a slice?" he asked her.

"Yeah," she said immediately.

The giant piece of pie topped with a decadent dollop of ice cream, arrived a couple of minutes later. The wonderful smell made Ami yearn to dive into it, but she controlled herself, and handed Dustin one of the forks the server had brought.

"Help yourself," he told her.

She shook her head, not wanting to make too much of a pig of herself. But when Dustin still didn't make a move to get some, she did. He reached across with his fork at the same moment, and their fingers touched. Their gazes locked.

Dustin forked a decent-size bite, but instead of eating it himself, he held it up for her. Eying her lips, he said, "Come on, open your mouth."

He cracked up, which made her laugh, too. She let him feed her, which was anything but funny. It was sensual and sexy. She licked her lips and caught the heat in his gaze as he stared at her mouth.

Danger, danger.

Didn't matter that she craved his touch, and dreamed about kissing him almost every night. The last thing she ought to be doing was leading Dustin on. Bad enough that she'd hurt him last month. So she forced herself to back away, and used her own fork. Much safer.

When the server delivered their bill, she grabbed it before Dustin could.

"No way." He shook his head and held out his palm.

"Sorry. This is my thank you for coming to my rescue tonight."

"That's my job."

Holding the check presenter out of his reach, she fished in her purse for her credit card. "I've got this."

Reluctantly, he gave up.

As they left the pub and strode across the parking lot, Dustin hooked her arm, stopping her before they reached his truck. "Can I ask you something?"

She gulped, pretty sure what the question would pertain to. "O-okay."

Exhaling loudly, he frowned. "I don't get it. Was I wrong about how good we were together?"

She dropped his gaze. "No, you weren't." No guy's kiss had curled her toes like Dustin's had. When he'd held her, it was as if she'd finally found her home. Sadness seeped through her.

He lifted her chin so she was forced to meet his stare. "Did I do something wrong?"

Tears threatened. "You did everything right. It isn't you. It's me. Well, not me exactly."

Tiny muscles around his jaw ticked. "Is there someone else?"

"No, well, yes." She huffed. "Not someone I care to date, no. It's…complicated."

He let go of her. "Kiss me, and then tell me how complicated it is."

God, she wanted to. Their bodies were a fraction of an inch apart. She could feel his heat, his desire. Or was it hers?

What could one little kiss hurt? Staring at his sensual mouth, those lips shaped like the perfect Cupid's bow, she couldn't stop herself. Standing taller, she slid a hand behind his neck and parted her lips. All thoughts of her parents, that icky vampire, her car breaking down, everything fell away. There was nothing and no one but the two of them, and a moonlit night perfect for romance.

Her eyes slipped lazily shut and all she could feel was his arms around her, then his mouth on hers. This wonderful, patient man wanted her so much—almost as much as she wanted him. The sweetness of apples and cinnamon lingered on his tongue. She threaded her fingers through his thick hair, and he growled his pleasure.

When they finally broke apart, she happily remained in his arms, not only for the warmth he provided, but for the comfort as well. Being so close to him had ignited sparks inside her that she hated to douse.

He stroked a thumb over her cheek. "You still haven't told me why you broke up with me."

Reality sucker punched her in the gut. She backed away. "Yeah, well…" She owed him an explanation. "Let's talk in your truck. It's freezing out here."

They got inside the Toyota and she drew in a deep breath for courage. "Okay, you're not going to like this."

Dustin listened as Amethyst spoke about her family, how her dad was a frustrated inventor who'd had no commercial success with his ideas, how money troubles had been a constant issue between her parents, and about her sister who'd left at sixteen because of all the strife at home. "I'm still confused about why that means you and I can't date."

Her brow knitted. "Because my mother is…a snob. Practically no one meets her ridiculously high standards."

So in her mother's eyes, he wasn't good enough for her daughter. "What about *your* standards. Isn't that more important than what she thinks?"

She wrung her hands. "It should be, but she's relentless. She browbeats my dad something awful. It's painful to watch. And she's almost as bad with me. You have no idea what it was like growing up with them constantly fighting."

He struggled to understand why her mother's approval was so important to her. After what his folks had put him through, he didn't give a damn what they thought of him now. "You're an adult, Amethyst, a strong, capable woman who has the power and intelligence to make your own decisions."

Her lips flattened. "I live in the apartment over their garage. I have to see them every day."

"Then move out. You do well enough at the Hair Scare, don't you?"

"I do. It's my parents who are struggling to make ends meet. Without the rent I pay them, they'd have a hard time financially. Plus..."

"What?"

She told him about Lawton—a wealthy vampire—and how he was likely to finance her dad's latest invention if she dated him. "He's going to be my date for the salon's Christmas party."

Pain throbbed in his head. He leaned back against the seat and rubbed the bridge of his nose. "So you're letting your parents pimp you out? And to a vampire, no less?"

She bristled. "It's not like that. I only want to keep the peace. And if there's a way for me to help my dad, of course I'll do it. They're my parents."

Putting her on the defensive hadn't been his intention, but clearly, he'd touched a nerve. "I understand that you want to do something nice for your father, but are you sure this is the way to go about it? You can't deny that there's something between us, something special."

She stared straight ahead. "I'd appreciate if you'd take me home now."

Darn, he'd gone too far. "If that's what you want."

Her only acknowledgement was a half nod.

When he turned onto her street a little while later, after a mostly silent drive, she said, "Just drop me here."

His chest constricted. "Are you ashamed of me?" He pulled to the curb four houses before hers and shut off the engine.

She flicked her gaze at him. "That's not it at all. I already told you the problem."

The real problem was that she needed to grow a backbone when it came to dealing with her mother. Although he wasn't in a position to give out advice on handling family relationships. He'd left home at seventeen. After the way his parents had treated him, he hadn't even gone back for a visit in the past eleven years, so Amethyst's ridiculous kowtowing to her mother's wishes baffled him. "You can't live your life for your folks. But I guess we all have our issues, myself included."

"I remember you telling me about your family, how they'd studied you like a lab rat." Her expression softened. "I won't lie, Dustin, I miss you. And yes, we have a strong connection. I'm honestly confused about what to do. Would you give me a few days? I need some time to think, and maybe get a reading from one of the other psychics at the salon."

"Okay." At least he had a chance with her, which was more than he'd had a few hours ago.

Hand on the door, she gave him a chaste kiss on his cheek. "Thank you."

Watching her walk down the street to her place, he wondered if she'd been exaggerating the demands her mother put on her, and the control the woman exerted. As Amethyst strode up the path to her house, the porch light went on.

Okay, maybe she hadn't been exaggerating. All he could do was wait, and hope for the best.

Monday morning Amethyst had a break between clients. As luck would have it, Mallory—the best tarot card reader in the shop—had an opening at the same time. Plus it was Petra's day off, and Ami preferred having a reading when her best friend wasn't around. After she'd witnessed her mom and Petra whispering the other day, she suspected the two were colluding about something. Perhaps Mallory could shed light on what was going on there. But the more pressing issue was what to do about Dustin and Lawton.

Amethyst sat at Mallory's table and waited as the nail tech cleared a few manicure supplies from the surface then wiped it down with disinfectant. "Thanks for doing this. If you want, I'll give you a reading later using my scrying mirror."

Mallory shrugged at the offer. "Don't worry about it. We'll work it out." Unlike the other readers at the salon, Mallory appeared to be the antithesis of a psychic. With her long blond hair and preppy style, no one would peg her as a tarot reader. She took her cards out of a drawer, and laid the green silk scarf in which they'd been wrapped on her table. Handing the deck to Ami, she said, "As you mix them, think about what you'd like to know."

Amethyst closed her eyes and concentrated on the two men, and her mother's wishes. After shuffling the cards a few times, she set it on the cloth and nodded.

Mallory spread the deck out. "Pick one."

After Ami had chosen five cards one by one, Mallory built a spread and widened her eyes. "Interesting. Let me guess. You're wondering about your love life."

"Mm hmm." That was apparent from the number of cards in the cups arcana, which were all about emotions, feelings and relationships.

"You have regrets that you can't seem to shake." Mallory touched the Five of Cups. "He's focusing only on the three spilled goblets, ignoring the two that are still full." She moved on to the next card, the Ace of Cups. "Ah, new love." She winked at Ami.

That could mean either man. She'd only dated Dustin for a few weeks, and Lawton was definitely a new addition to her private life.

Mallory narrowed her eyes as she peered at the spread. "You have to be strong." She tapped the Queen of Cups. "This probably represents your mother, or another spiritual counselor. She's psychic, and isn't above emotional manipulation."

Ami rolled her eyes. "Yup, that's my mom. Except she no longer has her psychic abilities."

Mallory raised a doubtful eyebrow. "This woman is definitely psychic, although we're talking about your future here, so maybe it isn't your actual mother. A mother-in-law maybe?"

Ami gulped. Dustin's mother was a scientist. Surely

he'd have mentioned it if she were also psychic. Could Lawton's mother be intuitive? Was she even alive? He'd said that he was almost two hundred years old.

"Interesting." Mallory pursed her lips as she stared at the cards.

"What?" Ami sat up taller.

"The man you're destined to be with forever is going to be at your side for an important event, very soon."

The holiday party?

"He's going to help someone you love," Mallory continued. "No, not just help them. He'll save them."

Lawton. Must be him, since he had the power to help her dad—in a way, saving him. She couldn't choose Dustin. The realization hit like a slap of icy morning air. She'd have to tell him, and deal with not following her heart. Dread washed over her. Her eyes stung but she refused to give in to her sadness.

Mallory gathered the cards up. "Anything else you wanted to ask?"

She'd had another question on her mind, but now she couldn't recall what it was. Didn't matter. Her dad needed her, and she had to help him. She'd just have to pull on her big-girl panties and put family before her own desires.

"I appreciate you getting my bike in so fast." Aiden shook Dustin's hand. "Darcy and I had planned to ride to the cabin yesterday but when the clutch wouldn't work, I figured I had a big problem on my hands."

Dustin brushed off his friend's thanks as he stashed the ticket behind the counter. "A broken cable's a quick repair. Besides, Monday afternoons have been slow around here since Thanksgiving."

Aiden took out his wallet. "What are the damages?"

"No charge."

When his friend protested, Dustin shut him down. "I couldn't sleep nights if I took money from a guy who gives most of his weekends to the Nocturne Falls Magic Scouts. Consider it my contribution to your troop."

Although in truth, he hadn't slept well since Friday night, when Amethyst had said she was going to think about dating him again. He just prayed her answer was yes.

As soon as his friend drove off the lot, Amethyst got out of the passenger door of a late model Honda sedan. Was the driver her vampire friend? His temples throbbed. He tried to see who was driving but with dark tinted windows, he couldn't.

She waved to whoever it was as the car pulled away then strode toward the entrance. Wearing a black skirt, silver boots and a lacy black top with a wool jacket over it, she was just as gorgeous as she'd been the other night.

Please let her answer be yes.

Heart thumping against his ribcage, he opened the door for her and breathed in her strawberry scent as she stepped past him. "Hey."

"Hi." She gave him the briefest smile. "How's my car?"

"Good to go. It was the alternator." He grabbed her key from the board and handed it to her.

Another customer came in. He rang the man up as Amethyst waited.

Finding the work order for her car, she picked it up

and read it as he finished with the guy. After the man left, she pointed to the paper. "This only has the cost for the part. What about labor?"

He shook his head. "I did it myself. The work's on the house." He knew better than to try to comp the price of the alternator for her. They'd had that argument while they'd been dating. Even then she hadn't wanted anything for free. Thankfully, she paid her bill without complaint.

Hoping for privacy, he started to walk her to her car, which he'd parked in the back of the lot, but she stopped in the doorway. "I can find it."

His hopes fell, until he glanced up and found a sprig of mistletoe hanging from the jamb. A few snowflakes blew past, setting a romantic mood. He took hold of her arm and eased her inside. "I was hoping we could talk."

Her eyelids shuttered. "I-I can't do this, Dustin."

His chest tightened. "The choice is yours."

When she met his gaze, desire sparkled in her pale blue eyes. She took his hand. "You have to believe that if I could, I would. But it's just not possible."

If that were really true, why hadn't she released his hand? Why was she still staring into his eyes with unmistakable attraction?

Their bodies pressed together, and she touched his cheek with a tenderness that took his breath away. He slid his hand around her waist, drawing her even closer.

Her gaze fell to his lips, and his mouth watered to taste her. But no sooner had he moved in for a kiss when she splayed her fingers on his chest and nudged him back.

"I want to. I really, really do. I just can't."

The sadness in her expression mirrored what he felt.

She shook her head. "We can't see each other."

Her words ripped through him. "So you had that reading you were wanting?"

Lips pursed, she nodded. "The cards said I'm destined to be with Lawton."

Lawton. Even his name gave Dustin the creeps. He scrubbed a hand over his face. "You should probably get home before the roads ice up."

Her throat twitched with a swallow. She dropped her gaze then hurried toward her car.

He didn't wait around to watch her leave. His gut was already tied up in knots. But he refused to throw his dignity to the wind by chasing after her or pleading with her to reconsider. He had to get his mind off of her. Aiming to do just that, he closed himself in the office and reached for the day's mail.

Spot rubbed around his ankles, purring. After a few seconds, she leapt onto his lap and nuzzled her face against his belt.

"How am I supposed to get anything done with you distracting me?"

She looked up at him and meowed as if she'd understood. Her eyes grew wide with mischief, and she hopped down, then picked up her toy mouse in her mouth and dropped it at his feet.

"You want to play fetch, huh? Just for a little while." He tossed the mouse and waited for her to bring it back. They repeated the game a dozen times before he hid the toy in his desk. She'd keep going for an hour if he was game.

As Spot curled up on her bed, Dustin finally got to his mail. There were half a dozen Christmas cards, but a red envelope captured his interest. The return address was from the Hair Scare. He tore it open and pulled out a folded flyer. It was an invitation, a masquerade holiday gala.

They'd probably sent it to all the salon's clients. Surely Amethyst didn't want him there. She'd probably invited that vampire her mother wanted her to go out with—Lawton.

He automatically clenched his jaw at the notion of any other guy dating her—a vampire, no less. She might not be safe with this Lawton person. He'd heard through the grapevine that some vampires who married mortals eventually bit their mate in order to make them vampires, too.

How could he be sure that Lawton wouldn't hurt her? All vampires had the potential to be dangerous. Just because the Ellinghams were upstanding members of the community didn't mean all vampires were. The idea of Amethyst being with that dude gave him the willies. He didn't know who Lawton was, but he sure as hell was going to find out.

And he knew just the person who'd be familiar with the guy. As luck would have it, Dustin was picking up that vampire's Maserati tomorrow morning for an oil change and tire rotation. He'd pick Julian Ellingham's brain, find out if Amethyst would be safe with Lawton.

Dustin parked his pickup in the parking lot at the Excelsior Saturday morning then headed into the lobby.

Lou, the beefy doorman glanced up from his newspaper. "Good morning, Dustin."

"Morning. I'm picking up Mr. Ellingham's car."

"Right. He told me you'd be coming for it." Lou fished out a keyring from the desk drawer, and dropped it into Dustin's palm.

"Is he home?" Dustin asked. "I need to speak with him."

Lou narrowed his eyes at him for a moment, then shrugged. "He's in the gym here, actually. Let me call him." Turning his back on Dustin, the doorman used his cell. "Mr. Ellingham, Dustin is here for your car. Says he'd like to talk to you. Right, I'll ask him." Facing Dustin, he moved the phone away from his ear. "He asked if you'd mind going to the gym. It's right here in the building."

"No problem."

Lou nodded then spoke into his cell again. "I'll send him over, sir." After he disconnected, he directed Dustin to the gym.

Minutes later Dustin found the sleek modern gym that would rival any free-standing facility. Spotting Julian Ellingham at the end of the long row of state-of-the-art cardio machines, Dustin headed along the padded floor.

Julian was running—almost as fast as Dustin could—on the treadmill. Watching him, Dustin recalled his endless sessions on similar machines in his parents' lab.

"Pick up the pace," his mother said. "Come on, son. I know you can do better."

Every day they'd insisted he run faster, lift heavier weights on the machines, do more chin-ups. They'd usually left him barely enough time to do his school work after all the tests they'd made him endure. Forget any social plans.

Unclenching his jaw, he waved to Julian, who

slowed his pace to a walk as Dustin neared the machine. "Sorry to interrupt your workout."

Julian's brown hair was damp and a bead of sweat slid down the side of his face. He used the towel on the side of the treadmill to wipe his forehead. "I was hoping for an excuse. Everything okay?"

"Fine. Any problems with the Maserati?"

"Not a one."

"Great." Dustin tried to think of a way to ask the vampire's advice without sounding like a stalker. "Off topic, I've got a question for you." He scanned the area, and thankfully found no one within earshot.

"What's on your mind?"

"I was wondering if you're familiar with a vampire named Lawton."

Julian nodded. "He fills in as Vampire on Duty on occasion. What do you need to know about him?"

Dustin scrubbed a hand over his chin. "Is he trustworthy? Has he ever hurt anyone? That kind of thing."

"Are you hiring him for a job? Or is this about a woman?" Grinning as if he already knew the answer, Julian pressed a button on the treadmill's control panel and the belt slowed then stopped.

"So you're psychic, huh?"

Julian laughed. "Nope, but I have some experience with feeling protective towards a lady."

Dustin nodded. "I just need to be sure that she'll be safe."

Julian slung his towel over his shoulder. "Wish I could tell you I knew him better, but I don't. Since most of us are hundreds of years old, we've all done things we're not particularly proud of. We always screen vampires before they're hired. Apparently nothing shady turned up."

Darn. He'd really hoped Julian could have provided a more in-depth character reference. "Well, thanks for your help."

"I can tell you that most evenings when he's not doing a VOD shift, he can be found at Insomnia, usually hitting on the prettiest women in the place."

Dustin had only been to the supernaturals-only nightclub a few times. "Maybe I'll check that out tonight. Thanks, Julian."

He waved away Dustin's gratitude. "No problem. What time will the Maserati be done? I'd like to take out my lady tonight."

He'd met Julian's wife, Desi, recently, a beautiful vampire who was apparently a Las Vegas star. "Early afternoon. I'll have my detailer spiff it up, on the house."

"I appreciate it."

He drove the sports car back to the shop, and made extra sure the Maserati was in perfect condition before returning it. Then he headed home for a nap since he planned to have a later night than he was used to.

Just before midnight he arrived at Insomnia. It had been a couple of years since he'd last been there, but judging by the number of cars outside the abandoned-looking warehouse, the club was busy as ever. He entered through the rusted steel door on the side of the building. Deceptive silence greeted him. A moment later, the doorman, Chet, greeted him.

"Evening, Dustin," the bear shifter said. "I haven't seen you here for a while."

"I open the repair shop at seven in the morning, so late nights aren't usually my style." Dustin wasn't used to seeing the hulking bear shifter in a suit. On the occasions Chet had brought his F-150 into the shop for service, he'd always been dressed casually. Dustin shook hands with him. "Good to see you." He stepped onto the elevator.

Chet reached inside and punched a code into the elevator keypad. "Same here. Enjoy your evening."

"Thanks." If he was there for purely social reasons, he might, but that wasn't the case. The doors closed and he descended to the basement. When the doors opened, loud dance music filled the air. He stepped into the club and checked out the eclectic crowd. As he strode to the bar, he glimpsed every kind of supernatural imaginable. It still struck him as odd to be around so many all in one place.

An attractive vampire smiled at him as he passed, revealing pretty impressive fangs. A few feline shifters strutted their stuff on the dancefloor, along with a gargoyle he'd seen at the fountain downtown. On his way to the bar, he noticed a couple of male vampires. Could one of them be Lawton? How would he know? He had no clue what the guy looked like.

Taking a seat at the bar, he checked out the bartender. Her pointy ears and small stature gave her away as one of the local fae.

She set down a black napkin in front of him. "Welcome. What can I get you?"

"Heineken Dark, please."

When she came back with his bottle a minute later, he set a twenty on the bar. "Do you know most of the regulars?"

Shrugging, she picked up the bill. "I guess. Searching for someone in particular?"

Leaning toward her, he kept his voice as low as he could, considering the level of the music. "A vampire named Lawton. Know him?"

Her eye roll was almost too quick to notice. "He's over there hitting on a witch with green and blue hair." She tipped her chin toward the VIP area. "I'll be right back with your change."

"Keep it." He carried his beer to a high-top table with a better view of the VIP section.

Lawton sat close to the witch, laughing, and leering at her. She didn't appear to be having the good time Lawton was.

Between the music and the din of the crowd, even his superhuman hearing didn't allow him to hear their conversation, but he was able to read the witch's lips when she called the vampire a jerk. She practically jumped off her stool and hurried away from Lawton.

It only took Lawton a few minutes to find another pretty woman to bother—one who appeared human. But Dustin knew better than to assume, especially here, since the club was exclusively for supernaturals.

Over the course of the next hour, he observed Lawton hit on four more women, mostly of the tipsy or full-on drunk variety. He'd seen enough. The guy was a slime ball. How could Amethyst's folks be okay with having the daughter that they supposedly loved, date someone like Lawton?

He hardly knew her parents, but he'd thought that they cared about her more than that, more than his mother and father had about him. Maybe not.

He couldn't just walk away and let her get involved with someone who seemed to be such an ass toward women. Thinking about the invitation he'd gotten to the

Hair Scare holiday party, a plan formed in his mind—a way he could make sure Amethyst was okay, at least the night of the party. Sure, he had a vested interest in trying to dissuade her from Lawton, and the last thing he wanted was to come off like he was stalking her. But despite that, he couldn't live with himself if he didn't do everything in his power to keep her safe.

5

"Would you hold the ladder still?" Petra asked Amethyst the night of the holiday gala.

Amethyst took in the tall metal archway that her friend had decorated with red and green Christmas ornaments, and loads of mistletoe. "Are you sure that won't fall over? I'd bet it weighs a ton."

Petra huffed as she tipped her chin toward the chandelier in front of the reception area. "Which is why I need your help with the ladder. I'm going to use wire to secure it so that it stays put."

That didn't seem like a great plan, but since Petra had gotten irritated with her a little while ago when Ami had suggested moving the food table close to the kitchen, she kept her mouth shut.

"You'll see," her friend said. "This place is going to look like a winter wonderland when people start showing up. Oh, and we have food coming any minute from Howler's and some desserts from Delaney's Delectables."

Amethyst held onto the ladder as Petra climbed to the fifth rung holding several pieces of wire. Even with the prospect of all that delicious food, Amethyst could barely muster any excitement about the party. As her friend threaded wire through the archway and the chandelier, Ami took in all the decorations. Twinkling strands of white lights strung through real pine garlands hung around the perimeter of the main room and the reception desk. The mirrors over each hair station had been edged with white spray-on frost, and the back wall was decorated with stockings bearing the name of each person who worked at the salon. Petra had even made dozens of paper snowflakes that she'd suspended from the ceiling using tape and white string.

The effect wasn't as authentic as Santa's Workshop, but the winter elves were experts at holiday décor since they maintained theirs all year long. Considering that this was Petra's first attempt at making over the Hair Scare for Christmas, she'd done a darn good job. The place really did resemble a winter wonderland.

Amethyst glanced at the clock. 7:20. T minus forty minutes. Soon Lawton would be here and she'd have to spend some time with him. Dread washed over her, but she did her best to shake it off. She had to make the best of this. That's all there was to it.

She tried to get into the holiday mood. "How many people are we expecting?"

"We had thirty-eight RSVPs. I think." She gestured toward the reception desk. "I wrote the number next to the appointment book. What's it say?"

Ami craned her neck around the ladder to see what her friend had written. "Um, it says eighty-three."

Petra gasped. "Uh oh."

"What?"

Descending the ladder, Petra scratched her head. "I

must have transposed the digits. I ordered food for forty people, and that's how many place settings I bought at the Party Depot."

Amethyst swallowed. "So we have only half of what we need?"

"About, yeah."

Ami jumped into action. "I'll call Howler's to double the order. And let Delaney's know we need more desserts. Maybe the Party Depot is still open. I can run over and—"

"They closed at six," Petra said. "I know. I can do a doubling spell."

Amethyst thought about Petra's spell disasters. Aside from the key fiasco, there was the time she'd done a weather spell to try to end two solid weeks of rain. The rain did stop—but was replaced by a rare October snowstorm. "I don't think that's a good idea."

But her friend waved away Ami's comment and disappeared into the back room. Before she could go after her, Mallory cornered Amethyst at the reception desk. "Hey, can you do me a favor?" Mallory asked.

Ami nodded. "What's up?"

"I was wondering if you have your scrying mirror with you."

Amethyst glanced at the door to the back room. Hopefully Petra was getting the food situation worked out. Mallory seemed concerned about something, and since she'd given Amethyst a reading last week, Ami felt compelled to return the favor. "Sure. Let me grab it. I just need to make two quick calls first." After she'd phoned Howler's and Delaney's to adjust the food orders, she strode to her station to retrieve the antique silver mirror from her drawer.

Mallory glanced around. Keeping her voice barely above a whisper, she asked if Amethyst would give her a quick glimpse into her future. "I just want to know if my twin's really moving out of my house soon. She said she is, but I need to be sure."

Amethyst unwrapped the mirror from the silk cloth she kept it in and drew a deep breath. She sat in her chair, cleared her mind, and focused her intent on divining the future, Mallory's future. Then she stared at the reflective surface. "Show me Mallory's sister, Jordan."

The mirror grew foggy. Amethyst felt the familiar pull for a moment. The salon faded away. She saw Mallory with her twin. Jordan stood at a door, suitcase in hand. "Thanks for putting me up, Mal." Then she headed away.

"I see her leaving, but I can't tell when that is," Amethyst told Mallory.

Mallory groaned.

"Wait, there's more." Ami saw snow flurries blowing through the air. "Soon, I think. Very soon."

"Awesome," Mallory said. "That means her new business will take off. Thank you."

Amethyst was vaguely aware of her coworker walking away. The mirror came into focus again. Instead of Mallory and her sister, though, Ami saw herself. She was kneeling next to someone who'd been hurt, and she intuitively knew it was a person for whom she cared deeply. But before she could make out who it was, the vision faded.

She redoubled her efforts to get back to the image. No luck. Concentrating on what she'd seen, she recalled that a piney scent had filled the air, and holiday music had been playing. The premonition must have been about something that was going to take place at the salon, on this very night. It was so unusual for her to get any information about herself. A chill ran up her spine.

Heart hammering, she struggled to return to the scene, but the scrying mirror merely showed her own reflection. She closed her eyes and tried to remember any details she'd seen. Whoever it was had been wearing black pants and shoes. The details were so faint. She couldn't be sure of anything.

The one thing she was positive of was that the person who'd been lying on the floor was someone she loved. Somebody close to her was in serious danger.

On the night of the party, Dustin parked a few blocks away from Hair Scare.

Last chance to back out.

Thoughts of Amethyst filled his mind. She probably had little to no information about this vampire her mother wanted her to go out with. But Dustin now knew enough about Lawton to concern him.

Amethyst was sweet and caring, while Lawson seemed like a hundred percent jerk. And there was no telling what the vampire might do to Amethyst if he got her alone. A chill snaked up his spine. No, he couldn't back out of this, not in good conscience.

Feeling a little like a stalker, he pulled the price tag off the Batman mask he'd bought at the costume store, and slipped it on. Then he brushed white cat hairs off his black pants. With a glance in his rearview mirror to be sure it was straight, he drew a deep breath, then headed toward the salon.

When he neared the entrance, he couldn't help but be impressed by the decorations. The only thing missing was the real-looking falling snow that Santa's Workshop sometimes managed, although how they pulled that off was a bit of a local mystery. Winter elf magic, he guessed.

Through the frosted windows he glimpsed at least fifty people inside the salon, maybe more. The big crowd would make it easier for him to go unnoticed. Stepping inside, he spotted Amethyst, who apparently had no desire to be stealthy in a purple mask that only covered her eyes. Her beautifully kissable lips were on full display, which only made it more difficult for him to be so near her.

Someone bumped into him, causing him to stumble, but he immediately caught himself.

"Oops, sorry about that." His friend Aiden patted Dustin's shoulder. Wearing a Phantom of the Opera mask that only hid part of his face, Aiden smiled at him. "You okay?"

Darn. He silently nodded as he quickly walked away. Last thing he needed was for his best friend to recognize him and call him out. Careful to avoid people that he knew—and more importantly, knew him—he made his way through the throngs and got to the refreshment table in the back of the salon.

Ami's friend Petra set a tray of coffee mugs next to the punch bowl. "Sorry, folks. We ran out of paper cups, but these work just as well."

Several platters of food on the other end of the table were nearly empty. Apparently they'd misjudged the number of guests. Guilt niggled at him for not replying to the invitation, but if he had, that would have blown the whole incognito-checking-up-on-Lawton thing.

He got himself a drink then found a dark corner that provided a view of most of the room. The majority of the guests' masks didn't completely hide their identity. He didn't see Lawton anywhere. Had Amethyst changed her mind about bringing the vampire as her date?

A tiny flicker of hope raised his spirits. Until Lawton walked in—sans mask—and headed straight for Amethyst. He kissed her cheek, and Ami blanched.

Dustin's gut twisted. Watching the two of them together was going to be torture, but he had to do it. Keeping Amethyst safe was more important than his feelings.

"I think your spell worked," a woman said.

He couldn't place her voice, but it sounded vaguely familiar. Covertly glancing toward the woman, he tried to figure out who she was but the mask covering much of her face didn't help. Standing next to Petra, the woman was shorter, and appeared to be a lot older than Petra. Curly brown hair, short and stocky. Maybe she was one of the hairdressers.

The pair leaned close and kept their voices low, but not low enough, since Dustin's superhuman hearing was almost as good as his cat's.

"I didn't think so at first," Petra said. "But Amethyst is here with the vampire, so maybe I finally got a spell right."

What sort of spell had Petra done on Amethyst? They were supposed to be best friends.

Both women chuckled.

Dustin was anything but amused. Clearly, the pair was up to something.

"I don't know how I can ever thank you for this, Petra."

Dustin realized why the other woman's voice was familiar. Another glimpse confirmed that she was Amethyst's mother, Colleen.

Petra huffed. "Ami would kill me if she found out what I did. I really hate to interfere with my friends' love lives, but I've got to admit, you were right. Amethyst was miserable before. I'm just glad I was able to help her get over Dustin."

Anger seethed inside him. Scanning the room for Amethyst, he found her with Lawton, who seemed to be invading her space. His arm casually draped over the back of her chair. Amethyst was clearly uncomfortable. Her smile was forced, and she was leaning away from the vampire.

How could her mother and her best friend—people who were supposed to care about her—be laughing and patting themselves on the back when Ami was clearly unhappy with the situation?

The burger and fries he'd had at Mummy's Diner a couple hours earlier felt like lead in his stomach. He'd planned to stay in the background tonight, but how could he remain silent for such a travesty, especially one that was so unfair to Amethyst?

"She needed to get over him," Colleen said. "I know what's good for my little girl, and Dustin wasn't the right man."

He couldn't keep quiet for another second. Marching over to the women, he ripped off his mask and jabbed a finger at them. "What did you two do?"

Both women gasped in unison.

"What kind of spell did you put on Amethyst?" He didn't care that other people could hear, or that the pair seemed afraid.

A worried expression passed between the women.

"Tell me," he growled. Someone grabbed his arm. Dustin spun around and found Amethyst's dad glowering at him.

"What's going on here?" Mr. Powers demanded.

Dustin yanked back his arm. "Using magic to coerce people you're supposed to love isn't okay, sir."

Mr. Powers darted his gaze between Dustin and the women. "I have no idea what you're talking about. Colleen, what's going on?"

Her throat twitched with a swallow. "We were just trying to help."

"Help who?" he asked.

Petra stepped between the husband and wife. "Amethyst was such a sad sack after you and Colleen made her break up with Dustin. I was merely trying to make her feel better with my spell."

Mr. Powers weaved around Petra and glared at his wife. "What's she talking about, Colleen? I would never presume to tell either of my daughters who they could date."

Colleen pulled off her mask and fisted her hands. "I was trying to help *you*."

"Me? By using magic on our daughter?" He pinched the bridge of his nose then turned his anger on Petra. "What was the spell?"

She wrung her hands. "Well, I found one to make her forget Dustin."

Dustin clenched his jaw.

"Because her mother asked you to do that?" Mr. Powers asked.

"Shhhhhh!" Colleen stage whispered. "You're making a scene."

"You bet I am." He wiped sweat from his reddened forehead.

Amethyst rushed over, her face flushed. "What's going on? I could hear you from across the salon." She widened her eyes at Dustin. "I didn't know you were coming."

Petra took Amethyst's hand. "Can you forgive me? I was only trying to make you feel better. That's why I cast the spell."

Amethyst squeezed her eyes shut for a moment. "Tell me what the spell was, the exact words."

"Let me think." Petra held a fist to her mouth for several seconds. "Okay, I've got it. I call to the powers below and above, north, south, east, west. In the name of love, heal Amethyst's heart, who is so dear. Heal all her pain, heal all her fear." She stopped and scratched her head. "I know there's more." She nodded. "I remember. I send her power, a heart of gold. I send her light and love untold. To heal her heart, to make it bright. Make her stop loving Dustin tonight. So mote it be." A big smile split her face, as if she'd just mastered a difficult task. But one look at her best friend and her smile withered. "Sorry, Ami."

Amethyst buried her face in her hands. "How could you, Mom?"

"That's what I'd like to know," her father added.

Dustin put his arm around her, offering what comfort she'd accept. He understood all too well the anguish of a betrayal by your own parent.

"We need Lawton to invest in your inventions," Colleen said. "And he took a shine to her the night he first met her."

Her father shook his head. "What about Amethyst? What about how she felt?"

Amethyst met her mother's stare. "I've always done as you asked. Even after you drove Emerald away. And now you've lost your other daughter."

"Ami, please," Colleen pleaded. "I did it for all of us."

Dustin's parents had told him the same thing, time and again. He tightened his grip on Amethyst. "Do you want to get out of here?"

Leaning against him, she nodded.

He led her under the mistletoe-covered archway, and heard creaking, like wood straining or cracking.

A moment later her mother ran after them. Grasping the metal on the side of the arch, she hooked Amethyst's arm to stop her. "I was only watching out for your interests."

"No, Mom. You were looking out for your own." Shaking her mother off, she sighed.

Another creak, louder this time. He followed the source of the noise to the chandelier above the arch. Small cracks in the ceiling stretched in every direction from the fixture. And they were getting bigger.

Before he could react, the arch and the chandelier came crashing down, and with it, a chunk of drywall from the ceiling. People screamed, and scuttled away. He shoved Amethyst out of the way, but the debris hit her mother on the back of her head.

For a moment, a cloud of dust obscured the scene. When it cleared, the full scope of the accident came into view. The metal arch lay on its side with pieces of the chandelier and chunks of drywall scattered around the reception area.

"Mom!" Amethyst kneeled next to her mother, who was partially buried under the debris, out cold.

Ami tried to move a huge piece of the ceiling off of her mom. "It's too heavy."

Dustin stepped around the mess, and grabbed the plaster, which still had most of the light attached. He easily moved everything aside then picked up Colleen and carried her to the sofa in the waiting area.

Aiden—an EMT and a Kachina healer—ran over and started checking Colleen over as Mr. Powers and Amethyst stood watching. The red gash on Colleen's forehead faded under Aiden's ministrations.

Lawton backed away, then mumbled something and left.

Good riddance.

Mallory hurried over and handed Dustin a wet towel. He wiped the dust and dirt off of Colleen's face and neck.

"She's coming to," Aiden said.

Her eyes fluttered for a second before she opened them and peered into his. "You saved me." She reached for his hand and squeezed it. Her face went pale, and her eyes glazed over. She appeared to be in some sort of trance for a moment. Then she gasped. "They're back."

"What is, Mom?" Amethyst sat on the edge of the couch.

"My psychic powers. They're back." Her expression changed to a calm serenity as she continued holding Dustin's hand. "You're going to make my daughter very happy. And she'll do the same for you."

Too stunned to speak, he just stared at Amethyst.

"I'm so sorry, Amethyst," Colleen said. "I don't know what came over me. I just pray that Petra can remove the spell."

Amethyst smiled warmly at him. "Her spell didn't work anyway. Maybe she jumbled the words. Who knows?"

Dustin pointed to a sprig of mistletoe still hanging from the ceiling over them. "Maybe the mistletoe's magic was just stronger." Shifting closer to her, Dustin cupped her cheek and brushed his lips over hers.

"Or perhaps it's our magic," Amethyst said. "I always suspected we had our own."

epilogue

One month later…

Spot jumped onto Dustin's kitchen counter as Amethyst finished stowing the leftovers from dinner in a plastic container. "Sorry, girl. No more human food for you." But with a glance over her shoulder at Dustin, who was washing the table, she retrieved the pouch of cat treats from the cabinet and slipped one to the feline.

"I saw that." Dustin dropped the sponge at the sink then wrapped Amethyst in his strong arms and pressed a kiss to the back of her neck, setting off delicious sparks inside her. "We can't both spoil her."

She twisted around to face him. "Thank you for inviting my parents to dinner tonight. That meant a lot to me."

"*You* mean a lot to *me.* Your folks are welcome here any time."

Could she adore him any more? Staring up at his ridiculously handsome face, she couldn't hold back a happy sigh. "Mom said that the only time she sees me lately is when she comes into the salon to get her hair or her nails done since I'm not staying at the garage apartment much."

He tightened his arms around her. "Is that a complaint?"

Amethyst shook her head. "She's been a lot easier to be around since she got hit on the head. I swear, it did more than just bring back her psychic gift. Her personality improved, too. Although I think that when she got hurt the first time—when she lost her psychic abilities—she became more abrasive. It just didn't happen all at once, so we didn't pick up on it. I wonder if that first whack on the head did something to make her ornery and super controlling."

"I guess that's possible." He stepped back and took Amethyst's hand. "I need to ask you a question."

She swallowed. They'd only been back together for a month. He'd given her a key to his place since she was practically living there already. Granted, things were amazing between them, but she wanted to be sure before they took things to a long-term commitment level. "O-okay."

"One of my venders asked me about the Cat Litter Master. He noticed it in my office when he came by this morning."

She nodded, unsure why he wanted to discuss her father's latest invention.

"He and his wife have five cats, and they're always harping on their kids to scoop the cat box. Of course, seeing that your dad's machine not only does that part, but also bags the mess, and replaces the litter, he was really excited. Said it would help keep the peace in their family if they had a couple of them."

She certainly understood that. There was a lot to be said for peace. Now that her folks seemed to be getting along better, she was thrilled. Emerald had even come for a visit last week. "Maybe my dad can make another one or two for them. I'm sure he'd love to make a sale."

His smile widened. "It's better than that. The man owns a company that builds machines—mostly the kind that have some function in an auto shop, and he was so impressed by the design that he wants to speak to the inventor about manufacturing and distributing Cat Litter Masters."

Amethyst cheered. "Oh my goodness. Why didn't you tell my dad about it over dinner?"

He shrugged. "I thought I should run it past you first. I didn't have time to do that since they were already here when I got home from work."

Dustin really was an amazing guy. She'd never had anyone treat her with such respect and caring. "We should call him. He'll be thrilled." The fact that he got along so well with her folks meant the world to her. She understood how hurt he was over the way his parents had treated him, but it still bothered her that they barely communicated. "Can I ask you a question now?"

"Sure."

Biting her lip, she sat him down at the table. "Family's important."

His brows angled to a V. "And?"

"Would you think about something, for me?"

He folded his arms over his chest. "What'd you have in mind?"

She went to the fridge and grabbed a water bottle, taking a sip as she sat back down. "I'd like for us to take a vacation this fall, maybe head north to see the leaves change in New England.

"Why there? We have fall foliage here."

She squeezed his hand. "Maybe it's time to mend fences with your family."

His lips flattened. Tension cut lines across his forehead. "I don't know."

"All I'm asking is that you mull it over. It's six or seven months away. What do you think?" She crossed her fingers.

"I think you're a beautiful, persuasive woman." He stood, pulling her into his arms as he did. "And I think that I love you very much. I'll give it some thought."

"Thank you." She couldn't ask for more. The man made her toes curl. Heck, her life was getting better every day since Dustin had come back into it.

"Who knows? We might have some news by the fall."

"News?"

He rubbed his thumb along her left ring finger, the only one on which she didn't wear any rings. "Maybe a new piece of jewelry."

Her heart fluttered. Barely able to suck in a breath, she gave him a kiss then started toward his bedroom, holding out her hand to him. "I love you, too."

His eyes darkened with desire. "I guess that call to your dad can wait a little while."

"Mm hmm." She waggled her eyebrows at him as he mated his fingers with hers. "Or a little longer than that."

THE END

The Psychics Say I Do

BY CANDACE COLT

Cousins Brianna Putnam and Jess Callahan are headed to the altar to wed the handsome falcon-shifter Ford brothers. But when the brides' plans run amok, even their psychic powers can't undo the chaos. The entire town pitches in to help, but will it be enough to pull off their Christmas dream weddings?

1

Two-step out of here? Or stay and apologize?

Guillermo's restaurant was closed for a private party. The longer Brianna Putnam stood outside the main dining room, the harder her heart pounded. She was sure it was louder than the overhead music and female laughter wafting her way.

Artful decorations covered the tables, color-coordinated in soft pinks, touches of gold, and rustic wood hues. Her cousin's wedding shower was well underway.

She had a good reason to be late. But she could count on one hand the number in this room who would give a flying fig.

She'd been in Atlanta almost a month with the love of her life, Connor Ford. He'd intended to get them back to Nocturne Falls hours ago so Brianna could change into something appropriate for an afternoon ladies' event. Not that she had a tea party dress anyway. Not her style.

But a last-minute meeting of the Ford Financial Group executive committee had run long, and not something Connor could afford to miss.

The delay had been worth every extra minute.

Connor had spent weeks convincing the old guard that he was capable of leading FFG. Today he'd been officially elected Chairman of the Board of the company his late father founded.

No small feat. He was by decades the youngest man in the room. He'd stood toe-to-toe with the most elite falcon shifters in the southeast. He'd held his own, and prevented a corporate take-over that would have ruined the Ford family.

Brianna could not have been prouder of her man if he'd won the US Presidential election.

Anxious to share the details with his brother, Connor had dropped Brianna off with a promise to pick her up after the shower.

That had sounded like a good plan. Until now. Every woman in the room was elegantly dressed. And here stood Brianna in her cropped ripped jeans and Atlanta Falcons sweatshirt. She squeezed her shower gift to her chest. The gift table was only a few feet away. She could sidle into the room, drop it off and be gone before anyone noticed.

Then later explain to her cousin, Jess Callahan.

Poised to make her run for the table, Brianna was startled by the touch of someone's hand on her back.

Busted.

"Oh, good. You made it after all." From behind, Delaney Ellingham's voice caught Brianna's ear.

"Uh. Hi, Delaney. We just got back. I was going to drop this off. I'm not dressed for the party."

Delaney put an arm around Brianna's waist. "Nonsense. You look adorable as always."

Before Brianna could come up with a clever exit line, they were through the threshold.

Delaney returned to her seat leaving Brianna standing in the center of the room. All eyes turned to her. For a long, eternal moment, the only sound was a single coffee cup returning to its saucer.

With sandpaper dry lips, Brianna grinned and made quick nods and waves around the room. Some of these women she'd met, but most were absolute strangers. Several turned to their table mates and didn't even attempt to hide their bewildered whispers.

A welcoming island amidst this sea of swirling sharks, Jess motioned for Brianna to sit in the empty chair beside her.

Beautiful in an autumn brown dress that complimented her gorgeous red hair, Jess stood and gave her cousin a quick kiss on the cheek. "I'm so glad you made it back in time."

"Sorry, I'm late." Brianna nodded across the table to Connor's mother and shower hostess, Solange Ford.

Jess leaned close to Brianna and whispered. "We got the text from Connor. We're so proud of you two. And, I'm so happy to have a friendly face in this room. Half these women are Solange's friends. I have no clue who they are."

Jess waved to the server to remove the stack of dirty plates in front of Brianna. "There's a ton of food left. Hope you're hungry."

Even Jess, who'd lived in Nocturne Falls most of her life, didn't know these women?

Relief poured over Brianna. "I'm starved."

She filled her plate with assorted tea sandwiches and salads from the buffet table then returned to her seat. As she spread a pink paper napkin across her lap, she sensed Jess's eyes staring at her.

Uh oh. The ring. She hadn't taken it off from the minute Connor put it on her finger. They'd planned to make their engagement announcement together. Certainly not in the middle of Jess's special day.

In all the hub-bub of the race to get here, she forgot to slip it into her purse.

Stealthily turning the stone setting toward her palm, Brianna hoped against hope…

"Is that what I think it is?" Jess said as she reached for Brianna's hand and turned the ring back around.

"That's a diamond." Unable to contain her glee, Jess's voice raised two octaves. "Connor finally came to his senses."

Heat spiraled up Brianna's neck. She wiped a sweat bead that wasn't the result of the jalapeno cheese dip she hadn't even tasted yet.

"What's this about my son?" Solange Ford's sonic boom shot across the table. The woman had the uncanny inability to keep her voice down. Once again, all heads in the room turned to Brianna.

"We were going to tell you later." Brianna scanned her cousin's face for approval. Jess's friendship was hard won. She didn't want to lose it now.

Jess couldn't be too surprised. After all, hadn't their time-traveling grandmother, Echo Stargazer, suddenly appeared to them in Solange's solarium and predicted grandchildren?

Of course, that was just a few weeks ago. Perhaps the Georgia custom was for people to date a while before getting engaged. Exactly how long was a while? And did that apply to supernaturals?

Brianna and Connor thumbed their nose at customs. They knew this was the right thing for them.

Giddy chatter percolated among the women again as Jess opened her gifts. Brianna's gut told her the conversation with Solange Ford wasn't over yet.

And it wasn't her psychic gift working overtime either.

2

Ryan Ford helped Jess carry gifts upstairs to their apartment over the Carpe Diem gift store. Though a fraction of the size of the Ford mansion, it was all theirs. Though Jess had no idea where they'd put all this stuff.

She and Ryan had spent weeks going through her grandmother's things and downsizing where they could. Echo may eventually come back from her sojourn to the 17th century and ask about them. But they would deal with that consequence when it arose.

At least now they could walk through the place without whacking their knees and hips on chairs, armoires, overstuffed chairs, and bric-a-brac.

"Stop saying you didn't know." Jess put an armload of gifts on the ottoman. She pushed Crealde the cat off the couch and took his place.

"You're convinced there's a conspiracy. Hate to tell you this, but there's not," Ryan said.

He sat next to her and gently squeezed his fingers into her tight neck muscles. "I'd think you'd be happy for them."

"I am. Really. If it makes them happy, then I'm happy."

Jess relaxed into Ryan's touch. She'd learned to shut down thoughts about his being a falcon shifter. This was her handsome husband-to-be giving her a loving massage.

"Umm. That feels so good," she murmured.

"Glad to be of service. Now, tell me why you're so worked up about my brother getting married."

"It seems sudden, is all. Brianna showed up the first week in October. Met Connor. Then bam. It's almost Thanksgiving, and they are engaged. Don't you think that's a little rushed?"

"We started dating in August, remember."

"But I've known you since I was a kid." And as a kid, she thought Ryan was the nerdiest geek on the planet. When she came home as a grown woman, she realized he was the *sexiest* nerdy geek on the planet.

"That's not the real reason you're upset. Out with it."

She was psychic. He was a shifter. Then how could he read her mind so easily? She took a deep breath and sighed. "You don't think she might be after his money, do you?"

"Come on, Jess. You don't really think that."

She'd come to love her curly-headed little cousin. But the fact remained she didn't know that much about her.

"I can't put it into words. Just a hunch," she said.

"Psychic hunch? Or plain old hunch?"

Jess turned the jade ring around her finger. Though tempted to take it off and unblock her clairvoyance, she decided against it.

Her grandmother, Echo Stargazer, didn't seem bothered by Brianna's sudden return. In fact, she was delighted. So why was it bothering Jess?

"When it comes right down to it, you know what I think my problem is?" She asked.

Ryan nibbled her neck. "Tell me." His breath in her ear set off fireworks.

"This was supposed to be our time. Now they'll share the stage with us. It's not fair."

Crealde, the behemoth cat, jumped up on Jess's lap and revved his B-52 purr engine.

"Even he thinks the 'it's not fair' argument is bogus," Ryan said.

Crealde looked up at Jess and blinked twice.

"Did you see that?" She lifted the cat and touched his nose to hers.

"Yep. He and I see eye-to-eye on this one," he said.

"Except yours are the same color."

"Hey, don't mock the cat. You know he's famous for those mismatched eyes," Ryan said.

Crealde shifted side-to-side on Jess's lap, kneading his mighty paws on her thighs. Then he settled into a ball, his butt facing her.

"I think you owe your cousin a heart-to-heart conversation. Don't ruin your brand-new friendship by acting like kids fighting over the same toy." Ryan gave her shoulders a squeeze. "If Connor loves her as much as I love you, there's room in this family for all of us. In fact, I think this is the best thing that's ever happened to the Fords."

"So, the secret's out. What's the big deal? We were going to tell them anyway." Connor opened a beer and offered one to Brianna.

Still full after shoveling in finger foods and cake all afternoon, she declined. "I don't think your mother is very pleased about this."

They bumped elbows as Brianna edged past Connor hiking a seat in the barstool at their tiny two-person breakfast counter. Connor's bungalow was great for a single guy. Cozy, but a little tight for two.

"Few things in this world please my mother. She'll come around. You know how she is," Ryan said.

Nobody had to explain Solange to Brianna Putnam. She'd witnessed the woman shift into a falcon. One minute Solange-the-human was hosting guests in her palatial living room. The next minute she'd shifted into a menacing predator.

"We did get engaged kind of quick." Brianna joined Connor at the counter.

"Regrets?"

"Not at all. But I wish I knew how to break this to my family."

"Just do it, Brianna. Call them up. Invite them to the wedding. They'll come if they want, or not. It won't stop us."

Brianna spun her silver infinity bracelet around her wrist. "I wish it was that easy."

Connor pulled his phone from his pocket. "It's six o'clock in the evening in Oregon. Tell me the number."

She grabbed the phone. "I can't. Not yet. Not now. I need more time."

"Time for what? To decide if this is the right thing for us?"

"That's not it. To decide how to tell my father that I'm marrying a falcon-shifter."

"Well, I wouldn't start the conversation off exactly like that."

"I'll make a deal. Give me three days, and we'll make the call, together. I promise."

"I'll hold you to it."

"Right now, I'd prefer you hold me, period."

3

Connor's Porsche whirred into the Ford estate driveway moments before Ryan parked his pickup behind him. The two couples stood on the front porch and exchanged nervous glances.

"You know we're acting like kids." Brianna tightened her grip on Connor's hand.

He broke her death grip and shook blood back into his fingers. "Ryan's the oldest. I think he should be the one to start the conversation."

"Why me? You two are the ones with the big honking surprise," Ryan said.

"It's not really a surprise, now is it?" Jess said.

"Here I am, the newly elected Chairman of the Board for one of the largest corporations in the country and my knees are knocking," Connor said.

"Maybe we lead off with the FFG deal. Mother's pretty darn excited about that. We'll keep talking that one up," Ryan said.

"That will take a full five minutes," Brianna said.

"Oh, hell. Enough of this. It's too cold to stand here yapping." Jess opened the door and led the way inside where the housekeeper, Sabrina, greeted them. Solange waited for them in the formal living room.

Though the house was comfortably warm, Brianna shuddered. When Solange accepted guests there, it was never good.

"I think we'll need alcohol to get through this," Ryan whispered to Sabrina.

"Got that covered. I'll bring in a tray about three minutes after you go in."

They linked arms like Dorothy, the Lion, the Scarecrow and the Tin Man and walked toward the living room in measured, uniform steps.

"You know we look like morons," Jess whispered.

"Yep," Ryan said.

"I hope this is the right thing to do," Connor said.

"I hope Sabrina set a timer," Brianna said.

Solange sat in the same overstuffed upholstered chair that she'd sat in the night the Ford family shifted into falcons to impress, or scare witless, the La Grande Bouche editor. That, and Sabrina's draoi gift to erase the man's memory had saved Brianna's bacon.

How could Brianna have ever considered writing a tabloid exposé on this wonderful town? It hadn't been for the tiny amount of money she would have earned.

Perhaps she'd come up with the insane idea to prove her father was right that his hometown was full of fakes and frauds. Maybe to gain his respect.

It didn't matter, now. It was all in the past. She looked over at Connor, still a bit sheepish in his mother's presence.

Cripes. Brianna had the same fluttery feeling in her gut that she did just before she watched the family's transformation. The first time she witnessed Connor shift.

Her butterflies released when she remembered that was the moment she'd fallen in love with her falcon.

"Why are you still standing?" Solange asked. "Be seated."

Her words thundered like orders, and all four sat as one on the massive leather couch across from her.

"I suspect you've drawn straws as to who will speak first. And I would guess that Ryan drew the short one," Solange said.

Amid Connor and Ryan's hemming and hawing, Brianna made up her mind to end this agony. She cleared her throat.

"Solange, we had planned to tell you about our engagement before it made headlines at the shower. I'm sorry for that," Brianna began.

"It's not your fault," Connor piped in. "Don't apologize."

He turned to his mother. "We'd hoped to share our news with you first. It didn't work out that way. It doesn't mean anything other than timing. We aren't ashamed of our decision. And it shouldn't come as a surprise to you." He glanced at his brother and Jess. "Nor to anyone else. And frankly, it isn't your concern."

Brianna split her attention between the conversation and the doorway. Where was Sabrina? As if waiting for her cue, the wonderful housekeeper entered with a tray of drinks.

Ryan proposed a toast. "Let's end the discord here and now. To my brother and Brianna. To my fiancé and me. And to you, Mother. May we all live long lives. Enjoy prosperity. Experience love."

They clinked their glasses and waited for Solange to take the first sip.

She cast an upward glance at the brothers and their mates. "And may I be blessed with many grandchildren."

It took both of Brianna's shaking hands around her glass to guide it to her lips.

"Feel better about things now?" Connor asked.

Outside by their cars, Connor, Brianna, Ryan, and Jess held a debriefing.

A November chill coursed through Brianna as she considered her response. The conversation with Solange had ended on a cordial and almost pleasant note.

She suspected Sabrina's delightful Swedish Fish cocktails had something to do with that. Smooth as a summer breeze, they slid down so easy. Fortunately, Brianna had the presence of mind to stop after one.

"She seemed calm," Brianna said.

Though the eye of the hurricane calm was more like it. Perhaps it was Brianna's lack of confidence that made her suspicious of everyone right now. It was way past time for her to kick that pile of nonsense to the curb. Why wouldn't she be worthy of marrying Solange's son?

"Oh, Mother will come around. Meanwhile, I have a proposition," Ryan said. "We haven't had a proper congratulation ceremony for the new FFG Chairman of the Board." He checked the time on his phone then tapped in a number. "It's still early. How about dinner at the Café Claude."

Ryan pushed his empty plate away and patted his full stomach. "I love this place, almost too much. I better watch it, or I won't fit in my wedding tux."

Jess punched his arm. "Okay, mister. I get the message. I'll skip dessert but only if you do."

Neither one of them needed to worry about how they looked or what they ate. Brianna never saw them once when they didn't look like high fashion models. What a knock-out wedding couple they would be.

Ryan leaned forward. "So, Brianna. Tell us how my brother popped the question."

"Honey, that's personal, don't you think?" Jess asked.

Brianna squeezed Connor's knee under the table. "Actually, we were at a Waffle Shack."

"They need one of those around here," Connor said. "Think the Ellinghams will go for it?"

Ryan shook his head. "Doubtful. Now back to my question. Brianna?"

"We'd been out late. I got a craving for fried chicken and waffles," Brianna said.

"I made an excuse to use the men's room and instead wrote a note for the server. When the bill came to the table, I pretended I'd left my wallet in the car. When Brianna opened the bill folder to pay, there it was. My proposal." Connor sat tall in his chair. "Pretty ingenious, huh?"

Brianna rustled through her purse and retrieved a plastic baggie with a paper napkin inside it.

"See?" She set it on the table and gently rubbed the edges flat.

In block letters, were the words 'I LOVE YOU. MARRY ME?' Though the word 'love' had nearly disappeared in a greasy stain.

"I thought the server had lost her mind. Then I realized it was from Connor," Brianna said.

Jess and Ryan exchanged unemotional glances.

"I told you it was personal," Jess said.

"Well, bro. I'm sure feeling the passion," Ryan said.

Brianna reverently refolded the napkin and placed it back in the little bag, then in her purse. Those five words meant more to her than all the money in the world.

"I think I'll powder my nose," Jess said. "Join me, Brianna?"

"Why is it that women always go in twos to the john?" Connor asked.

The women shared knowing glances. Time for a little girl talk.

Jess finished washing her hands. "I hope you know we are..."

The blast from the hand dryer drowned out the rest of Jess's sentence. Brianna hoped it was something encouraging.

The women stood in front of the mirror reapplying lipstick and dabbing powder on their faces. It was, after all, what they'd set out to do. Wasn't it?

Then why did Brianna think there might be another shoe about to drop?

"So, have you talked about a wedding date? In the spring, perhaps? Or late summer?" Jess snapped her lipstick case shut and blotted her lips with a tissue.

Kablam. The other shoe.

"We haven't decided yet." Accepting Connor's proposal and buying a ring had been amazing events in themselves. She was getting used to being a fiancé. Becoming a married woman seemed a bit distant.

"Your wedding is the most important thing to us right now," Brianna said.

Jess who had been staring at Brianna in the mirror's reflection, turned to her cousin. "You mean that, don't you?" She asked in a quiet tone.

Did Jess think Brianna was back to steal her thunder? Was that why this impromptu bathroom meeting?

Brianna touched Jess's arm. "Why wouldn't I mean it? A wedding day belongs to the groom and bride. Getting married is a big deal in my book. And you two are perfect together. Just as I feel Connor and I are."

They stepped aside so a woman could wash her hands. The stranger seemed to stifle a giggle.

Jess scrunched her eyes as she flashed a tight-lipped smile to the handwasher. "Come on Brianna. Obviously, this isn't a good place for a private conversation."

"Thought you two had ducked out the back door," Connor said as the cousins took their places at the table.

"There was a line." Brianna gave Jess a broad smile.

"Yeah, a long line," Jess said.

5

Brianna didn't know the first thing about what went into wedding planning. The next day she gratefully accepted Jess's invitation for lunch. Then she would go with her for a final wedding dress fitting at Corette Williams' Ever After Bridal Boutique. Maybe she'd pick up some pointers.

In October, when Connor had taken her on the whirlwind meet-and-greet around Nocturne Falls, he'd avoided taking her into the boutique. Now she knew why. It was a lovely shop. But it was all about weddings. Not a Connor thing at all.

While Jess was in the dressing room, Brianna wandered through the store. Racks of dresses in all lengths, sizes, and styles. She'd never imagined there were so many ways to combine fabric, beads, and lace. She thumbed through a photo album of other dresses Corette had sold. Brianna recognized several clients from around town, including Delaney.

"Well, what do you think?" Jess had stepped up on a riser surrounded on three sides by mirrors.

Brianna's breath hitched. She didn't know what to

think, let alone say. Jess Callahan was stunning.

The only thing that compared was the gown that Duchess Kate had worn when she married Prince William. No. This was much better.

Dazzling white, the mermaid style dress fit Jess like a second skin. The graceful skirt flounced just below her knee. Seed pearl lace rounded her shoulders, covered her arms, and ended just before her knuckles. In the mirror's reflection, Jess could see it was backless, cut to the waist.

Then the image blurred.

Jess had stepped down off the small riser, came to Brianna's side, and clasped her hands. "Are you crying?"

Brianna sniffed twice and shook her head. "Something in my eyes." She sniffed again.

"Aw, Brianna." Jess enfolded her cousin in a hug.

"The dress." Brianna held her arms out to her side. "Be careful."

"This dress can handle it," Jess said.

They embraced in a tight, long hug.

"You look…" Brianna searched for the right word. "Amazing." The only word she could say to describe Jess.

"Wait till it's your turn," Jess said.

Corette stepped up to them. "I understand you are Connor's fiancé. Congratulations. And I would be honored to help you select and order your dress. Have you set the date yet?"

Brianna shook her head. Excitement braided with fear. A date to get married? Was this a real conversation or a dream?

Suddenly her feet felt like ice blocks.

"Not yet," she said.

6

Brianna swiped her hand across the kitchen counter, knocking her tumbler of tea to the floor. Muttering curses, she grabbed towels to mop up the mess.

Thanksgiving was over, and Christmas was three weeks away.

No matter what she did to distract herself, Brianna's mind kept coming back to the fact that this was the first time in her life that she wasn't in Portland with her family for the holidays.

It was a Putnam tradition to have Christmas Day lunch in Chinatown. She was in high school before she realized Peking Duck wasn't on every Christmas day table.

Connor shut his laptop, left his tiny desk in the corner of their bungalow, then scooped Brianna into his arms. "The closer to Christmas we get, the crazier you've been acting. What's going on?"

Connor's embrace had become her haven. Where she felt safe and protected. She edged her arms out of his bearhug and then wrapped them around his waist.

"Nothing's going on," she mumbled into his chest.

Brianna straddled panic like a horse that she knew was going to kick. Sooner or later.

She loved Connor over the moon and back. But she missed her family, even to an extent her father.

And this whole wedding thing was scaring the socks off her.

She rolled her eyes up to meet Connor's gaze. "Have you ever thought about eloping?"

Brianna swore she heard a voice somewhere shrieking *'Noooooo.'* Impossible.

Connor pressed back to arm's length. "Are you serious?"

Not really, but it would solve some serious problems.

"I'm all mixed up. I don't know what I want. Jess makes this all look so easy," she said.

"Look, this wedding is about what *we* want. Not what somebody else wants, or what they are doing, or how they run their show. Nobody's forcing you to decide the date. But you need to tell your family. You asked for two extensions on that three-day promise to call them. Are you dragging your feet because you aren't sure you want to get married?"

"Oh, hell no. That's not it at all." She threw her arms around him again and squeezed with all her might.

"Okay," he wheezed. "It's tough being away from your home this time of year. I get that. Christmas has been hard for us, too, since my father died. But you think it's fair to your mother to keep this secret?"

No. It wasn't fair, and Brianna felt horrible every time she ended a phone call to her mother without telling her. Brianna had skirted around the subject when she'd explained that she was spending Christmas in Georgia to attend her friend's wedding.

She'd dodged her mother's questions about what town, knowing that even mentioning Nocturne Falls would set off a nuclear explosion.

Her mother had always been her closest confidante, and Brianna was holding back on the most important news she'd ever had.

Despite how her father railed against his hometown, she loved it here. It was a picture-perfect place to celebrate Christmas. If her mother could see it, she'd feel the same way. Brianna knew it in her heart.

"I'll make the call tomorrow, I swear." She hid her hands behind her back and crossed all her fingers.

Brianna walked the five blocks from the cottage to downtown. Making the turn to the Hallowed Bean, she was hit head-on by a brisk wind gust. She pulled her jacket collar around her neck. Winter was just around the corner. No better way to greet it than a latte.

People inside the Bean were backed up to the door. Cripes. She'd promised Connor she'd get to the bank before ten-thirty. No time for lines.

She passed up the bank lobby coffee intending to stop by the Bean and try her luck again. Finished at the bank, Brianna stepped up her pace. The Bean's morning crowd should have thinned by now. It was down some, but still packed. Then she saw the sign: *Free Samples of Yuletide Cinnamon Latte.*

Well, no wonder. And a latte would have made laundry day tolerable.

The shortcut back to the bungalow took her past the Carpe Diem. Jess's car was in the driveway. Maybe there was a chance for a fresh cup of coffee after all. Throw in some cinnamon and sugar and voila.

Brianna went through the front door to the shop and greeted the staff. Then she went upstairs to the private apartment and tapped on the door.

"Hi there. Come on in." Dressed in a denim work shirt and jeans, Jess looked ready to tackle one of her famous home repair jobs.

"Am I interrupting?" Brianna asked.

"Not at all. I just finished changing out the light switch in the bathroom. Join me for coffee?"

The fairytale princess and all-around handy woman changing a light switch? Of course. Why not?

Crealde greeted them in the kitchen. Unfortunately for him, sitting in the middle of the table was apparently unacceptable in this house.

"Shoo, you little tyrant," Jess said. "You know better."

In his characteristic laissez-faire style, Crealde stood, stretched, yawned and sauntered to the table edge. Looking over his shoulder before he expended another ounce of energy, he gave a quick head shake and jumped to the floor with a thud.

Brianna went to the door. "Want out, buddy?"

Crealde shot her an indignant scowl easily interpreted as, 'in this weather?' then sashayed toward a bedroom.

As the coffee brewed, Jess sat across from Brianna at the table. "See what I've put up with? We've been battling almost twenty years. He's a little more respectful around Nana, but not much."

"How old is he?" Brianna asked.

"We have no idea," Jess said.

The girls shared a comfortable laugh.

"Think grandmother will be back for the wedding?" Brianna asked.

"She told us she would be. She keeps her promises," Jess said.

"I hope she stays long enough so I can get to know her better. She seems very nice."

"The best. Looking back, I don't know what I would have done if she hadn't taken me in after my parents died."

Brianna dropped her gaze to the table. If her father hadn't been such an ass, Jess would have lived with them.

Jess put her hand on Brianna's. "Oh, I'm so sorry. I still sometimes forget my uncle is your father."

Brianna drew in a long breath and let it out slowly. "I think it would have been fun to grow up together."

"Me too, now that I know you. But you're here now, and you're going to marry Connor. That seals our relationship even better."

Over the delicious fresh coffee, they chatted about the wedding and how the details were coming together. It seemed to Brianna that Jess had it all under control. She knew she'd be a basket case at this point.

"When Connor and I finally pick a date, would you consider helping me plan the wedding?"

"Would I? I'd love it. Have you given any thought to a date?" Jess asked.

Brianna shook her head. "I haven't even told my parents that I'm engaged."

Jess took a sip of coffee, put down the cup and stared into Brianna's eyes. "Because Connor and Ryan are shifters, right?"

After a long pause, Brianna answered. "Yes. You know how my father feels about this town. He raised my brother and me to think everything here was fake. Now I know that was his way of dealing with the disappointment that he didn't inherit the psychic gift. How in the world could I tell him I'm marrying a falcon?"

"The longer you put it off, the harder it will be. I have an idea. How about I get back to my super-woman chores and you sit right here and give them a call. What is it, four hours difference? It's about eight in the morning out there, right? Sounds like a good time."

Brianna stammered excuses. They'd be at breakfast. Her father in his chair, her mother pouring coffee and fixing his two fried eggs, over easy. Wheat toast, butter substitute. She couldn't call now. It would upset his routine.

"We don't have a date yet. I should wait until we do." Good out. The middle of this charming sunny kitchen wasn't a good place for the phone conversation, anyway. She'd write out a script later and practice. Yes. That's a much better idea.

Jess crossed her arms and leaned back. "You're stalling, cousin. If the date is holding you up, then set one. What are you waiting for, anyway?"

"Connor and I haven't given it a lot of thought."

"Well then, I have another idea. How about December twenty-seven."

"You mean next year? But that would be on your anniversary. That's not right."

"I don't mean next year. I mean this one."

"That's crazy. That's *your* wedding day."

"Exactly. What do you think about a double wedding?"

7

"A double wedding? You can't be serious. Who came up with that idea?" Connor dropped into his recliner.

Brianna sat on the floor beside him. "Actually, it was Jess."

Connor cocked his head and shot her the falcon stare. Cute, but scary at the same time.

"Seriously, it was hers. I was just about to call my mother and tell her. Then I realized we hadn't flown it past you and Ryan yet. She's telling him tonight."

"How nice of you to '*fly*' it past the grooms. We can't impose on their day, honey. Don't you want your own wedding day?"

An incoming text on Connor's phone saved her from answering. Probably Ryan. Intensely focused on typing a reply, Connor didn't see her slip into the bedroom.

Sitting cross-legged in the middle of the bed, she spun her phone around on the chenille spread. A double wedding. In her wildest dreams, she'd never considered this. She could see Jess walking down the aisle in that fantastic dress. Taking the hand of her prince.

Brianna wondered what she'd wear. At this late date? Yoga pants, perhaps. Did she have any white ones?

'Make the call.'

Who said that? Brianna snapped her gaze to the door. No one was there.

'You're as stubborn as your father. I said make the call.'

"Grandmother." More a statement than a question.

'You betcha. You'll have a fanny full of splinters if you ride this fence much longer. Eloping is not an option. And a double wedding will be the most spectacular event this town's ever seen. Economical for me. One trip. Two brides with one stone, so to speak.'

"I guess you aren't in body tonight."

'Too much work just to give you a piece of my mind. You call and tell them. Let the chips fall. One way or the other, it won't matter a hoot. You and Connor have your life to live. You can't go 'round worrying about the little stuff. Got me?'

Brianna turned her silver bracelet. It didn't block her thoughts from her grandmother at all. No use in trying.

"I got you. But you said you'd be here, right? In your real body."

'Yes, in my real body. I wouldn't miss this for anything. And your dress is going to turn heads. It will fit you perfectly.'

"You mean Jess and her dress, right?"

'No, honey. Yours. You'll know when you see it. Now get with it. Get that call made. I'm out of here.'

Among the many things it took getting used to in this town, Echo Stargazer popping in and out was one of the craziest.

She picked up her phone and tapped the contact for her mother.

"Please don't go to voicemail. Please. Please."

"Brianna? I was just thinking about you."

"Hi, Mom. You got a minute?"

"And what did Connor say?" Jess sat on Ryan's lap and played with his wrong-way lock that bobbed between his eyes.

"He's about as gobsmacked as I am. But if it's what you want."

Jess gave Ryan a tight hug as she kissed the top of his head. "Absolutely. The more I think about this, the better I love the idea."

"Have you looked at the calendar lately? Three weeks and counting, and don't forget Christmas."

"That's not going to be a problem. This is Nocturne Falls. Magic happens."

"Yeah, and sometimes something else happens."

"Oh, ye of little faith. I've got this."

"That is exactly what frightens me."

Jess tipped Ryan's chin to hers and planted a soft, loving kiss on his lips. "A little fright occasionally, keeps the spark in a relationship."

"Umm. There are other ways to light the spark." Ryan pulled her back into his arms to finish the kiss.

A persistent buzz on Ryan's phone alerted him to an incoming call. "Not now," he murmured.

"Go ahead. It might be important," Jess said.

Ryan ran kisses over Jess's arm as she reached for his phone on the end table. "It's Brianna."

Jess hopped up and took a seat on the sofa. "It's me. I've got his phone. What's up?"

"Yours went to voicemail. You'll never guess who dropped in tonight," Brianna said.

"Oh, I think I might. Nana?"

"Yep. And guess what else?"

"No telling."

"I called home. My father wasn't there, but Mom was. She's delighted. And guess what else?"

Ryan had taken a position behind Jess and was massaging her neck and shoulders. Jess relaxed her head into Ryan's hands. He kissed her forehead. Her cheeks. Nipped at the top of her ears.

Jess was melting. He was ready, and so was she.

It was just about time for Brianna's guessing game to end. "Could we maybe talk about this tomorrow?" Jess asked.

"I invited them to the wedding. And she said they'd be here."

Jess sat ramrod straight and stayed that way even after the call ended.

The man who wanted no part in raising his only sister's orphaned child. Was he going to show up at her wedding?

Nana, wherever you are, you better have a special trick up your sleeve. Nobody, but nobody, is going to spoil this wedding day.

'Oh, ye of little faith.'

"I'm holding you to this, Nana."

8

"Um." Corette Williams tapped her pencil on her scheduling book. "December twenty-seventh. Why don't you look at some of the gowns I have in the store. I can alter them amazingly fast."

Jess and Brianna looked at each other and shook their heads. They'd seen all the ready-to-wear dresses. No. This dress had to be special.

They left the boutique and walked along the chilly sidewalk. Since morning, the skies had turned overcast, and tiny flakes of snow blustered around them.

"If I were four inches taller, I'd be the right weight and fit into a size ten," Brianna said.

"Phooey on that. You're fine just as you are. Just ask Connor," Jess said.

"What do you suppose grandmother meant when she told me the dress would fit perfectly?" Brianna asked.

"I have no idea. If you want, I can take off my ring and try to see it. No promises," Jess offered.

"That's sweet. But I want to do this straight up. No magic. No using the psychic gifts. The regular, old-fashioned normal human way."

Brianna could only imagine what was going through her mother's mind with the news that her daughter was getting married. In Nocturne Falls. And the conversation with her father would have been a disaster.

He might decide not to show up at all. And not a problem for Brianna. But she hoped her brother and mother would come. It was, after all, her wedding day.

The cousins stepped out of the way as a couple pushing a stroller passed.

"You remember what Nana told you the night she appeared in Solange's solarium?" Jess asked.

The day her time traveling grandmother appeared out of nowhere from another dimension? That day? As though Brianna could ever forget.

"'When I know something, I know it,'" Brianna said.

"She's nothing if not a straight shooter. Hang in there. We'll find the right dress. There's lots of time."

Oh, sure. Loads and loads.

The next stop was Howlers Bar where Jess had arranged to hold her reception. The owner, Bridget Merrow, had included clever menu workarounds that met Ryan's vegetarian preferences and Jess's penchant for anything beef.

Neither excited Brianna. She'd been raised on Pacific Northwest fish. Her mouth watered for a grilled freshwater trout. Or a melt-in-the-mouth wild salmon.

"Any chance we can add some fresh fish to the menu?" Brianna asked.

"Wow. I'd love to," Bridget said. "But I don't know if

we can get an order in here by then. I can call around, but no promises."

At Delaney's Delectables, Delaney pulled out her sketchbook and went over Jess's cake details. Delaney had taken a swatch of the beaded lace from the gown and worked it into a design. The topper would be marzipan white roses. Ryan's groom cake would be devil's food with mocha cream cheese frosting.

"Now, Brianna, what were you thinking?" Delaney asked.

The question of the day. What *was* she thinking? Jess was so organized. So detailed. So prepared.

And Brianna was so behind the curve.

"Honestly? I love hummingbird cake. But can you make the whole cake out of that? It would weigh a ton."

"Here's a thought. If you want layers, we make the top two hummingbird. The top is for you to freeze. The second one is yours to eat at the reception. Then the other layers can be more traditional and I think will please your guests. What embellishments were you thinking about?"

Embellishments? Brianna kept flipping pages in Delaney's binder of past designs hoping something would jump out at her.

"I think this might be a little overwhelming, right Brianna?" Jess asked.

Totally. "How did you manage this, Jess?"

"I guess it's the analytic side of me. I'm a list maker and decision tree thinker. Let's start with the easy questions. Modern or vintage?" Jess said.

What a good idea. "Vintage."

Jess led Brianna through a dozen more questions while Delaney took notes. Eventually, Delaney had a full page of ideas and quick sketches. And Brianna was beginning to feel much better.

"Now, how about the groom's cake?" Delaney asked.

Deer in the headlights moment. Groom's cake? Did Connor Ford have a favorite cake? Cripes. She had no idea. She'd never seen the man eat cake of any kind.

"How about I talk to Connor and get back with you?" Brianna said.

After a long afternoon, Brianna suggested they stop by the Poisoned Apple Pub for a drink. Sipping rosé, Brianna ticked off a list of what still needed to be done. For each, Jess had at least two solutions.

"We still have time to get printed invitations mailed out, but it's going to be a close call. There's a printer here who can get them ready in a snap. Do you have a list?" Jess asked.

"Of guests?" No. Not even on her mental list.

Jess laughed. "That was my hardest thing to do. How about I send you mine? Then you and Connor can go through it. Or, you can always send an announcement after the wedding. We only invited two hundred. I imagine only a hundred fifty or so will be there."

A hundred fifty? People? Watching her get married? Was it the wine causing her head to swirl?

Jess pulled up a website on her phone. "You might want to set up something like this."

Brianna scrolled through the 'Jess and Ryan's Special Day' web page. Engagement photos. Wishlists. Comment section. All themed to her shower colors.

This was almost too much to take in. She waved to the bartender for another glass of wine.

"I can't possibly get all this done in three weeks, Jess."

"Oh, sure you can. Everyone will pitch in. My webmistress is amazing. She can whip up a site in a couple of hours. We can get some photos taken. Easy peasy."

Easy peasy for who?

Where could they hold a double wedding? Connor, Ryan, and Jess, had graduated from Harmswood Academy. Since Solange was a big donor, reserving space there for one wedding had been a no-brainer.

Could Harmswood handle a double wedding? Jess piled this on top of her *how-will-we-do-this* stack of questions.

'Oh, ye of little faith.'

Jess and Brianna sliced their gaze to each other.

'Nana,' Jess silently mouthed.

Brianna nodded.

'Stop fretting on the details, precious girls. Your frenetic energy is driving me nuts. I feel it clear over here. This should be the happiest time of your lives. After all, it's a one-time thing. Or it better be. Now both of you, slow down. Take a breath. Who cares about invitations and cakes? Marry the boys, for God sake.'

"But, Grandmother," Jess started.

'Nope. I'm not listening to any more of this. All for now.'

Jess's phone pinged. A text from Brianna.

"You know her best. Is she mad?"

"Don't worry. It won't last long," Jess typed.

"Can she hear text messages?"

Jess replied, "Don't know."

The cousins put down their phones and drank their wine in silence.

Then both phones pinged at the same time.

"Apparently, she can," Brianna said.

An identical message followed by three little yellow smiling faces appeared on both screens.

'Ciao, my precious girls.'

9

While Connor grilled chicken outside, Brianna flipped through her list. If the technique worked for Jess, maybe it would work for her. Jess was happier to flow with the moment. This organization thing felt like walking through the mud.

At least she had more 'done' than 'to do.'

Two still stood out like beacons.

Wedding dress.

Groom's cake.

It was digging into her heart that she had no idea what kind of cake Connor liked. What else didn't she know about him?

She turned to a new page and started another list. Favorite color? Last book he'd read? Who was his best friend in Nocturne Falls? Did he have a favorite movie? What did he think about Peking Duck for Christmas Day?

"Honey, can you move that paperwork over?" Connor held the platter of barbeque, looking for a place to put it.

Startled, Brianna covered the Connor-list and took her notes to the sofa.

She'd put out three different salad dressings but noticed Connor ate his dry. No French. No Blue Cheese. No Thousand Island. A discovery for the list?

He peeled the skin off his chicken. She made a note to add that to the list.

"I never saw you do that before," she asked.

"What?"

"Don't you like the skin?"

"That's a weird question."

"And the dressing. Don't you like any of those?"

"Huh?"

"Do you like duck?"

"Brianna, how much did you and Jess drink this afternoon?"

"I'm trying to learn more about you."

Connor's laugh filled the room. "I burned one side of the bird, so I took off the skin. I forgot to put dressing on my salad. I'm not a big duck fan. Anything else?"

"What's your favorite cake?"

"Good God, woman."

"No. I have to know what cake you like."

"It's that important?"

She nodded.

"Lemon."

"Lemon pound cake or plain lemon cake?"

"I don't care which kind. Are these the final qualifiers? Or is there a next round?"

"Nope. That's all I need."

"Speaking of need."

In an exaggerated southern accent, Brianna cooed, "Why, Mr. Ford, whatever do you mean?"

"Well, I'm not talking about lemon cake."

10

The traditional Ford Christmas began with a Christmas Eve buffet. The evening ended with opening presents at midnight, and then sleeping in until late morning.

Completely *bassackward* for Brianna. But when in Nocturne Falls, or make that, when in Solange's house, it's best to follow protocol.

Christmas morning, just after dawn, Brianna slipped downstairs to grab a few quiet moments alone by the brightly lit tree. In two days, she was going to be Mrs. Connor Ford. Or maybe she'd take the name Brianna Putnam-Ford. Or just keep it Brianna Putnam.

No matter what title she adopted, she would be a married woman. And to the most wonderful man she'd ever met. Once her mother got over the falcon-part, she'd realize what a fantastic son-in-law she had. Brianna's brother, Samuel, would finally have a big brother. She couldn't wait to show him the real Nocturne Falls.

Then there was her father.

The last message from her mother had confirmed

their travel plans. They'd be in town tomorrow, and leave the twenty-eighth. At least they'd be here long enough for the wedding.

"Merry Christmas." Jess joined Brianna on the couch. "Mind my company?"

"Not at all. I need somebody to pull me out of my nostalgia trip."

"I'm right with you. I miss Nana like you wouldn't believe," Jess said.

"This is about the last quiet minute we'll have together for a long time. Before things go bonkers around here, can I tell you how much your friendship means to me? I didn't make a great impression when I hit town. You didn't have to offer me any kindness. I wouldn't have blamed you if you didn't." Brianna's voice broke.

"Don't get emotional or we'll both lose it. You've been a wonderful addition to this family. And how Connor's changed because of you still blows my mind."

"He's had the same effect on me. I was pretty much a wild child before he came into my life."

"Merry Christmas, ladies." Connor, dressed in sleep shorts and no shirt, joined them. "You're still wild when the need arises."

"Connor Ford. Please." Heat bloomed over Brianna's face.

"Where's the woodman?" Connor asked.

"Sawing logs upstairs," Jess said.

Connor muffled a laugh. "That was a good one, Jess. Wood artist. Woodman. Sawing logs. Get it?"

After a wide yawn, Connor excused himself to the kitchen. "I need coffee."

Jess stepped to the tree and picked up wrappings

they'd strewn around last night. "Here's another present. How'd we miss that?" She read the gift tag. "It's for you."

"Me?" Brianna examined the box wrapped in white tissue and curly red ribbon. Just *Brianna* on the tag. Had Connor slid this under the tree?

"Should I open it?" Brianna asked.

Jess made a face that clued Brianna to go ahead.

The ribbon and paper slipped off like butter. The box seemed to have weathered many years. She took a deep breath, lifted the lid, then opened a layer of tissue paper.

"Jess," Brianna whispered. "Look."

"What is it?"

Brianna gingerly touched the edges of the garment and raised it from the box.

"It's the most beautiful dress I've ever seen," she said.

Jess gasped. "This is impossible. I thought that was lost or tossed out."

Brianna pulled the dress all the way out and held it against her.

In pristine condition, layers of antique ecru lace draped in graceful tiers, stopping just mid-calf. The soft waistband would flatter anyone who wore it. The sleeves were a single layer of lace that flared from the elbow to the wrists. The cute V neck would frame a pearl necklace like it was meant to be there.

And it was Brianna's size.

"I love it," Brianna said as she hugged the dress. "Where do you supposed it came from?"

"It's Nana's wedding dress," Jess said.

Jess had to be kidding. Her grandmother's dress

shows up here? Now? Then, remembering Nana's psychic conversation in the bar, and text message from the other side, Brianna shrugged. No end to the surprises.

"I have to try it on," Brianna said.

Connor reappeared from the kitchen with a carafe of coffee and three mugs.

"What's all the discussion about?" He asked.

Brianna quickly re-boxed the dress. "Just girl talk."

"Did you know Sabrina's in the kitchen?" Connor asked.

"Thought she had the day off?" Jess said.

"I did too." Connor handed each cousin a mug of coffee before he sat down between them. "But she's apparently been hard at it for hours. She just took a bird out of the oven. And you'll love this, Brianna. It's a duck."

After a fabulous brunch, including crispy Peking duck, Connor and Ryan loaded their cars with gifts. Brianna and Jess stayed inside to thank Solange for her hospitality, and Sabrina for culinary magic.

The brothers came back inside, their legs covered in snow. Connor, the shorter of the two, had a white dusting up to his knees.

"We need to get back to town. This snow is piling up fast," Connor said. "Not sure how good the roads will be and the Porsche sits low."

Snow? "That must have happened overnight," Brianna said.

The county highways back to Nocturne Falls were in

good shape from early plowing, but the snow was still coming down strong. Once back in town, Brianna couldn't believe her eyes.

Always quaint and charming, downtown looked like something from a storybook. Twinkling lights, snow-capped roofs. It figures there was no crowd at the Hallowed Bean now, but she wasn't in the mood for coffee.

"I don't even know if there's a snow shovel in the garage," Connor said as they pulled into their driveway. "I'm not driving any farther till I see."

Brianna pushed open the passenger door, sweeping back a pile of snow. She hiked her foot out and watched as it, her lower leg, then her knee all disappeared into the thick white blanket.

"Uh, Connor?"

He'd already reached the front porch but turned around. His eyes flashed wide open. Then he started laughing.

"Oh, sure. Laugh. You think it's funny being short?" She tugged one foot out and stepped forward knee deep again.

"Here." Connor came back, grabbed her hand and together they slogged to the porch. "You go on inside. I'll look for a shovel."

Forty-five minutes later, Connor came inside. "I haven't seen this much snow up here in a long time."

Brianna had been watching a TV weather station. "They say we'll get another foot, at least."

"If we don't lose power, we'll be fine," Connor said. "But we won't be getting out much for the next day or so."

"Day *or so*? We get married in on the *'or so'* day."

"Imagine that." He pulled Brianna in for a hug. "Stop fretting. It will work out."

"You're all cold and wet," she said as she wiggled away from him.

"How about a shower?"

"I think you should," she said.

"I meant the two of us."

"First get out of those wet clothes," she said.

"Yes, ma'am."

11

The weather forecast had it all wrong.

The next morning, Brianna had jumped out of bed early to look out the window. They'd predicted another foot. Missed that by a mile. There were at least two more feet of snow on top of what had already fallen on Christmas.

How would she get out today for all the last-minute details?

She checked her phone for messages and found a boatload.

Delaney. Can't get into the bakery today. Sorry.

Corette. Snowed in. Can't get to the store. If you needed alterations, sorry.

Florist. No fresh flower deliveries until further notice. Sorry.

Guest regrets. Sorry. Sorry. Sorry.

Then the worst news. Her mother's text. They were stuck in Atlanta. The Georgia Highway Patrol said all roads to the mountains were unsafe for travel.

She was getting married tomorrow if she had to crawl to the altar.

A new text pinged.

Jess. A roof leak in Howlers'. Won't be ready for reception.

Fine. Simply fine. Okay. All they needed was the judge. They had their license. The wedding would happen.

Somewhere.

And her grandmother would be here to see it. Snow wouldn't stop her.

"Chin up, babe. We'll pull this off if Connor and I have to dress in sweatpants." Ryan rinsed the cat food can in the sink and dropped the empty in the recycle bin.

Jess crossed a line through 'tux pick up' on her list. She couldn't believe the store was closed today. "This stupid snow was not in my plan."

"Mother's okay with us holding the ceremony at the mansion."

"Well since it will probably just be two brides and two grooms, Solange and Sabrina, that shouldn't be a problem. At least the judge said he'd be here. He's the smart one with a four-wheel drive."

"A couple of my buddies said they'd lend a hand with their trucks. I'm going out with them later to get some chairs and tables for the reception and take them out to Mother's. Want me to run any errands for you?"

She shook her head. "At least I had the good sense to get my dress before Christmas."

After Ryan left, Jess went to the bedroom where the dress hung in the closet. Crealde sat on the floor in front, facing the closed closet door.

Knowing his affinity for catching his claws in chintzy lace and for opening doors at will, she warned, "If you so much as think about it, Mister. So, help me."

He looked over his shoulder. She swore he had a look of sympathy on his furry face. Well, she wanted it to be sympathetic. This cat had three waking faces. Sleepy. Angry. Skeptical.

Nope. Crealde had no sympathy.

She escorted him out of the room and shut the door. Then she slipped on the wedding dress. She ran her hands over it, feeling each pearl as it crossed her palm. It was the perfect dress. And, by damn, it was going to be a perfect wedding day.

Hellfire or blizzard.

12

Sabrina was a miracle worker.

Solange stood awestruck at how the living room looked. Sabrina had directed the removal of the living room furniture and the placement of the chairs Ryan and his friends had brought.

Ryan had spent hours in his old woodworking studio in the estate's garage to fashion candle holders from scraps of oak and birch. Sabrina had found candles of all sizes in the pantry and placed the rustic candelabra in strategic locations around the room.

Connor had brought in evergreen boughs from the woods behind the estate. Sabrina had placed them on either side of the hallway leading into the room.

Solange could only imagine how it would look with the lights dimmed, and the fireplace stoked, flickering candles, and aroma of fir and pine. Sabrina had transformed the Ford living room into an enchanted chamber fit for King Arthur's court.

And Brianna and Jess's wedding.

Solange went upstairs to help the cousins dress. Jess had styled her hair into an uplift with a couple of loose tendrils. Brianna's natural golden curls circled her head like a halo.

"You are lovely beyond words," Solange said in a hushed tone.

The cousins shared the mirror. "We are, aren't we." Jess giggled.

"But you need a little something else. I'll be right back," Solange said.

"Ready," Brianna asked.

"Yep. You?" Jess said.

"Absolutely," Brianna said. "Wonder how the guys are doing?"

"Connor's probably playing video games. Ryan's sketching a new project. I don't think they suffer from nerves much."

Their laughter was interrupted by Solange's return. She carried a velvet drawstring pouch.

"Let's see how these look on you." She reached into the bag and pulled out two tiaras. "Choose the one you'd like to wear. My wedding gifts to you."

Brianna and Jess looked at each other, wide-eyed and open-mouthed.

"Are those…," Brianna stammered.

Jess finished the question. "Real?"

"There was a time long ago when the boys' father and I attended some of the most elaborate shifter balls you can imagine. Over time, formal dress up parties went out of style. I want you to have them."

"You pick first, Jess," Brianna said.

Jess chose the one with a triangle of diamonds topped with an emerald. It slid into her hair effortlessly.

Brianna hesitated to even touch the one for her. It was

a jewel-encrusted headband with a swirl of diamonds and pearls at the top.

Sensing Brianna's hesitancy, Solange placed it on Brianna's head.

"Now then, look in the mirror," Solange said.

"Oh, my God," Jess said.

"We look like princess brides," Brianna said.

They took turns hugging Solange.

"Oh, that's quite enough. Now, I believe I hear the music," Solange said. "It's time, my dears."

"Where the heck is Nana?" Jess said as they descended the long stairway to the first floor, followed by Solange.

"She promised," Brianna whispered.

They stopped at the foot of the stairs to give their dresses one last adjustment.

"I want you to see something." Solange opened the double doors to the dining room.

"The cakes made it? And all the food? How?" Jess raced forward to inspect them.

"Mine and Connor's are here, too," Brianna said.

"Delaney found a way to get to the shop yesterday. She didn't want you to know, just in case something happened at the last minute. And Bridget enlisted the Sheriff's department to escort her and the food here. It took a little help from the county to clear the roads out this far." Solange lifted an eyebrow. "I can be very persuasive."

Brianna raised a silver lid covering a large platter. "You're kidding? My salmon?"

"That took a little more doing. Bridget found a supplier who could overnight ship a smoked salmon from Oregon. I had a sample. It's very tasty, for cooked," Solange said.

Brianna laughed. If it was falcon approved, it must be good.

"I guess that's the last of it," Jess said.

"Did you think you wouldn't have flowers?" Echo Stargazer stood behind them holding the brides' bouquets. Fully human. Rosy-cheeked. And dressed in a beautifully embroidered silk Chinese robe.

"No crying. You'll spoil your makeup." Echo handed each bride a white rose bouquet. "Now, let's get this party started."

Outside the closed doors to the living room, Jess and Brianna locked arms with Echo.

"You know, Brianna," Echo teased. "You look almost as good as I did in that dress. It held up well for over fifty years, don't you think?" Echo's eyes danced.

"It's just like you told me it would be," Brianna said.

"Someday we'll have that long talk about my '*knowing*.' And guess what, I'm back for good. So, plan on it, honey," Echo said. "And Jess, it kills me to know I'm losing my precious. But, those two men are about the hunkiest things on the planet. If I was a few years younger..."

A cold blast of air from the open front door startled them.

Brianna's heart stopped. Three people stood on the front porch. She tapped Echo's shoulder to turn around.

"Grandmother, you won't believe this," she whispered.

"Honey, I bet I will," Echo said.

13

"It's been a long time," Echo said.

A tall, broad-shouldered red-haired man stood in the doorway with a woman and another younger man.

"Mother," he said in a low voice.

"Come inside and shut that damn door. It's cold," Echo said.

Brianna felt Jess's hand on her back. "It's going to be fine, Brianna."

"I'll let folks know we're a little behind." Solange opened the door to the living room and gently shut it behind her.

Willing her feet to move, Brianna went to her mother and squeezed her so hard the woman gasped for a breath.

"How?" Brianna whispered in her mother's ear.

"Long story. Rented a truck," her mother whispered back.

Brianna hugged her brother and introduced him to his grandmother. Tears flowed down the usually stoic woman's face as she embraced him.

Her father, quiet through all this, had stayed back, leaning against the door.

Brianna walked to him. "Thank you for coming, Daddy."

He gave a silent nod. "I brought them, but I'm not staying."

Echo stood beside Brianna. "Why would you come this far and not attend your daughter and niece's wedding?"

"You know why," he muttered.

"Because you're a stubborn ox," Echo said.

"Daddy, Grandmother. Enough. Not today. Daddy, you are more than welcome to stay and witness this. Or sit in the driveway. Your choice. Make your decision now. I'm getting married in a few minutes, whether you like it or not," Brianna said.

"Oh, I almost forgot." Brianna's mother reached into her purse and pulled out a small jewelry box. "I wore this at my wedding. I want you to have it."

Brianna opened the box. A knot swelled in her throat.

A pearl necklace.

"I'm shaking. Somebody help me put this on," Brianna said.

Jess fastened the clasp. "It's like the necklace was meant to be part of this dress."

Echo smiled and nodded.

Solange stuck her head into the room. "Ready?"

"Mom, Samuel, go on inside. Solange will find your seats." Brianna turned to her father who still stood by the door.

Echo wiped her tears, then took a position between her granddaughters, Brianna on her left elbow, Jess on her right. "Ok, girls. This is it." Then she looked down at Brianna's feet.

"That's what's been bugging me," Echo said. "When I got married in this dress, back in the day, I was barefoot.

Oh, well. That was the sixties."

"Really?" Brianna thought a moment then kicked off her satin pumps. "They're killing my feet anyway"

"I couldn't agree more." Jess kicked off hers followed by Echo.

Something caught the corner of Brianna's eye. She turned to her father who was taking off his shoes, and his heavy coat. "Or me either."

He slipped his arm around Brianna's. "Think there's room for four of us to walk down that aisle?"

"Son, we'll make room," Echo said.

Brianna finally realized the music was live and not recorded. How in the world had a three-piece chamber group made their way here? Only in Nocturne Falls.

Solange opened the door and announced the arrival of the brides as the music changed to a wedding processional.

Brianna's breath caught and she tightened her grip on her father's arm.

The room, bathed in candlelight, was packed. Connor and Ryan, smiling and handsome in their separate ways, were dressed in suits. Not sweats. A roaring fire burned in the fireplace. The path ahead was lined in fresh tree boughs.

"Did you know how this was going to end all along," Brianna whispered to her grandmother.

"Oh, ye of little faith."

THE END

The Meddlesome Misadventures of Merri and Bright

BY ALETHEA KONTIS

Fairy Merri Larousse never intended to become one half of a famous prankster/matchmaking duo with winter elf Polaris Brighton. Little did they know, the best match they would make would be their own!

1

It all started with a note hidden in a book.

Technically, it started with Samson Sol. That annoyingly handsome summer elf had threatened to burn Merri's book bag to a crisp if she didn't let him copy her Chemistry homework. Merri's reaction had been quite enough to get Professor Beketaten's attention.

Samson said he was "just kidding." He didn't get in trouble, oh no. The popular rich boys never got in trouble.

Merri, on the other hand, was immediately banished to the library. She was to translate the first two songs of the Finnish epic *Kalevala* and discuss the importance of Ilmatar…whoever or whatever that was. The assignment was doubly horrible because Merri hated English class. Chemistry was her true passion. Potions and solutions were topics at which a flower fairy could excel. English bored her to tears. The only thing that class was good for was staring at Samson Sol's wild blond hair and amber eyes and perfect tan skin. Bloomin' daisies, that boy was beautiful. He totally knew it too.

Jerk.

The note fell out of the book the moment she slid it off the shelf, fluttering to the stone floor like an autumn leaf.

I dare you, the note said. *I dare you to play a prank.*

Instead of wondering who had written the note or how it got there, Merri considered the challenge. She'd never pulled a prank before in her life, though she was certainly the kind of outcast who would. Merri just didn't care that much about the other kids at her school, and they didn't care about her. She'd never sought the kind of attention drawn by pranks.

But to be asked anonymously…and to pull it off anonymously…the entertainment value would be hers alone. And if she failed, no one would be the wiser. It was tempting. Too tempting.

By the time the horn blew to signal the change of classes, Merri had both finished the assignment and decided on her prank. She would do it during Chemistry, her last class of the day. With all those chemical ingredients lying around, Chem lab would be the best place to hide her magical signature. Plus, she already knew Samson hadn't done his homework. Let him think that whatever transpired was his fault.

It's not like he'd get in trouble for it.

This afternoon's experiment was to study surface tension by blowing bubbles made from varying mixtures of dish soap, water, and glycerine. Merri had played out the whole scene in her head: She'd go up to Samson and make up some fake apology about earlier, distracting him long enough for her to get her hands on his bubble wand.

In the end, she didn't even have to do that. Prom

queen poster girl Taylor Hayden provided enough of a distraction all on her own, asking everyone their opinion on the haircut she'd treated herself to during the lunch break. (She only received compliments, of course. Anyone smart enough to see through her thinly-veiled attempt at fishing was also smart enough to keep their mouth shut.)

Merri passed by Samson's abandoned lab bench on her way up to the crowd at the front of the classroom. She reached out, casually drew her index finger along the length of Samson's bubble wand, and concentrated.

Dandelion, she thought to herself.

When the time came for them to blow a bubble from the first solution, Merri waited. She wasn't disappointed. The moment Samson put those perfect lips to his bubble wand, tiny bubbles burst out like dandelion fluff blown to the wind.

And they didn't stop. They kept on coming, tiny and perfect, like bubbles blown from a machine. Samson was confused for about ten seconds before he took advantage of the situation. He began running around the classroom, spreading his bounty everywhere. Teens turned into children: chasing bubbles, kicking bubbles, piling bubbles on top of their heads, making fake beards. They laughed and they danced. Samson climbed up on a stool and held the bubble wand over Taylor's head. She spun gleefully in the shower of bubbles beneath it.

A few bubbles flew in front of Merri's face. She popped them with a pencil and smiled.

"Enough of that nonsense!" Professor Bowers called from her desk at the back of the classroom. She rose from her seat...and then something weird happened.

The bubbles froze. They just sat there for a moment,

suspended in midair. Then, as one, they dropped like stones. No, not stones. Glass. Every single bubble fell to the floor and shattered.

But not like glass. *Ice*. Merri watched as the delicate shards on the lab bench before her instantly started to melt. What on earth…?

Merri hopped off her own stool, fully intending to walk over to Samson's table and see if she could figure out what had gone wrong with her spell. She made it halfway before she remembered that it wasn't only water on the floor. There was a good deal of soap and glycerine, too.

On her fourth step, her boot slipped. Samson, who had similarly hopped down off his stool, slid backward in her direction. They crashed together in an ungraceful bobble of limbs, finally ending up on the floor.

"Are you all right?" Samson said to her. He actually sounded like he cared.

"I think so." Merri rubbed her head. She had banged it against something hard. Most likely Samson's own noggin. "Nice trick you got there."

Samson waved his bubble wand, which seemed to have exhausted its supply of bubble-making solution. "It's all in the wrist. Want some help up?"

Suddenly he was being nice to her? He had definitely hit his head, too. Merri looked out across the room, where all the other students were sliding into one another. She pulled her knees into her chest and hugged them. "I think it's safer down here for now."

"You might be right." Samson stretched out his long legs beside her and leaned back against the lab bench. Together, they watched the rest of their classmates—and professor—flail about like drunken penguins on an ice floe.

Eventually, Professor Bowers got control of the situation and ordered everyone back to their tables. Merri got to her own feet before she realized Samson had his hand out, offering to help her again. He could be so kind when he wanted to be.

"Here," he said instead. "For luck." She caught the now-dormant bubble wand he tossed to her.

Did he know she'd been the source of the prank? No. No way. She chuckled at the bubble wand and smirked. "Gee, thanks."

Professor Bowers began to lecture from the white board—there was no going back to lab now, but she seemed determined to maintain the focus of her class. Merri pulled her notebook out her of her book bag, just as she slipped the bubble wand inside. It was a cheap and silly memento, but it would always remind her of this first prank, well played. That challenge of the anonymous dare had been accepted, and accomplished, with no one the wiser.

Or so she thought.

He was waiting for her after class, leaning casually against the pillar like a shadow come to life. Where Merri dyed her hair and clothes with henna and indigo, he had been born with hair as black as an inkstain. His "Used to be Everything" t-shirt looked fresh from a concert. His black jeans still had a crease. His Doc Martens didn't have a mark on them. His white skin stood out in contrast, even paler than his cold, silver-gray eyes.

"Well done," he couldn't have said. Because Polaris Brighton didn't speak to her. Polaris Brighton didn't speak to anyone.

She was about to tell him she had no idea what he

was talking about when he added, "I have a proposal for you. Walk with me."

Merri was too shocked and too curious to think of anything else to do, so she started walking. She glanced at him out of the corner of her eye as they strolled to the courtyard—he was a hard boy to look at. Not that he wasn't as handsome as Samson; if anything he was more so. But where Samson had the warm, welcoming demeanor of a summer elf, Polaris Brighton was cold, even for a winter elf. His features were angular and perfect, as if he'd been sculpted from snow, and he was as distant as the star he'd been named after. If Samson was a flame, Polaris was an iceberg, with great hidden depths that no one dared brave the frozen waters to discover.

Merri was turning out to be quite the daring fairy today. She kind of liked it.

"You have a rare talent," Polaris said as they approached the fountain. "You're already an aloof and detached sort of person..."

That's the pot calling the kettle black, thought Merri. It was something her mother always said, but she hadn't truly understood the phrase until now.

"...which makes you exactly the type who would pull pranks like the one in class today. But you're also highly intelligent. No one would ever suspect you were the instigator." After all their classes together, this brief speech was the most Merri had ever heard him say. His voice was deeper than she'd thought it would be, and softer, but still condescending.

"No one except you, obviously," she said.

Polaris grinned, and the wickedness of it chilled her to the bone. "It takes one to know one. You remember the roosters?"

Last fall, right after the start of the school year, several roosters had been discovered running amok through the halls of Harmswood, each labeled one through five. Over the course of several weeks' worth of crowing alarm clocks, 1, 2, 3, and 5 had been caught. Even after several more weeks of searching, Rooster 4 had never been found. No one had ever taken credit for the prank, and to the best of Merri's knowledge, no one had ever been caught.

"That was you?" It was impossible to keep the awe out of her voice.

"The one and only," he said with surprising humility. "With your help, I'd like to do more."

Merri thought back on the bubbles, how they had all frozen in midair at the end. *Frozen.* That had been Polaris's doing, of course. She had not intended to do anything more. How was she going to get out of this without admitting why she'd played the prank in the first place? "But..." she started to say.

"But you did this all because you're secretly in love with Samson Sol and the idiot doesn't even know you exist?"

Merri's jaw dropped. The winter elf's words cut like a knife. Even her mother couldn't see straight into her soul like that.

"Merriaurum...sorry, what's your middle name?"

"Grandiflora," she managed to croak.

"Merriaurum Grandiflora Larousse," he said formally. "I hereby propose that we join forces. Together, we shall perpetrate shenanigans the likes of which Harmswood has never seen...and doubtless will never see again."

"What do I get out of this?" she asked before accepting.

Polaris shrugged. "Considerably more chances to 'accidentally' get tangled up with that fool Samson Sol again."

As much as she hated to admit it, she wouldn't mind at all if that happened. She narrowed her eyes. "And what do *you* get out of this?"

He paused before answering, as if considering his confession. Merri decided she wouldn't participate in this partnership if he decided to lie to her. With twelve little brothers and sisters, Merri was sure she'd be able to tell if he was lying.

Polaris sighed. "Let's just say I wouldn't mind getting similarly tangled up with a certain future prom queen."

Merri managed to stop her jaw from dropping again. He had a thing for Taylor Hayden? That pretty little bit of nothing with fluff for brains? Granted, most of the male population at Harmswood—and most of the females, for that matter—wanted to walk hand-in-hand with beautiful, boring Taylor Hayden. Merri didn't understand any of them, but to each their own. Polaris's interest made even less sense. Dating Taylor just seemed so...beneath him.

But it wasn't for her to judge. She had promised herself not to partner up with him if he'd been lying, and he definitely wasn't lying about his crush on Taylor. No one would lie about admitting something as ridiculous as that.

She stuck out her hand. "It's a deal," she said. "But my name is Merri. No one but my grandmother calls me Merriaurum."

"In that case, I'm Bright," he said. His handshake was soft and firm and cold. "Nice to meet you, partner."

That same afternoon, they decided what their first prank would be: changing the horn-signal for classes. They planned carefully—if they made the mechanics too simple, then they would be too simply undone. They decided that each alarm should have its own sound, and that each spell to manufacture the sounds needed to be different. It took them a week to plan.

"One of the spells shouldn't be a spell at all," Merri whispered to Bright. They sat together in the library, heads bent over their books as if deep in study. "That way, the administration will spend all sorts of time trying to trace a spell that doesn't exist."

"Brilliant," Bright replied. "I assume you have something in mind?"

The next day, the sound of a noisy herd of elephants preceded first period. A banshee wailed to announce lunch. Throughout the day, students were greeted with wind chimes, car horns, a baby crying, a manticore's roar, a plague of locusts, and Wagner's *Ride of the Valkyries*. One by one, each sound was discovered and stopped (though that same baby cried for three days straight—Merri had to give Bright points for that one). The teachers lost most of the day to unproductive students awaiting the next "horn."

The pièce de résistance, however was an ear-shattering *"cock-a-doodle-do!"* that greeted the residents of Harmswood first thing the following morning. A live rooster was eventually discovered in the room where the school announcements were made. On his side, the number four was painted on his russet feathers in bright blue.

Neither Merri nor Bright had orchestrated a run-in with Samson or Taylor—this first collaborative stunt was purely an exercise to see if their partnership would work. But they did hear later about two students who had visited the Head Witch, oddly disturbed by the false manticore's roar. They had arrived at her office as strangers and left as a couple.

"We managed to match up someone, anyway," Merri murmured to Bright as she passed him on the stairs. "Too bad it wasn't the intended targets."

"Let's still call it a win, shall we?" It was amazing how he always managed to sound so full of himself with that overly formal way of speaking.

"We shall," Merri replied with equal pomp as she continued down the stairs.

The rest of that semester was the most fun Merri could ever remember having at Harmswood. Probably because she'd never really had a friend before. She actually cared about getting up in the morning. She studied harder in class. She even chatted excitedly during her mother's weekly phone call. Not about Bright, of course, but about everything else.

The pranks were tremendous. They snuck smelly things into at least thirty vents in both the boys' and girls' wings. They had Salvatore's deliver a pizza to Professor Beketaten's class three times in one day. They wrote a spell based on old Fortran code that alphabetized every keyboard in the computer lab.

They were always sure to cover their tracks, but they didn't totally avoid their own gifts—Merri once used her flower fairy skills to stuff one student's locker full of goldenrod. Bright once used his winter elf talents to freeze pennies to floors all over the school.

But there was an odd side effect to their shenanigans: every time they played a prank, a couple was created from two people who otherwise might have never noticed each other. Merri and Bright kept trying to fabricate scenarios involving themselves and Samson or Taylor, but it never worked. The universe seemed set against them.

Like today, when Merri and Bright found themselves locked together in the janitor's closet.

"You were supposed to wait until we were in the hall to freeze the hinges!" Merri scolded as she yanked on the door's handle.

"I'm sorry," he said. "That door wasn't supposed to be closed in the first place!"

Merri sighed and sank down to the floor. "It will thaw eventually. I'm just sad we can't run around and see the looks on everyone's faces."

"We can imagine them, though, can't we? Besides, this way, we *definitely* won't be suspected of anything." He smiled as he settled himself beside her. That grin wasn't half as disturbing to her as it once had been. "So...got any siblings?"

"I'm the oldest of twelve," she said. "It's about to be thirteen."

"Wow! And...congratulations."

It was nice to be able to shock him for a change. "My family is crazy huge," she said. "Being locked in a closet with only one other person is a dream come true in our house. What about you?"

"Oldest of three boys. And that's quite enough, thank you very much."

They had chatted little in passing since that first conversation, in dark corners between classes, hidden in the bushes by the courtyard fountain, and at the library. They hadn't wanted to broadcast their partnership, so they'd never before had the chance to get to know one other.

That closed door was one of the best things that had ever happened to Merri. For the first time, she got to talk about her giant odd family back in South Carolina with someone other than a relative. In return, Bright told her about his high-born parents' impossible standards, the family lodge in Vermont, and the extended family they visited in Tasmania every summer break. Which made perfect sense—it was winter down there while it was summer up here.

The more they talked, the more *real* Bright seemed to her. Much less like the untouchable rich-boy celebrity act he put on in public. Oh, he was still too beautiful for words, but she wasn't scared of him anymore. He bloomed before her like a bed of violets after the spring thaw. Any coldness between them now came only from his winter elf nature.

By the time Merri and Bright emerged from that closet—long after the doors had come unstuck and the traffic in the hallways had died back down—they were the best of friends.

And more determined than ever to get their schemes to work.

2

"Come on, Thuban," said Taylor.

"Yeah, Thuban, don't tease," added her little sister. "You published another half-page article in the school paper right before fall break."

"You can't expect us to believe you have *no idea* who the Mad Bandits are," said Taylor.

Bright's younger brother held up his hands—the skin of his palms glowed white in the firelight. "I can't reveal my sources," Thuban said with feigned innocence.

The gathering of young people around the fire pit groaned. Several of them threw marshmallows.

"Hey, now! Cut that out!" Thuban protested, laughing all the while.

Well, he brought that on himself, Bright thought as he stepped away from the gathering. Thuban wouldn't reveal his sources, because he didn't have any. Every "fact" in every piece his brother had written about the Mad Bandits had been fabricated out of thin air. Merri and Bright would chuckle over the articles…and then use the headlines to papier mâché the Head Witch's ceremonial broomstick.

Even with Thuban's recent exposé, the Harmswood administration was no closer to revealing the identities of the Mad Bandits after all these years. The only consensus so far was that there had to be more than one prankster, but exactly how many could never be settled upon.

Thuban had been the one to name them, back when he was but a lowly op-ed writer for the *Harmswood Gazette*...but only because Bright had given him the moniker. "Why don't you write something about the Mad Bandits?" Bright suggested one morning over breakfast.

"The who?" his clueless brother asked.

"You know, the ones who keep pulling all the stunts at school. The Mad Bandits. Isn't that what your friends are calling them?"

"Of course. Sorry, it's early." Much like their mother, Thuban was never one to admit he was ignorant about anything. "Should I be pro- or con-bandit?"

"Does it matter?" Bright asked before he walked away. There was no more to discuss. The seed had been successfully planted.

The major downside to Bright and Merri's secret partnership was that it had to stay at school. The younger Brighton brothers always invited handfuls of friends to the family lodge near Stowe over fall break. The only person the eldest Brighton brother wanted to invite was the one person he couldn't admit to knowing in public.

It was too bad, too. Merri would have loved the colors of New England in October. She'd spent all her life in South Carolina and Georgia. There were seasons in the South...but nothing like up here. Especially during peak leaf season. On the flip side, he'd much rather be back at school with her, plotting the final tricks of their senior year. He'd challenged her to come up with a solo prank over the long weekend while he was away with his family. He could only imagine what amusing mischief she'd devised in his absence.

"Star light, star bright," an airy voice said behind him. "Don't wander off too far or you'll get eaten by a goon."

Bright turned to see Taylor standing just behind him, her long red-gold hair illuminated by the fire they'd left behind. The game she referenced was one they'd played as children, taking turns as the "goon" that chased the others through these very woods. Well, Taylor and her sisters, Bright's little brothers, and whatever friends had come to the lodge on vacation. Bright never took part in those reindeer games. They teased him with "Star light, star bright," because he always stayed so far away from the rest of them.

Even as a child, Taylor had been exquisitely beautiful. Her other two sisters were pretty enough—Hayden witches always came in threes—but Taylor possessed a rare inner grace that only magnified as she got older. Even in these shadowed woods she looked like a doe caught in a shaft of light.

As far as money and position went, Taylor Hayden was his equal. His parents would definitely approve of the match. But she was a lively sort of person, always chasing after mindless entertainment. She was much more likely to end up with one of his far more gregarious brothers.

"Why are you wandering out here all alone?" she asked. "Are you still too good to play with us lowly brats?"

Bright didn't know how to answer. Merri would have said "yes" without hesitation, and the thought made him want to laugh.

"Your cider's cold." Taylor took the mug he'd forgotten he held in his hands. "Here." She whispered a spell and blew across the top of the mug before returning it to him, piping hot.

Bright stared at her. "Why are you being nice to me?"

Taylor rolled her eyes. "Because I want something, silly. Why else?"

"Hmm." Bright sipped at his mug before his cider got cold again. "Out with it."

"I want to play a prank on Samson Sol, and I want you to help me."

Bright was so shocked by her declaration that he almost spat out the cider. "Why me?" he managed to ask.

"Because you don't care about anybody," she said. "No one would ever suspect you. And there are already so many Mad Bandits running around our school now, I figure I might as well join them."

Bright wanted to argue with every sentence she spoke, but he bit his tongue. Yes, there had been a few copycat jokers over the years, but their deeds had always been subpar, and they'd always been caught. Meanwhile, he and Merri had become masters of the craft.

"Why Samson?" He had to ask. Seriously, why did every girl in school fall for that sunburnt surfer-boy knucklehead? That elf had about as much depth as a kiddie pool. How could anyone tolerate someone so boring?

"Because he hasn't asked me to the Midwinter

Masquerade, but I know he's going anyway. I want him to think that whatever girl he brought instead gave him bad luck."

Bright wasn't sure what to say to that either. He and Merri had never discussed the exclusivity of their partnership, but only because neither of them had ever been approached in this way.

But wasn't this his end game? To orchestrate events so that he got tangled up with Taylor? For the first time, and for whatever reason, Taylor was paying attention to him. Surely Merri wouldn't begrudge him this one small deed, whatever it was. Especially with so little time left before graduation.

Taylor sighed. "Bright, if you're in, then you need to say so out loud. You forget, the rest of us can't see inside that busy brain of yours."

His brow furrowed. Merri never said such things. She always let him think in peace. Weren't people supposed to think before they spoke? It was his own fault that he thought so much. Some folks had so little patience that they filled in the silence themselves before he ever spoke a word. Which suited him just fine—he could go for days without having to speak a word to anyone. Except Merri.

"Yes," he said finally. "I will help you."

He wasn't sure how he was going to tell Merri. He met with her the first day back, during the lunch period, at their secret spot by the hollow tree in the woods. She waited for him there, her lunch already spread out on her blanket. She was growing out her hair—it was bright cornsilk blonde at the roots and fading reddish-black to her shoulders. Her hands were clasped before her, and she was grinning from ear to ear. Bright wondered if she realized her giddiness had made the clearing behind her bloom with foxglove.

"So what have you been up to while I was away?" He folded his legs on the blanket beside her and offered her one of the Cokes he'd brought with him. "I expect a full report."

"Aye aye, captain!" She bounced a little in her excitement. Bright forced himself not to laugh, but he really, really wanted to. "I actually came up with two things. One is a surprise for later, but you're going to love it. Trust me."

In his whole life, no one had ever given Bright a gift that wasn't obligatory. Merri had no clue what a godsend she was to him. She was clever and talented, and she thought outside the box. She knew the limits of her own magic, but only because she was constantly testing them. The more adept she became, the more she inspired Bright to challenge himself.

"Whatever it is, I'm sure I will love it," he said. "And the other business?"

She sipped her Coke and relaxed a bit. "The other thing is all set to go, but I do need your help cementing the deal."

Bright allowed himself to grin this time. Merri had the chops to invent complex pranks on her own, but it felt nice to be needed. "Go on."

"I need you to officiate the marriage of two ghosts."

Bright chuckled into his Coke bottle. "Never a dull moment with you, is there?"

"Oh, but you'll like this one." She brightened up again, like sunshine on snow. "I've convinced a ghost mariachi band to follow Dean Zuru around for Dia de los Muertos."

"Because doing something like that on Halloween would be too obvious," said Bright.

Merri waved her hands. "Every copycat in Harmswood will be planning some lame trick for Halloween. This prank has so much more class."

"I agree," said Bright. "It's definitely worthy of the Mad Bandits. But...who is it that wants to get married? One of the ghosts in the band?"

"The lead singer's sister, Bianca," said Merri. "She's fallen in love with a Chinese soldier from the Han dynasty."

Bright shook his head. Only Merri. She always did have more ghost friends than live ones. "I assume the feeling is mutual?"

"Oh, yes. They're a wonderful couple. Met in the biography section of the library over a mutual love of flowers and poetry and sword fighting." She waved her hands again. "But that's beside the point. They want to get married, and I can't be the one to do it."

"Why not?"

Merri sighed. "Because, despite all their differences in time and space and culture and religion, they can only agree on one thing: that they have to be married by a man."

Bright burst out laughing—something he only ever did around Merri. "I promise to fulfill my manly duties."

Mari smirked at him. "Don't get me started. But the trade-off will be so much fun! The band will follow Dean Zuru from sunup to sundown, except for lunchtime, when they'll perform a full concert in the cafeteria. Bianca taught me some dances—I'm hoping to get up enough courage to ask Samson to dance with me.

Bianca can teach you too, if you want, and then maybe you can ask Taylor."

Bright set his Coke aside. There would be no better time to bring this up. "Speaking of Taylor and dances…"

"Yeah? You come up with something new?"

"Sort of," he said. "Taylor asked me to play a prank with her during the Midwinter Masquerade."

"Wow," said Merri. "You mean while your crew was up at the lodge this past weekend?"

When Merri said "your crew," Bright knew what she meant was, "all the popular rich kids." Even if he'd been able to acknowledge their partnership, Merri wouldn't have fit in with that crowd. Heck, *he* didn't fit in, and he belonged there.

"Right out of the blue," he said. "She just walked up and asked me."

"Wow," Merri said again. "Do you think she suspects…?"

"No," Bright said before she could finish. "She asked me because I'm apparently the last person anyone would ever suspect."

Merri lifted her bottle in salute. "Second-to-last," she said. "So does this mean you're going to the Midwinter Masquerade with her?"

"Of course not," he said. "She's going with my little brothers and a bunch of other people. Besides, I assumed you'd be going with me."

Merri froze with the Coke bottle halfway to her lips. "Wouldn't that defeat the purpose? Isn't the whole point of our partnership that we can't ever be seen together?"

Bright shook his head. "I don't mean 'go-with-me' go with me, I mean…ugh, how do I explain this?"

"Polaris Brighton," she said pertly. "Are you inviting

me to *not* go to the Midwinter Masquerade with you?"

He blew out the breath he'd been holding. "*Thank you.* That's exactly what I mean. It is our last year, after all."

"I was thinking about that," said Merri. "You know, all the Harmswood alumni are invited to the Midwinter Masquerade. Maybe we should come back every year and pull a prank. Just for old times' sake."

"You can," he said as he unwrapped his sandwich. "I know one thing for sure—our shenanigans have been the only good thing about my time here. Once I leave Harmswood, I never, ever want to come back to this school again."

He wore a silver bowtie with his tuxedo because he knew Taylor would be wearing silver. His brothers did the same. He and Thuban and Alrai looked like three versions of the same black-haired, fair-skinned elf: the athlete, the journalist, and the CEO.

He may have been the youngest, but Alrai's shoulders were almost twice the size of his brothers'. Thuban's fingers were, as always, perpetually stained with ink. And Bright was...perfect. Pressed, polished, and not a hair out of place. Just like his father. Just as he was supposed to be.

He'd bought a wrist corsage for Merri. He wasn't sure why. She'd said she had a surprise for him, though he still didn't know what it was. Maybe he just wanted to return the favor. When he'd walked into Enchanted Garden and seen the black-eyed Susans—Merri's favorite—surrounded by miniature black roses, he knew the corsage was supposed to belong to her.

Taylor and the rest of her friends met them in the courtyard. She spotted the box right away and assumed the flowers were hers. She gave Bright a perfunctory kiss on the cheek as she took the box from him, didn't even stop talking to his brothers as she slid the corsage onto her wrist. It clashed with her silver dress, but she didn't seem to mind.

Bright was too stunned at the kiss to take it away from her. He simply pulled the silver mask down over his eyes and joined the party.

The low-level prank Taylor had asked him to do for her—she'd never planned to help, he should have known—was set up and ready to go. A mesh canopy of white and silver balloons had been rigged to drop idyllically upon the guests once the masquerade had started. It hadn't been too difficult to fill one of those balloons with ink. It would be tougher guiding the balloon to its target once the canopy collapsed, but the gymnasium was kept cool enough for Bright to manipulate a few icy drafts with no problem.

Bright looked forward to watching Samson get his just desserts, so much so that he forgot to be afraid of Taylor. As soon as the alma mater was finished, he pulled her into his arms for the first dance. Taylor laughed and danced with him, her red-gold hair shining in the dim lights.

But all she could talk about was Samson.

Taylor pulled Bright close and whispered in his ear. Her breath was sweet. The feathers of her mask brushed his cheek. "Do you see him yet? They'll pull that canopy at any second. We need to find that no-good two-timing elf before it happens."

Bright had already located the target. Samson was

dancing on the opposite side of the gym. His partner was some tall, curvy fae girl. Her floor-length gown only had one shoulder, and a line of ruffles down the back. Between the golden dress, golden mask, and her short golden pixie cut, she almost looked like an award statue come to life. Samson Sol and his new Trophy Girlfriend. It was all too perfect.

As the song came to a close, Taylor dragged Bright closer to their victims. They had a front row seat when the ink balloon came crashing down on Samson's tawny head. His partner got just as splattered as Samson, from golden hair to the toes of her golden shoes.

"What the..." Samson sputtered as he and his dance partner pulled the masks from their faces. "Taylor?"

Taylor's evil laugh turned to a shriek. "That's what you get for dancing with another girl, you selfish jerk!"

"I didn't ask her, baby, I swear. She asked me. It was just one dance..." Samson continued to plead his case to Taylor, but the words melted away in Bright's ears the moment he realized exactly what fae girl Samson had been dancing with.

Merri.

She'd cut her hair...and where had she gotten that dress? She wiped her cheeks with the back of her hand. Those kaleidoscope blue eyes glowed against the blue-black mess, staring him down. Even splattered with ink, she was the most beautiful woman in the room. Was this supposed to be his big surprise?

Oh, gods. His heart sank.

"Merri," he said softly. "I'm sorry."

At Bright's declaration, Taylor raised a hand to shut Samson up. Merri caught sight of the corsage on her wrist. The black and yellow of the black-eyed Susans mocked them both. A look of…pain?…crossed her face, but it was gone in an instant. Merri's bright eyes moved from the corsage, to Taylor, to him.

"Goodbye, Polaris," was all she said before she turned and walked away. The crowd parted to let her leave.

Taylor finally noticed the corsage as well, the plain wildflowers and black roses that had no business on her wrist. They matched the black and gold vision of the girl now walking away.

"This was for her," she whispered. "Oh my gosh, Bright, I'm so sorry. I never would have interfered if I'd known."

"Known what?" Bright asked in a daze.

"That she's in love with you, you idiot." Taylor pulled the flowers off her wrist and shoved them back into Bright's hands. "And if you know what's good for you, you'll go after her, right this second."

Bright stared at the flowers in his hand. The black-eyed Susans stared back. Taylor was spouting nonsense. Merri wasn't in love with him. Oh, she was plenty mad at him, sure, but she wasn't in love with him. That was ridiculous. It wasn't what their partnership was about.

"What are you waiting for?" Taylor asked.

"Taylor's right," said Samson, dripping ink on the gym floor like a fool. "You should go, man."

Bright grimaced. The last thing he wanted was unsolicited advice from surfer-boy Samson. "She'll be fine," he said. "She just needs to cool off. We'll talk about it tomorrow."

But there was no tomorrow. Merri wasn't in class the next day. She wasn't in the library, or the courtyard, or in the woods by the hollow tree. Not even the ghosts knew where she'd gone. By winter break, he heard a rumor that she'd gotten her equivalency diploma and gone back to South Carolina to help her mother with the new baby.

She didn't call him. She didn't write. Merri had said her goodbye. He just hadn't realized it would be the last one. Like he hadn't realized she'd loved him all that time. Like he hadn't realized how much he loved her back.

The last semester of school was torture. Without Merri, it was painfully obvious just how alone he was in that place. So he went back to quietly not caring about anything or anyone. Not caring made everything hurt a little less.

Taylor and Samson got back together, and broke up, and got back together again, and Bright didn't care. He took his midterms, and then his finals, and he didn't care. He interned at his father's investment firm and sat in on conference calls and board meetings and he didn't care. He assembled in the gym and marched with his fellow classmates down to the athletic field to rehearse graduation, and he didn't care.

As the seniors crested the hill, Bright began to hear whispers, then giggles, then shouts of joy. He pushed through the crowd so he could see the sight for himself. Within the pristine, spring-green athletic field had been planted another sort of grass, but much darker green. From their vantage point at the top of the hill, the students could read the giant words it splashed across the field as plain as day:

CLASS OF MB

"Class of the Mad Bandits!" someone cried out, and everyone in the senior class cheered again. Everyone, that is, except Bright. Because he knew that M and that B didn't stand for "Mad Bandits."

This had been the surprise she'd kept so secret. Merri's gift, just for him, fashioned by her own flower-fairy hand. Her last prank, immortalizing them both. The last secret shared between them.

And he wished to the heavens that he didn't care.

3

Four years later

It was autumn again. Merri could tell because the pine needles were falling, everything was flavored with pumpkin spice, and Cassiopeia was talking to dead people.

Mother had named the thirteenth Larousse baby Cassiopeia Merrisandra. An exquisite, complicated, and possibly doomed name, but she'd grow into it. For now they just called her Cass, or Sippy, or whatever else they felt like that day.

Cassiopeia had pointed ears and those telltale Larousse eyes, but her curly locks were black where her siblings had fair hair. This was a trait shared among many fae thirteenth children, Mother explained, because their spirits were closer to the veil. Especially the ones born between All Hallows and Midwinter.

Merri kept watch over her littlest sister at the Nursery-Nursery, where she'd taken a job after leaving Harmswood. At the Nursery-Nursery, young ones played in a natural, greenhouse-type environment. The idea was that being surrounded by flowers and trees and natural light was more conducive to education than being cooped up in tiny rooms with no windows. It was also a better place for paranormal children who might accidentally burp acid, or set fire to their paper, or turn a friend into a toad, or walk up to Merri and say, "Bianca has a message for you."

Merri blinked at her little sister and pulled the strands of hair out of her mouth. "Bianca who, Cassafrass?"

"Bianca from Harmswood," Cassiopeia said, and then stuck her thumb in her mouth instead.

Right, thought Merri. *Ghost Bianca.* Merri helped her sister make a better choice about where to put her fingers. "What did Bianca say, sweetheart?"

"She says you havta come to the dance 'cause Bellamy needs your help," she said quickly, and then promptly ran away to join her friends beneath the apple tree.

Bellamy needed help? That was almost as odd as a ghost friend delivering a message through her baby sister. Bellamy was the happiest and most generous of all the Larousse siblings. If life gave Bellamy lemons, she opened a lemonade stand that saved the world. Merri couldn't imagine what predicament Bellamy could be in that required any sort of help, never mind her meddling oldest sister's.

But Merri loved her crazy fairy family and would do anything for them. Windkin fae might be flighty flibbertigibbets, but they would never abandon one of their own in a time of need. Bianca knew that.

Merri let out a great sigh. She hadn't planned to

attend Harmswood's Midwinter Masquerade this year. Or ever again.

The first year, she'd gone back to the dance just to prove that she could. She wanted to remind herself that she was still a Harmswood alumna, despite not participating in the graduation ceremony with the rest of her class. Admittedly, a small part of her also wanted to see if Polaris Brighton stayed true to his word to never come back.

He did.

She wasn't sure if she was happy or sad that her former partner-in-crime was nowhere to be found on the school grounds. The emotional confusion didn't last long. She decided that she wanted to pull one more prank, all on her own. Nothing big or drastic or showy, just a small thing. To reclaim her territory. To remind herself that she didn't need Bright to get away with mischief. To remember that she was still capable of having fun.

That year at the Midwinter Masquerade, every bathroom in Harmswood sported an "Out of Order" sign. It led to a little confusion, a lot of chuckles…and Professor Beketaten running off with the custodian. Apparently, Mr. Zimmer had spent the last ten years secretly memorizing his way through the poetry section of the library, a trait that swept Merri's former English teacher right off her feet, once she was satisfied that all the toilets were functioning properly.

The year after that, Merri's prank once again made a match. And again the year after that. Yup, she still had it. And yet, she was forced to admit that her schoolgirl stunts didn't amuse her the way they once did. Laughing alone wasn't quite what it used to be.

This Midwinter, she planned to save the money she

would have spent on the periwinkle dress in the window of Glinda's Closet and stay at home. Except now, Bellamy needed her.

Leave it to family to throw a wrench in your plans, thought Merri. Well, at least she already had the dress picked out. Besides, without family, who else would stand up for her?

No one, that's who.

She kissed Mother and all the little ones goodbye, caught a bus down to Georgia, and arranged for one of her brother Asher's coworkers to pick her up at the station. It was sweltering. When she arrived at Harmswood, she made a beeline for the restroom closest to the library. She figured she could at least catch up with Bianca while she got ready.

Bianca was thrilled to see her old friend. She told Merri about the rest of the library ghosts, the mariachis, and wedded life—*afterlife*—with Xiao Wu.

"He's strong and wise and calm, which is so strange for me," said Bianca. "My family is full of singing and dancing and yelling and flying."

"Sounds a lot like my family." Merri fixed her lip gloss in the mirror. She wondered if her own temperament would follow her into the afterlife. If she became a poltergeist, she could continue playing tricks on people...

"You know, I would never have put you and Xiao together," Merri admitted. "But you really are a perfect match."

"Speaking of," said Bianca. "Xiao still asks about Bright. You never hear from him?"

"No." Merri ran a hand through her short hair, so that it didn't look squashed flat from hours against a bus seat. Whatever her feelings for Polaris Brighton had been, they'd faded over time into a dull heartache, like one might have for a lost toy, or an old home. Their time together was a beautiful memory she could never relive. That was all.

But she still couldn't bring herself to say his name out loud.

"His loss," said Bianca, "because you are amazing."

"Thanks." Merri did a twirl in her gown for good measure and Bianca clapped.

"You can leave the rest of your things here. I'll keep an eye on them. Just don't forget your mask." Bianca's ghostly form hovered over to where Merri's glittery mask lay beside the sink. "And you should get a move on. Hubble said he would meet you in the courtyard, by the fountain."

Merri stopped with the mask halfway to her face. "Who?"

"Hubble," said Bianca. "Bellamy's friend from the drama club. I think he has something planned for tonight. But it's Hubble. He's always organizing something."

Merri smirked. "Sounds like this Hubble and I have a lot in common. Is he the guy my sister's sweet on?"

"Oh, no," said Bianca. "That would be Tinker."

"Wait...you mean her best friend Tinker? The goblin? Are you sure?"

"I'm sure Hubble will explain it all," said Bianca.

Merri sighed dramatically. "Doesn't Xiao Wu have a nice calm brother I could maybe set her up with instead?"

Bianca giggled and waved her out the door. "Shoo! Go on, don't be late!"

Mask in hand, Merri slipped on her dancing shoes

and hurried out of the restroom. She slowed her pace when she exited the library, as she hit the wall of heat. Was Nocturne Falls under a spell or something? Georgia had never been so hot this late in the year.

She fanned her face with the mask as she walked, her heels clicking on the cobblestone path. Why couldn't this Hubble have met her somewhere air conditioned? Was he a fire elemental of some sort? She was so lost in thought that she arrived at the fountain before she knew it.

On the other side of the fountain stood Polaris Brighton.

Merri halted midstep. They stared at each other in silence.

As many times as Merri had imagined this moment, she had no idea what to say. And he had never been the one to start a conversation.

Did he look older? As far as she could tell, he looked exactly the same as the night she'd walked away from...everything. That same cold beauty: same black hair, same haunting eyes, same sharp jawline. He might have even been wearing the same bespoke suit and expensive silver bowtie.

Merri gritted her teeth. Well, at least one of them had changed.

A crease between his eyebrows was the only indication that he had no idea she'd be here either. Merri wracked her brain. She had to say *something,* or they might be stuck here forever.

Thankfully, a short cloaked figure slipped through the gap in the hedge. His hair and skin were the silver-gray of a winter elf's eyes—a kobold, she guessed—and he carried a garment bag over one arm.

"I'm Hubble," he said quickly, "and I'd love to chat, but there's not much time. Which stinks, because I've always wanted to meet the legendary Mad Bandits." He looked from Merri to Bright and put his free hand to his heart. "This is a real honor. I'm a huge fan of your work."

Merri's heart stopped. This was definitely not the conversation she'd been expecting. "How did you find out?"

The kobold shrugged. "Hindsight's twenty-twenty, especially when you know what you're looking for," he said. "You do enough research, put enough class lists together, read enough articles…" He waggled a finger at Bright. "Getting your brother to publish about you was a masterstroke, I have to say. And you"—this time he pointed to Merri—"did you know it took them almost a year to erase your parting shot from the athletic field? Only a flower fairy could have been so precise."

"Does anyone else know?"

Merri flinched. It was as if she could feel Bright's voice against her skin, and it hurt all over.

Hubble looked offended. "I'm a fellow miscreant, sir. Not a jerk."

Merri might have enjoyed this worship of her past accomplishments if she wasn't so annoyed. The oppressive heat didn't help matters. "What does all this have to do with my little sister?" she asked him.

"Right, sorry. The short version is this: Bellamy and my best friend Tinker are in love with each other, and pretty much have been forever, and—circumstances being what they are—this dance is their last chance to actually say so. And it needs to be said."

Merri met Bright's eyes across the fountain again.

Too much of that story sounded like their own sad tale.

"I've set them both up with costumes—"

"Costumes?" Merri asked.

Hubble grinned. "Bellamy should be arriving at any minute, and I'm about to go get Tinker."

"It sounds like you already have everything under control," she said.

Hubble shook his head. "I can dress them up and get them to the dance, but I need help getting them *together*. Preferably alone. If left to their own devices, Tinker and Bellamy will happily stand at arm's length for the rest of their lives."

"Probably a good idea since goblins are allergic to fairies," Merri quipped.

"Normally, I'd agree with you," said Hubble. "But tonight, I don't think that's going to be a problem."

Merri sighed. The kids must have gotten their hands on an anti-allergy spell or something. Ultimately, the details didn't matter. "Fine," she said. "I'll get them together. On one condition."

"Yes! Wonderful! Anything! What?"

This kid was too excitable for his own good. "I want to talk to the goblin first. I'm not setting him up with my sister if he's not good enough."

"Deal," Hubble said too quickly. "'Cause you're going to love him, I promise. He's a real prince."

She admired his loyalty. "And how will I recognize him?"

"Don't worry. We'll make a grand entrance."

Merri raised an eyebrow.

Hubble sighed. "He'll be the annoyingly tall and handsome one in the goblin mask." And with that, he dashed off into the night.

Without a backward glance, Merri turned and headed for the gymnasium. The sound of Bright's perfectly-polished Italian leather shoes followed her.

"We're *legendary*," he said. "How about that?"

Merri said nothing.

"You said you'll get them together," he said.

Merri continued to ignore him.

"You said *you'll* get them together. Not *we*."

"There hasn't been a *we* for a very long time," Merri replied without turning around. "Not that you care, but I've been coming back here every year and pulling off similar stunts just fine without your help. I can handle this without you too, thank you very much."

"Just because you didn't see me, doesn't mean I wasn't there."

Merri tripped on a raised stone in the path, caught herself, and kept walking. The thought that Bright might have been there any—or all—of those times she'd come back to the masquerade, watching from afar, silent and distant... It was exactly the sort of thing he had done in the past, before they had ever been friends in the first place.

But it made sense. Every prank they pulled together in school had inadvertently matched up a pair of unsuspecting individuals, and every prank Merri pulled at Harmswood in the years since had had the same side effect. Bright *had* been there, and she should have realized that. Merri gritted her teeth again and silently cursed at the sky.

Whatever scar tissue had healed over her broken heart ripped right back open again.

Merri stopped in front of the gymnasium door and settled her mask over her eyes. "When Hubble makes his grand entrance, make sure you're dancing with Bellamy. I'll grab Tinker. If I decide he's really as in love with my sister as his best friend seems to think, I'll get him over to you. Then we'll switch off and be done with this." *And done with each other*, she didn't add. *Again*.

Bright put on his mask and gave a small salute. "Aye aye, captain."

Merri grimaced behind her own mask, remembering all the times she'd said that to him, back in their heyday. He'd used those words on purpose, she knew. She wished he'd stop doing stuff that hurt so much.

The gym had been decorated to look like an idyllic winter landscape, complete with a copse of silver-white birch and a star-filled sky. Atop a pillar in the center of the room was a picturesque snow globe. Merri smiled. Not only did this landscape have Bellamy's signature all over it, but it had obviously been decorated by someone very much in love.

Bright looked out over the sea of students scattered across the snow-filled scene. The black and white and silver of him blended in perfectly with the surroundings. "Which one is Bellamy again?" he asked her.

"She's got wings," said Merri. As soon as she spotted Bellamy in the crowd, she couldn't help but laugh. "And currently looks like she belongs on top of a wedding cake."

Bright gave a low whistle at the giant silver-and-white gown. "Some costume. I can't wait to see the groom."

For half a second, they were old friends again and the years melted away. And then a young blonde wearing a black silk dress and too much eyeliner leapt into his arms.

"Brighton!" she squealed. "Taylor told me you were

coming, but I didn't believe her! Come meet my friends so I can make them all jealous."

Bright looked pleadingly at Merri, but she said nothing as Taylor Hayden's shallow little sister led him into the trees.

Some things never changed.

Someone struck up the Harmswood alma mater and Merri sang along under her breath, all the while keeping an eye on her sister. Bellamy was surrounded by friends, a luxury Merri had not experienced during her time at school. Merri recognized Bellamy's roommate, Lian, and her best friend Kai, who was flanked by two incredibly handsome young men. One of them looked like a werewolf.

The other looked like Samson Sol.

Merri had heard that Kai had a serious boyfriend now, but she couldn't tell which one of these boys it was. They both stood protectively close to her. When the school song finished, Kai took the dark wolf's hand and began to dance with him. The tawny-haired boy followed, not far behind.

"You teenagers are always in love with the wrong person," Merri muttered, and then stalked across the dance floor to save this poor boy from himself...and save Kai's relationship in the bargain.

The closer Merri got to him, however, the more a strange feeling washed over her. She was suddenly seventeen again, throwing caution to the wind and asking Samson Sol to dance with her. She was determined to prove to herself once and for all that the crush she'd had for Samson paled in comparison to the love she felt for Bright...right before she'd become the butt of Bright and Taylor's little joke.

What a fool she'd been.

Merri gave herself a mental shake. She wasn't that silly schoolgirl anymore. She grabbed tawny-boy's shoulder and spun him around so that he was dancing with no one but her.

"I'm Merri," she yelled over the music.

"Merry meet," he said, completely misunderstanding. Was that a British accent? Oh yeah, fourteen-year-old Merri would have had a massive crush on this kid.

"Bellamy's sister," she yelled again, pointing at herself.

"Ah," he yelled back with a nod. "I'm Owen."

Merri smiled, nodded, and kept dancing. She spun this way and that, but try as she might, she couldn't get Owen to step more than six feet away from Kai.

Drastic times called for drastic measures. Merri grabbed Owen's hand and pulled him toward the birch trees. "Come on, let's dance over here." She didn't care if he understood her. Thankfully, he didn't resist the change of location.

She didn't let go of his hand until she'd pushed him right in front of Taylor's little sister. "Owen, you know Taylor, right?"

"It's *Heather,*" the pretty girl yelled.

"I *know,*" Merri yelled back. This time she grabbed Bright's hand and dragged him away.

"Wasn't that a little rude?" he asked.

"Trust me, those two deserve each other." It was only fitting that the Taylors and the Samsons of this world be forced to endure each other's company, if only for one dance.

"If you say so..."

Merri didn't want to start a conversation. "Now go dance with my sister."

She shoved Bright in Bellamy's direction and went to linger by the gymnasium door. The sooner Hubble made his grand entrance, the sooner this painful and awkward night would be over with.

Four years. Four years had passed since that horrible night, and Bright still couldn't get out of his own head long enough to talk to Merri. Actually talk to her. What was *wrong* with him?

Well, whatever it was, he could figure it out later. Right now he was on a mission. A Mad Bandit mission. That old thrill returned to him and rushed through his blood.

He weaved through the throng of dancing students to where Bellamy was chatting animatedly with her friends. Honey-blonde hair done up with white flowers, big kaleidoscope blue eyes…even without the wings, he would have recognized her as Merri's sister in a heartbeat.

He gently touched her on the elbow and she spun around to smile at him. Her face was covered with an organic mask of glitter and white feathers and happiness, and she looked genuinely adorable. If anyone deserved to have a magical night, it was this young woman. At that moment, Bright promised himself that he would do whatever he could to make that magic happen for her.

"You're Bellamy, right? I'm Polaris Brighton." He held out his hand and she shook it politely, but he could tell she was trying to place him.

He pulled her aside, so that he didn't have to yell over her friends. "I'm..." A friend from school? A former partner-in-crime? The guy who ruined her life? How did he explain?

Words, don't fail me now... "I'm in love with your sister."

Amazing.

Amazing how it just came pouring out like that.

Amazing how easy it was.

Amazing how he meant every single word.

Bellamy's smile at his declaration made the gymnasium's wintry landscape shine all the more. "Bright," she said in recognition. "Yes, I know about you. Even more than Merri thinks I do."

The soft bit of South Carolina in her accent was completely charming. "Oh, my," said Bright. "I believe this is a story I need to hear."

"Only if you promise not to tell," said Bellamy.

"I solemnly swear," he said with as much mischief as he could muster.

"I read her diary once," Bellamy confessed.

"As all good sisters should." Bright tried not to grimace. He could only imagine what scathing words a young Merri Larousse might have written about him once upon a time.

"She was so much fun back in those days. So alive. And then..." A shadow seemed to fall over Bellamy's face.

"And then she left school," he finished.

"It was such a difference," said Bellamy. "She

became more and more quiet and withdrawn. I hoped it was a phase, like some sort of depression after leavin' school. But Mom said that Merri had been that way before, back when I was too young to remember. She said that maybe happiness had been Merri's phase, and now it was over."

Her words were like a dagger in his heart. "So you read through her diary to find out what caused it," he surmised. Merri was lucky to have such a caring and generous soul as a sibling.

Bellamy nodded. "Whatever the happiness had been, I wanted to give it back to her," she said. "Turns out, it was you."

Bright wasn't sure it was possible to feel worse than he did right now. It was time for his own confession. "She was my happiness too."

"What happened?"

Bright shook his head. "I screwed up."

Suddenly, the gymnasium doors burst open. A short plague doctor walked through, followed by an African god and a wicked Red Death. The plague doctor threw his arms wide with a bang and a shower of bubbles.

"HEAR YE, HEAR YE!" The voice of the infamous Hubble rang out from behind the mask, magically amplified. The DJ stopped the music.

Bright chuckled. He *had* been warned. "Nice grand entrance."

Bellamy stood on her tiptoes in an effort to peek over the crowd. "That's my friend Hubble," she said proudly. "He doesn't do anythin' by half."

"An admirable trait," said Bright. "Wish I had more of that."

"Me too," Bellamy replied with a sigh.

As soon as Hubble finished his announcement, the DJ struck up a waltz. A romantic fairy tale dance, perfect for putting two soulmates together. *Well played, Sir Hubble. Well played.* Bright held his hand out to Bellamy. "Do you waltz?"

Bellamy nodded and put her hand in his. "Merri taught me."

Of course she did. Many years ago, in the dark woods by a hollow tree, it had been Bright who'd taught Merri.

At first glance, Bellamy's massive ballgown looked too stiff for dancing, but in the thick of things, the fabric of her skirt was a blur of shimmering movement. In those first few steps and turns, Bright decided how he was going to put his spin on Merri's matchmaking machinations. If there was ever a setting where a winter elf's particular traits would come in handy, it was this one.

He twirled Bellamy, mindful of her wings, and when she settled back into step she asked, "Do you think you could make Merri happy again?"

"I want to," he said.

"Then I will help you." He recognized the look of resolve on Bellamy's face—he'd seen the same one on Merri enough times to know. "She's here tonight. I'm goin' to dance you over to where she is, and then we'll strategically change partners."

Seeing as that's exactly what he and Merri had planned to do to *her*, Bright was totally on board with Bellamy's idea. "If you can do that, I promise to do everything in my power to make Merri happy."

"That's all I wish for," she said.

Bright almost warned her about wishing on stars,

but he decided to save the teasing for another time. "I just have one question."

"Only one?" Bellamy's smile lit up the room again. "What's that?"

"Assuming I can get back into your sister's good graces..." He stepped to the side and spun Bellamy around once again. Her skirt sparkled about her like a flurry of new-fallen snow. "How would you feel about being *my* sister?"

Bellamy threw back her head and laughed so hard that one of the white blossoms fell from her hair. It was a true fairy laugh, one that sounded like a river of tinkling bells. He remembered Merri laughing like that, before he ruined everything.

"Oh, my dear, sweet Bright," she said. "Bein' a sister is one thing I am *very* good at."

Bright spotted Merri dancing in the crowd with her tall partner. It looked as if Merri was teaching him the steps as they went along, but he seemed to be a quick study. They were getting closer, so Bright guessed that Tinker had passed whatever test Merri had put to him.

Bright managed to catch Merri's eye, and she nodded. Confirmation. Now all they needed to do was the partner exchange...

...and in one quick turn, it was done. Bellamy and Tinker were off together, to sink or swim on their own.

Merri was in his arms now, like a dream come true. Bright never wanted to let her go. Granted, it was a little like dancing with a mannequin.

"Let's get out of here," she said with a fake smile.

"I just need to do one thing first," he said, holding her tightly. Because in order to pull off the mischief he'd planned, he needed a little more than his own magic.

He absorbed her energy through their joined hands, and then directed it toward Bellamy and her beau. A gust of cold wind whipped through the gymnasium.

Merri's ice-cold fingers tightened around his. "What was that? What did you do?" She looked around. "Where's Bellamy?"

"She's fine," said Bright. "I did a sort of...twist on a classic winter elf communication device."

Merri narrowed her eyes at him, waiting for him to explain further.

Bright couldn't help but smile. He loved seeing that look again, too. "I put them in the snow globe."

He could tell she wanted to laugh at that, but she managed to quash whatever joy had reared its ugly head. "Great," she said. "Now we can leave."

She started to pull away from him, but Bright didn't let her. He remembered his conversation with Bellamy, the ease with which he'd been able to confess his feelings for Merri, and he held on. "We need to talk first."

Without letting go of her hand, he pulled her out of the gymnasium and into the oppressive heat. He took her with him across the courtyard, past the fountain and past the library, all the way to the outer edge of campus and into the woods. When he reached the hollow tree, he finally let her go. He turned to her and took a deep breath...but the words were gone.

To her credit, she didn't turn and run. She folded her arms across her chest and stared at him. And waited.

And waited.

Say something, he yelled at himself. How did one fix the biggest mistake of one's life? He couldn't afford to screw this up, but here he was, already doing it. *Say something.*

She rolled those exquisitely blue eyes. "So I guess you and Taylor obviously still talk," she said, breaking the silence. He wanted to kiss her for that. Maybe he should.

"You know our families have been friends forever," he said instead. "She's actually engaged to my younger brother. The journalist."

"Thuban became a professional journalist? Good for him!" Once again, she shoved that joy back down in its box. "Though I'm not sure I ever understood what you guys saw in Taylor."

"I'm not sure I did either," he said softly.

"You want to hear something crazy?" she asked. "I don't hear from you in years, but it still makes me sad knowing that you talk to her more than you talk to me." She shook her head. "It shouldn't, but it does."

Finally, *finally*, the words burst out like a flood. "Merri, I don't talk to *anyone*. I left here, went on to university, and graduated with no friends. I work at my father's office now, just like he planned from the day I was born. I have a secretary. I send emails and *she* talks. I attend meetings, and the board members talk. The only person in my life I've ever *wanted* to talk to was you." He threw his hands up in the air. "And I'm so terrible at it, that I only seem to be able to do it when I'm arguing with you."

"Okay, then let's try this," she said. He could hear the frustration in her voice. But she didn't turn and walk back to the school, so he continued to hope. "I'll ask questions and you answer."

He braced himself. "I'm game if you are."

"First question," she said. "Why haven't you spoken to me in four years?"

He took another deep breath of humid air. "You

know when you screw up, and there's this window of time in which you could fix it...but that time passes, and then you feel like it's too late to fix it...and then more time passes...and then it's been four years?"

"Hmm." Merri pursed her lips. "I'm not sure I know exactly, but I suppose I can guess. Second question: Have you really been at all the Midwinter Masquerades?"

"Yes." Every nerve in his body was on fire. He was terrified of screwing this up again.

"And you continued not to speak to me because...you thought it was too late to fix things?" Those kaleidoscope eyes pierced his soul.

"Once upon time, when I was a clueless eighteen-year-old idiot, I hurt the one person who meant the most to me, and she walked out of the room. Little did I know, she was actually walking out of *my life*." Bright looked up at the sky through the bare trees and silently asked whatever stars were out there to help him get through this. "I was worried that however I tried to make it up to you, I would just end up causing you more pain. And I did, didn't I? I saw you wince at the fountain when you saw me, and again before we entered the gym. Being forced to touch me on the dance floor hurt you. And I'm hurting you now just by making you stand here."

Her gaze dropped to the ground. "Yes," she whispered to her shoes. "It shouldn't, but it does."

"Merri," he said. "I want to apologize."

"You did," she said without looking at him. "I remember quite clearly. The last words you said to me were 'I'm sorry.' I'll admit, it was cold comfort when I had to throw away the dress I'd just spent a huge chunk of my savings on."

"My most magnificent Mad Merri, I will buy you a dozen new dresses, every color of the rainbow, every year for the rest of your life to make up for that night. But that's not what I need you to forgive me for."

"You don't need my forgiveness, Polaris."

Polaris. She'd called him that the night she walked away. He never thought someone could hate their given name as much as he did right now.

"But I do," he said. "I need you to forgive me for taking so long to realize just how deeply I was in love with you."

"What?" She looked up at him again. He wanted to stare into those magical eyes for the rest of his life.

"I was so thickheaded that I didn't realize it until that moment. What did I know of love? I had nothing to compare it to. My relationship to my family has always been one of obligation." The more he spoke, the faster the words came. "Taylor is a fine person, but she was never going to be enough for me. I was more in love with the idea of Taylor than Taylor herself."

Merri almost smiled at that. Maybe she'd realized the same thing about Samson.

"*You* were the only true friend I ever had," he said, "so I thought what I felt for you was only friendship. But when you stood there, covered in ink from that stupid balloon, staring at me with fire in those amazing blue eyes, I considered what it would be like to lose you. And it scared me to death."

"Why didn't you come after me then? Or ever?" Her heart was in her voice now. "Why didn't you do *anything*?"

"I was scared," he said. "I'm still scared. I know Bellamy is. Maybe you are, too. But I think maybe when a person is in love, they have to take some risks."

He spread his arms out wide.

"So here I am, risking it all. I love you, Merri. I'm sorry it's taken me this long to say, but I love you. I always have. And I don't want to live without you anymore. I want to show you Vermont in the fall. I want to show you Tasmania in the summer. I want to see South Carolina in the spring and have dinner with all twelve of your brothers and sisters. I want to dance with you and laugh with you and go on crazy adventures with you and not know what's happening tomorrow with you. Most importantly—I don't want to spend the rest of my life in silence."

Merri took off her mask. "There's only one problem."

Of course. Somehow, he had screwed this up, like he knew he would. "What's that?"

She stepped closer to him. So close. "We're going to have to be quiet for a few minutes longer." She touched his cheeks with her fingers, sliding them up to remove his mask, and then she kissed him.

He froze in shock, and in the moment it took for him to recover, she giggled against his lips. He cupped her face then and kissed her back with all the love he had inside himself. He felt her whimper in the back of her throat—or maybe it was him—and her body sank against his. He wrapped his arms around her tightly, so tightly, never wanting to let her go, and shielding her from the cold.

Cold?

Bright reluctantly broke off the kiss. The heatwave had ended. Snow had begun to fall on their heads and faces and all around them.

"My winter elf," Merri said, and then didn't say anything more as he kissed her again.

Somewhere on campus, alarm bells began to shriek.

This time, both of them laughed.

"What did you do now?" he asked.

Merri looked back over her shoulder. "Seriously, should we be worried?"

Bright refused to loosen his grip. "Only that our legacy might be overshadowed by Hubble. Oh, and maybe this." He took one of her hands in his and got down on one knee. "Merriaurum Grandiflora Larousse…"

"Yes?" she whispered. He felt her hand tremble ever so slightly in his own and it gave him courage. He *did* say he was risking it all. He *had* promised Bellamy he would spend the rest of his life making her sister happy. He just needed her to say that word again.

"Would you do me the honor of…helping me create an ice bridge so we can drive your brother's pumpkinmobile onto the roof of the library?"

Merri threw her head back and laughed that full laugh of a flower fairy, half earthy woman and half tinkling bells. She pulled Bright to his feet. She slipped his mask back down over his eyes, and then put hers on as well. "I thought you'd never ask."

They kissed again, there in the woods by the hollow tree, with the fat snow dancing waltzes all around them.

And so the Mad Bandits of Harmswood lived happily ever after.

THE END

The Sorcerer's Christmas Miracle

BY CATE DEAN

Tami Bennett came to Nocturne Falls to help her best friend, Lidia. It was supposed to be temporary—until she laid eyes on Jack Cross, sorcerer. As much as she wants to deny it, she's falling for him. When Lidia's werewolf fiancé is in trouble, Tami asks for Jack's help. She knows that if he succeeds, she could lose her only excuse to stay—and lose the one man who has come close to stealing her heart.

Christmas in Nocturne Falls was, in a word, magical.

Tami wandered along the streets, twilight creating an atmosphere that was fun and spooky at the same time.

She loved it here. She also knew that she should leave, before she became attached. Her life was in California, her job as senior librarian waiting for her. She had put off leaving long enough.

Pushing that out of her mind, she headed for Harrison Grey's store, The Grey Wolf. She was meeting Lidia there, probably for their last morning coffee and gossip session—

"Stop it," she muttered. "You had a good run. It's time to go home."

She shook off the depression that threatened at just the thought of leaving and pushed the door open. Her greeting lodged in her throat when she saw Lidia, on the floor and holding what looked like an unconscious Harrison.

"Tami—oh, thank heaven. Can you lock the door and flip the sign?"

After doing both as fast as she could, Tami ran across the store and knelt next to Lidia.

"What happened?" Up close, Harrison looked even worse—white, shaking, sweat running down his face.

"He's trying to shift. It's the full moon," Lidia whispered, her voice edged with tears. "This is the worst I've seen it since we've been together. He's losing control, Tami, and I can't help him."

"Are you okay here?"

Lidia nodded. "He's over the worst. With my magic almost at full strength again, I was able to cast a calming spell when I realized what was happening. Why?"

"I need to talk to someone who might be able to help."

"Not Jack Cross?" Tami could feel the heat flush her cheeks, at just the mention of his name. "I already talked to him about Harry. He said he couldn't help."

"I tend to be more persuasive than you, sweetie." She kissed Lidia's cheek and stood. "I'll go out the back. Take care of him, and I'll be back as soon as I can. Did you need anything?"

"He'll be hungry once he's—done."

"I'll swing by Howler's and get some burgers."

"Thanks, Tam."

"Anytime. Call me if anything happens, okay?"

"I will." Lidia had her head bent over Harrison before she finished saying the words.

After waiting another minute, to make sure Harrison wasn't going to start shifting again, Tami headed through the back room, sprinting down the alley as soon as she cleared the door.

Lidia was well on her way to regaining her power, but Tami wouldn't leave now—not until she knew that both of them would be all right. She headed straight for the only man who could help her make it happen.

Jack Cross had rented a small apartment near Delaney's Delectables, claiming he'd wanted to stay long enough to make sure the gargoyle, Eli Saunders, wouldn't relapse after he'd been poisoned.

Tami snorted, smiling when a couple of kids in superhero costumes stared at her. He had been just as blindsided as she had been when they'd met—and that same jolt of attraction drove through her every time she saw him. No one could have been more wrong for her, but she would use the attraction to get what she wanted.

The door to the building came into view, and Tami stopped, long enough to take a few deep breaths, and brace herself for the shock of need. Then she walked into the small foyer and straight to the apartment at the back of the hall. Before she could talk herself out of it, she knocked on the door.

"Go away." Jack's deep voice filtered through the door.

"I'm not here for me, Jack Cross." Liar, liar. "Can you open the door? Or do you want all your neighbors to hear what I have to say?"

The door jerked open, and Jack appeared, wearing jeans and a rumpled, white button down shirt. Tami cursed under her breath and ignored her pounding heart.

"What do you want, Bennett?" He'd called her that since their first electric meeting—probably to distance himself. From what she could see, it wasn't working.

"Can I come in?"

After he glared at her for an endless minute, with those intense hazel eyes, he stepped back, giving her just enough room to squeeze past him. She jumped when he slammed the door.

"What?" he said, his voice a low growl.

"I have a favor to ask."

His laughter made her fingers itch—and not with the need to touch him. More like the desire to strangle him. The man was infuriating.

"A favor? What makes you think I would even consider listening?"

"It's for Lidia Reston."

Jack's humor faded. "Is she all right?"

"Yeah. I didn't mean to panic you. She's doing great, actually." Jack had helped Lidia find the way back to her magic, and Tami would worship the ground he walked on for that. "I came to ask you to help her fiancé, Harrison."

"The werewolf who can't shift."

"Yeah—well, he tried to shift this morning, to greet the full moon. I need your help, Cross. He needs your help."

His eyes narrowed, and he crossed his arms. He might as well have said no; his body language shouted the word, loud and clear. "I can't help him."

"I thought you were the great and powerful sorcerer."

His nostrils flared, and Tami knew she'd hit her mark. "I have skills, and power, but I can't change the fundamental nature of a supernatural."

"But it has nothing to do with his nature. You don't know what happened to him?" She was surprised that Lidia hadn't said anything during one of her sessions with Jack. He shook his head. "He was stabbed by a rival with a silver knife, in the middle of a shift."

Jack frowned, studying her. "It was an injury? Even with a silver knife as the weapon, he shouldn't have lost his ability to shift."

"Gotcha." Tami smiled. "You're interested now, aren't you?"

His frown reappeared. He pushed off the door and stalked past her. "Stop doing that."

"Doing what?"

He moved so fast she didn't have time to react.

Between one second and the next, she found herself pinned to the wall, Jack towering over her. "Reading me like my thoughts are written on my face. You're a mortal."

"What does that have to do with anything?" Tami wanted to sound angry, but her voice betrayed her, rasping out of her throat.

"No mortal has ever—" He cut himself off, staring at her. "Why are you here?"

"I just told you. Harrison needs your help." She let out a sigh when he raised his eyebrows. "I want to know that both Lidia and Harrison are okay, but I have to leave soon, before—"

Before I fall in love with you and want to stay here.

"Tami." Jack's quiet voice jerked here back. He held her arm, worry darkening his eyes. "Come and sit."

"I'm okay."

"You're whiter than the ghosts running around town." He smiled, the half-smile that always left her heart pounding. "Sit. Please."

The please startled her, and she let him lead her to the surprisingly nice sofa. If she looked past the hideous green and orange plaid—which wasn't easy—it looked almost new, and was pretty comfy.

Tami didn't realize how much that one thought had affected her, until she was off her feet. Jack sat next to her, his proximity making it even harder to catch her breath.

"What makes you think I can help Harrison?"

"Your reputation." She managed to take in a head-clearing breath. "The fact that you helped Eli. Your kind of spectacular display last month when you ran off a banished dragon."

He raised his eyebrows. "How do you know about the dragon?"

"I was in the park when it happened."

"Right." With a sigh, he leaned back. He looked tired, the lines bracketing his mouth deeper than Tami remembered. Not that she'd noticed. "I haven't approached the subject with Lidia, but now that I know how Harrison lost his ability to shift..." His voice faded, and he studied her.

"Don't leave me in suspense, Cross. Can you help him get his mojo back?"

"Mojo." His lips twitched. "Well, there are limitations to what I can do—"

Tami pressed one hand over her heart. "Wait—limitations? You?"

"Is that sarcasm?"

"Got it on the first try." She winked at him. He was so serious that teasing him was too much of a temptation. "Sorry, I can't seem to help myself around you."

"I am honored."

She burst out laughing. "You're getting the hang of it." When he didn't even crack a smile, she cleared her throat. "Look—Harrison needs help. Lidia said he's getting worse, losing control and trying to shift every full moon. Can you talk to him, see if you can do something?" She hated begging, but for her best friend, she'd beg.

"You want me to speak to him now."

"Now would be good. You might be able to get some vibes from him, since he just tried to shift."

"I will go and speak with him, see if I can detect any vibes. No promises," he said, when she opened her mouth to thank him. "I have never come across a situation like Harrison's before now. I can't guarantee that I will be able to do anything for him."

"But you'll try. That's all I need to know right now, Cross." She stood, moving to the door. "Just do me a favor—don't make promises you can't keep. I don't want to get Lidia's hopes up, then have you not be able to help him."

"I would never—" He cut himself off. "You do poke at my temper, Bennett, and I have a hard time figuring out why."

"Dense," she muttered, and started to open the door.

Jack caught her around the waist and pulled her back until she was plastered against his chest. His deep voice sent need coiling through her. "I am hardly dense, you beautiful, exasperating woman." His breath heated her throat, his arm tightening when she tried to pull away. "You are a distraction I never planned for, and don't want."

"Then let me go." She gasped when he turned her to face him, so much heat in his eyes she should have become a pile of ashes, right there.

"I want to, Bennett." He cradled the back of her head, leaning in until his breath caressed her lips. "But my heart won't let me."

He kissed her, his assault on her senses a slow, sexy build. By the time he finally freed her, she had both hands twisted into the front of his shirt, her knees like rubber.

"Why did you—" She cleared her throat, her voice husky. "What was that?"

"I thought I was the one in the room with the density problem." He leaned in. "I kissed you, Bennett."

"Stop it." *Don't stop, ever.*

"Which is it, Bennett?" The half-smile was back, sexy and infuriating. Then what he said hit her.

"Did you—can you read my mind? The answer better be no, sorcerer."

"I don't need to when you fling your thoughts at me." His half-smile turned to a full smile, and she knew she was in trouble. "The answer is no, Bennett. I can't read minds—but I can hear the thoughts of others I am—damn it." He let her go and backed across the room.

"Others you're what?"

His nostrils flared, anger sparking off him. "Connected to. Stop smiling at me."

"Sorry." She wasn't sorry, at all. But she figured he probably knew that, too. "Will you go?"

"As soon as you leave."

"Afraid to be seen on the street with me?"

He almost snarled, but he obviously took it as a challenge, because he grabbed a worn leather bag off the counter that separated the kitchen from the living area, and slung it over his shoulder.

"Very little scares me, Bennett." He stalked over to the door and yanked it open. "After you."

She walked past him, relieved that he'd agreed to at least talk to Harrison—and so aware of him she found it hard to focus.

Leaving Nocturne Falls was probably the smartest thing she could do. Jack Cross turned her brain to mush—which wasn't the ideal state for a librarian.

Jack strode along the street, unable to ignore the

stares of the tourists—or the presence of the woman beside him.

Tami Bennett had become an unwanted distraction, a reason to leave. Yet he stayed, aware that he could run into her every time he left the safety of his apartment. She loved to wander, she had told him after nearly running into him outside Café Claude.

Her penchant for wandering seemed to place her directly in his path on a regular basis.

Putting his attraction for her aside, he had found, to his surprise, that he was enjoying his time in Nocturne Falls.

Being able to live openly as a sorcerer, outside of the enclave he had created for himself and sorcerers like him, gave him a sense of freedom he never expected to find in small town America. Before Sophie Mead had barged into his life again, he had been toying with the idea of moving to England. Eccentricities of all kinds were generally accepted there.

Tami's laughter pulled him out of his thoughts. He smiled when he saw the reason; three children dancing around one of the vampires, begging him to transform into a bat. He did not look amused.

"I love it here," Tami said, her voice wistful. Jack glanced at her, swallowing when he saw the green aura surrounding her, shot through with the grey of sadness. He'd seen it since the moment he touched her, and the reason had kept him from pursuing her. "Cross?"

"Here." He met her eyes, another punch to his heart. They were the rich, deep blue of the lake near his childhood home.

"I need to stop in at Howler's and grab some food."

"I will accompany you."

She grinned at him, and he wanted to kiss her.

Fool.

"I'm honored. We can get lunch for us, if you want."

"I would like that." He realized he had skipped breakfast, intent on finishing the ancient book he'd found during his last trip to New York.

They walked into the bar, and Jack unconsciously created a thin, invisible wall. He had learned at a young age that his sensitivity to emotion could cripple his power—a disability that had worsened after a deadly mistake in his youth. Creating a barrier before he came in contact with any type of crowd gave him protection, and control.

Control was paramount to a sorcerer.

"Okay, Cross?" Tami touched his arm.

He stared down at her hand. She shouldn't have been able to reach in past his wall, not without retaliation. When he finally understood why, she had let him go and moved to the bar to place her order.

Jack had already let her in.

He would never be able to shield himself from her. Not completely.

The realization nearly had him bolting. Instead, he forced down the need to run, and waited for her near the door. Emotions swirled around him, some pushing through the cracks in his wall. Happiness warred with resentment, joy, need, envy, and the raw emotion of the supernaturals.

"Jack."

He jerked at Tami's voice. Judging from her face, she had spoken his name more than once.

"Sorry."

"What's wrong?"

He shook his head, and led the way out of the bar. The cold breeze wrapped around him, helped cleanse the emotions still clinging to his skin.

"Talk to me, Cross."

"I am sensitive to emotion." He refused to look at her, walking just ahead of her, his gaze focused on the tourists. "Enclosed spaces amplify the sensitivity."

"Why didn't you say something? Jack." She grabbed his arm, forcing him to stop. When she stepped in front of him, he finally looked at her. The concern that rolled off her surprised him. "Why didn't you tell me?"

"A sorcerer does not— "

"Stop spouting that claptrap."

He raised his eyebrows. "It is hardly—

"Talk like a normal person, not a textbook."

With a sigh, he rubbed his forehead, fighting the headache that threatened. "Can we walk while I do?"

"You bet." She moved to his side, juggling the large brown bag so she could take his hand. "Talk."

Her touch distracted him, but he didn't want her to let go. He twined their fingers together, then took the bag from her, fighting a smile when her eyes widened. The breeze lifted her sun-streaked brown hair off her shoulders. Long, silky hair he had wanted to touch since the moment they met.

"Control is paramount, especially when a sorcerer begins training. The more powerful we are, the more chance there is that we can kill someone if we lose control."

"Is that why you were hiding out, holed up with a bunch of people like you?"

"That is part of it." He let out his breath, and continued, sure that he was about to push her away for good with his next words. "I killed, Tami."

Her silence left him cold, and he started to free his hand. She tightened her grip.

"Keep going."

He glanced at her, expecting disgust. Instead, he found sympathy in her eyes, the warmth of it finally reaching him—and he realized the cold he felt was his own barrier. Creating it had become such an unconscious act, an almost daily habit living here, that he hadn't noticed its presence.

"I was nineteen, and proud. I was also arrogant, and so sure of my power, I didn't think rules and restrictions applied to me." He sighed, remembering the impetuous, foolish boy he had been. "One of the other boys in the coven challenged me, and I accepted."

"A duel?"

"Of power. It was a way to show off, to gain allies. There were rules, but we both agreed to duel without them." Jack swallowed, staring straight ahead. "I lost control, and the spell I threw killed him."

"Oh, Jack. I'm so sorry."

It was easier when she called him Cross.

"I was punished, my power shackled for five years."

"What?"

"Trust me, it was better than the alternative, which would have been my immediate death. There are consequences for losing control, and they have to apply to everyone."

"Okay. So that was like sorcerer prison."

He smiled. "Sort of."

"What happened after the five years was up?"

"I left, and joined another coven. One led by Sophie's father. When I openly disagreed with his methods, he tried to have me killed. I left and formed my own enclave. One where sorcerers could practice in peace, learn from each other, and find a place to live without persecution."

"Do you miss it?"

"Sometimes. But I've locked myself away too long. Spending time here has shown me that the world has changed, that we aren't the freaks we used to be."

"You wouldn't even stand out in LA." She smiled at him, and squeezed his hand.

His heart responded, and before he could stop himself, he pulled her in and kissed her, right in the middle of the sidewalk, in front of anyone who might be walking by.

"Wow." Tami whispered against his lips, then leaned back enough to meet his eyes. "Just when I think I've got you figured out, Jack Cross, you go and surprise me again." She kissed him, hot and fast, then stepped back and led him around the corner. He followed, more than a little dazed by her passion. "We're almost to the store. I'm going to take you in through the back, since Lidia had me lock up the front."

Power hummed through Jack, clearing his head, and he nodded, letting her go. He started building a stronger wall than he had used at the bar, since he would need more protection between him and the werewolf's pain.

Jack followed Tami through the back room, halting just inside the store. Pain slammed into him; old pain, overlaid with desperation and fear. It took all his control to keep that pain from shattering his barrier.

"Jack." Tami stood in front of him, like a beacon of light.

"All right," he muttered, handing her the bag before he stepped around her.

Harrison Grey knelt in the middle of the floor, Lidia next to him. She whispered as she gently rubbed his back, and Jack felt another wave of pain roll off Harrison.

"Hi, Jack," Lidia said, and held out one hand to him. Her fingers shook, and he wanted to comfort her, but any contact could weaken his already cracked barrier. Harrison's pain was so much stronger than he had anticipated. "Thank you for coming."

"I don't know what I can do, Lidia, but I will try."

"No one can help." Harrison's deep, pain-scratched voice brushed over Jack's skin. "I've spent my life trying to break free."

"Before you dismiss me, I would like to examine you."

With a sigh, Harrison nodded.

Jack scanned him, with both his gaze and his power. He skipped over the ring on Harrison's right hand, then came back to it when a sense of discord snagged at him.

"Where did you get the ring?"

"I've had it for years. I used it as a focus when I started trying to shift on the full moon."

"Take it off."

Harrison raised his eyebrows. "Why?"

"I sense something." Jack was not used to anyone questioning him, or his power. "The ring may be working against you."

"It was a gift, from my father. He wouldn't give me anything that would hurt me."

"And he may not have known there was anything wrong, when he gave you the ring." Jack held out his hand. "Take it off."

"I have more control with it." Harrison pushed to his feet, Lidia following him up. "Thanks for the consult."

Jack stood, not wanting to let go. There was something off with the ring, but he wouldn't know what until he could touch it. "I was asked to help you. Please let me do so."

"And I said thanks, which was a nice way of saying get out."

"Harry!" Lidia smacked his chest. "He's trying to help."

"And he helped you, love." Harrison framed her face, the love between them so bright that Jack wanted to turn away. "But this is different. I'm crippled, and no sorcery can heal that."

"You won't know unless you give him a chance."

Harrison shook his head. "I want to go home, get some sleep." He kissed Lidia, then let her go and headed for the back room. "I'll meet you at the car."

Lidia watched him grab the bag of food and walk into the back room, then she turned to Jack. "I'm so sorry. He can be stubborn—mule-headed stubborn. I'll talk to him." She reached out her hand, and Jack took it this time, letting his barrier fade. "Please, don't give up on him."

"It will take more than a simple 'get out' to chase me away."

"Thank you." She hugged him, then turned to Tami. "Thank you, for bringing Jack here. And for the food."

His and Tami's meal had just walked out with Harrison, but Jack kept that to himself.

"Call if he changes his mind," Tami said, hugging Lidia. "Or if you need any help."

"I will. You can go out the back—I'll make sure the

lock is set to engage when you close the door. Love you, Tam."

"Love you back, sweetie." She watched Lidia run across the store before she turned to Jack. "Sorry. I guess that was a giant waste of your time."

"Maybe not."

Tami raised an eyebrow. "What did I miss?"

"His ring. I believe it may be the reason he started shifting again."

Tami didn't say anything on the way back to Jack's apartment, but she had questions.

Oh, did she have questions—and she wasn't leaving until she got answers. By the time Jack unlocked the door to his apartment, she was ready to burst.

He blew every question out of her head when he yanked her inside, slammed the door, and kissed her like he was dying and she was his salvation.

She was happy to oblige.

By the time they came up for air, Tami was shaking, and Jack didn't look all that steady.

"Sofa," he muttered, and stumbled across the room, taking her with him. He pulled her down and tucked her into his side, his face buried in her hair. "I need to catch my breath."

She didn't like the way he sounded.

"Jack." When he didn't answer, Tami leaned back until she could see his face. Pain deepened the lines around his mouth, darkened his hazel eyes. "Headache?"

"Yes."

"My mom used to get them all the time. Can I help?"
He hesitated, then nodded, flinching at the movement.
"Okay." She moved to the other end of the sofa, and patted her lap. "Lay down, your head here."

After hesitating long enough that Tami thought he was going to refuse, he finally stretched out on the sofa, resting his head on her thigh. He closed his eyes when she gently pressed her fingers against his temples, massaging in a slow, clockwise motion.

His soft groan told her that it was working. Her mom used to give the same sound of relief. When he relaxed against her, the rock hard muscles in his shoulders easing, she moved her fingers up, sliding them into his hair.

He opened his eyes. "What are you doing?"

"Giving you the full treatment, sorcerer. Relax—it won't hurt."

"You don't need—"

"I do. I talked you into helping him. The aftermath is on me. Now, relax, and let me help you."

He swallowed, and closed his eyes.

Tami understood. Even as she gently massaged his scalp, the feel of her fingers sliding through his thick, dark hair left her a little breathless. She took advantage of his proximity—and the fact that he wasn't trying to walk away from her. He'd been doing that since their first meeting, so she had never been able to study him like this, without interruption.

Jack Cross was an incredibly good looking man, with high, sharp cheekbones, long, dark lashes that she'd kill for, and the intense, intelligent hazel eyes that studied her like she was a unique specimen he'd never seen before.

She smiled at that thought, and moved slowly back to his temples, finishing with a few gentle circles.

"Okay," she whispered, not wanting to wake him in case he had nodded off. Her mom had, more than once.

But Jack hadn't; he proved that by reaching up, twisting his fingers into the front of her shirt, and tugging until they were almost nose to nose.

"Thank you, Bennett."

She smiled. "You're welcome, Cross."

Still smiling, she closed the space between them, kissing him upside down.

It was—interesting, and not nearly as sexy as it looked on screen. When she started to pull away, Jack's hand held her in place. She gave in to the kiss, aware that leaving him was going to hurt more than leaving Nocturne Falls. Much more than she thought it would.

Jack finally freed her, both of them fighting for breath. He sat, taking her hand as he stood. Her heart skipped when he headed for the short hall—and his bedroom.

"Jack—"

"I didn't plan for you, Bennett." He cradled her cheek. "But my heart won't allow me to let you go."

"I—what am I supposed to say to that?"

He kissed her forehead. "Say yes, Bennett, to staying with me. Until you have to leave, I want you here."

"Who are you, and where did you stash Cross?" His laughter warmed her, and helped calm her jumping nerves.

"Spending time with Lidia and Harrison forced me to face my own feelings about you."

"Oh? Like what?"

"The fact that I have them, for one."

"Took you long enough."

His laughter rumbled through her. "You are a constant surprise."

"I don't like to be predictable. I also don't do this on first dates."

"This isn't a date."

"Well—never mind, then." She stood on tiptoe until their lips met. "I accept your offer, Jack Cross."

He kissed her until her head spun, then swept her up into his arms, leaving her breathless as he carried her to the bedroom.

They were devouring cold pizza in the middle of Jack's obscenely huge bed when Tami's cell rang.

She froze, a slice halfway to her mouth. "That would be Lidia—or my mom."

She slid off the bed and picked up her jeans, digging her cell phone out of the back pocket.

Please don't let it be Mom.

Their bitter fight about Tami heading here to help Lidia still hurt, and she really didn't want yet another rehash. Relief had her smiling when she saw Lidia's name on the screen. "Hey, Lidia."

"Tami—are you still with Jack Cross?" Panic shot through her voice.

"Yeah. What's wrong, Lidia?"

"Harry's—trying to shift again."

Tami could hear the ugly, pained snarls in the background.

"Where are you?"

"My house."

"We're on our way. Don't try to stop him, Lidia, you hear me? He'll hurt you."

"Just hurry. Please."

Jack was already on his feet, dressing. "How bad?"

"I could hear Harrison, sounding really wolf-like." She pulled on her jeans, and finished buttoning her shirt.

She was still adjusting her second sneaker when Jack grabbed her hand.

He paused long enough to pick up his leather bag and sling it over his shoulder, then strode to the door, almost dragging her after him. When they hit the sidewalk, he started to run. Christmas décor and brightly dressed locals blurred as Tami ran past them, focused on not tripping, or getting left behind because she slowed Jack down.

Thankfully, Lidia lived on Cauldron Lane, one of the side streets near the center of town. It took less than five minutes for them to reach her front door. Jack opened it without knocking, and sprinted toward the kitchen in the back.

Tami caught up with him in time to see him approaching Harrison, who had partially shifted. His left side was trying to become a wolf, while his right stayed human. Tami moved to Lidia's side and gently backed her toward the doorway. Just in case.

"He's never changed this much," Lidia whispered, leaning against Tami. "I can feel his pain, Tam."

"Jack will help him, sweetie."

Jack stood in clawing distance, which terrified her. But he looked calm, almost serene. "I'm going to take the ring off, Harrison, and prove to you—

"No." His snarling denial raised the hairs on Tami's arms. "It keeps me from harming Lidia."

"Who told you that?"

Harrison frowned—or tried to. "The ring—"

"I believe the ring has a spell in the stone. One that has finally been released, and is causing your shifts. Please let me help you."

Harrison glared at him.

"Harry, please." Lidia's choked voice snapped his head around. "We need help."

Harrison closed his eyes, and Tami's throat tightened when she saw the tears sliding down his cheek. He hunched his shoulders, and held his human right hand out to Jack.

"I will remove the ring," Jack said. "Then I can remove any—"

With a roar, Harrison swiped his clawed left hand.

"Jack!" Tami's desperate shout soundtracked his retreat.

He almost made it.

She screamed when Harrison's claws dug into Jack's left arm, hauling him up and forward—right into Harrison's grip.

Instead of trying to free himself, Jack leaned in, and Tami understood why. He was still trying to get the ring off Harrison's finger.

"Harry—let him go!" Lidia yanked out of Tami's grip and marched forward. "I mean it. You let him go right now!"

Harrison stopped growling and lifted his head, blinking at Lidia. Jack took advantage of the distraction, dropping to his knees with a pained shout. Sweat slicked his face, but his hand stayed steady as he pulled the ring off Harrison's finger—and jerked free of the claws imbedded in his left arm.

Forgetting everything but her need to get him away from the werewolf, Tami darted forward and wrapped her arms around Jack's waist, jerking him back. They both hit the floor, hard.

Jack moaned, gripping his left arm.

"Let me see," Tami whispered. She pushed up to her knees and leaned over him, swallowing when she saw the blood soaking his sleeve. "Hold still."

"Worse than it looks," he muttered. "Help me sit."

"I'm sorry." Harrison's raw voice sounded completely human. "I'm so sorry, Jack." He appeared in front of them, his clothes torn and bloody, his face paler than Jack's. "I should have believed you."

Jack opened his right hand, revealing the ring. Shaped like the profile of a wolf, the single stone that had been the wolf's eye was cracked now, smoke curling out of it. Jack bent over his hand and muttered a few words Tami didn't understand.

The smoke dissipated, and the stone broke, falling out of the ring. It had been a dark gold topaz, but now it looked like it had been pulled out of a fire.

Lidia reached for the stone, her hand freezing inches above it. "A changeling spell." She stared at Jack. "How did you know?"

"Negative spells are always marked with a smear. Not many can sense it, but I've always been able to. The spell is also recent." He looked at Harrison. "How long have you been shifting?"

"This is the third full moon." He sighed, his big hand enveloping Lidia's shoulder. "I should have listened to Lidia after the first time, but I thought it might have been a fluke."

"What happened three months ago?"

Harrison started to shake his head, but Lidia touched his wrist. "You ran into Jared. He said he wanted to apologize, remember?"

"Right." Harrison ran one hand through his sweat-damp hair. "We shook hands, and I felt—I thought I had imagined it at the time, but I thought I felt what I could only describe as hate."

Jack studied Harrison. "This Jared is the shifter who injured you."

"Yes. His apology seemed suspicious at the time, but he told me he was trying to make amends, change his life." Harrison shook his head. "I believed him."

"Harry was also sick for two days after that meeting." Lidia took his right hand, her thumb rubbing his ring finger.

Jack frowned. "Was this Jared wearing a ring?"

"He was. The handshake was awkward, now that I think about it. Almost like he wanted our rings to connect."

"And transfer the spell." Jack cradled his injured arm. "He paid a great deal for that spell, and more for the ability to pass it to another object."

Lidia leaned against Harrison. "I really thought he'd leave you alone, after what happened in the alley."

Tami raised her eyebrows. "Elaborate."

Smiling, Lidia looked up at Harrison. "He pounded Jared, trying to get to me."

Normally, Tami would have rolled her eyes at the sappy look Lidia had on her face. But right now, she understood, since she was on the edge of dragging Jack straight to Dr. Sophie Mead.

"I will be fine, Bennett." His deep, quiet voice

brushed over her skin. "Sorcerers heal more quickly than mortals."

"Yeah, if you don't bleed to death first." She turned to Lidia. "Do you have a dishtowel you don't mind losing?"

"Oh—I'm so sorry." She raised her hand and snapped her fingers. The dishtowel hanging next to the window over the sink sailed across the kitchen, landing in her open hand. "Here you go."

"Thanks." Tami folded it, pressing the makeshift bandage against Jack's arm, ignoring his protest that he was fine. "I never thought I'd see that again."

"Me, either. It feels amazing." She smiled at Jack. "Thank you, for everything you've done."

"I'm not finished." He turned to Harrison. "Do you want to shift?"

"I—yes. More than almost anything." He gripped Lidia's hand. "Can you—would you be able to help me?"

"Was your block because of an injury? Tami told me," he said, when Harrison frowned at him. "I need the truth, or I can't help you."

"Yes. Jared stabbed me with a silver knife while I was shifting."

"How old were you?"

"Twelve."

Jack frowned. "Your family never tried to reverse what happened?"

"They couldn't. The poison from the knife—

"Had nothing to do with your inability to shift." Both Harrison and Lidia stared at him. "Do you feel pain, when you try to shift?"

Swallowing, Harrison nodded. "The same hot, tearing

pain I felt when I was stabbed. But it's amplified, so much that I can't breathe, can't think."

"I believe I can help you. It will mean going back to where the injury occurred."

"I can do that."

"Harry." Lidia cradled his cheek. "Are you sure?"

"I am not complete, love. I want to be that, for you, for our family. Whatever it takes, I'm willing to try."

She kissed him, and Tami fought to keep from crying. Her best friend's relationship with the werewolf had always bordered on sappy, but their love for each other had been obvious from the beginning.

Jack cleared his throat. "I will need a few supplies from my apartment. Can you meet me there tonight?"

"Tonight?" Lidia frowned. "He just— "

"Yes," Harrison said. "Name the time, and we'll be there."

"Seven." Jack started to stand, and cursed under his breath. "Bennett, can you give me a hand?"

"Sure." She clapped her hands, grinning at his raised eyebrows. "Sorry—couldn't resist such an opening." She helped him to his feet, keeping her arm around his waist when he swayed. "I think we'll be needing a ride."

Jack shook his head. "I will be— "

"Face down on the sidewalk."

"I'll drive you," Lidia said. She kissed Harrison, then moved to Jack's other side. "Go upstairs, Harry. I want you to rest, or you don't get to go tonight."

"Only if you join me."

"Fine. Now go." Lidia pointed to the doorway, waiting until Harrison left before she spoke again. "Thank you, Jack, for offering to help him. I don't think it's a good idea."

"It is not your decision to make, Lidia." His voice was gentle, but she still flinched.

"If it doesn't work—he already thinks he's half a man because of this. I can't—I won't have him lose what ground we've gained the last few months."

"If I can interrupt," Tami said. "I think *not* trying will hurt him more, Lidia. Knowing that he can't shift, if what Jack wants to try doesn't work, will be much easier to live with than wondering for the rest of his life."

"You're right." She sighed, then raised her voice. "If you're eavesdropping, Harrison Grey, you won't get dessert for the rest of the year."

Tami laughed when the sound of feet on the hardwood floor echoed through the hall—heading away from them. "How did you know?"

"He agreed much too fast. And dessert is me." She winked at Tami, laughing when Jack coughed, obviously uncomfortable. "Let's get you home, Jack."

After pretending to lie down, Jack waited until Tami left before he rose, heading for the hidden compartment he had constructed in the back of the closet.

His left arm still ached, and would for several weeks, but a quick glance showed him the raw scars already forming on his bicep. He would mix a drink to help with the blood loss before Tami returned.

As he whispered the unlocking spell, he let his mind drift, and it inevitably led to her.

She was the woman he never thought to find. The woman he never wanted to find.

His life was easier without the complication of a relationship, and the messy emotions that always came with it. Tami was different, because she didn't demand anything from him. She could have wrapped him around her finger with a few words, but she had clearly been as hesitant about their attraction as he had been.

Spending today with her drove home the fact he had been avoiding all these months. He was in love with her.

"Fool," he muttered, and yanked the door open.

Gathering what he needed for tonight focused him on the moment. He would use his amulet, to help counter the weakness from his recent injury. Because it had been delivered by a supernatural, the wound affected both his body and his power.

The others didn't need to know. Since they had never seen him work his power, they would assume he always used his amulet. One of his fellow sorcerers would have known in a heartbeat that something was wrong; he hadn't needed a focus for years.

He knew Tami was at his door before she knocked.

Cursing, he slid the chain holding the amulet over his head and gathered up his supplies, heading for the living room. She would get impatient if he didn't answer right away.

The knob started turning as he reached for it. He yanked the door open before she could finish turning it, and met her startled gaze.

"Sorry," she said. "I thought you might still be asleep."

"I was—in the bedroom." He almost told her about the compartment. Like he could trust her with the information.

"And not asleep." She brushed his cheek. "You look terrible." Her smile softened the words.

"Bennett." He didn't know what to say to her, how to end something that meant so much to him.

She seemed to sense his thoughts, and lowered her hand, breaking contact.

"No need to let me down easy. I have to leave soon, anyway." She managed to keep smiling, but Jack felt the pain behind it. The ache that he had caused, by caring for her. He blocked that ache, before it threatened to burrow deeper. "Stop looking at me like that, Cross. You have a werewolf to heal."

"Right." He reached up to rub his forehead, and sucked in his breath when hot pain shot through his left arm.

"That arm needs to be looked at." She cupped his elbow and gently eased his arm down. "I know you're the great and powerful, but even your kind gets banged up every once in a while."

"My arm is fine, Bennett." He couldn't stop the smile at her teasing. "Are you ready? Lidia and Harrison will be here any time."

"Knowing Harrison's almost obsessive need to be early, they're probably walking up to the building right now."

Jack lowered the wall he'd thrown up, just enough to reach past the door. "You were wrong." He leaned in, unable to keep from kissing her again. Just once more. "They're inside already."

"Oh." She sounded breathless, her blue eyes dark. Before he gave into temptation and kissed her again, Lidia and Harrison appeared. Tami headed straight for Lidia, taking her hand. "How are you?"

"Scared. I'm so glad you're here."

"Me, too."

Jack turned away from them, adding the supplies to his bag before he carefully settled the strap on his right shoulder. The amulet warmed against his skin; he muttered a spell, letting the quartz draw his words in, hold the spell until he needed it.

By the time Tami turned to face him, he was ready. He nodded, and she took a deep breath.

"Okay, she said, smiling at Lidia and Harrison. "Let's go do this."

Tami had never ventured outside of Nocturne Falls, and the forest surprised her.

It was thick, dense, and almost spookier than the town that celebrated Halloween every day. She fought the desire to turn around and run back to town.

Like he knew, Jack took her hand. His warm fingers twined with hers, his touch soothing. She knew that their time together was short, so she planned to enjoy every second—even when they were walking through a forest that could have been in the opening scene of a horror movie.

Harrison stopped in a clearing, his face so pale he almost glowed in the moonlight. Lidia gripped his hand, and Tami had to constantly force down the need to jerk her friend away, in case he started to shift.

So far, he stayed human—which proved Jack's theory about the ring.

Jack freed her hand and stepped forward. "Is this the place, Harrison?"

"Yes." He took a shaky breath. "I haven't been back since that night."

"I understand this is difficult. Stand away from him, Lidia. I want you and Tami to stay at the edge of the clearing." He met Tami's eyes. "No matter what happens, make sure she stays."

"I will." She grabbed Lidia's arm and pulled her away from Harrison, dragging her before they got halfway across the clearing. "Lidia—"

"I have to stay with him—let me go—"

Tami used the advantage of her height and picked her friend up, carrying her to the trees. "Stop, Lidia, please. He wants to keep us safe—all of us."

Lidia let out a choked sob, and sagged against her. "I can't lose him, Tam. I just can't."

"I won't let that happen, sweetie." She gathered Lidia into her arms. "I trust Jack, and I know you do."

Rubbing Lidia's back, Tami looked over at Jack. He stood next to Harrison, handing him what looked like a necklace.

"Put this on," Jack said. When Harrison hesitated, he crossed his arms. "I need you to trust me, or this won't work."

"I do." Harrison took a shaky breath, and slipped the chain over his head. An amulet rested against his chest, with a clear, round quartz in the center of the triangle. "It feels warm."

"It's supposed to. Where was your wound?"

"My right shoulder." He laid his hand on his shoulder, and looked at Jack. "Tell me what to do."

"Defend yourself."

Jack pulled a knife out of his bag and raised his arm.

"No!" Lidia leapt forward, fighting when Tami caught her. "Let me go!"

Tami wanted to, but she had to believe in Jack, believe that he wouldn't hurt Harrison—

She almost let go when Jack swept the knife down.

Harrison shouted, catching Jack's wrist. The blade—the silver blade—hovered inches from Harrison's shoulder.

"What are you doing, Cross?" she muttered—and grunted when Lidia's elbow hit her ribs. She tightened her grip, silently apologizing.

"Shift, Harrison." Jack's voice was perfectly calm, but Tami saw his arm trembling, sweat sliding down his face. "Shift, as you did that night."

"I didn't—" He twisted his grip, but Jack moved with him, the knife moving closer. "Why are you—doing this—"

"You're stuck, in that moment. You need—to move past it."

Jack let out a pained gasp when Harrison's grip twisted again, fiercely this time.

The amulet started to glow, and Tami felt the familiar tingle of magic brushing her skin.

"Harry!" Lidia fought Tami's grip. "What are you doing—"

Harrison's furious roar cut her off—right before he shifted.

Lidia froze, which was a good thing, because Tami was too busy staring to hold on to her.

She never thought about what the shifters she'd met over the past months did when they actually *shifted.* Watching Harrison change from man to wolf left her heart pounding, and terrified for the sorcerer trying to help him.

Harrison as wolf was huge, his claws so long and sharp they could pierce Jack like the knife he still held. Snarling, Harrison shook Jack's wrist. The knife flew out of his hand, leaving him defenseless.

Tami sprinted forward just as Harrison pinned Jack to the nearest tree, those long claws wrapped around his throat.

"Harrison—you have to let him go." She couldn't believe she was talking to a werewolf, never mind practically ordering him to give up his prey. "Look at yourself. You're a wolf—he helped you with that. Please, let him go now."

She stumbled back when he glared at her, tripping over the uneven ground. Lidia stepped in front of her, arms crossed, the familiar glow of her power surrounding her. That only happened when she was furious.

"Harry Grey. Let him go right now." He blinked, looking down at her. His wolf dwarfed her by almost two feet, but she didn't even flinch. "I mean it. He risked his life to help you—this is *not* how you repay him." When he didn't move, she marched forward and smacked his furred arm. "Harrison! Shift back right now."

He did, only a little shaky when he became human again. "Lidia—"

She threw herself at him, and he let go of Jack to catch her. Tami rushed past them, grabbing Jack's right arm as he slid down the tree.

"Hey," she said. He looked awful, bruises already marking his throat.

"Hey," he whispered, and flinched, reaching for his throat.

She stopped him. "That was the dumbest thing I've seen in a long time. What were you thinking?"

"He needed to—relive the attack, and win this time."

"So, you decided that you could play rival werewolf, after being injured just hours before."

"Well, yes."

She laid her forehead against his. "You're crazy, sorcerer. I like that about you."

"I like you," he whispered. "That could have—gone better."

"You think?" She eased back and met his eyes. "Can you stand?"

He nodded, killing her doubt by not only standing, but walking across the clearing, with only her arm for support. She wouldn't mention that he stumbled a few times before they reached the trees.

Lidia and Harrison walked ahead of them, her arms wrapped around his waist. For the first time, Tami noticed just how tiny she looked next to Harrison, but how strong she was for him, had always been, since they first met.

She wanted that kind of relationship, but she had to fall for a sorcerer. Her, a mortal, with one of the most powerful men in the South. It would never work.

"Time to go home," she muttered.

"What?" Jack's raw voice snapped her head up.

"I talk to myself. Didn't I tell you?"

He smiled, and her already aching heart cracked more. "I figured that out, in the bedroom."

Heat flushed her cheeks as she remembered their time together. It would have been easier to let him go, if he hadn't treated her with such care, with such—love.

Idiot—you already fell for him.

Tami and Jack were a block from his apartment when he stopped her.

"Cross—what's wrong?"

"You are."

She yanked her hand free and took a giant step back. *"What?"*

"I'm not doing this right." He scrubbed at his face, and met her eyes. He looked beyond exhausted, but those intense hazel eyes were sharp and clear. "I want you to wait until I'm finished. This isn't easy for me."

"Spit it out, Cross, before you fall over."

He sighed, and moved in until he could take her hand, studying their twined fingers. "There's a myth, in my family, passed down from one generation to the next. This myth claims that we always see the aura of the person meant for us."

"You don't believe it."

"I didn't—until I saw your aura, the first time we met."

"Oh." She swallowed. "That must have been a shock."

"One that has taken me until now to move past." He looked at her, his hazel eyes intense. "Here it is, quick and dirty. I love you, and if you will have me, I'd like to marry you."

It took a minute for his words sink in. Then *what* he said finally registered.

"That was the least romantic proposal I've ever heard." Tami pulled out of his grasp and crossed her arms, her heart pounding so hard she was sure he could hear it. "Try again."

With the half-smile that she had fallen for, he nodded, and lowered himself to one knee.

"Tami Bennett." Her eyes widened when he pulled a ring out of his pocket and held it up. "I'm afraid I can't let you go."

"How—when—Cross..." Tears stung her eyes, and she blinked, mortified when they slipped down her cheeks.

"I have been lost, Bennett, since the moment we met. My heart refuses to give you up, and for once, I agree. Please give me an answer, before I stiffen up and can't stand."

She let out a watery laugh, then sank to the sidewalk. "I wouldn't want that. You're sure, Cross? I'm the 'until death do us part' type, so there's no backing out of this."

"According to family myth, you were meant for me. I love you, and I never expected to care for a woman enough to say those words."

"I'm honored."

"That's not—sarcasm?"

"Not this time." She smiled. "You have so much to learn, Cross."

"As long as you will be the one teaching me." He took her hand, and slipped the gorgeous teardrop sapphire on her finger. "Say yes, Bennett, and I will stand at your side, no matter what trouble you find."

"I'm not the only trouble attracter, sorcerer."

He leaned in, until his breath warmed her lips. "Then we should have an interesting life."

"Yes, Cross. You know the answer is yes." She cradled his cheek. "I fell the second I saw you."

He smiled. "It's good to know I am not the only hopeless romantic kneeling on the sidewalk."

He was still smiling when he kissed her.

THE END

The Witch's Snow Globe Wish

BY LARISSA EMERALD

When a letter is delivered by mistake to clairvoyant witch Telia Kraft, she must return it to its rightful recipient, a handsome vampire neighbor, the very guy she had dated over the summer until he dropped her without a word. Jake Newburg is shocked to learn of his brother's upcoming Christmas wedding in Nocturne Falls and rashly asks Telia to accompany him to the event. For once, he needs to stop second-guessing himself.

1

The off-road course rose before him, two laps to go and he was neck and neck with the werewolf. Jake Newburg grinned to himself. Racing made him feel alive. His modified wheelchair allowed him to sit low and lean forward. His biceps strained as he pushed his hands against the wheels in rapid succession. Sweat streamed from his forehead. His tank-style shirt clung to his pecks and back. Throaty laughter peeled from his lips as his gain lengthened.

He was going to win this. Crossing the finish line felt exhilarating.

"Awesome race," Billy said, clapping his hand in Jakes and tugging the grasp until their wheelchairs clanked and their shoulders touched.

"It sure was, thanks," Jake replied.

They both reached for their water bottles to replenish the fluid they'd lost. "Are you going to the Steeple County race over New Years?" Billy asked.

"Yes. I've sent my race entry."

"Excellent. See you then."

Over by his Suburban, Jake hit the button to raise the

backend of the vehicle. He pushed his body from the wheelchair and stood, using the side of the SUV near the tail light for support until he could reach in the back for his cane. He loaded the racing chair and closed the electronic door. His arms felt a tad weak as he leaned onto the cane while he made his way to the driver's seat and slid behind the steering wheel.

Today had been an outstanding day. He started the engine and headed home.

If only he could feel this alive every day.

"Christmas is in three weeks, Mom. I'll come home a few days before, and we can shop then," Telia Kraft pinched her cell phone between her chin and shoulder as she slid the mail from the box, including a small package. The snow globe she'd ordered, a quick check of the label confirmed.

She lived on the outskirts of Nocturne Falls in a section of homes with large, wooded acre lots. It was a hefty trek back up the drive to the house. Her mom lectured about the importance of being together as a family over the holidays the entire way.

Back inside the house, Telia held the phone aloft and sighed heavily. Ever since her younger sister had left for college, mom had been going through empty nest syndrome. This meant she was pressured to fill in the missing togetherness time.

Her parents lived in Atlanta. Abigail attended the University of Georgia not far away. Holidays were a big deal for mom. And even though Telia was twenty-seven her mother insisted everyone be home for Christmas.

And honestly, she liked that.

She dropped the mail on top of the stack on the counter with the intention of getting to it when she paid bills on Thursday. The pile of letters and mailers didn't sit right, though, and spilled onto the floor. "Okay Mom, I promise we'll have enough time to make it a fabulous Christmas." She peered at the envelopes scattered at her feet. "Love you too."

After she pressed the end button, she opened the package with anticipation. As a child, she'd collected snow globes, but it had been a long time since she'd gotten a new one. A few weeks ago, she'd found a lovely Christmas scene that spoke to her in a Facebook ad and she'd ordered it.

Inside the box and styrofoam packaging she found another box of polished cherry wood. As soon as she lifted the top to reveal the snow globe, a tingle washed over her. The scene captured the perfect family setting, gathered around the fireplace, complete with a Christmas tree and dog.

Her heart melted with longing. "I wish..."

She swished the snow and watched it fall, and then set the snow globe in a safe place at the back of the counter. She would find the ideal spot to display it later.

With a sigh, she bent and picked up the fallen letters, repositioning them on the counter. As she went to set down the very last one, she froze glancing at the soft-white envelope. Her hand shook a little as a mixture of joyful and fretful emotions pulsed off the envelope into her fingers. Her witchy powers included picking up and reading information off of inanimate objects, such as how the person felt or thought about things in their life. And sometimes even from the person themselves, *reading them* as it were. She flipped the envelope over to see who it was from. No return label. Plus the missive was addressed to Jake Newburg, not her. He lived two doors down.

She knew because they had dated over the summer.

Sucking in her lower lip, her gaze skimmed the letter pile then moved to her computer where she needed to get back to work. As a virtual personal assistant, getting her client's marketing out in a timely manner was vital. More important than sorting through mail or delivering a wayward letter.

However the imprint on the missive nudged her to finish the job of delivering the letter. Her fingers pinched the envelope. It was meant for Jake. She should take it to him even though the idea of seeing him made her tummy anxious. They'd been introduced at the Red, White, and Boo by realtor Pandora Williams. At first, she thought they'd hit it off. He gave her good vibes. Until Jake had dropped her like a hot potato, although he'd never said why. He'd just stopped calling.

The muscles along her spine tensed. Delivering this note was going to be so awkward. But she really need to suck-it-up and get it done. She sensed the letter was some kind of invitation…and time sensitive. How many days had it sat on her counter, undelivered? The date stamp in the corner was smeared and illegible. So there was no way to tell.

She decided to take the letter to her neighbor right now and avoid further delay. With a sigh, she headed back out the door, feeling a tad pleased to gain control over her propensity for procrastination. She almost had a skip in her step as she walked the driveway to the street. Two doors down shouldn't take that long to achieve.

Plus it would count for her exercise.

With her job as a personal assistant, she was sedentary way too much.

She approached the drive, double checking the numbers on the envelope just the make sure it was Jake's. Yes, this was it. The house couldn't be seen from the street. Gravel crunched beneath her feet as she moved down the drive that curved around between thickly wooded trees. She inhaled the fragrant aroma of the forest. A few of the oaks appeared very old.

An air of isolation and remoteness wafted around her. My goodness, he had a long drive. She'd forgotten that.

Finally, she came upon the house constructed, or decorated, in flagstone siding. It had the appearance of an English cottage. She traipsed up the steps and knocked on the solid wood door.

The place was well kept. She liked that about Jake. Not a cobweb in sight. She craned her head back scrutinizing the corners near the ceiling. Actually, she had liked a lot of things about him. Too bad it hadn't worked out for them.

The door clicked open. She snapped her head down to discover the heartstoppingly attractive man standing before her. *Where was his wheel chair?*

"May I help you?" he asked, his brows lifted in recognition.

"Um, yeah. Your mail was delivered to my house by mistake." She handed it to him.

"Thanks. It was nice of you to drop it by." He glanced at the envelope.

Telia felt a pinch in her neck as she tilted her head back to gaze at his dark brown eyes. *Big mistake. The vampire was alluring and sexy as ever.* "It looks like an invitation."

"Yes."

"Aren't you going to open it?" It wasn't curiosity that made her nosy exactly, but more like the item spoke to her, making her need to nudge him in order to see the task complete.

He lifted one muscular shoulder and let it fall. "It's from my brother."

"I think he's getting married," she blurted out.

His brows shot up and a throaty laugh erupted from his lips. "Say what?" As if to verify if she was correct, he ripped open the envelope with clean manicured fingers. His jaw dropped. "Camille Nahuel and Nathaniel Newburg…Joyfully request your presence…In a celebration of our love." He stared at the ceiling. "Awe crap."

"This isn't good news?"

"They're getting married here, in Nocturne Falls. This weekend."

He didn't go into more detail, just pulled his lips to one side. Somehow it made him look even more handsome. She bit her lip. "I'm sorry you don't have more notice. The invitation may have sat on my counter a little longer than it should have."

As if coming out of his inner thoughts, he blinked. "Don't worry about it. I appreciate that you delivered it to me. Thank you."

"No problem." She rotated to leave.

"Wait. Would you like to go with me to the wedding on Saturday?"

His invitation startled her. She paused to peer over her shoulder, meeting his intense dark coffee brown eyes. He brushed a lock of sandy blonde hair from his forehead, waiting for her answer. There was nothing timid in the way he stood there, nor did she feel sorry for him, and yet it didn't feel right to turn him down. And so she answered, "Sure. It will be nice to get out."

"Good. I'll pick you up at 6:00 P.M. The ceremony will be held by the falls."

"Okay. That sounds like it will be beautiful," she said. She lowered her lashes and then brought them up once more to peer at him.

"Yeah." But his definition of beautiful was standing right in front of him. From her strawberry-blonde hair framing her heart shaped face to the way she looked over her perfect shoulder to the V of her shirt and the pendant that rested against her delicate skin. She had what he thought was referred to as peaches and cream complexion. There was a softness and sensitivity about her that was so appealing.

But she always seemed to know too much about him. Maybe it was the witch in her.

He watched her walk away, waiting until she rounded the bend and moved out-of-sight before stepping backwards and closing the door. He stood there for a moment, staring across the room at the grandfather clock. One of the few things he'd hauled around with him from place to place when he'd moved over the last century.

He had shocked himself with his invitation, asking her to go with him after he hadn't called her in months. He didn't know exactly why he'd asked her. It had simply been impromptu. Something had drawn him to her, and that, coupled with the sudden realization that he didn't want to attend his brother's wedding pathetically alone had spurred him into action.

Regret was a foolish emotion. Especially remorse for what one had not done. Yet, he seemed to get caught wishing he could change things. So he'd learned to act, to trust his instincts, and never to second guess himself. The past couldn't be changed, only the future.

Jake considered the opened invitation. A spray of white flowers, magnolias perhaps, with dark green leaves outlined in gold embossed filigree curved around the names.

Scratching bear claws. His brother was getting married. A December wedding right here in Nocturne Falls. He exhaled a cleansing breath of air as he flipped the invitation front to back several times, taking in the lovey-dovey ambiance clinging to the fine paper. He inhaled deeply of the scent that lingered on it, the spicy masculine aroma of Nathanial and a softer, sweeter feminine fragrance. He liked the latter. He and Nate had always appreciated similar things. Up until their falling out, that is.

He didn't really dislike his younger brother. Actually, quite the opposite. The thing was, after the war had put him in a wheelchair, he couldn't abide Nate's pitiful guilty mug. So he'd left Terror, Minnesota, and after years of bouncing around the country, eventually he'd settled in Nocturne Falls.

And life had been good. Peaceful. Uneventful. Yes, okay. The founding family of Nocturne Falls was vampires. The Ellingham's. He was a different offshoot of vampires than them. But that was neither here nor there. They got along just the same. Hugh was a standup vamp and they had become close friends.

Besides, Jake's adventures had pushed his body, if not his social circle. The people he hung with were others like him, who surged beyond their physical limitations.

What his brother didn't know was that over the past six months his body had slowly been healing, little by little. When he'd come across Nate in February at the Mardi Gras ball, he had still been in his wheel chair. He couldn't dance. Didn't want to anyway. In Nate's mind, the chair defined him.

That couldn't be further from the truth.

Nate had immediately whisked his culprit out of Nocturne Falls to Terror. Jake hadn't had a chance to converse with his brother, catch up, or set him straight. Even after that, he'd thought he would have an opportunity to talk with him, perhaps when Nate came back into town to visit the girl he'd been with. But the word was that Camille had moved to Terror to be with Nathaniel.

So there had been no revealing conversation between him and Nate.

He grabbed hold of the cane and pushed off, balancing his forward step.

It was about time he closed the distance between them, though.

2

When she got home, Telia went straight to her closet and flipped through the dresses, trying to decide what to wear to the wedding. She had called Caroline Linzer during her trek home to find out more about the wedding. If anyone would know, it would be Caroline, who owned Crazy Critter Pets store. Sure enough, Caroline would be the maid of honor.

The event was semi-formal.

Telia wrinkled her nose. Nothing looked appropriate for a December wedding. And her wardrobe was mighty scarce. Her job kept her at the keyboard, so it didn't matter what she wore. Sweatpants and sweatshirt were her preference.

A whirl of anticipation circled through her at the prospect of going shopping. Yes, she needed a reason to buy a new Christmas outfit. And she would choose a dress she could also wear when she visited her parents. She smiled to herself, pleased she had agreed to accompany Jake to the wedding.

She was over him, so it was no-big-deal.

If she worked hard and got her client's marketing

campaign done then there would be time to visit Misty's Boo-tique this afternoon. That was enough motivation to skip lunch and work continuously.

She set up three blog hops, plus a social media campaign with awesome prizes. Author Roxy St. James, one of her clients and a local author, had given her a generous budget to work with.

By two-thirty, she had accomplished all of the items on her list, with plenty of time to shop before the stores closed.

She phoned her friend Alice Miller to see if she'd like to meet her at Misty's. It had been so long since they'd been shopping.

Later, as she tried on several dresses some of her excitement faded. What was she thinking agreeing to attend the wedding with Jake? She wondered if she was once again simply giving in to what was expected of her. To fall in line with what other people expected of her.

She needed to face who she really was. A witch with sympath tendencies.

Agnes bounced into the shop shaking her head, sending the teal and purple streaks in her hair waving. "You're being too tame, girl." She peered at Telia through her big, round, black-rimmed glasses, and her bright blue eyes squinting. "Try something bold, yet chic." She glanced around. Like that, she pointed to a gorgeous long dress in dark green on a display mannequin. She sauntered over the display rack and removed a dress in Telia's size, then held it out. "Here."

Telia complied, changing in the dressing room and then modeling it for Agnes.

Agnes whistled when she came to the three-way mirror. "There you go. *That's* the dress, sweetheart."

Her heart skipped faster. The gown hugged her figure, but not too tight. The neckline was off one shoulder, with a dynamic lightning-bolt design. A slip of fabric draped over her upper arm.

"Wear that gown and he'll be yours forever."

"What if I don't want him forever?" she quipped. She turned and looked at the dress from all angles. *But she did want him, didn't she?*

Jake paced, the tip of his cane striking the ground in an even thud. With practiced balance, he compensated by tightening his shoulders and back as he leaned on the cane. Maybe he shouldn't go. After all, he hadn't returned the online RSVP until a mere three days ago. His brother and fiancée probably had not even seen it. Wouldn't plans already be set?

He glanced at the clock. It was time to pick up Telia. He tensed the muscles along his jawline. He'd already made a commitment to her. And he kept his commitments…not that it mattered if his brother thought otherwise.

He drove his SUV to her place, got out of the vehicle and lumbered to the front door where he rang the doorbell. As he waited, he noted how cheerful the porch looked. Christmas lights adorned the railing, framing the veranda. Snowflake decorations hung between the posts, sparkling with iridescent glitter.

Jake inhaled a shaky breath. This was so not him. He faced death defying speeds, climbed grueling cliffs, and jumped out of airplanes to ride the wind. But let him need to converse with a gorgeous, sweet female, and, well, that frightened him.

He rang the doorbell. A holiday tune chimed. He grinned. She really got into this, didn't she? The door opened. His jaw dropped. Oh. My. Gods. She was stunning.

Her brows shot up as she looked at him. "The cane adds a debonair touch. I like it."

"That's good, I guess."

He nodded, sweeping his gaze the length of her. She wore a sleek dark pine-tree green dress. It had an angled neckline showing the tempting view of her shoulders. How he'd enjoy running kisses there. It was sleeveless and the figure-hugging fabric clung in all the right places. A slit up to the mid-thigh showed one leg. Sparkly shoes covered her delicate feet.

She looked sexy as hell.

"Too much?" she asked.

"No. You look striking. The color suits you perfectly, setting off your hair."

"Thank you. I hope my mom approves when I wear it to a Christmas event." She moved past him out the doorway. "Then again, I've promised myself not to let her opinion bother me."

"I'll go set her straight," he said, then thought better. It wasn't his place to interfere.

But the comment seemed to be okay because her smile brightened. And that outshone everything.

"Be careful. My mother's a crafty witch."

"Warning noted." He extended his hand indicating for her to precede him.

He escorted her to the passenger side of the Suburban and held the door for her, feeling her eyes on him as he walked around to the driver's side and got in behind the wheel. A hint of self-doubt niggled at him.

His movements weren't smooth and fluid as they once had been. He started the SUV and drove.

"I imagine the wedding will be small," he said.

"Probably. But Camille had made a lot of friends while she was here. Her dance studio was popular."

"Yes, of course." Although that was one place he'd had no interest in going.

The evening was like most others as he drove through town, the spectators milled about. Saturdays were the busiest. And Jayne Frost's shop was rockin'. By the door, an elf held a sign reminding people that there were only seventeen days until Christmas.

"I need to go shopping there," Telia said. "I'll probably be able to find a special present for my sister."

He didn't have anyone to shop for, which was a sad and lonely thought.

It was a clear, bright evening, making the drive to the falls quite pleasant. The sun dipped behind the trees. The sky dimmed to a peachy glow, then faded into a tinted blue-gray curtain as stars peeked out.

He turned off the road onto a smaller, gravel drive. There were a number of cars already there, parked in a designated area of grass marked off by a rope.

"The place seems magical," Telia said, exiting the SUV and standing beside him.

A golf cart pulled up next to the cars. "Want a ride to the falls?" Sam Kincaid asked with a smile.

"Sure," Jake answered and then waited for Telia to slide across the seat. Another couple sat on a bench in back and Ivy Merrow took the front seat. "What about Hank?" Sam asked.

"He's going to talk with the groom first. He's giving the bride away, you know," she explained.

"Where is he?" Jake asked, looking over his shoulder.

"Over in that camper," she pointed at the RV among the trees.

Jake clenched his jaw and swallowed hard. "Wait," he said to Sam, and then touched Telia's hand. "I need to speak to my brother. Do you mind going ahead and finding seats?"

Her smile was sweet. "I don't mind at all. Take your time."

Jumping off the cart, he headed toward the camper, tension winding inside of him with every step. He didn't want to put a damper on the wedding. He just wanted to set things right between them. To let Nate know that no matter what, he could count on him. That the past was the past. He didn't harbor bad feelings for Nate.

And the bottom line, he wanted his brother to be happy. It was the reason he'd hit the road in the first place. Nathaniel had made himself responsible for Jake's injuries. No matter how Jake denied that. It didn't matter. And the truth was Jake couldn't stand Nate's guilt. So he'd left town.

He knocked on the door. It opened. Nathaniel stared down at him.

She didn't have a problem going alone to seat herself. When Jake had touched her hand, his emotions had zinged straight into her. Hot and raw and confrontational and painful. He was sad and yet determined. Hesitant and yet bold.

Whatever had transpired between Jake and his brother needed to be resolved. For Jake's peace of mind.

Telia turned her attention to the wedding decorations. She stepped from the golf cart. The setting was spectacular. An arch of flowers and netting framed the falls in the background. The water drummed a soothing rhythm, sending a misty spray over the rocks. About forty chairs made up the bride's and groom's sections. Twinkling lights filled the surrounding trees. She speculated for a second how it had been accomplished. A generator perhaps. Her guess was confirmed when she noticed a DJ table off to the side playing music and inconspicuously checking the microphones.

Up the bank, on a large flat area, a huge tent was set up for the reception, with more lights and seating and tables. The place was beautiful.

"This is gorgeous," she said to Ivy as they approached the seating area. "I think I've discovered my new dream wedding." As soon as she'd said it, she wished she could take it back. She hadn't meant to share that she even thought about finding Mr. Right. A tiny nervousness set her insides into a twitter because she wouldn't want them to think of her and Jake that way. As a couple. Even though the thought intrigued her more than a little.

"Would you like to sit with me?" Ivy asked. "Hank will be giving Camille away. She doesn't have family, you know. And we grew fond of her after she'd moved to town. We sure have missed her dance classes.."

Telia open and closed her mouth to protest Ivy's assumption that she and Jake were a couple. She said nothing. Instead, allowing the idea settle over her.

And she liked it.

"Yes. I'm sure that will be fine."

Ivy led the way, selecting a seat in the front. They chatted at how all this had been accomplished. Ivy speculated that Corette Williams may have had a hand at pulling this off.

Telia intended to find out. Just in case. One day when she was the bride this may be exactly what she wanted.

3

It seemed to take forever before Hank stepped forward within the doorframe. A fistful of tension settled in Jake's gut. This wasn't how he'd envisioned making amends with his brother. Not at all. And adding to the situation, he didn't intend to mess up Nate's wedding.

"Hi," Hank said, lumbering out and down the trailer steps. "He cleans up pretty good." Hank clasped Nate's shoulder as he strode past.

Jake nodded. He entered the motor home. Standing next to the kitchen counter, Nate turned his head. Their eyes met and held, and all the old childhood memories came rushing back, and like that, he was a proud brother again. Yet he knew it wouldn't be that easy.

"I wanted to come offer my congratulations before you got too busy," Jake said, walking into the tight space that made up the kitchen.

Nathaniel's eyes settled on Jake's legs. "What the…"

Jake glanced to Val Langdale, the law of Terror, a dangerous dragon shifter, and next to him stood his cousin Patty. He stared at her for a millisecond, realizing how long it had been since he'd been back to Terror. She'd grown up.

Recovering his composure, he shot his thumb over his shoulder. "Do you mind if I speak to my brother for a moment alone."

Val shrugged. "No problem. We don't have long anyway. I'll wait for you down the walkway, Nathaniel." As he walked passed, he paused, saying, "It's been a long time, man. Good to see you."

"Likewise." Jake offered up his hand and tapped knuckles with Val.

Inhaling and exhaling a long slow breath, Jake said, "I wanted to clear the air. I didn't get a chance to when you were here earlier."

Nathaniel crossed his arms over his chest. "You've got my attention. You better talk quick."

"Right." He leaned both hands forward, taking some of his weight onto the cane. "About six months ago, I felt a change. My body started slowly healing. Actually, I don't use the chair much anymore. Except at the races I attend. It really depends on how tired I am."

"You could have told me."

"You're right. I've been living in my own world. I was wrong to shut you out. I wanted to apologize. And…and tell you I'm proud of you, and happy you've found a mate."

Nathaniel hung his head for a long moment, then looked up and smiled. "Camille is extraordinary. Wait 'til you meet her." Suddenly a smitten, lovesick expression overtook his brother's face. "We're good. We can catch up later. Now, I have to get married." He tugged on his formal jacket, giving the lapel an extra jerk. Then he closed the distance between them. "Will you stand up with me?"

Jake was shocked and pleased by the invitation. After all he'd put Nate through, how could he make such an offer? He sighed. His brother was a better man than he. "I'm not dressed to impress."

"Doesn't matter. The ceremony isn't like that. Everything that's been done has all been handled long distance by Camille through her friends here in Nocturne Falls and a wedding planner. Corette Williams did the dress. Caroline helped arrange everything out here. Delaney made the cake. Everything has fallen into place. But it's not a formal deal."

A smile tugged at his mouth as Jake draped an arm around Nate's shoulders, pulling him closer. "Okay. Of course. I'd be honored."

He exited the camper in front of Nate. Together they walked to the rear of the seating area and met up with Hank. He wondered if he should make a quick trip to give Telia the heads up that he would be standing with his brother. At that moment, she glanced back at him. He gave her a wave. She smiled warmly, and he thought she understood. She seemed to have an extra sense like that.

Another golf cart drove up with Camille and Caroline and an unfamiliar woman and dropped them off. The red headed woman was the wedding planner, he guessed given the way she took charge.

"My brother will be my best man," Nathaniel informed the group.

The red-head nodded and didn't miss a beat as she lined up the procession. "Okay. Jake and Camille. Then Nathaniel. Then Hank and Camille." Everyone took their places. "Good. We're ready."

"Not quite," Nate said. "Where's Spook.?"

The planner shot him a quizzical glance.

"Our dog," Camille enlightened her.

The woman held up a finger as if to say wait-a-minute. She walked over to the side and came back with a Jack Russell on a leash, extending it to Jake. "Here. You will escort Spook to the front. He has the ring attached to his collar."

What the heck? Now he'd seen everything. A dog in the wedding? This woman had altered his brother big time. He wondered how that was possible. Jake peered over his shoulder at Nate who shot him a thumbs-up.

Slowly, Jake took the leash.

To his surprise, Spook was well behaved. The music began to play and the dog trotted on Jakes right while Caroline looped her arm in his on the left.

As they progressed down the aisle, Spook initially stole the show. The audience turned, ooing over the cute pup. Jake couldn't blame them. Spook was adorable with one brown patch around his eye and a complimenting brown ear on the other side of his head. He walked tall, well, as tall as a Jack Russell could walk.

When Jake got to the front, he separated from Caroline each taking their places. He peered into the audience. Hugh and Delaney Ellingham, along with Julian and Desi Ellingham, sat in the front row of the groom's side. That was an unexpected surprise, since they didn't have family to attend.

It was nice to see the turnout for Camille. She'd obviously touched a lot of people. The music changed. Nate marched down the aisle, his back straight and head high, acknowledging a few people along the way with an almost imperceivable nod.

The music altered again, turning soft and melodic.

Everyone rose as heads turned to glimpse the bride. They watched as Hank escorted Camille, glowing and radiant, down the aisle. She sparkled in a champagne colored dress. As she took her place beside Nathaniel, Telia marveled at her gorgeous dress. The back was framed in lace that hugged her shoulders and dipped low into a wide V down to her waistline. The skirt comprised of layers upon layers of tulle netting. Corette Williams had outdone herself.

Telia tried to imagine the style of dress she'd choose one day. She'd heard that Corette used her witchy abilities to match the perfect dress to its bride. She would do alterations on the spot. Camille's dress did indeed look like it was perfect for her, and her alone.

Telia sighed in longing and appreciation.

The ceremony was performed by Jake's cousin who introduced herself. The couple recited the vows they'd written. Then Nathaniel called Spook to him, taking the ring from a pouch attached to his collar. The vows were said and the rings exchanged. The tiny lights dimmed in a magical wave. It took a few seconds for Telia's eyes to adjust. Above the mist of the falls, a moonbow showed in full splendor. Soft colors washed over them.

"You may kiss your bride."

Telia's breath caught at the beauty of the moment. The soft light of the moonbow ensconced the couple as Nathaniel gathered Camille in an embrace that culminated with him twisting her to the side in a dip and bending over her.

A collective sigh whispered through the audience. Slowly the miniature lights grew bright. The music played and the crowd clapped as the couple moved happily down the aisle.

Her eyes met with Jake's. He seemed more relaxed than she'd ever seen him. As if knowing his brother was happy lifted his spirits.

"Please join us for the reception inside the tent," his cousin said.

Jake waited for Telia at the back so they could go to the reception together. He worried how she'd feel since he had joined the wedding party. Would she be upset because he'd deserted her during the ceremony? That hadn't been his plan, but he couldn't say no to his brother. Surely she would understand.

"That was beautiful," Telia said as she approached him.

He set a hand on her shoulder and ran it along her arm. "I'm sorry I couldn't warn you about standing with my brother. It was unexpected."

"No big deal. I figured it was something like that."

"Thanks for understanding."

"Really, you don't owe me an explanation."

He shrugged. "Yes, I do. I asked you to come with me."

She shook her head. "It's not like it's a real date, you know."

He left that comment alone. He had some explaining to do, he supposed, as to why he quit asking her to go out. He had wanted to call her a hundred times since those few dates. But he'd been in a wheel chair then, plus his head wasn't in a good place. He hadn't even known how to make a move on her then. She deserved more than someone with his level of problems. But now…He thought about the idea a moment. His recovery had occurred over the past six months. Actually, he didn't understand his new situation, however he was thrilled.

He'd been given a second chance for a full life. He intended to make the best of it. And hadn't his feelings for her been the driving force to asking her to accompany him to the wedding?

Don't waste this chance.

He turned his head to watch her as they walked and slipped a hand to the curve of her spine. He wanted to touch her more. Spend more time with her. Love her more.

But was he deserving enough?

"Don't you need to get pictures taken?" she asked when they arrived at the reception area.

"I don't think so. Nate didn't mention anything about pictures." He glanced around, observing the layout. "Would you like a drink?"

"Sure. Red wine, please."

He nodded giving her a lopsided grin. "Coming right up."

She watched him as he strolled to the bar that was set up in a back corner. He was the same man she'd dated six months ago, yet different. She'd like him then. He was kind, playful, and sexy as hell, even in his wheelchair. He oozed charisma. Still did. And she was still smitten.

But he'd dropped her once, so she wasn't ready to go running back to him. She couldn't take this not-a-date too seriously.

On an exhale, she turned her focus to the reception. The tent was huge, candles burned on tables draped in white linen, more miniature lights twinkled like fireflies around the edges, disappearing into the surrounding foliage. A DJ played music from one corner. A dance floor occupied the center with round dinner tables positioned around the perimeter. All very elegant and perfectly done.

Jake returned and handed her a glass of wine.

"Thanks."

"Let me introduce you to my brother."

"I'd like that."

He guided them to the bride and groom standing near a table set at the front of the make-shift room. "Nathaniel, congratulations again, brother," Jake said, shaking Nathaniel's hand, drawing him into a half hug and bumping shoulders.

"Thanks." Nathaniel stepped back. "Have you met my wife Camille?" He laughed, low and rumbling. "I'll have to get used to saying that."

"It's a pleasure," Telia said "Everything about the wedding is gorgeous. You are stunning. What made you have the wedding here instead of at the new wedding chapel."

"The new wedding chapel is fabulous with its themed rooms and all, but I wanted an outdoor wedding. Plus the falls is my favorite place in the area."

The DJ announced the couple and called for the first dance. Nathaniel and Camille took center stage and struck a pose. What a stunning couple. The sound of a tango filled the tent as they twirled around the dance floor. They had chosen the perfect dance.

"I recall them dancing at the Mardi Gras Ball. They had captured everyone's attention." She pinned Jake with a look she hoped said she expected him to take her a time or two around the dance floor.

"Oh, no. Don't look at me like that. I'm not dancing."

"You don't have to do the tango. Just shuffle your feet and hold me," she said, her tone far more sultry than she'd intended. But she wasn't sorry. Her body tingled at the thought of being kissing close to Jake. She hid her boldness behind finishing the remainder of her wine.

He leaned in closer to her. "If I hold you, I won't let go this time." His eyes held hers, intense and serious.

She wet her lips. "Promise?" Her voice wasn't pleading but challenging, a dare.

The music ended and another slow, melodic tune began. To her surprise, Jake set his cane on the back of the nearest chair, put their empty glasses on the table, and held his hand out for her to take. Her lips spread into a wide smile.

Dragonfly wings, yes. She placed her hand in his and followed him onto the dance floor. His left hand went around to her back, and felt warm and secure, his right hand warmed her palm and held it curled inward close to his chest. They danced as a number of other couples joined them. But to her…they were the only couple there.

His lips brushed her forehead. After a while she worked up the courage to ask, "Why did we stop dating?"

His feet paused, then resumed. "I'm not the right guy for you."

This time she stopped. "You do recall that I can sense emotions, don't you? What you said isn't true. You don't believe that."

"I thought your gift was only with objects."

"Partially correct. But your jacket is something you've touched and holds your imprint."

"I see." He thought for a moment. "Well, then, I didn't want to burden you."

"Okay. That's more like it. But you should have let me decide what is a burden and what isn't. I really lov…liked you." She caught herself before she said the big "L" word.

The notes of the song drew out and faded. He leaned closer, taking her lips in a slow kiss. And just like in the romance novels she marketed, her toes curled. Her recollection of what they'd been discussing got all jumbled.

"Don't do that again," she said.

"What? Kiss you?"

"No, leave and not call. I moped for weeks waiting for your call."

"I'm sorry. I was a jerk."

"Yes, you sure were." She laced her fingers in his hair and drew him down to kiss her again.

"I understand, though. Dealing with emotions sometimes isn't easy."

Just then, something wedged in between them, forcing their legs apart. Telia glanced down as a dog wriggled at her ankles. "You did an excellent job taking care of the dog during the wedding."

"His name is Spooks."

"Cute. His name goes with your brother's town. It's Terror, Minnesota, right?" She led the way to a table and selected a seat.

"Yes. That's where I grew up. And if I recall, you're from Atlanta?"

She was pleased he remembered some details they'd shared when they had dated. "My parents still live there."

Dinner was announced and the guests sought tables according to place cards. Hugh and Delaney Ellingham were at their table, along with Pandora Williams and Cole Van Zant, and Hank and Ivey.

Pandora slid into the seat beside Telia. "Look at that, two red heads at one table."

Telia smiled awkwardly. She didn't consider her strawberry-blonde hair red, but she knew her mother and others did.

Pandora winked, leaning close to Telia, saying confidentially, "I knew you two would hit it off."

"Yes. We see each other every now and then," Telia said, shooting a glance at Jake.

"Delaney, I saw the wedding cake. It's beautiful. You're so talented," Telia remarked, striving to turn the attention to someone else.

Pandora agreed, "I don't know how you find the time with the new little one."

"Thank you," Delaney said with a slight blush rising to her cheeks.

"How is the baby doing," Telia asked.

Delaney's smile widened. "Oh my goodness. He's all cuteness and love. And what an appetite he has. Auntie Tessa is watching him this evening."

"It must be nice to have so much family around," Jake said.

"Yes, it sure is," Delaney replied. "I don't know what I'd do without them, or my fabulous husband." She placed her hand on Hugh's arm. "Having the right person by your side means the world."

Telia could feel the contentment oozing from the couples at their table as they all unanimously agreed. Each couple leaned into one another, each seeming to relive their own story and wedding. Telia caught Jakes eye. Could he be the one for her?

The flutters she felt in her tummy thought so.

A few minutes later, the food was served. She recognized several of the servers from Howlers that were working, placing elegant entrees of fish and chicken on the tables. "I wonder if Bridget is expanding her business to include catering?" Telia said. "She seems to have done a number of weddings lately."

"I don't know but she always does such a super job," Pandora added.

Everyone agreed as they dug into their food. Telia followed suit. Although she was less concerned with eating and the reception and more interested in getting Jake alone to perhaps see if the chemistry they'd shared before was still there.

5

Jake had a dilemma.

He wanted to rekindle the relationship he'd so carelessly thrown away months ago. It had not been his best move. He realized now that part of the reason he'd been so miserable since the end of summer was because he'd ignored his heart. Falling for Telia had not been one of those head-over-heels deals. Instead, it was more fitted to absence makes the heart grow fonder. He had missed Telia. Nothing showed him that more than being with her now.

Perhaps they would cut out early. The guests had finished dinner and were dancing and celebrating. But before he could leave, he needed to do one more thing.

Speak again to Nate. He wasn't going to let his brother leave this time without having a meaningful conversation with him.

The bride and groom were mingling separately. He leaned to the side and spoke into Telia's ear, so she could hear him without raising his voice over the music. It was a good chance to be close to her. He inhaled her floral scent. "I'm going to talk to Nate. Feel free to join the group on the dance floor." He grinned at her as he stood, stepping back.

"Oh, I will. Don't worry about me." She could feel his longing to seek some sort of forgiveness from his brother. He wanted closure, she thought.

There was another emotion wafting off of him. Desire. And he seemed to have something else on his mind, too. Her.

Telia slid away from the table, standing. She looked amazing in her long, dark-green dress. She sought out Agnes Miller on the dance floor, along with the group of witches from the Nocturne Falls coven. Camille and Caroline joined them in a rockin' all-girls dance.

Nathaniel stood to the side watching the women. Jake approached him, leaning on his cane more than he would have liked. That one dance he'd had with Telia had been exhausting on his muscles, with the control it required to keep his steps in tune with hers and his balance in check. But he wouldn't have missed holding her close, feeling the pure pleasure of having her warm and soft against him for anything.

"I really appreciate you being here," Nate said.

Jake nodded. "We're family. Listen," he held his arms out, cane in hand. "The healing started to kick in about six months ago…about the middle of July. When you were here in February, I was still totally in the chair. But even then, I'd been living my life, pushing myself, entering wheel chair races, doing rock climbing, going parasailing, doing whatever I wanted to do."

"I'm glad to hear it. But you never came home."

"It wasn't because I blamed you. I don't. I just couldn't stand the guilt you were carrying. It ate at me. The war, the accident…none of that was your fault."

"I know." He glanced across the space to the women dancing. "Camille has made me realize a lot of things. One of them is, I can't control everything."

Jake bumped his fist against Nate's shoulder. "It's about time someone made you see reason. I'm happy for you." He gave him a bear hug.

"Thanks. Camille makes me feel good."

"Does she now?" Jake lifted a brow, peering at his brother.

The corners of Nate's mouth almost touched his ears, his smile was so big. "Yes, in many ways."

Standing side by side, they watched their women walk over to them. He paused in mid-thought. Their women? Telia wasn't exactly his, yet. But maybe.

He had pushed her away before. He wondered what would happen if he let go of his angst and allowed his feelings to grow.

Jake escorted her home after the cake was served. Telia walked slowly to the door, not wanting the enchanting evening to end. He hung his cane on the doorknob and drew her closer. "Thank you for going with me."

"My pleasure."

"If I ask you out again, will you accept?"

"That depends, on if you promise not to just disappear on me again. I like you, Jake. I—"

He smothered her mouth with his. She could feel the genuine deep sense of need in him. An explosion of desire, she ignited with a flare of passion so intense it scorched them both. She tugged at his neck, dragging him closer, pressing her body against his so he molded to her every curve. "Come inside," she urged, her voice husky, her mouth suddenly dry.

"Lead the way."

The front door closed behind them with a click. She plucked two bottles of water off the kitchen counter as she passed and padded straight into her bedroom. Jake followed. There was no sense pretending she didn't want what he wanted. Because she did.

She had the rest of the night to get reacquainted. Besides he had a lot of making up to do.

One thing she'd discovered about vampires, they went long into the night and woke late in the morning.

He had a bit of whisker growth by the time they actually got out of bed. Which accounted for the little bit of burn she felt after their morning sex. But it was worth it. She stretched. So worth it.

He rolled her over toward him, sheets and all, and kissed her forehead, then cheeks, then lips. "Okay, my clairvoyant witch, can you read my emotions now?"

"Horny. You want to do it in the shower."

"Wow. You're good." He gave her bottom a squeeze.

"Come on," he said, taking her with him off the side of the bed. It took him a second to solidify his balance. She used a wave of magic to start the water running in the next room.

"Tricky."

"You haven't seen anything yet."

Later, after they ate breakfast, Jake was getting ready to head home. He didn't fully dress. There was no point in donning the formal jacket again. "I'm going to a mountain ride this evening, want to tag along?" he asked.

"Will I be able to watch you?"

"Yes."

"Just don't expect me to join in. I hate heights."

He gave a low chuckle. "And I thought witches loved to fly."

"Not this one. And the broomstick thing is fake."

A pleasant chuckle rumbled through his chest. She saw him to the door where he kissed her goodbye.

"I'll be back at six."

Closing the door, she leaned her back against the wood, thinking, what a difference a day could make. She practically skipped into the kitchen to get another cup of coffee. She felt that fantastic.

On the counter, she noticed the snow globe that she had yet to place in a decorative spot. She lifted it and gave it a twirl, watching the snow float as she walked into the living room. Looking around, she settled on end table right beside where she usually sat. That way she could give the globe a swirl whenever she needed a pick-me-up.

She spun around, went to get her cup of coffee and returned to sit and dream over the snow globe.

6

The mountain Jake drove to was not far outside the city limits. They took a dirt back-road that wound through dense trees. A group of about six vehicles already had arrived. At the top, the area of this park opened up to huge flat rocks that had been worn by time and Mother Nature.

They were at different stages of unloading their wheelchairs. Some guys were already set up and rode around investigating and testing their special chair or bikes. The one thing they all had in common was fat wheels.

Jake's bike was a three-wheel configuration with two large wheels on each side and a small wheel in back. He seemed to have more difficulty moving about on this rough, rocky terrain than he did last night. But once he strapped into the bike and donned his safety helmet, he was like any other person. Brave, bold, brazen.

She liked this side of him. He reached his hand around the back of her neck and brought her to him, kissing her soundly.

"We'll ride for about an hour," he told her.

She nodded. He propelled the bike with his arms and hands. No wonder his upper body was so ripped—with a workout like this, who wouldn't be.

She took a seat on some rocks, making sure she was out of the way and yet could see. He was remarkable in his strength. She discovered she loved watching him. He wore a plain white t-shirt and looked handsome as ever.

The memory of running her hands over those hard muscles and plains couldn't be denied and wanted to run her palms over his pecs again.

But her feelings were more than just physical attraction. He touched her right down to her soul. She'd known it the first time they'd dated, and she knew it now.

He had a resilience about him she admired. He was the type to run away and suffer in silence. She'd gleaned that from him early on in the way he'd tried to keep her out, not totally willing to share himself. But she also detected a stubbornness not to give up.

Over the past six months, he'd encountered a change. As if in healing his spine, other parts had been healed as well. He probably didn't even realize it. However, she sensed that essence of completeness.

Leaning her back against another larger rock, she enjoyed watching him as the sun began to set. Sometimes the wheels of his bike would do a wheelie or bounce over a hard stretch of rocks and she'd hold her breath. How easy it would be to roll over the edge? She inhaled sharply at one risky moment when he went airborne.

Even though he appeared to have control, her nerves were a mess by the time he finished and stored the bike in the SUV. Because honestly, now that she'd found Jake, she couldn't bear the thought of losing him.

A week later, they were returning from the Christmas concert at the fairgrounds. It had been a pleasant evening, the weather was crisp. They snuggled beneath a fur blanket and drank hot chocolate. She was getting used to these perfect evenings.

"How about an ice cream on the way home?" Jake asked. "We can stop by I Scream."

"Ooo, yummy."

"I take it that's a yes."

"Yes." She chuckled. "But can we get it to take out? I'd like to go park by the falls. The moonbow was so beautiful at Nate and Camille's wedding last week, I'd like to see if it is there again."

"Okay. What flavor?"

"Hmm. Orange You Crazy."

"Got it. Sit tight."

Telia rolled down the SUV's window. Hank and Ivy strolled by, they'd also been at the concert. "Hey, great minds think alike," Telia said.

"Yep. Nothing like a little treat on the way home."

Jake exited as Hank and Ivy entered. He delivered her ice cream cone through the window and did a dramatic bow as he handed it to her. Then he came around and dropped into the driver's seat again.

He drove while they ate their cones. A short time later they were parked at the falls. She hadn't even finished her ice cream yet. They sat for a while until it was gone. Then he said, "I have an idea. Come on."

He got out and went around and helped her with the door. "Let's sit on the hood of the Suburban. We can relax against the windshield and watch the mist."

"Okay."

He lifted her by the waist and positioned her on the hood. Then he went to the driver's side and jumped up in one fluid motion.

"You're pretty good at that. And strong," she commented.

He smiled and the tips of his fangs glistened. "Vampire perks."

They leaned back at just the right angle to view the clear sky and stars and moonbow. The crisp December air rolled off the water. He swung his arm around her shoulders and she curled into him. The sounds of night creatures intensified, mingling with the beating rhythm of the waterfall.

She purred a contented sigh. "This is so nice, I could drift into sleep."

"Go ahead."

"Naw. It would be a waste of a perfect snuggle."

He drew her even closer and kissed her until she felt that familiar warmth melt in her belly. No one else had made her feel this way, as if he gave her breath. And this time she could sense the same love in him.

"Telia, I—"

Telia's cell phone rang. She wanted to pretend she hadn't heard it. "My mother," she whispered. "I'm supposed to leave this weekend for Christmas."

His muscles beneath her palm tensed.

"Interested in coming with me?" she asked.

He pushed to a sitting position. She raised up to join him. The electricity circling between them intensified, a swirl of unity. Holding her hands he searched her eyes in the light of the moonbow. He swallowed.

Ask me.

"Telia, will you marry me?"

"Yes." It was a simple yet powerful word, and it held all her dreams and expectations.

Her vampire of few emotions, his smile was the most vibrant she'd ever seen. He drew her into a vigorous embrace. "I'm not letting you go, ever," he promised. "I love you." This time his kiss was long and slow. When it ended, he said against her mouth. "We'll go to Illusions tomorrow." Small kiss. "I want Willa to create a special ring for you." Little suck on her lips. "Exactly what you want."

Her phone rang again. With nimble fingers, he drew it from her pocket. "Tell her you're bringing a guest, if that's okay with you."

She nodded.

"Hi, Mom." He nuzzled her neck. She couldn't think when he did that but she gave him more access anyway, because it felt so good. "Yes. I'm leaving Friday. And I have a Christmas surprise. I'm bringing a guest." She suppressed a moan and moved away from him for a moment. She gazed into his deep brown eyes. "You'll see."

7

Telia led him by the hand into her childhood home. The place sat among a neighborhood of Victorian gothic style homes. It was large and spoke of money. He had the feeling that Telia had not wanted for anything growing up.

"Mom. Dad. I'm home," she called as they entered the vestibule. She twisted to face him, whispering. "I know they're here."

"Sweetie," her mother came rushing down the staircase.

Her dad and sister were on her heels. They all stopped like bumper cars when they caught sight of Jake.

She slipped her arm around his back, as he did hers. "I'd like you meet my fiancé, Jake Newburg."

Her mother glanced at her husband. "A wedding. Did you hear that, Bart. Our baby is getting married." She took the rest of the steps at a rapid speed.

"We're engaged. And we plan to take our time, so cool your jets, Mom."

The rest of the family made their way down the stairs and joined in greeting Jake and making him feel welcome.

"Have you set a date," her mother asked.

"Mom. No. For now, let's just focus on having a wonderful Christmas," Telia said.

"It will be whenever your daughter wants," Jake said, flashing a smile at Telia.

The sight of his fangs set her mother back on her heels. "Okay," she said with a raised brow.

Her dad stepped forward clapping Jake on the shoulder. "Let's go in the family room and let the girls make their plan of attack for shopping tomorrow. It's been a tradition since Telia finished college and set out on her own."

Telia watched the two men disappear into the other room.

A few minutes later, after her mother had proposed the shopping for tomorrow, they joined the guys. As they entered, Telia paused, admiring the poignant scene of her family gathered around the fireplace. The guys with a drink in hand, in conversation. The lights twinkling on the Christmas tree. Her sister adding a new ornament on it. The room was warm and cozy and full of love.

The snow globe, she thought. She had her own snow globe scene right here.

She strolled to Jake and slipped into his waiting arms.

THE END

Magic's Frost

BY SELA CARSEN

Lonely werewolf Dima Samarin looks forward to watching his favorite winter elf every morning at the Hallowed Bean. He rescues her unfinished novel from the perils of spilled cocoa, and becomes her hero. Elin Bergstrom's day job is at Santa's Workshop, but she secretly writes sci-fi novels on the side. She accepts Dima's invitation to the Christmas Ball, but when their date gets derailed by a drug deal gone bad, this elf isn't about to stay on her shelf. Sometimes a werewolf can use a little helpful frost magic to win the day, and save their date.

1

Dima Samarin paid for his drink and slipped into his favorite seat in the furthest corner of the Hallowed Bean. This was his favorite time of day. He'd been waiting at the door when the first, sleepy-eyed employee arrived to unlock and set up for the morning. Technically, the little coffee shop didn't open for another half an hour, but they'd grown so used to Dima that they let him wait inside, out of the chill, while they went about their work.

They knew he was an *oborotyen,* a Russian wolf shifter, which meant he could tough out a Siberian winter as long as there was enough to eat. But this was Nocturne Falls, Georgia, not the Rus fae world. Here, it was considered rude to leave someone standing on your doorstep.

He appreciated their kindness.

Over his nearly fifty years, he'd learned to appreciate kindness. There was so little of it in the world.

But it wasn't just the great coffee that made this his favorite moment of the day. That was always the moment when *she* walked in.

Like him, the pretty blonde winter elf was accustomed to the cold, but she seemed to embrace the seasonal spirit with knit caps and gloves, long scarves, and crazy sweaters. For the last two months, he'd learned to sit and wait, enjoying the mildly illicit thrill of watching her strip off her layers until she was bare-headed and bare-handed, her long, elegant throat exposed.

She ordered the same thing every day—hot chocolate with a hint of peppermint—and every morning, she would wrap her hands around her cup, close her eyes, let the steam warm her face, and make this happy little humming sound as she smiled before her first sip. And every single morning after she took that tiny slurp, her brilliant blue eyes would fly open, she would suck in a breath, and whisper to herself, "Hot!"

It seemed like his day couldn't end until she burned her tongue.

Opposite from everyone else trickling into the little shop, he was just coming off his shift as a bouncer at the local nightclub, Insomnia. It was a good job. Not a lot of action because the supernaturals who frequented the place generally knew how to behave. And if they didn't figure it out quickly enough, they soon learned they didn't want to be in a position where he was the one who laid hands on them.

But mostly, it was sitting at the door, checking to make sure only members and no humans made it inside. The member's only club was strictly for supernaturals and their guests. Situated in an old brick industrial building that used to be a gasket factory, the first level was filled with rusting manufacturing equipment to fool any humans who went exploring. A ride in a well-hidden freight elevator would lead supernaturals in the know down to the basement where he waited at the reinforced door to let them in.

It was a pretty swanky spot. Hardly the rough pine bar, sawdust floor, and sour beer type of dump he'd grown up in. Insomnia was all moody lighting and sleek, industrial decor with plush leather seating, and thumping techno music. The club stayed busy until nearly dawn to accommodate the more nocturnal of their kind. Not really his kind of place at all, but as far as jobs went, he was happy.

But Dima much preferred this cozy little coffee shop where he stopped every morning after getting off work.

Exactly on schedule, he heard her whisper, "Hot!"

She pulled out a beautiful, handmade bag he knew she'd purchased from one of his neighbors, Carina Valdis. A Norse soothsayer who saw the future in her weaving, getting something from her, like commissioning a piece from Willa Iscove's jewelry shop, held some significance.

Carina had given him a small wall-hanging as a housewarming gift when he moved in. Her smile had been warm, and the bottle of vodka her boyfriend, Rodion Czernovitch, had held out to him, had been perfectly iced.

He remembered her words now, though he'd thought them strange at the time. "I saw clear blue skies for you, Dima. I hope you like it."

It turned out that the color of the wall hanging was almost exactly the color of his winter elf's eyes.

Dima quietly snorted into his coffee cup. *His* winter elf.

He didn't even know her name because he, one of the toughest creatures in either the mundane world or in the Rus, was too…what was the word…*trus*. He was too chicken to ask.

Today, she didn't pull out the sleek little laptop that she usually carried. Since the first day she'd walked in, she would set up her laptop and spend precisely one hour typing with occasional pauses to sip at her cooling cocoa, or simply to stare into space. Today, however, the bag bulged with a stack of papers almost two inches thick. Bright red slashes and margin scribbles covered half the pages that she set aside before she pulled out a red pen and tapped it against her pink lips.

He'd figured out that she was a writer of some kind, and this must be how she fixed and edited her work.

Dima watched, fascinated, as she bent over the pages, her brows drawn into a frown as she worked. His fascination meant he wasn't paying attention when the mom with a young toddler and a stroller-bound infant slammed her giant diaper bag into the cafe table where his elf worked.

The too-hot mug of chocolate wobbled in a slow circle before it finally tipped, splashing dark liquid all over the papers.

There was a moment of terrible silence before the bubble burst.

The toddler screamed. The mother began to repeat, "Oh my gosh, I'm so sorry, Oh my gosh" over and over And the baby, disturbed by the panic, began to wail.

His elf just sat there in shock, all the color leached from her face as the paper soaked up the chocolate.

No.

Nope.

This wasn't happening.

Elin Bergstrom's traumatized brain flashed back to an old Reese's commercial. "Get your novel out of my chocolate! No, get your chocolate out of my novel!"

The noise penetrated her thoughts first. So. Much. Crying.

Children cried when they got upset. She understood that. But did it have to be at that decibel level? Trained sopranos couldn't hit those notes. And the woman in front of her kept repeating the same words like a mantra, clutching a giant bag to her body as her children shrieked.

They were not going to be any help at all.

Instead, the dark giant who'd caught her eye months ago, was up and moving. He grabbed a roll of paper towels from the barista and started wiping up the sea of chocolate that seeped into her papers. Her novel. Her chocolate covered novel with the ruined paper center.

He didn't say a word, which was good because she couldn't have heard him over the weeping, wailing, and gnashing of baby teeth coming from both children and mother.

She closed her eyes for a moment and took a deep breath. Chocolate and coffee from all over the shop, the shot of peppermint she liked to add to her cocoa, the smell of paper and ink, and warm animal. Dog.

Growing up with sled dogs, some of her fondest childhood memories were of falling asleep in a pile of warm huskies. But since it was coming from the man in front of her, still quietly stemming the tide of cocoa, she had to figure him for some breed of werewolf.

She'd always thought werewolves were sexy.

Elin opened her eyes and was immediately caught in a gaze as icy blue as any winter elf's.

"Thank you," she whispered.

"You're very welcome." His voice was shockingly deep and warm, with an intriguing hint of an accent. She'd have liked to listen more, but the babies were still shrieking.

"Ma'am, are you all right?" Elin didn't have children, but she would be genuinely horrified if the little screamers had actually been injured by her spilled drink.

"We're fine. No one's hurt, but I'm so sorry," said the harried mom, on the verge of tears herself. "I didn't realize the bag would swing so wide."

"It's just some paper." Elin smiled and clenched her fist as she lied through her teeth. It wasn't just paper. It was the last year and a half of work, finally printed out for editing. She'd been working all weekend, marking up gaps and mistakes and flaws with her red pen, and she was nearly halfway through the very first science fiction novel she'd ever finished.

"Just some paper," she repeated. "You're sure everyone is all right? The chocolate was pretty hot. Anyone splashed or burned?"

Anyone other than her, because the shock had finally worn off and she could feel a slight, stinging burn through the wool of her trousers that was quickly cooling into unpleasant dampness.

She stood and pulled her sweater down to hide most of the stain. Luckily, she'd worn the tunic-length sweater with the light-up Christmas tree on it. She hit the button on her collar that made the sewn-in lights twinkle, and immediately, the shrieking stopped.

Mom lifted the baby from the stroller and swayed a bit to soothe it, and Elin offered to hang the huge diaper bag from the handles to get the dangerous weapon out of the way. Then she pulled a peppermint stick from her own bag, unwrapped it, and offered it to the toddler clinging to his mother's leg. He'd quit bawling, but his cheeks were blotchy and tear stained and he rubbed his sticky nose on Mom's jeans.

He glared at her as if she was the cause of the chaos, but relented enough to grab the candy and jam it in his mouth.

"Say thank you, Danny."

The kid glared at her some more.

Elin kept the smile glued to her face until they moved on, Mom scurrying out of the shop while everyone gave her a wide berth. Finally, she blew out a big breath and let her shoulders slump.

The giant had finished mopping up the table while she dealt with the family, and was wiping off his hands.

They both stared down at the sodden mess of her edits.

"Can you save them?" he asked in that wonderfully deep voice.

"I don't know." She shrugged and tried to crush the gaspy feeling that always came before a sob.

"Are you all right?"

Elin nodded. She didn't trust her voice anymore, and she couldn't get her thoughts organized enough to know what to do next.

"Hey." He stood closer now and he smelled wonderful. Like chocolate and coffee and warm spices and dog. She wanted to huddle into that luscious scent and not come out until Christmas. But he was a total stranger.

He opened his arms and she walked right into them.

Some part of her brain tried to ring an alarm bell, but she ignored it. Yes, this had "inappropriate" written all over it, but Elin needed a hug, and this man with his broad shoulders and delicious smell who had helped clean up her mess was offering.

She closed her eyes and leaned in as his arms closed around her. Not too tight, not too loose, and without a second's hesitation.

With her eyes closed, Elin buried her face in his dark gray sweater and let her senses take over. His heart beat strong and steady and a little fast, but his breathing was deep and even. His body radiated heat, and she rubbed his sweater with her cheek, enjoying the softness of cashmere on her skin.

"You smell like peppermint." His breath moved her hair and it tickled.

But that was no excuse for what came out of her mouth. "You smell like coffee and dog."

He stilled, and in a wild leap, she pushed back. "Oh no, wait. I didn't mean to say that. It's not how it sounded. It's good. I like those smells."

Awesome. Babbling. Forty-six years old and she was babbling. Heat washed over her face and down her neck, and she knew she was blushing in swaths of bright red.

This day couldn't get any worse.

"I'm so sorry." She couldn't bear to look at him. "Thank you so much for all your help. I really appreciate it." She shoved a pile of papers into her bag and slung it over her shoulder. "I… I have to leave now. Work. Right. Leaving now. I'm sorry. Goodbye."

Elin hauled the bag over her shoulder and practically ran for the door, hoping only that she wouldn't trip on the way out.

If he called after her, she didn't hear him over the sound of her own mortification.

2

When a woman rubbing her cheek against your chest tells you that you smell like a dog, it's time to reconsider your life choices.

And your brand of deodorant.

Dima stood in the middle of the coffee shop, his arms aching with emptiness, and watched his winter elf run away.

Never run from a werewolf. It just makes him want to chase.

He took the first long step of the hunt, when a flutter caught his eye. She'd only grabbed the stack without any markings. The thick pile of papers soaked with chocolate and red ink still sat atop the little cafe table.

A predator's grin stretched his mouth.

"*Wolves of Fenrir* by Elin Bergstrom."

The title caught his interest almost as much as the author's name. This was going to be easier than he thought.

He gathered up the wet pages carefully, then strolled back to his slightly shabby apartment, nodding to his neighbors as he went in. He pulled out the drying line he'd hung on his kitchen wall and stretched it to the hook on the other side of the living area. Then he got out his basket of mostly unused clothespins and a hair dryer, and got to work.

Two hours later, the pages were mostly dry. A couple were probably unsalvageable, but for the most part, the cocoa had dried and flaked off, leaving the wrinkled pages light brown and chocolate scented, but legible.

And they were good. He hadn't meant to start reading, but the first page had drawn him in. Even with the red marks and arrows and margin notes, he was completely absorbed by the story and the characters. The futuristic, science-fiction world she had built with her words was astonishing in its detail.

He needed to find her, if only to get the rest of this story.

Dima showered again, put on a different deodorant, and set off for Santa's Workshop, the Christmas shop where most of the winter elves in town worked.

He deftly avoided the sales-elves who asked, "How can I help you?" relentlessly at anyone who might accidentally make eye contact. Finally, he made it to the back of the store and found someone he recognized. Jayne Frost, an occasional guest at Insomnia, was in conversation with an earnest looking elf carrying a tablet, but she broke off when she saw him.

"Dima! How's my favorite bouncer?"

"Doorman, Ms Frost. I'm fine, and you?"

"It's almost Christmas Eve. Couldn't be better. You look like you're on a mission." Jayne was nice and normal-friendly, not manic like the ones on the sales floor. He guessed working retail over the holidays made people crazy in different ways.

"You could say that. I'm looking for Elin Bergstrom. Is she here?"

Jayne raised a blue eyebrow. She'd quit disguising her hair and even with the blue, she fit right in with the young tourists who dyed their hair all the colors of the rainbow, and some the rainbow had never thought of.

"She is. First time she's ever been late to work, but she's here now."

Jayne was looking at him now with a cooler expression, and he felt a hint of frost in the air. Nothing a Siberian werewolf would even blink at. "She left something at the Hallowed Bean. I'm just returning it."

She stared. He looked back steadily until she came to whatever decision she needed to make. She nodded.

"Sure. She's in the back. I'll go get her."

He nodded his head politely. "Thank you."

While he waited, he looked around. This was where she spent her days and that made it interesting. He'd never been one to do a lot of Christmas shopping, and now he remembered why. This place was filled with crazy people.

Aside from being crammed with toys, the shop was also filled to the rafters with holiday tchotchkes and knick-knacks, decorations and wrapping, and more tree ornaments than he'd ever seen in one place. Half the shelves were covered with red, green, and gold glittery things, where others featured the blue and silver he preferred.

Christmas in the Rus was very different from the American holiday. *Ded Moroz,* or Father Frost, and his granddaughter, the beautiful snow maiden, *Snegurochka,* didn't travel until Three Kings Day because the Rus, like it's mundane Russian counterpart, used the Julian calendar. Although it had never been outlawed in the Rus as it had in Russia, the holiday of his youth was much more toned than this insane rush to purchase happiness.

But as he looked around at the smiling people, he thought perhaps his small tree could use a new ornament or two.

Finally, someone tapped his shoulder.

"Can I hel—" Her eyes widened. "It's you."

"It's me. My name is Dima Samarin. You must be Elin Bergstrom."

She held out her hand, and he grasped it gently, struck again by her bright beauty. "*Zimneye nebo*."

"I'm sorry?" She cocked her head to the side slightly.

"Your eyes. They're the color of the winter sky."

She blushed again. Not the wild, agitated color he'd seen earlier, but a pretty pink flush spread from her cheeks out to the tips of her pointed ears.

He hadn't let go of her hand, and she left it there. It felt good to touch her again—something he'd been craving since the moment she ran from his arms in the shop.

"Is there…is there something I can do for you?" she finally asked.

He'd nearly forgotten why he was there. Dima held out the folder with her papers in it. "I found these at the coffee shop. You left them behind when you—" He didn't want to say "when you ran," so she said it for him.

"When I took off like a crazy person?" Her self-deprecating chuckle charmed him.

"I wouldn't say that."

They paused and he watched the pink fade until it was only in her cheeks.

"I'm sorry I said those things. It's not what I meant."

He smiled, and thought he hadn't smiled this many times in a day in quite some time. "It's all right."

"No, it really isn't. It's just that my family raised sled dogs and I've always found the smell comforting."

His heart gave a great thump and his smile grew. "Then I'm honored."

There didn't seem to be anything else for him to say and an awkward silence descended. At least, as much silence as could fall in a store where the noise level was a nearly criminal assault.

"Are you going to the Christmas ball tonight?" he finally asked out of desperation.

She shook her head. "No. I'm not seeing anyone and I didn't want to go in a group."

Dima picked up the extremely helpful information she'd dropped and ran with it. "I hadn't planned on attending, but would you like to go with me?"

Winter elves, with those pointed ears, had hearing nearly as acute as his own, and Jayne stepped over. At least she'd quit trying to pretend she wasn't eavesdropping.

"You could take the afternoon off if you need to go find a gown. I know Misty's Boo-tique has some beautiful gowns available."

"Gowns?" Elin's pale blonde eyebrows rose.

"It's a formal event," he said. "Is that all right?"

"It's been a while since I had a chance to wear something really nice."

He looked her up and down and smiled again. "I think you look nice."

"Oh good grief." Jayne grinned. "You guys are gonna

give me a toothache. And that's saying something for a winter elf."

Dima mock frowned at Jayne. "Are you still here for a reason?"

"Yes, I'm trying to move this along, so Elin can go dress shopping."

"Shouldn't I actually say yes, first?"

How had her life suddenly taken a backwards leap in the timeline back to high school?

For a second, she wondered whether to nurse that spark of indignation that flared up—she was perfectly capable of making her own decisions—but decided to be amused instead.

Either way, there was no way she was going to turn down Dima's invitation. Especially not when he delivered it in that perfectly yummy Russian accent.

Even with his dark skin, she could tell when a rush of warmth hit his cheeks. His slight smile deepened. "Ms Frost has always been a troublemaker. Ms Bergstrom, I'd be honored if you could attend the Christmas Ball with me this evening."

Jayne stood behind him, nodding and waving her hand at her face, miming that she should accept because he was hot. She wasn't wrong.

Trying to keep from laughing at her boss's antics, she accepted. "I'd love to. Thank you for asking."

Dima turned around. "I think we've got this. You can go now." Elin chuckled at Jayne's patently false huff, belied by the happy gleam in her eye.

"I'm sorry for the late notice," he continued once

Jayne had retreated. "Will you be able to find what you need?"

"I'm sure I will." She'd make a dress out of green velvet curtains if she had to. "What time?"

They settled the details and she very much enjoyed the view as he walked away. Oh, he was nicely put together. From the sigh she heard beside her, she wasn't the only one watching. She elbowed Jayne. "Don't be a lech."

"What? I can look. How'd you meet Dima, anyway?"

"He goes to the Hallowed Bean in the mornings when I'm there. We never even talked before today."

"What did he bring you?"

Elin suddenly realized she'd been hugging the chocolate-scented pages of her manuscript. "Oh, it's nothing. Just a project I'm working on."

"Some computer thing?" Jayne didn't mess with the store tech, and left all the IT end of the shop squarely in Elin's lap—which was right where she liked it.

"Yeah, some computer thing."

"Well, no more computer things today. You have a gown to buy." Jayne gave Elin directions to the dress shop and one of the local beauty salons, the Hair Scare, if she wanted to do any sprucing up.

Elin dashed up to her apartment to make a call to the shop and the salon to let them know she was coming, and she put the pages aside to look at later.

Half an hour before Dima was scheduled to pick her up, she was almost ready.

Elin put the finishing touches on her make-up and admired the new haircut that made her wild curls look tamed and elegant. She was already fastened into the fancy undergarments that sucked in the parts of her that weren't quite as firm as they had been twenty years ago, and she'd very carefully rolled on the silky sheer stockings she'd bought on a whim.

The whole day had been one whim after another—what was a pair of stockings?

Her gaze strayed again to the dress that hung behind her door. It had been a splurge, but the pale blue gown molded gracefully over her curves from shoulder to knee before flaring out in a gentle swirl of glittering fabric that didn't quite brush the ground. When she'd walked into the shop, it was the first thing that caught her eye. The fit had been perfect from the get-go. And the shoes she'd found—sleek kitten heels covered in gleaming crystal beading—were both comfortable and on sale.

If Santa had taken out a billboard that said, "Go the ball!" the signs couldn't have been more clear.

Nerves fluttered up in her belly, not for the first time that day. It had been quite a while since she'd dated. She'd gone out a fair bit, but she'd never found anyone that made her want to stay. This was the first time in years that anyone had made her nervous, and she wasn't sure if that was good or bad.

But even if nothing else worked out, the dress and the shoes were fabulous.

If she just sat around and dwelled until it was time to put the dress and shoes on, she'd make herself crazy, so she decided to do some reading. Her eyes landed on the packet Dima had brought to her.

She breathed them in. They smelled like chocolate. Chocolate and Dima. Not only were all the pages there, but they had all been dried and cleaned off, which was very sweet. As she flipped through the sheets, however, she was suddenly struck by something new. Little dashes of a different handwriting, written in small caps with purple ink.

"Props to Heinlein."

"Gibson's Neuromancer, *Ch 8, might help clarify the tech."*

"Like this twist on Stephenson's Cryptonomicon.*"*

She'd only used red ink. These were not her edits.

The note on the last page read, "When is this coming out? I need to know what happens next!"

He'd read her book.

She was trying to wrap her head around the realization that he was the first person who had ever read her work when her phone dinged.

It was a text from Dima. "Sorry. Work emergency. Can't make it tonight. Really sorry. Would have loved to see your gown."

Oh. No. He. Didn't.

He'd thrown her too far off balance to get away with running now.

Elin shoved her phone down the side of her long-line bra, fastened on the gown like armor, and stomped out of the Santa's Workshop building like she was leading a crowd of pitchfork-wielding medieval peasants.

No Russian werewolf was going to get away with reading her work, then standing her up. Not when she looked this amazing.

It is on, Dima Samarin. You'd better hope you're armed.

3

Dima swallowed down the disappointment that lodged in his throat as he wrote the text to Elin.

She'd never talk to him again, and he couldn't blame her.

He tucked the phone into the inside pocket of his tuxedo jacket and turned back to Chet.

"I called the ambulance. I can't imagine how we missed him when we closed up last night."

The big bear shifter shook his head. "I don't know, either. He's lucky to be alive after laying on the bathroom floor all day."

Dima leaned down to put the back of his hand against the young fae's forehead. "I think that may have been what saved him. Keeping him cold while this garbage was trying to burn him up from inside."

The boy on the floor was a good looking young man, rather more pretty than handsome, but he'd grow into it. If he lived.

Chet was going through the kid's pockets when he paused. "Huh. This can't be good."

A small, clear plastic baggie held three little pills.

The fae didn't get sick, so they weren't prescription meds, which left only one option.

Dima took the baggie from Chat and lifted it to his nose.

Bitter. Hollow. Chemical.

Madness.

The drugs held no particular scent of death, but he imagined that if you took enough of them, a trip to the afterlife wouldn't be far behind. He wondered how many had been in the bag to begin with. If there were three left, was this simply a large purchase or was the victim also the dealer? Too many questions, but no answers were evident.

"What is it? Ecstasy? Some kind of uppers or downers?" The bear's voice dropped to a rough rumble. Chet was a pretty affable guy, open and friendly with the patrons, and easy to work for until something happened to change his mind. Dima hadn't seen the big man get angry like this in a long time. Heads would roll.

"It can't be. Illegal drugs don't affect supernaturals at all. There would be no point in taking them."

"Then what is it?"

Dima frowned. He'd heard about something coming through the border at Volshev from his neighbor, Rodion Czernovitch. Rodion had belonged to the Border Crossing Patrol until he'd come to Nocturne Falls to recover from an injury received in the line of duty. He'd settled here with Carina, and was the newest member of the Nocturne Falls Sheriff's Department.

"Cold Pill. I can't be sure, but my neighbor used to guard the fae/mundane border down in Volshev on the Trinity River. He mentioned something about a drug that was starting to come over that only affected other supernatural creatures. In Russian, it's *koldunya pyl'*. It means 'magic dust.'"

The word that slipped from Chet's mouth was one Dima fully endorsed.

Sirens touched the edge of his hearing and he let Chet know the ambulance was near. The bear nodded. "I'll let them know where to pull in so we don't advertise the place to anyone watching."

Dima crouched next to the young fae and contemplated the outcome of poor life choices until he hear Chet's voice announce his return, along with the footsteps of several other people. One set of steps in particular caught his attention.

High heels were not generally the footwear of choice for emergency service personnel. And they usually didn't smell like chocolate and peppermint.

Elin walked in behind the stretcher and immediately turned her blue eyes to him. He held out his arms and she walked into them as if she belonged there.

"Dima, what happened?"

"What are you doing here?" Their questions stepped over each other, and he answered first.

"I was called in just after I finished getting dressed. This young man was found on the bathroom floor. It looks like he's OD'd on something."

One of the paramedics perked up. "OD'd? On what? He's fae."

Dima handed over the baggie of pills, minus one that he pocketed. Perhaps it was only that he was Rus, but though he knew the sheriff would be on his way, he was never able put all his trust in the police. Dima wanted to check with a few sources to see if he could find out more on his own.

"We found this in his pockets."

"Any idea what it is?"

Dima and Chet shook their heads. Good. They were thinking on the same lines—there was no point in speculating, and the last thing they needed was for information to leak before they had all the facts.

The woman took the pills and went back to work.

He kept his arm around Elin and stepped over to his boss. "I need a couple of minutes."

Chet nodded, his eyes speculative. "You bet. He's on his way, so don't go far."

"He" was the owner of Insomnia, one who preferred to remain in the shadows and leave the day to day, or rather, night to night, management of the club in other capable hands. He'd want to be here for this.

Dima nodded and walked with Elin to a door that led to a small alcove behind the building.

Finally, he was able to admire her. She'd taken his breath away when she arrived. The blue gown fit her figure perfectly, not too tight, but molding itself along slim, delectable curves that she'd always hidden under those crazy Christmas sweaters. Her blond curls were piled up in a complicated looking mass of tendrils he wanted to touch and unravel. She was wearing more makeup than she had been earlier, and it made her eyes sensuous and deep. And her lips were slick and red and he wondered if they tasted as good as they looked.

"What are you doing here?" he asked, after taking in the beautiful sight before him.

"I..." She blinked those wide eyes and the pink flush from this morning returned. "I feel like an idiot."

"What happened?"

"I got mad. That's it. I got angry when you texted.

I'd just realized that you read my work, and then you stood me up, and I put the dress on and stomped over here in a big snit to tell you off." She put her hands on her cheeks. "I'm so sorry. I can't believe I did that."

"I don't blame you for being mad. Believe me, I didn't want to send that text, but I'm not going to get out of here for a couple of hours."

"I know. That poor boy. Do you think he'll be all right?"

"I don't know. I hope so, but he was here all day by himself." Dima frowned. "I'm not sure how that happened. Chet and I both checked the bathrooms. It's procedure. What one person may miss, another will catch."

Something about the situation was bothering him. There was no way both he and Chet would have missed seeing someone lingering past closing time. Even if they didn't see him, they would have smelled him.

He put the dilemma to the side and concentrated on what was in front of him.

"You look beautiful." He'd have been so proud to take her to the Christmas ball, so happy to see her glitter under the lights.

"Thanks. You look very handsome in your tuxedo."

"What a pair we make, all dressed up, standing in an alley."

"At least no one's covered in hot chocolate this time."

Dima leaned in a little and sniffed. "But you do still smell of chocolate and peppermint. My two favorite flavors."

Elin hadn't had this much fun flirting in years. "That's something we have in common."

"That, and excellent taste in science fiction."

In all the fuss and her mortification over stomping down here like a toddler throwing a tantrum, it had slipped her mind that he'd read her story.

"I nearly forgot. I was supposed to be mad at you about that, too."

"Mad? Why? It was very good reading. And I think your edits and notes are going to make it even better."

"You weren't supposed to read it. No one's read it before."

He smiled, his teeth bright in the darkness. "Then I'm honored. How many others have you written?"

"Others? Oh no, this is my first. It took a long time to write it and I...well, I had a little too much wine the other night. I got brave enough to pitch it to some agents and editors on Twitter and it must have worked because I got a couple of requests. I'm putting the finishing touches on it and I'll send it out at the end of the week."

She was still stunned that anyone had liked her rather tipsy pitch, but when not one, but two agents had asked her to send in her synopsis and the first three chapters, she'd been over-the-moon thrilled.

"So I'm on a date with a soon-to-be-published author."

It sounded too good to be true, so she deflected. "No, you're standing in an alley with a desperate writer in a ball gown."

"Same thing."

She laughed a little and he stepped closer.

"I like your laugh." His voice was quiet and husky, with that trace of Russian accent sliding over her skin.

"I like your smile." Elin's voice was quiet, too.

But the smile she liked so much faded. "I don't smile often. Not until you. But you should know something. I'm not…"

"Not what?" she asked when he stopped, obviously struggling with what he wanted to say next.

"I'm not nice."

It was the last thing she expected to hear from him, and she was surprised. "I disagree."

"Excuse me?" He obviously wasn't expecting that for an answer.

"I think you're very nice. You were nice to me at the coffee shop. You dried my pages and wrote interesting comments. That was nice."

His brows drew together. "Maybe I'm only nice to you."

"Nope. Sorry." She shook her head at his cute frown. "I've sat in the coffee shop watching you for weeks. You're nice to everyone. You help them carry things, you open doors, and I've seen you pay it forward more than once. Dima, I hate to break it to you, but you're actually a pretty nice guy. I wouldn't be here otherwise."

"You came here to yell at me."

She waved his comment away. "Maybe. But I was only that angry because after all the sweet things you've done, it shocked me that you could stand me up via text."

"About that. We should probably get you home. I'm going to be here for quite a whi—"

Elin was all set to argue with him when he broke off. She knew he was a wolf, but the proof was shifting in front of her. Dima hunched and writhed as his bones cracked and reformed. He grew unnaturally tall as his arms lengthened and sharp claws sprouted from his fingers. White teeth became fangs as his face elongated into something murderously lupine.

A werewolf. Not the kind like most of the other wolf shifters in Nocturne Falls who changed into large wolves. She was reminded forcefully that there were many kinds of shapeshifters, and Dima was from the Rus. He was a creature part wolf, part man, all monster.

He spun, putting her behind him, and the growl that rumbled through his body made her every cell vibrate.

With a deep sniff, he called out, "Come out, come out, wherever you are." The children's rhyme had never sounded so ominous, delivered in an inhuman snarl.

A bright light blinded her for a moment, and when it faded, it left residual flashes that made her vision untrustworthy. A voice, light and sweet with an Eastern European accent, intruded on her confusion.

"I only want what's mine. Give me the rest of my stash, *oborotyen*."

Dima growled. "You're the one peddling Cold Pill?"

"You know what it is, then? Want a taste? I can hook you up."

Elin couldn't figure out where the voice was coming from. One moment it was in front of her, the next, it echoed high above her against the brick walls.

"That kid nearly died. Is that how you keep your clientele? Kill one and the rest will line up?"

"He was stupid. I warned him, but he took too much." Now it was off to her right.

"Doesn't sound like you'll be getting much repeat business."

Dima stayed in front of her, but swung his arms out,

trying to catch the voice that seemed to come from all around them. It was a clever little spell because she was completely disoriented.

"Hey, I left him where you could find him. He'll probably live, but I didn't have time to check his pockets. I'm just here to grab what's left of my stash and I'll let you go. No need for you or your pretty lady to get hurt here."

The growl intensified. "You really shouldn't have said that."

Dima backed up until her back touched the cold brick wall of the building. One of his clawed hands reached down and touched her thigh, squeezing lightly to convey a message. *Stay back.*

Dima stepped forward, still searching for the voice that hummed a happy little tune. The sound continued to bounce off all the walls, but she had an idea. Elin was a computer nerd who write sci-fi novels on the side. But she was also a winter elf. She might not be as powerful as Jayne or Dima, but she wasn't helpless, either.

She bent down to grab a handful of dust and gravel, trying not to think of her fresh manicure, and brought it to her mouth. Taking a deep breath, she pulled on her winter magic and blew a steady stream of Arctic air. Ice stuck to each particle as it flew from her palm and dusted everything in the alleyway.

Including the drug dealer.

The small, dark man was perched on top of the half-wall that divided the alley in sections. He wasn't anything she'd seen before, but Dima's growl intensified.

"*Chuma*. I should have known you'd be mixed up in spreading this plague."

"Just doing my job. And you, Dima Samarin. I thought you'd died a dog's death years ago."

"Perhaps you will tonight."

The little man was nimble and quick, but Dima was amazing. Elin stepped back to the wall where he'd left her and watched as the two tumbled and grappled with deadly intent.

She'd never seen a real fight before, and the silence of it struck her. But for the sliding of feet, the slap of a well-aimed blow, or the occasional grunt, neither combatant made a sound.

Dima had been born fighting. First to protect himself from the harsh environment he'd grown up in. Later, it became a marketable skill that he'd put to use in ways he wasn't always proud of.

He might be getting older and a little slower than he used to be, but he made up for it with years of skill. And a stubborn determination not to look bad in front of Elin.

Out of the corner of his eye, he saw her watching them.

But far from shrinking away in horror, his bloodthirsty winter elf's eyes were narrowed, and her fists were clenched. She swung against a mock opponent and half-shouted encouragement. "Get him, Dima! Knock him down!"

He was so startled, he took a sharp jab to the cheek that split the skin. That got his attention.

He was done with this fight. In a set of practiced moves, he struck with all his muscle behind each blow. In seconds, the *chuma* was down, bleeding from his mouth and nose, out cold on the ground.

She whooped in joy and ran to him. He barely caught her as she leaped into his arms and began planting smacking kisses on his face.

The door to the alley slammed open and Chet barreled out, followed by Sheriff Merrow and a couple of his deputies, including Rodion.

Dima shifted with a thought, Elin still wrapped around him, and he clutched her more tightly as he stepped back into the shadows and put her back against the wall.

He brought one hand up to the back of her neck to hold her still, and kissed her, at least partly to get her to pay attention, but mostly because he needed to kiss her as much as he needed his next breath.

She had brought him warmth and joy and laughter today. More than he'd had in his life in years. She was fierce and fiercely intelligent, and he wanted nothing more than to get closer to her. Closer than they were right now with her chocolate and peppermint flavored mouth under his, her hands sifting through his hair, and her legs wrapped around his waist.

When she finally pulled back, her eyes were shining and soft, and her lips gleamed in a tremulous smile.

"This is not how these things usually turn out." Sheriff Merrow's dry tones brought them back to reality.

The *chuma* started to come around with a moan. Dima let Elin slide to the ground, then he put one foot on the plague-bringer's chest.

"Found your dealer. *Chumoi* are beings of pestilence. They bring sickness and disease wherever they go. Not surprisingly, they're frequent dealers in the drug trade, though I've only ever seen them deal to humans before."

"Did he tell you where he got the stuff?"

"Not yet." He reached down and picked him up.

In moments, the *chuma* told them everything. How he was supposed to start carving out territory for the new drug, and that he was getting his supply shipped in from Volshev.

Rodion, the former Border Crossing officer, grimaced. "Sheriff, there are people in my old unit who could use this information."

Merrow nodded, then turned to the dealer. "This is the beginning and the end of Cold Pill in Nocturne Falls. We're going to make sure everyone knows what happened here. And we're going to throw the book at you so hard, your boss's will feel it in the Rus. You will not bring your plague here."

The owner of Insomnia came down to join the Sheriff, and both men let go of the tight hold they kept on their human appearances. The nightmare creatures growled, "Never again. Not in any way. Clear?"

The *chuma* whimpered and nodded. "I'll tell them, I swear. Never again."

Dima let him go, and Rodion cuffed him, then hauled him to the patrol car.

After all the chaos, it seemed that things wrapped up fairly quickly after that.

The ambulance left with the overdose victim, who had finally started to come around. The sheriff and his deputies left to take the dealer to jail. And Insomnia's owner went back inside with Chet to lock up.

The chilly night air carried no sound as Dima watched her, watching him. A spot of icy white touched her wild curls and he looked up. Snow. Nocturne Falls was close enough to the Blue Ridge Mountains that it wasn't unusual to get a flurry every now and then. Of course, the entire state would come to a screeching halt, but for now, it was perfect.

Elin turned up her face to the pretty flakes and smiled, and he wondered at the turn his life had made since this morning.

Finally, she broke the silence. "What a day, huh?"

"Yeah." He wanted to bite his tongue. *Witty response, wolf.*

"I kind of liked it."

His eyes widened. He hadn't expected that, but then, Elin hadn't done anything he'd expected today. "I did, too. I really enjoyed reading your book."

"Thanks. I really enjoyed kissing you."

A laugh burst from him. "Have you always been this direct?"

"No. That's the benefit of not being in my twenties anymore, I think. Most of my regrets are about the things I didn't say. I like to think I've outgrown that."

"I like it." Dima grasped her waist and stepped nearer. "I liked that kiss, too. We should do it again."

"Practice makes perfect?"

"Something like that. We should also practice actually going out on a date. I don't think we have that part down yet."

"But we're good at spilling hot chocolate." She raised her hands to his battered tuxedo jacket and smoothed down the collar.

"And we're good at taking down plague-dealers. Your blowing ice trick was great." His thumbs slid up and down her sides and he enjoyed the shape of her.

"I'm not sure I want to practice that anymore, though."

"We can practice staying in while you write your next book and I make dinner."

"I think we're getting somewhere now." She smiled and he dropped his forehead to touch hers.

"Is tomorrow too soon to start practicing?"

"Tomorrow is perfect. Walk me home?"

It was his pleasure. He was going to enjoy finding out all his winter elf's secrets and quirks. And he'd never see snow again without thinking of a touch of magic's frost.

THE END

About the Authors

Fiona Roarke is a multi-published author who lives a quiet life with the exception of the characters and stories roaming around in her head. She writes about sexy alpha heroes, using them to launch her first series, Bad Boys in Big Trouble. Next up, a new sci-fi contemporary romance series. When she's not curled on the sofa reading a great book or at the movie theater watching the latest action film, Fiona spends her time writing about the next bad boy (or bad boy alien) who needs his story told. Visit Fiona's website: www.fionaroarke.com.

USA Today Bestselling Author **Jax Cassidy** followed her dreams to Paris, then Hollywood to pursue a film career but managed to fall in love with penning sexy romances and happy endings. She is Co-Founder of Romance Divas, an award winning writer's website and discussion forum. Jax is also known as one-half of the retired writing team of Cassidy Kent. She is represented by Roberta Brown of the Brown Literary Agency. To learn more about Jax, visit her online at www.jaxcassidy.com.

Born and raised a Jersey girl with easy access to NYC, **Kira Nyte** was never short on ideas for stories. She started writing when she was 11, and her passion for creating worlds exploded from that point on. Romance writing came later, but when it did, she embraced it. Since then, all of her heroes and heroines find their happily ever after. She currently lives in Central Florida with her husband, their four children, and two parakeets. She work part-time as a PCU nurse when she's not writing or traveling between sports and other activities. She love to hear from readers! Visit her online at www.kiranyte.com.

Wynter Daniels has authored more than three dozen romances, including contemporary, romantic suspense, and paranormal romance books for several publishers including Entangled Publishing and Carina Press. She lives in sunny Florida with her family and a very spoiled cat. After careers in marketing and the salon industry, Wynter's wicked prose begged to be set free. You can find her online at www.wynterdaniels.com.

Candace Colt decided it was time to write her memoir midway through eighth-grade. The last line was, "And now the climax of my story"… Any surprise this little girl grew up to write romance novels? After careers in education and health care, Candace now writes contemporary and paranormal romance. In between, she practices Tai Chi and yoga. And if there's a drum circle in town, she's there! Her heroines are savvy independent females who don't need men cluttering up their lives, that is until the right one comes her way. Candace lives in a small town on the Florida Gulf Coast where she lives her HEA every day. Visit her online at www.candacecolt.com/books/.

Alethea Kontis is a princess, author, fairy godmother, and geek. Author of over nineteen books and contributor to over twenty-five more, her award-winning writing has been published for multiple age groups across all genres. Host of "Princess Alethea's Fairy Tale Rants" and Princess Alethea's Traveling Sideshow every year at DragonCon, Alethea also narrates for ACX, IGMS, Escape Pod, Pseudopod, and Cast of Wonders. Alethea currently resides on the Space Coast of Florida with her teddy bear, Charlie. Find out more about Princess Alethea and the magic, wonderful world in which she lives at http://aletheakontis.com/.

Cate Dean has been writing since she could hold a pen in her hand and put more than two words together on paper. She grew up losing herself in the wilds of fantasy worlds, and has had some of her own adventures while tromping through the UK, and a few other parts of the world. A lover of all things supernatural, she infuses that love into her stories, giving them a unique edge. When she's not writing, she loves cooking, scaring herself silly in the local cemeteries, and reading pretty much anything she can get her hands on. Learn more about her and her books at http://catedeanwrites.com.

Larissa Emerald has always had a powerful creative streak whether it's altering sewing patterns, or the need to make some minor change in recipes, or frequently rearranging her home furnishings, she relishes those little walks on the wild side to offset her otherwise quite ordinary life. Her eclectic taste in books cover numerous genres, and she writes sexy paranormal romance and futuristic romantic thrillers. But no matter the genre or time period, she likes strong women in dire situations who find the one man who will adore her beyond reason and give up everything for true love. Larissa is happy to connect with her readers. Stop by and say hello at her website: http://www.larissaemerald.com.

Sela Carsen was born into a traveling family, then married a military man to continue her wandering lifestyle. With her husband of 20+ years, their two teens, her mother, and the cat, she's finally (temporarily) settled in the Midwest. Between bouts of packing and unpacking, she writes paranormal and sci-fi romances, with or without dead bodies. Your pick. Follow Sela Carsen online at http://selacarsen.com.

Made in the USA
San Bernardino, CA
08 November 2018